ALECOS

Titles available in this series

Yannis
Anna
Giovanni
Joseph
Christabelle
Saffron
Manolis
Cathy
Nicola
Vasi
Alecos

Greek Translations

Anna

To Fiona
To bring back happy
memories of Florida.

ALECOS

Beryl Darby.

Beryl Darby

JACH

ISBN 978-0-9574532-0-3

Printed and bound in the UK by Biddles,
part of the MPG Books Group, Bodmin and King's Lynn

First published in the UK in 2012 by

JACH Publishing
92 Upper North Street, Brighton, East Sussex, England BN1 3FJ

website: www.beryldarby.co.uk

For Jackie, Jeorjina, Anita and Elita.

2007
Saturday 22nd September

Lambros put both the dogs on their leads and began to walk up the road to Vasilis Iliopolakis's house. The dogs sniffed at the verges and would have liked to be released to investigate the interesting smells further, but he gave them a tug and reluctantly they continued their progress.

On reaching the gates both dogs became excited and Lambros smiled. That probably meant Mr Vasi was there. Lambros keyed in the code for the gates and once inside the dogs became quite frantic to be released.

'Hold on,' he grumbled. 'If he's there now he'll still be there in five minutes time.'

To his surprise, once free the dogs did not go racing up to the house, but began to sniff at the grass next to the wall and amongst the shrubbery, gradually making their way further up the driveway.

Lambros followed them. He had obviously been incorrect in his assumption that Vasi was there and now he had rounded the curve of the drive he could see no sign of Vasi's car. The dogs were still sniffing, their noses close to the ground like bloodhounds, lifting their heads and scenting the air every few steps.

It gave Lambros an uneasy feeling. Was someone lurking in the grounds? He would have to make a full investigation of both the grounds and the house before he commenced with washing the windows. He certainly did not want to be surprised by an intruder, despite having the two dogs with him.

As he reached the top of the drive he stopped and looked at the scattering of paint chips that littered the ground. What had Mr Vasi been doing? It was unlike him to leave such a mess behind him. He was such a meticulous man; never left anything out of place. Lambros shrugged. He would sweep it up before he started the windows. If a wind got up it would be dispersed all over the place and he didn't relish the thought of having to collect the small pieces from the grass by hand.

Lambros called the dogs, who were sniffing anxiously around the flakes and chippings, and made his way to the rear of the house. Once there the dogs mooched from place to place, not showing any particular interest in the smells they encountered.

Commanding them to stay Lambros opened the patio door with his key and then the kitchen door. He stood and listened. Everywhere was quiet. He removed his shoes and padded through the ground floor in his socks before mounting the stairs and entering every room up there. There was no sign of anyone.

'Damn dogs.' He cursed them silently. They had made him jittery for no good reason. He returned to the kitchen and replaced his shoes. He would just sweep that mess up; then make a start on the windows. He placed a bowl of water for the dogs on the patio and called them over as a signal that they were released from his command and could roam as they pleased.

Lambros opened the door to the shed and removed the stiff broom and a dustpan and brush. He returned to the front of the house and began to sweep the flakes of paint into a small pile. Once collected together he swept them into the dustpan and emptied them into the garden rubbish bin.

He had almost finished the ground floor windows when he heard the buzzer that indicated someone wished to open the gates. The dogs barked and raced down to the gates, where they stood daring an intruder to enter the premises. Lambros sighed. It would be quicker to go round to the front of the house and see who was there than take off his shoes to enter the kitchen and answer the buzzer. He would probably have to go down to the gate anyway.

Lambros threw his sponge into the bucket and walked around the house and down the drive. He frowned and quickened his step when he saw the local policeman standing there impatiently.

'I need to come in,' called Christos.

'What for?' asked Lambros.

'Instructions from Heraklion. Can you tie those dogs up?'

'Give me a couple of minutes. I'll take them back to the house and shut them in.'

Once again the dogs sniffed at the grass and shrubbery that bordered the driveway and Lambros called to them impatiently. Reluctantly they joined him and he opened the patio door, ordered them inside and closed it firmly. Unhurried he walked back down to the gates where Christos was waiting for him.

'There's no one here except me. I doubt if I can help you.'

'I only need to come into the grounds. It won't take long.'

Lambros keyed in the code for the gates and opened them wide enough for the policeman to squeeze his bulk through. 'Well, you're in. What now?'

'Where does Mr Vasi usually park his car?'

'At the top of the drive, of course, but he's not here now.'

Christos nodded and walked up the tarmac, studying it as he went. 'Did you notice anything unusual this morning when you arrived?'

Lambros looked at him, puzzled. 'What do you mean by unusual? The dogs seemed a bit excited and unsettled. I thought they knew Mr Vasi was here.'

'Were you expecting him to be here?'

Lambros shrugged. 'Sometimes he's still around when I arrive.'

'But not today?'

Lambros shook his head. 'If he was his car would be here.'

'Can you show me exactly where he parks when he is here?'

'About there.'

Christos bent down and began to examine the ground. There were no signs of any flakes of paint. He straightened up and mopped his brow.

'I'll be off now and leave you to your work.'

Lambros looked at the policeman in disbelief. 'Is that it? Is that all you wanted to look at?'

Christos nodded. 'Thanks for your help. If you'd just release the gates again for me I'll be on my way.'

Once back inside his police car Christos radioed the police station in Heraklion. 'I'm at the Iliopolakis house now. I've been in to the grounds and spoken to the handyman there. He saw nothing untoward when he arrived this morning. There's no sign of any paint or metal chippings.'

Thranassis smiled. 'That's it, then. I'm charging him.'

'Marianne? It's Saffron. We're at the police station in Heraklion. They've arrested Vasi. I don't know why, but I think it's something to do with an accident that happened last night. I don't know what to do. Help me, please, Marianne.'

'Which police station? There's more than one in Heraklion.'

Saffron looked around wildly. 'I don't know.'

'All right, Saffron. Go back inside and ask whoever is on the front desk to speak to me.'

'They won't understand.' Saffron choked back a sob.

'Just hand them the 'phone and wait until they give it back to you.'

Saffron nodded.

'Did you hear me, Saffron?'

'Yes. I'm on my way back in now.'

The officer on the desk looked at her in surprise as she spoke into her mobile 'phone and handed it to him. Without taking his eyes off Saffron he gave Marianne the address of the police station and handed the 'phone back.

'Marianne?'

'I'm here, Saffron. I want you to go outside and wait. I'm going to telephone Vasilis now. I'm sure he'll come straight down and sort everything out and look after you. When I've spoken to him

I'll telephone you back and you can tell me what has happened.'

'Thank you, Marianne.' Saffron leant against the wall. She felt quite faint with relief.

It seemed an age to Saffron before Marianne telephoned her back.

'Are you still at the police station?'

'I'm standing just outside the entrance.'

'Stay there and Vasilis will be with you very soon. What's happened?'

'I'm not sure. We were driving to Heraklion and there had been an accident. Someone had gone over the side into the ravine. The police stopped Vasi and then asked him to drive to the police station with him. They seem to think he was involved as there is a scrape on his car.'

'A scrape? How did that happen?'

'I don't know. We saw it when Vasi drove me home last night. It wasn't there earlier. Vasi certainly hadn't done it whilst he was driving. He said he would take it in to the garage later today. He was in a hurry to get to Heraklion to see the bank manager; then we were going to lunch with Cathy and Vasilis. He said he needed to talk to his father; something to do with being refused a loan to buy a hotel.'

'Which hotel did he want to buy?' asked Marianne curiously.

'He changed his mind and then he found out the owners had sold it to the man at the bank.'

'Which hotel?' repeated Marianne.

'The Imperia.'

'Why was he interested in that one? It's hardly a going concern.'

Saffron hesitated. She felt uncertain that she should tell Marianne Vasi's plans. 'He had some ideas to get it back on its feet.'

'And the bank refused to back him?'

'I don't know the details, Marianne. Vasi said the bank would let him know when they had examined the accounts for the hotels and told him to return a couple of days later. When he did so he found the bank manager had bought it from under his nose.'

'Wow! I bet Vasi was furious.'

'No, he seemed amused that the manager had bought it, but very annoyed that he should have been told the hotels did not provide enough collateral. That was why he was driving up to Heraklion. He wanted to go to their head office and ask for an investigation into the refusal.'

'I'm not surprised. I'm sure Vasi would not have asked if he thought there was any doubt that he would get a loan. No doubt Vasilis will soon sort that out! But why are they holding Vasi at the police station?'

'I don't know, Marianne. They took us into separate rooms and asked me how the scrape on the car happened. I couldn't help them. I just said it was there when Vasi came to drive me home last night. I'm not sure if they believed me. I've got to report to the police station in Aghios Nikolaos with my passport within twenty four hours.'

'Don't worry about that. It's just a formality. Uncle Yannis can take you in tomorrow morning.'

Saffron bit her lip. 'I'd rather be with you or Giovanni. Uncle Yannis won't be able to explain anything to me.'

'We'll sort something out. I expect Vasi will take you anyway.'

'If he's been released by then.'

'Of course he will be,' replied Marianne confidently. 'Once Vasilis has had a word with them they're bound to release him. There's obviously a misunderstanding somewhere.'

Stelios watched the news on the television anxiously. There was only a brief mention of the accident that had occurred on the main highroad from Aghios Nikolaos to Heraklion. As soon as the hotel along the road from his lodgings had opened he had sauntered in casually and made his way to the pay phone.

He had dialled the number for the police station in Heraklion and asked to speak to a senior officer, saying he had important information regarding an accident that had taken place, refusing to give his name or any details of his location.

'Just write down what I tell you. I saw a dark saloon car speeding on the highway. As it rounded a bend it hit another vehicle and forced it through the barrier into the ravine. The registration numbers were eight, zero, two. I didn't have time to read any more.'

'Could I have your name, sir?'

'No. I've told you what I saw. A dark saloon, registration eight, zero, two. Have you got that written down?'

'Yes, sir, but if you could give me your name, please.'

The line went dead as Stelios replaced the receiver and the officer glared at it in annoyance. He didn't like anonymous calls; it looked as if he had not done his job properly and asked for the caller's details before taking the message. He sighed heavily. He would have to pass it through to Thranassis, although he knew the man would berate him for inefficiency.

Stelios watched the news one more time; then decided that Vasi may not have left his house yet. That could explain why there was no mention of anyone helping the police with their enquiries. He would drive up to Vasi's house and if his car was there he would make another call to the police from a different location.

He picked up his car keys and slipped them into his pocket. As he did so he remembered that his own car was damaged and sprayed with paint. He did not want to draw attention to himself by driving it to a garage for repair until he was certain that Vasi had been arrested and charged. He would take the bus to Elounda walk up the hill and have a quick look at Vasi's house to see if there was any sign the man was around.

Vasilis placed his arm round Saffron's shoulders. 'Are you all right? The police didn't touch you?'

Saffron shook her head. 'They were very courteous. Found an interpreter and offered me coffee.'

Vasilis nodded. 'Sometimes they can be a little rough and heavy handed. Do you want to come in with me whilst I speak to them?'

Saffron hesitated. She knew she would not understand the conversation between the police and Vasilis, but she felt nervous about standing outside alone any longer. A number of people had looked at her speculatively as they passed by.

'I'll come with you.'

Vasilis nodded and strode inside the police station leaving Saffron to follow him. She leaned against the wall whilst Vasilis demanded the attention of the officer in charge.

'I am Vasilis Iliopolakis. I understand you are holding my son and I should like to know the reason why.'

The desk officer gave Vasilis a bored look. 'Name?'

'Vasilis Iliopolakis.'

'Your son's name. You've already told me yours.'

'His name is the same as mine. I understand he came here voluntarily to answer some questions. I should like to know why he has been detained.'

The officer shrugged. 'Presumably he did not answer the questions to our satisfaction.'

'I should like to speak to the officer who has detained him.'

'He's busy.'

'And so am I! Please be good enough to ask him to come to the desk and speak to me. I am sure there is a misunderstanding and my son should be released immediately. If he refuses to release him I shall be telephoning my lawyer and instruct him to sue you for wrongful arrest.' Vasilis was trying hard not to lose his temper.

The officer glared at Vasilis. It would be better for him to risk Thranassis's wrath than risk being sued by Vasilis Iliopolakis. The man had considerable influence and unlimited money at his disposal. He lifted the telephone receiver, turned his back on Vasilis and spoke rapidly.

'Superintendent Solomakis will be free in about half an hour.'

'Very well. I am taking the young lady to the taverna opposite and I will return to wait for him.'

The officer nodded and looked back down at the form he had been completing.

Vasilis rubbed his hand over his forehead and walked to where Saffron was waiting for him. 'I have to come back in about half an hour. I suggest we go over and sit outside the taverna and you can give me a few more details.'

Vasilis ordered orange juice for Saffron and an ouzo for himself. 'You're sure you wouldn't prefer a glass of wine?'

Saffron shook her head. 'They may want to question me again and I don't want them to think I've been drinking. Thank you for coming out. I'm so relieved you're here.'

'Vasi should have 'phoned me.'

'He may not have been allowed to.' Saffron drank half her orange juice and Vasilis waited until she had put her glass down.

'Now tell me exactly what has happened.'

'We were driving along the main road. A car appears to have gone over the side into the ravine. A bit further on Vasi was asked to pull over. There are scratch marks down the side of his car, but they were there last night. The police asked him to come here and make a statement and now they won't let him leave.'

'What are these scratch marks? How did they happen?'

'Yesterday we drove to Palekastro where we had lunch and then on down the coast to Vai to have a swim. We drove back to Elounda and later Vasi collected me and we went out for dinner. Afterwards we returned to the house and watched a film.' Saffron felt her cheeks burning. She did not want to admit they had gone straight up to Vasi's bedroom. 'When we went out to the car for Vasi to drive me home I noticed there was a long scratch all down the passenger side of the car. He could only think that someone had come into the grounds and vandalised it. We had neither of us seen it earlier. I said he ought to report it, but he said that would be useless. We had neither of us heard anything or seen anyone around. He said he would take it in to the garage later today. He wanted to get to the bank in Heraklion this morning and also to talk to you.'

Vasilis patted Saffron's hand. 'I'm sure there's nothing to worry about. The police like to make life difficult for us sometimes. If they don't release Vasi when I have spoken to them I'll be phoning my lawyer.'

Vasilis drained his glass and walked across to the police station whilst Saffron sat in an agony of apprehension whilst she waited for him to return. He was talking on his mobile as he approached her.

'I need you down here *now*, Lakkis.' Vasilis frowned when he heard the answer. 'Cancel your appointment. This is more important. I'll explain everything when you arrive. Vasi is being detained by the police. It has to be a trumped up charge. I'll be at the taverna opposite the police station and I expect you here within twenty minutes.'

Vasilis closed his 'phone and sat back down opposite Saffron. 'My lawyer is on his way. They are charging Vasi with dangerous driving, causing an accident and endangering life.'

Saffron gasped. 'That isn't true. The accident had already happened when we passed the scene and it was nothing to do with Vasi. They were winching the car up so it must have occurred some hours earlier.'

'Tell me exactly about Vasi's car, Saffron. How bad are the scratches?'

Saffron frowned. 'They looked worse when I saw them in daylight. They're all along the passenger side, in some parts the paint has gone completely. They're not in a straight line, more a series of jagged lines, some wider than others.'

'How far up are they? Near the wheels or the door handles?'

'About half way, I suppose, maybe nearer to the door handles. Some of the chrome trim had been ripped off.'

'Were any of the lights smashed or the wing mirror damaged?'

Saffron shook her head. 'Vasi wouldn't have driven it with that kind of damage. I'm sure he would have ordered a taxi for me last night and arranged to hire a car today.'

Vasilis nodded. 'I agree. Now when my lawyer arrives I will

16

want you to tell him exactly the same as you have told me. He speaks good English,' Vasilis added as he saw the look of consternation that crossed Saffron's face. 'What time did Vasi take you home last night?'

'I'm not absolutely certain. About two, maybe two thirty. Why?'

'Lakkis will want to know and he'll also want to know from the police what time the accident happened.'

'If it happened earlier than that will they believe that we spent the evening at Vasi's house, your house?' Saffron corrected herself. 'If it happened later how can Vasi prove that he returned straight home?'

'I'm sure someone will have seen him in the early hours. The taxi drivers work all night during the season taking the tourists back to their hotels. Do you remember seeing any?'

'Some cars were around, but why should they have noticed us?'

'How much had you had to drink? You may not have realised Vasi was driving erratically, but the taxi drivers would certainly have noticed.'

'I had a glass of wine at lunch and Vasi had a beer. We shared a bottle of wine with our meal. That was all. We were neither of us drunk.' Saffron frowned. 'They did ask for my driving licence and wanted to know if I had driven Vasi's car. I had the feeling they didn't believe me when I said I'd never driven it.' Saffron shrugged. 'That may have been my imagination because of using an interpreter.'

'What else did they ask you?'

'Why I was in Crete, where I was staying, how long, the usual sort of questions. They asked to see my passport, but I don't carry it with me. I offered to return with it tomorrow or they could telephone Giovanni and ask him to bring it up. I was frightened they might put me in a cell until they had seen it.' Saffron gave a wan smile. 'They finally decided I could leave but I have to take my passport to the police in Aghios Nikolaos within twenty four hours.'

Vasilis nodded. 'To see your passport is just a formality; nothing to be concerned about. It is not a crime not to be carrying your passport.' Vasilis looked at his watch. 'I wish Lakkis would hurry up.' He pulled his mobile 'phone from his pocket. 'I'll telephone Cathy and tell her we'll all be delayed for lunch.'

Vasilis tapped his fingers impatiently on the table and looked around constantly for the arrival of Lakkis, finally rising to his feet and waving as he saw his lawyer weaving his way across the road amongst the traffic towards them.

'Sit down, Lakkis. Do you want a drink? I'll tell you briefly what has happened as I know it and then Miss Bartlett can tell you her side of the story. She's English, by the way and doesn't speak Greek.'

Lakkis extended his hand to Saffron and refused Vasilis's offer of a drink. 'I've managed to delay my appointment for a couple of hours, but I need to get back to my office as soon as I can. I promised clients I would telephone them back and I haven't had the opportunity yet.'

Vasilis nodded and related how he had been telephoned by Marianne and asked to come to the station where Vasi was being detained. Once there he had spoken to Officer Solomakis and been told the charges they were proposing to bring against Vasi.

Lakkis raised his eyebrows. 'And the lady; how is she involved?'

'Saffron was with my son yesterday until the early hours of the morning. She will repeat to you all that she has told me and answer any questions you may have.'

Lakkis nodded. 'Very well.' He turned to Saffron and began to speak fluently in English. 'I understand from Mr Iliopolakis that you spent the whole of yesterday with his son. Please tell me exactly how you spent your time from when he met you until he returned you to your home.'

Saffron felt herself blush. She had no intention of telling anyone exactly how they had spent some of their time.

'Vasi was considering purchasing the Imperia hotel. He was expecting the bank to advance the capital to him but they refused to give him an immediate decision and he was to return on Wednesday. He asked Mr Palamakis to have a look at the hotel and when I met

Vasi yesterday he said he had changed his mind. Mr Palamakis had advised him not to buy it. Vasi told me he had tried to visit the owners to tell them before he collected me and they were not there. He wanted to try again before we left the area for the day and they were in. Vasi came back to the car after just a few minutes and said the man from the bank had told the owners Vasi could not afford it. Vasi was very cross about that and we drove into Aghios Nikolaos so he could go and see the bank manager. After that we drove to Palekastro and had a late lunch. Afterwards we went to Vai, had a swim and spent the remainder of the afternoon on the beach. When we returned to Elounda I went back to my relative's house to shower and change and then Vasi collected me in the evening and we went out for dinner.'

Saffron deliberately missed out that between returning from Vai and going to Yannis's house she had spent two delightful hours with Vasi. 'We returned to his house after dinner and watched a film. I think it was about two in the morning when we went out to the car for him to take me back home. It was then that I saw the damage to his car. All down the passenger side there was a long scrape. I know Vasi had not scraped against anything and if it had happened when he was parked in Elounda I would have seen it then.'

Lakkis nodded. 'And the events of this morning, madam?'

'Vasi asked if I wanted to come up to Heraklion with him. He said he wanted to collect the accounts disk from the Central, visit the bank and speak to his father. I said I would be happy to spend my time in the museum whilst he was busy. As we drove along the main road the traffic was being held up and each way was allowed through in turn. We saw someone had driven off the road and that was causing the congestion. A short distance further on a police car waved Vasi down and examined the car. They then asked Vasi to drive to the station and make a statement regarding the damage.'

'And you are quite certain the damage to the car did not happen at any time whilst you were with Mr Vasi?' Lakkis's dark eyes bored into Saffron.

'Positive. The first time I saw it was in the early hours of the morning when Vasi was about to drive me home.'

'Can you describe the extent of the damage to me, please?'

Saffron repeated the description of the scrape marks that she had earlier relayed to Vasilis.

'It was dark, of course, and it looked worse when I saw it in the morning.'

Lakkis turned to Vasilis. 'You do not have security lights?'

Vasilis shook his head. 'We have a high wall around the property, security gates and the dogs. Security lights would continually come on as the dogs moved around at night.'

'So why did the dogs not alert your son to an intruder?'

'The dogs are with the gardener at present. There is not always someone at the house to look after them.'

Lakkis turned back to Saffron. 'You didn't take a photograph, I suppose?'

Saffron shook her head. 'It never occurred to me. Should I have done?'

Lakkis shrugged. 'It may have been helpful.' He rose and pushed back his chair. 'I will speak to the police. I may be some time. Do you wish to meet me later?'

Vasilis looked at Saffron. 'I'll take Saffie back to my apartment to be with Cathy. I'll come back and wait for you here, and I'll expect Vasi to be with you when you return.'

Vasi sat with Mr Tsilikadis feeling much more confident now the solicitor was with him and he knew his father was looking after Saffron.

'I honestly have no idea who scraped my car. It had to have been done deliberately, but why should anyone want to damage just the passenger's side? Why not do both sides?'

Mr Tsilikadis did not answer the question. 'Tell me exactly how you spent your time yesterday, from when you returned from Vai until you were requested to come to the police station this morning.'

20

Vasi sighed. 'We returned to my house so I could shower and change, then I took Saffron to her relatives.....'

Mr Tsilikadis held up his hand. 'The young lady says you took her straight to her relatives' house. She didn't mention returning to your house until after you had dinner.'

'She probably didn't think that was relevant. The car had not been damaged at that point.'

'Quite.' Mr Tsilikadis smiled to himself. 'So after you had showered and changed you drove your companion to the house where she is staying. Where is that, please?'

'The house that belongs to Yannis Andronicatis. She's a relative.'

'And you returned and collected her at what time?'

'About eight. We went along to Elounda waterfront and shared a bottle of wine in a taverna before walking further along and having dinner at one of the restaurants.'

'What time did you leave the restaurant?'

'Probably about eleven thirty. I didn't look at the time.'

'And would anyone at the restaurant remember you being there?'

'I expect so. We have been there on a number of occasions.'

'And after you left the restaurant?'

'We returned to my house and listened to some music for an hour or so.'

Mr Tsilikadis raised his eyebrows. 'Are you quite sure about that?'

Vasi nodded.

'The young lady said you watched a film.'

Vasi swallowed and his face reddened.

'Maybe you would like to think again about your activities when you returned to your house?'

'We went up to my room.' Vasi's face reddened further.

'I cannot help you unless you are completely honest with me. Would that also be the real reason why the young lady did not mention her visit to your house earlier in the day?'

'I expect so,' mumbled Vasi.

Mr Tsilikadis nodded. 'I trust you will advise the lady to admit to spending her time in your room. If the police should decide to investigate further and find a discrepancy in your stories they will not believe anything else you tell them. What time did you finally take the lady back to her own lodgings?'

'Probably about two in the morning.'

'And that was when you saw the damage to your car.'

'Saffron drew my attention to it. She noticed it when she opened the passenger door.'

'And you are quite certain it had not happened earlier, when you were having your meal possibly?'

'Absolutely certain.'

'After you had taken the lady home what did you do then?'

'Returned to my house and went to bed.'

'Can you describe the amount of damage on your car to me? Is the door buckled?

Vasi shook his head. 'There are a series of long scrapes and the trim is missing.'

'What about the wing mirror and the lights?'

'There's no damage to them.'

'And you believe this happened when you were parked in the grounds of your house?'

'I'm sure it did. There were flakes of paint on the ground along that side.'

'What did you do about that?'

'Nothing. It was dark. I planned to sweep them up this morning, but I couldn't see them and I thought they had blown away and dispersed during the night.'

'Are you certain you parked your car in exactly the same spot as before?'

Vasi shrugged. 'I may not have done.' He frowned. 'I suppose I could have parked over them and that was why I thought they had blown away.'

'So it is quite possible the paint is still on the ground?'

'It should be unless it really has blown away.'

'Is there anything else you think you should tell me before I have a word with that policeman? I am going to demand that he either releases or charges you. No don't worry,' Mr Tsilikadis smiled as he saw the concerned look on Vasi's face. 'If they decide to charge you I'll immediately apply for bail.'

Superintendent Thranassis Solomakis read through Vasi's statement again. He wished they had more details about the man who had telephoned earlier and said he had witnessed the accident. Why hadn't the man alerted the emergency services immediately? Why had he waited until eight in the morning before placing his 'phone call and why had he refused to give his identity?

Thranassis sighed. He supposed he should be grateful to the anonymous caller. He had at least identified the car as belonging to Mr Iliopolakis and the vehicle did have scratches along the passenger side. The explanation for the damage was flimsy. Why would anybody bother to climb over a wall into private property to vandalise the car?

'Now he's spoken with his solicitor we'll charge him formally. No doubt the solicitor will apply for bail immediately and I'll place it as high as possible. It's Saturday afternoon. His father won't be able to get to a bank, so he'll be spending the weekend with us. Any news from the hospital?' he asked of Makkis.

The officer shook his head. 'Nothing yet. They said they'd let us know when the man regained consciousness.'

'Check again. I expect they're busy and have probably forgotten.'

With a sigh the officer dialled the number and waited, finally shaking his head at Thranassis. 'Still unconscious.'

Mr Tsilikadis rose to his feet as Thranassis returned to the interview room. 'I take it my client is free to leave?'

Thranassis shook his head. 'We will be detaining Mr Iliopolakis whilst we continue with our enquiries.'

Mr Tsilikadis glowered at the Superintendent. 'What exactly are you charging my client with?'

'At the moment the charge is dangerous driving and causing an accident that endangered life. There may be further charges depending upon the victim's condition.'

Vasi paled. 'I had nothing to do with the accident.'

'Your car has been identified as the one being driven erratically that forced another vehicle through the safety barrier.'

Vasi shook his head. 'There must be a mistake. I was not on that road at any time yesterday.'

'I am applying for immediate bail for my client,' Lakkis spoke firmly.

'The banks are closed until Monday,' replied Thranassis smugly.

'I am sure that will be no problem.' Lakkis spoke confidently. 'There are cash points where money can be withdrawn.'

'Bail will be set at twenty five thousand Euros. Mr Iliopolakis will stay here until the full amount has been guaranteed.'

Lakkis tried not to show his concern. It was an enormous sum and Mr Iliopolakis was hardly likely to have so much cash readily accessible.

'Very well. I shall return as soon as possible. In the meantime Vasi, do not volunteer any further information to the police.'

'Do I have to be locked in a cell?' asked Vasi. 'Can't I just wait in the reception area? I won't try to run away or anything.'

'Now you have been formally charged I have to lock you in a cell until your bail money has been produced. I will now ask you to empty your pockets and a receipt will be given to you for your possessions. These will be returned to you if you are released.'

Vasi looked at Mr Tsilikadis who nodded. 'That's the usual procedure, Vasi. Your father is waiting for me and I'm sure we shall be back within an hour with the bail money. You just have to be patient.'

'Ask my father to look after Saffron, please.'

Mr Tsilikadis strode across the road to the taverna where he could see Vasilis sitting, swinging his beads nervously.

'They've charged him with dangerous driving and causing an accident. I've applied for bail and it's been set at twenty five thousand Euros.'

'What!' Vasilis rose to his feet. 'How dare they? He had nothing to do with the accident.'

Lakkis Tsilikadis shrugged. 'They must feel pretty certain of the case against him. The immediate problem is how to get hold of such a large sum of money on a Saturday when the banks are closed. The cash machines certainly won't let you draw out that amount.'

Vasilis pulled out his mobile and dialled Cathy's number, cutting her enquiries about Vasi short. 'Open the safe and tell me how much cash there is in there,' he ordered. 'Do it now, whilst I wait.' Vasilis wrote down the sum on the serviette in front of him. 'Vasi's fine. I'll call you later,' he promised.

Lakkis raised his eyebrows.

'I don't keep that kind of money sitting in my safe at home.' Vasilis smiled grimly and keyed in the number for the beach hotel. 'This is important, Aristo. Tell me exactly how much the hotel has taken in receipts this week.'

Vasilis waited for the answer. 'Have you banked it?'

'No, there's no problem, Aristo,' he replied to the man's anxious question. 'I can't explain now. I'll call you later.'

Vasilis turned to Lakkis. 'I'll 'phone the Central. I expect they banked yesterday as well, but at least I'll know the amount I can ask the bank to release to me.'

'But the bank is closed,' protested Lakkis.

Vasilis did not answer him as he was busy writing down more figures on the serviette. He added them together and frowned. There should be enough to raise the bail money by drawing out from the hotel accounts provided he was able to contact Stavros Tanakis and get the manager to agree to open the bank vault.

It took a considerable amount of time for Vasilis to convince Stavros that he needed access to the money immediately and could not wait until the bank opened on Monday. Lakkis kept looking at his watch and finally telephoned the client he had arranged to meet that afternoon to offer his apologies for being delayed indefinitely.

'We'll take your car,' Vasilis announced as Lakkis finished his telephone call. 'I'll pick mine up when we come back.'

'Where are we going?' asked Lakkis.

'To my apartment first, then to the bank. Stavros will meet us there.'

Vasilis was no more than a few minutes inside his apartment and came out carrying a holdall. Lakkis looked at him in surprise.

'Is that a case of clothes for Vasi?'

Vasilis shook his head. 'Hopefully he'll not need a change of clothing. This is to put the money in from the bank. Twenty five thousand is rather too large an amount to put in my pocket.'

Lakkis parked in a space reserved for bank employees and he and Vasilis waited on the steps until Stavros appeared.

'You realise this is most irregular,' he said by way of a greeting.

'It's an emergency. I can't have my son locked in a police cell over the weekend for the sake of a few Euros.'

'We'll have to go in at the side entrance. The main door can only be unlocked from inside.' Stavros led the way around the building and unlocked a door marked with a hazard sign for high voltage electricity. 'Take no notice of that,' he waved his hand. 'It's to deter unwanted intruders.'

Vasilis and Lakkis followed him inside and a short distance down a passage. He keyed in a code set in the wall and opened the security door.

'This will take a few minutes,' he said as he seated himself behind his desk and turned on his computer. His stubby fingers jabbed at the keys as the machine came to life, finally bringing up the accounts for Vasilis's hotels on to the screen. He ran his hand over his chin as he studied the figures.

'The bulk of the money could come from the Central. Your beach hotel and the Katerina should have sufficient to make up the balance.' Stavros swung himself around to face Vasilis. 'I have no access to the bank vault and I doubt if you'd want to carry that kind of sum around in cash with you.'

'I have a holdall with me.'

Stavros looked at the bag. 'You'd need something a good deal larger than that and I doubt if you'd be able to lift it. I'll move the money from your account into a bank holding account and then issue you with a guaranteed bank credit note. You'll be able to put that in your pocket.'

'Whatever.'

Stavros created a new account and keyed in a code to transfer twenty five thousand Euros from the account for the Central hotel to the bank. He frowned in consternation as the screen began to flash with the information 'insufficient funds' and cancelled the transaction.

'I must have pressed the wrong key,' Stavros mumbled and repeated the procedure getting the same result. 'I don't understand. There must be a malfunction on the computer. The balance on the account is quite sufficient, but when I try to withdraw I'm unable to do so. Let me see if I can put through a debit on another account.'

Vasilis sat with a growing feeling of frustration. He should have asked if there was a time limit in which he had to produce the bail money.

Stavros shook his head. 'There doesn't appear to be a problem anywhere except on your accounts. The computer is refusing to allow me to enter any debit transactions for your hotels. I can only imagine that the credits that have been paid in have not been verified through the system yet.'

'So what can I do? I need the money for my son's bail immediately. He's totally innocent of the charge against him and certainly doesn't want to spend the weekend in jail.'

'Well,' Stavros Tanakis considered. Mr Iliopolakis and his son were two very influential customers. He did not want them to move their accounts elsewhere due to a malfunction of the computer. 'I suppose I could raise a loan against your property.'

'Then do so.'

'I'll need a guarantor. It's Saturday so I'm not able to complete all the usual formalities of taking up written references. If it can wait until Monday there will be no problem and the computer could even be functioning correctly again by then.'

'It can't wait. I've told you that. Can't you act as a guarantor for me?'

Mr Tanakis shook his head. 'I'm not allowed to do so. I'm breaking all the rules as it is. Have you a colleague in the business who would guarantee you temporarily?'

Vasilis pulled out his mobile 'phone. There was only one person he knew who might be willing to trust him for such a large sum.

'Giovanni, I need some help. Vasi has been arrested for dangerous driving. It's all a mistake as he was nowhere near the area. He's being held at the police station and his bail has been placed at twenty five thousand Euros.' Vasilis heard Giovanni gasp. 'I know it's extortionate and ridiculous. I'm at the bank in Heraklion. Stavros opened up as a favour for me, but we have a problem. The computer is malfunctioning and it won't let him withdraw any money from any of my accounts. He's agreed to give me a bank loan, but I need a guarantor. It will only be until Monday. Would you be willing?'

Giovanni hesitated. He had no reason to doubt the veracity of Vasilis's statement, but if the man was in financial difficulties Giovanni could end up bankrupting their own business. Strictly speaking it was not even his business, it belonged to his uncle. 'Can I speak to Mr Tanakis?'

Vasilis handed his mobile to the bank manager and Stavros repeated Vasilis's request to Giovanni and explained that the only problem was the computer.

'I assure you, Mr Pirenzi, the money is on Mr Iliopolakis's account, but I am unable to access it. To grant him a temporary loan

I need a guarantor. I'm sure the technicians will have sorted out the problem by Monday and you will be released from the charge on your property immediately.'

'How quickly do you need my decision?'

'Immediately.'

Giovanni tapped his fingers on the counter at the taverna. He would have liked to discuss the problem with Marianne and his Uncle Yannis before giving the bank manager an answer.

'I suppose so. Yes. I'll guarantee Vasilis Iliopolakis for twenty five thousand, but I need to speak to him again.'

Stavros nodded his head towards Vasilis and handed him back his mobile.

'Thank you, Giovanni. I can't talk now, but I'll telephone you as soon as Vasi has been released and we're back at the apartment. Saffron? Oh, yes, she's fine. She's with Cathy.' Vasilis wiped the sweat from his brow and closed his mobile 'phone.

Mr Tanakis entered another programme on the computer and copied a loan document, inserting Vasilis's name and Giovanni's as the guarantor. He waited until it had printed and pushed it across the table to Vasilis.

'I'll need your signature.' He indicated the space. 'Mr Tsilikadis can sign on behalf of Mr Pirenzi as he's a solicitor.'

Vasilis signed his name with a flourish and Lakkis inserted his own, adding per pro.

Now what happens?' asked Vasilis.

'I'll issue you with a promissory note against the loan.'

'Won't the police station want cash?'

Stavros shook his head. 'They'd have nowhere to store it safely until the banks opened. They would then need to arrange a collection by a security firm.' He entered another password that gave him access to a programme that was only available to him and two other members of staff and printed off a promissory note, the name of the bank heavily embossed at the top of the sheet and watermarked throughout with the bank's name. He signed it and handed it to Vasilis.

'Provided the police don't try to verify it there should be no problem,' he smiled.

'What do you mean? You said this was as good as money.'

'It needs two signatures on it to be legally acceptable, but I doubt if the police know that.'

Vasilis opened the holdall and withdrew a quantity of notes held in a rubber band. 'Thank you for your trouble. I appreciate it.' He passed the bundle to Mr Tanakis and placed the note safely into his wallet.

Stavros smiled and eyed the money greedily. It was always worthwhile doing a favour for Mr Iliopolakis.

Superintendent Solomakis accepted the credit note without questioning the number of signatures on it. When he had placed the bail for Vasi at such a high amount he had certainly not expected Mr Iliopolakis to be able to raise the sum within a couple of hours. He had hoped he would have the young man in the cells over the weekend and be able to elicit a full confession from him. He hated hit and run drivers, having lost his sister to one when she was walking along the side of the road to school. They were no better than murderers

He frowned at Mr Tsilikadis whilst he waited for Vasi to be released and brought to the reception area. 'Mr Iliopolakis will need to be available for further questioning. We will be keeping his car here until we have completed our examination of it as it is considered as part of the evidence against him.'

Vasi appeared and smiled with relief. His possessions that had been removed from him earlier were placed on the desk and he was asked to check they were complete and sign for their return.

'Mr Iliopolakis, I have told your solicitor that we will be holding your car as evidence and you must be available for questioning. You will report to your nearest police station every day and you may not leave Crete without applying to us for permission.'

Vasi frowned. 'How long will those restrictions last?'

Thranassis looked at him keenly. 'Did you have plans to leave the country?'

'In November. I have arranged a trip to England.'

'Your vacation may well have to wait until our enquiries are completed. You will be advised when the reporting requirements are lifted.' Thranassis gathered his papers together and walked out of the room leaving the door open.

Mr Tsilikadis hurried after Thranassis. 'I would like to take photographs of the damage to Mr Iliopolakis's car.'

'We have taken photographs.'

'Then I would like a copy of them on behalf of my client.' Mr Tsilikadis spoke firmly and looked challengingly at Thranassis.

Thranassis scowled. If the car suffered any further damage whilst in the hands of the police Mr Tsilikadis would be in a position to claim compensation from them. He pulled a file out from beneath his desk, removed the photographs and handed them to Makkis.

'Make a copy of those and get Mr Tsilikadis to sign for them. I have other work to do.'

Mr Tsilikadis waited impatiently for Makkis to return. He removed the photographs from the envelope Makkis handed to him and showed them to Vasi. 'Have a look at those and tell me if they look accurate to you. If you disagree with any of them tell me now and we'll insist that we take our own photographs.'

Mr Tsilikadis waited whilst Vasi scrutinized the photographs. Finally Vasi shook his head. 'They're about as accurate of the damage as I remember.'

The lawyer placed the envelope into his briefcase. 'Let's go and find your father. He said he would wait in the taverna across the road.' He took Vasi's elbow. 'Come on; before that Superintendent changes his mind about you leaving.'

'So where do we go from there, sir?' asked Makkis, as Mr Tsilikadis and Vasi left the station. 'That man who claimed to be a witness could be a publicity seeker and making up the information.'

Thranassis snorted. 'If he was making it up how did he know the car was a dark saloon and give part of the registration number?'

'Maybe he has a grudge against Mr Iliopolakis. He could have vandalised the car and then taken advantage of the accident happening to implicate him. Shouldn't we ask all the force to keep their eyes open for damaged cars and pull the owners in for questioning? We could put out a message to the garages, those who specialise in repair jobs, and ask them to let us know if anyone takes a car in with damage on the passenger side.'

Thranassis scowled at the sergeant. 'I think it more likely Mr Iliopolakis had a grudge against the victim. He's the manager of his local bank and he'd refused a loan to Mr Iliopolakis earlier in the week.' He was convinced that Vasi was guilty, but without a confession and only information from an anonymous caller he knew he would have to investigate further. 'I'm hoping the victim will regain consciousness and be able to give us a description of the driver or at the very least the car he was driving. We'll ask the local news channel to appeal for that witness to come forward. They're bound to broadcast the accident.'

Mr Tsilikadis took Vasi's elbow and steered him across the road to the taverna where he could see Vasilis sitting,

'What took you so long?' he asked.

'It's no good trying to rush the police force, you know that. There's nothing more I can do now until they call Vasi for questioning again. He has to report to a police station every day and cannot leave Crete without permission.' Mr Tsilikadis raised his hand and began to hurry back to where his own car was parked as he sensed Vasilis was about to ask him to return and argue further with the police chief.

'Send me your bill,' Vasilis called after him.

'I certainly will,' Lakkis muttered.

'Thank you, Pappa. How's Saffie?' asked Vasi immediately.

'She's at home with Cathy. I thought it more sensible to take her there than have her sitting here with me for hours.'

'How did you know I'd been arrested?'

'When Saffie was told she could leave the station she telephoned Marianne to ask for help. Marianne 'phoned me and I came straight down. When the police wouldn't release you I called Mr Tsilikadis.'

'I'm glad you did. I was worried they were going to keep me in a cell indefinitely.'

Vasilis nodded. 'I'll want to know all the details when we get home. I only know what Saffie told me.' He took some change from his pocket and left it on the table for the waiter to collect.

Saffron's face lit up with relief when she saw Vasi walk through the door with his father. He took her hands in his.

'Thank you for telephoning Marianne. I would probably still be sitting in the police station otherwise.'

'What would have happened if you had been alone?' asked Saffron.

'Oh,' Vasi tried to brush the idea aside, 'they would eventually have allowed me to make a telephone call. I really would like something to eat. I wasn't offered anything at the station and I'm ravenous.'

Saffron nodded. 'Cathy and I haven't eaten yet. I couldn't face anything. I'll help her get a rather late lunch ready.' Saffron tried to smile, but she still felt quite sick. She had been so frightened when she had been separated from Vasi and questioned.

Vasilis motioned to Vasi to sit down. 'I need to speak to you about your bail money.'

Vasi smiled. 'I'm convinced that policeman thought you wouldn't be able to raise it and he'd have me in prison over the weekend.'

'It was quite a close call. I persuaded Mr Tanakis to open up the bank, but he wasn't able to take any money from our accounts. He thought it was a computer malfunction, but he tried a couple of other accounts and said there was no problem with those. He finally agreed to the bank giving me a loan and I had to 'phone Giovanni to ask him to guarantee me.'

Vasi frowned. 'According to Alecos there wasn't enough collateral to give me a loan to buy the Imperia.'

'How much did you ask for?'

'Eighteen hundred and fifty thousand. If you estimate the value of the Central or the Hersonissos hotel either one of them is worth more than the loan I wanted for the Imperia.'

'So why should he refuse? You have plenty of collateral.'

'That's what I told him, but he wouldn't listen. He said he would have to have your approval before he could agree to include your hotels to guarantee me. He also said he would need to approach the Head Office in Heraklion regarding the way we ran our accounts and I should come back later in the week for their decision. In the meantime I asked Mr Palamakis to have a quick look at the property. He advised me not to touch it as there was far too much work that needed doing. I called at the Imperia to tell the owners I had changed my mind and they had already sold it to Alecos.'

Vasilis frowned. 'What did he want it for? His family have never invested in property.'

'I think that was just to spite me. He insisted I explained my proposals for the hotel and he thought he would capitalise on them.' Vasi grinned. 'It has definitely rebounded on him. I returned to say I'd changed my mind about buying and you should have seen his face. I think he'd gambled on me wanting it enough to pay him an inflated amount for the property.'

'So why did you need to go to the bank?'

'I wanted to find out if Alecos had really approached them and if they were dissatisfied with the way our accounts were conducted. If it was just him being malicious I was going to ask to have him disciplined and have a written apology from them. Our reputation was at stake.' Vasi spoke indignantly.

'I'll certainly want an explanation from the bank,' agreed Vasilis.

'I think it would be a good idea to visit the Central and have a look at the accounts ourselves. Mr Tanakis couldn't understand why he was unable to put through the transaction on our accounts. We don't want to accuse the bank and then find there was a discrepancy somewhere in our accounting.'

'We ought to have something to eat first?' Vasi's stomach was rumbling uncomfortably. 'Then I'll telephone Dimitra and ask her to meet us there?'

'Is there any need?'

Vasi shrugged. 'I just thought she'd be considerably quicker than either of us. She's so familiar with the system she could work it in her sleep.'

Vasilis gave his son a questioning look. 'Dimitra is completely trustworthy isn't she?'

'I've always thought so. I know I split the files up as a precaution and she shouldn't be able to access some of them, only the authority to collect a back-up from the individual hotels at the end of the day.'

Vasilis nodded. 'Phone her when we've eaten and ask her to meet us at the Central as soon as possible.' Vasilis rose from the table and went out to the patio where Cathy and Saffron were waiting for the men to join them in a late lunch.

Dimitra was not amused at having to return to the hotel on a Saturday afternoon. Alecos would be arriving shortly and she wanted to have their evening meal prepared so she would not have to spend time in the kitchen when he arrived. She tried to telephone him on his mobile and was told there was no signal. That probably meant he was driving towards Heraklion at this moment. The road rose and fell between the mountains and it was often difficult to use a mobile.

She wrote a brief note addressed to Alecos and stuck it on her front door. Once he had seen it he would probably 'phone to find out how long she was going to be at the hotel or come there to find her. No doubt it was something to do with the computer failure at the bank that Alecos had tried to rectify the previous day and it could be useful if he did arrive at the Central so he could answer any queries for Mr Iliopolakis.

Dimitra hesitated. It was possible the computer at the hotel had malfunctioned and it could be wise to take the back-up she kept at home with her. That way Mr Iliopolakis would be able to appreciate what a conscientious employee she was and deserved an increase in her salary. Thankful that Alecos had returned it to her the previous evening she slipped it inside her handbag before locking her door and walking to the end of the road where she was sure she would be able to hail a taxi.

Vasi switched on the computer in the office, typed in his password and opened up the accounts for the Central hotel. He pored over them, scrolling back over the last three weeks, finally shaking his head.

'I can't see any problem there. There's no sudden increase in expenditure or drop in income. I'll have a look at the beach hotel.'

'I ordered forty new umbrellas for round the pool and on the beach,' Vasilis reminded his son. 'The invoice for them may have been paid this month.'

Vasi shrugged. 'That shouldn't make a lot of difference, unless Aristo tapped in some extra zeros,' he grinned. 'Even if he did, the error should have been picked up by Dimitra when the accounts were balanced.'

Vasi closed the programme and opened the one for the beach hotel; again he could not see any reason for the bank to say the account was not being properly administered. Having paid the overheads for the hotel there was a healthy balance showing on the account.

'The invoice for the umbrellas is listed as outstanding.' Vasi pointed to the item showing on the screen with his pen. 'Now, let's have a look at Hersonissos.'

He scrolled up and down the entries, finally closing the programme and entering his password for the Katerina hotel at

Aghios Nikolaos. Dimitra arrived as he studied the entries and stood hesitantly at their side. Vasi acknowledged her with a brief nod of his head, closed the document and opened the accounts for the hotel in Elounda.

'Have you had any problems with the computer this week?' asked Vasi.

'Not with our computer. I think there was a problem at the bank with their system.'

Vasi raised his eyebrows. 'What was that? Do you know?'

'Something about transferring money between your accounts and the computer operator had run into problems.'

Vasilis frowned. 'I didn't ask for any funds to be transferred. Did you, Vasi?'

Vasi shook his head. 'I asked for a loan, not a transfer.'

'I wish we could access our account at the bank,' grumbled Vasilis. 'If the bank made a transfer in error that could have made Alecos think we had a cash flow problem and also account for the problem I had this morning.'

Vasi looked at Dimitra. 'How did you know the bank had a problem? Did it show up on our computer?'

Dimitra reddened. 'Alecos told me.'

'What exactly did he tell you?'

Dimitra's blush deepened. 'He said the computer operator at the bank had managed to delete your file whilst he was completing a transfer for you.'

Vasi stood up and faced Dimitra. 'So why did Alecos tell you? Surely it was a bank matter.'

'He thought I might be able to help.'

'How?'

'By replacing the information for him,' Dimitra mumbled, embarrassed.

'And did you go to the bank and do that?'

Dimitra shook her head. 'I allowed Alecos to borrow the back-up so he could do it.'

Vasi let out his breath in a hiss. 'How dare you do that without the permission of my father or myself?'

'I'm sorry,' Dimitra's eyes widened in fear, certain she was going to be dismissed immediately. 'I didn't see any harm. Alecos said it would save the man from being sacked. I thought I was being helpful.'

'Helpful to Alecos, no doubt!'

Vasilis held up his hand. 'Wait a minute, how did you get hold of a back-up? When you have run the disk off for all the hotels' accounts you give it to me and I lock it in the safe. The balances on the accounts are brought forward and the details of the finance for the previous week are deleted from the computer. No one has access to that back-up unless they have the code to the safe and the key to that strong box.'

Dimitra hung her head. 'I keep a back-up of my own.'

Vasilis frowned. 'You do? Why?'

'Alecos suggested it could be a good idea for me to have one in case the computer ever failed and the details needed to be recovered. He said they take a back-up every day at the bank. They send one to the Head Office and keep one in the branch. If they need to restore files they can do it easily instead of having to repeat all the previous work.'

Vasi shook his head. 'With a current back-up stored in the safe there is no need for you to have one as well. Where is this back-up now? Does Alecos still have it?'

Dimitra opened her handbag. 'He only borrowed it for a day. He returned it to me last night.'

'Then I think we'll have a quick look at it.'

Vasi inserted the disk into the machine and waited until it was loaded. He ran the cursor up and down and could see no immediate error. He gave a sigh.

'The only way to check this properly is to run off a paper copy of all the transactions for the hotels for the previous week, maybe two, just to be on the safe side. It's going to take time.'

He filled the printer with paper. 'When this is finished we'll get the back-up from the safe and check the paper copy with the figures on that.'

'Couldn't we use the machine in reception to run the back up from the safe?' asked Vasilis.

Vasi shook his head. 'We would need to have the machines next to each other. By the time we had disconnected and reconnected it would be no quicker than having a paper copy. It's also easier to tick things off with a paper copy. You tend to lose your place when you try to do it from a screen.'

Dimitra stood uncertainly beside the two men. Should she tell them that the quickest way to check would be to add the columns of figures and then cross cast?

'There is a quicker way,' she volunteered.

Vasi looked at her. 'How?'

'Add the columns and do a cross cast. Take the balance from the previous week, deduct the debits, add the credits and you should end up with the current balance.' She saw no reason why there should be an error but if Vasi and his father wanted to check for accuracy her way would save a considerable amount of time.

'You do it,' Vasi ordered and relinquished his position at the computer to Dimitra.

Her fingers skipping expertly over the keys, Dimitra began to add the columns. Having completed the debits she moved on to the credits and was surprised when she saw the debit total was more than that shown for the credits. She had not noticed any excessive expenditure, but when she added the previous week's balance the account was no longer in credit. She frowned.

'I don't understand. There must be an error that has slipped through on one of the hotel accounts.' She reddened. 'I must have carried a figure over incorrectly.'

'How can you find out?'

'I'll need to go into the separate hotel accounts and check them in the same way. That should show it up immediately.'

Vasi nodded. He had a sick feeling in the pit of his stomach. He hoped it was where he had eaten his lunch too quickly and had nothing to do with the figures not balancing.

Dimitra was beginning to feel frightened. On each of the hotel's accounts the debits were greater than the credits, which then made the final balance incorrect. She was certain that they had all the accounts had balanced correctly when she had copied the disk, once for herself and another for Vasilis Iliopolakis to place in the safe. What had Alecos done? She licked her dry lips.

'Maybe this disk is corrupted where I let Alecos borrow it to use at the bank. He may have placed some sort of security code on it that hides certain transactions. If you brought me the other one from your safe, Mr Iliopolakis we could check that.'

'I want a paper copy of this one,' said Vasi firmly and pressed the key to start the printer running.

Dimitra sat and watched as the sheets of paper slid out onto the tray. A smile of relief spread across her face. 'I know what it is. It's the transfer. The money has been taken but the figures have not been recorded.' She let out a sigh of relief. 'The one from the safe should show the figures correctly before the transfer took place.'

'There should not have been a transfer.' Vasi spoke sharply. 'Neither my father nor I authorised a transfer. If one hotel had needed some extra funds we would have telephoned each other before we approached the bank and asked them to complete the transaction.'

'Maybe another hotelier asked the bank to complete a transfer and the bank entered your account number by mistake,' suggested Dimitra. 'That could explain why Alecos was so worried about it.'

Vasi glanced at her sceptically. He remembered the stricken look on Alecos's face when he had refused to purchase the Imperia hotel. An incredible thought crossed his mind. Had Alecos actually bought the property with funds from the Iliopolakis hotels? He shook his head. Surely it could not be possible.

The paper accounts were still running out of the machine when

Vasilis returned with the disk from the safe. Vasi looked at his father. 'I'm not going to bother with this cross checking that Dimitra showed us. I'm going to run off a paper copy and then we'll sit and check the figures manually.'

'Is it alright if I 'phone Alecos and tell him where I am?' asked Dimitra. 'I couldn't get a signal on his mobile so I left a message for him on my door. I'd like to make sure he found it.'

'Ask him to come to the Central. I want to ask him about this transfer and bank error.'

Dimitra smiled brightly at him. 'Why didn't we think of that before? I'm sure he'll be able to explain exactly what has happened.'

Vasi did not answer her. He had a feeling Alecos would have a very plausible excuse whereby he was unable to meet them at the hotel with an explanation.

Dimitra frowned as she closed her mobile. 'I still can't contact him. I'm surprised he hasn't 'phoned me here. I wonder where he is.'

Vasi waited until the printer had finished spewing paper, covered in figures, on to the receiving tray. As Dimitra stretched out her hand to retrieve them Vasi stopped her.

'Don't touch them. I want to make sure they're all there and in order.'

Dimitra looked at him sulkily. 'I'm obviously not much use to you. I might as well go back home. After all, it is supposed to be my day off.'

'No. You can go to the bar and bring a couple of bottles of beer back with you.'

Dimitra glared at the back of Vasi's head. She was an employee, not a servant. With a loud 'Tut!' she tossed her head and walked towards the bar whilst Vasi inserted the disk from the safe and gave the command to print.

He removed the sheets from the tray and laid them carefully to one side. 'When Dimitra returns she can put a large red cross on each sheet so we know which disk the pages came from. I don't want them to get muddled up and have to run them all off again.'

'I could start doing that,' offered Vasilis.

'Pappa, you're the boss. You give mundane jobs like that to your employees.' Vasi smiled. 'Remember the jobs you told me to do for the first few weeks? You could go and find out if there's a suite free. We'll need space to lay all this paper out.'

Dimitra returned still looking disgruntled. She placed two open bottles of beer beside Vasi and took a mouthful from the third that she held in her hand.

'Thanks.' Vasi lifted the beer and drank deeply. 'If there's a suite free we'll take all this upstairs so we have enough space to lay it out and check it properly. In the meantime you place a large red cross on the top of each page of the papers from your copy disk, but make sure you don't get them out of order.'

Vasilis returned, confirming they could have their choice of three empty suites and seized upon the beer gratefully.

'We'll take a couple more beers up with us, then the hard work will begin. We'll check each corresponding page to make certain the figures agree and that way we should find the balance discrepancy.'

'What do we do when we find it?' asked Vasilis.

'We'll have to wait until Monday and ask the bank to look at their records again. Once we've double checked with them we can do an appropriate contra-entry and everything will agree.'

Dimitra continued to place a red cross on each of paper. How she wished she had never agreed to lend Alecos the disk. Once Mr Iliopolakis and Vasi had been to the bank there were bound to be questions asked and Alecos would no doubt be in trouble, although he had acted in his employee's best interest. She would ask to go outside the hotel and see if she was able to get a signal for Alecos's mobile. At least she would be able to send him a text message and warn him, even if the signal was not strong enough for them to have a conversation.

Saffron cleared the table after their lunch and Cathy placed any remaining portions in the fridge.

'I've no idea how much longer they will be at the bank, but they'll probably appreciate a snack when they return. Vasilis said they are running off a disk and need to check the figures for the hotels for last week. Apparently Dimitra has been making a disk each week as well as the master copy for Vasilis and she lent it to Alecos. Now the figures don't balance.'

'These glitches happen with computers occasionally. All our hospital appointments are kept on them. One day I was handed my list for the day and I was seeing the same person every half an hour. The operator hadn't looked at it, just run it off and put it in my tray. I don't know what she had done, but it wouldn't let her change the names and eventually she wrote them out for me by hand.' Saffron smiled. 'There's a lot to be said for pen and paper.'

'I'm so glad I was never expected to learn how to work a computer. Vasi has tried to show me, but I really do not understand. I can just about manage to send an e-mail to Marion.' Cathy shrugged. 'Now I don't really need to do that. I can pick up the telephone as she's on her own again.'

'Why couldn't you telephone her before?' asked Saffron curiously.

'When Adonis was stationed on the army base she would come down to stay with me for a few days each week. I really missed her when they moved to Rhodes.' Cathy sighed. 'We had been such close friends for so long. She was also my nurse after my accident. For a while I could telephone and chat each day, then her husband said we were spending too long on the 'phone together. I tried 'phoning when he was at the base, but her mother-in-law always told him when he came home and then he would get angry with Marion. We arranged that she would call in at a network shop whenever she could and we would e-mail each other.'

'Why didn't she buy a mobile?'

'Adonis said she didn't need one and by then she was too frightened of his temper to defy him.'

'Poor girl. I can sympathise with her. I was frightened of Ranjit sometimes and I could never tell Marjorie. It would have worried her so much. At least Marion had you to confide in.'

'It was a small thing after all the care she had given to me. Had she not arranged to bring me to Crete I would never have met Vasilis. I would probably still be stuck in a wheelchair in England feeling sorry for myself if Marion had not been such a bully.' Cathy smiled happily; then frowned. 'Of course, if we hadn't come to Crete she wouldn't have met Adonis.'

Saffron was longing to know more about Marion, but did not feel she should pry. She knew she would feel very hurt if a friend passed on personal information about her marriage to Ranjit to an unknown person without her permission.

'Was your spine injured when you had your accident?' she asked instead.

Cathy shook her head. 'There was nothing broken, thank goodness. Badly bruised, of course. It was my legs that suffered the worst damage, multiple fractures. I had to be cut out of my car. The specialists kept telling me I would walk again, but I didn't believe them.'

'Do you still see a specialist?' asked Saffron.

'Not now. There's no need. Everything that was broken eventually mended. Of course, now I'm older I have arthritis.' Cathy sighed deeply. 'I shall probably end up in a chair again one day.'

'Does that thought worry you?'

'It certainly doesn't excite me! I just have to accept it and be thankful for every day that I don't need it. Now we're living here I have to admit it is much easier. No stairs and the ground is relatively level outside. I don't think I could manage to walk up the hill from the village now. At least when I *do* have to depend upon a chair again I can have an electric one and be reasonably independent. There are so many old people over here who can just about stagger to their door and spend the day watching the traffic go by. Either they cannot afford an electric chair or where they live it would be impossible to use one.' Cathy smiled brightly. 'Why are we talking about such a depressing subject? Tell me about this hotel that Vasi was so keen to buy. What was so special about it?'

Vasilis called over the figures taken from his master disk to Vasi who had the papers marked with a red cross spread out before him. Dimitra sat miserably in an armchair. She had tried to text Alecos and had been unsuccessful in contacting him again. It was unlike him to forget to charge his mobile and if he had he could have contacted her from a pay 'phone. She could only think his mobile 'phone had been stolen and he had not realised. She chewed at her finger nails. Alecos should certainly have arrived at her apartment by now so why had he not come to the hotel? She was worried that the note she had left had blown away and he was sitting outside annoyed that she was not there as arranged. That brought her full circle back to wondering why he had not tried to telephone her.

Vasi frowned. 'There's no credit on my sheet for that date.'

'Let me see.' Vasilis pulled the sheet of paper towards him and compared it with the one in front of him. He ringed the amount on his copy and passed the paper back to his son. 'Carry on calling. Let's see if some others turn up that are not on your copy.'

For a further half an hour Vasilis called the figures across ringing the figures that Vasi said were missing. The balance for each day read correctly on both print outs, but when Vasi did the calculation manually the figures disagreed. Finally he took a blank sheet of paper and wrote the individual amounts down and added them up.

'Where are those figures Dimitra produced?' asked Vasi. 'Let's see if the difference between the credits and debits that she had equals our figure.' A few moments later Vasi threw his pen down on the table. 'To the cent.' He frowned. 'Now, if you deduct the sum of those credits from the total on your print out it agrees with mine, yes?'

Vasilis nodded agreement.

'And if I add the total of the missing credits to my figure that then agrees with your total?'

Again Vasilis nodded.

'I now take the debits from the credits, add the previous week's balance and we both agree.'

Vasilis shook his head. 'You've written down the wrong figure for the opening balance.'

'No I haven't.' Vasi looked at back at the page. 'Tell me the figure you have.'

Vasilis called out the numbers slowly and Vasi threw his pen down in disgust. 'Someone has tampered with these figures.' He looked at Dimitra. 'Did you change anything on this disk before you lent it to Alecos?'

'Nothing. I checked that the overall statement balanced before I ran off two copies as usual and gave one to Mr Iliopolakis.'

'So the only other person who had access to these figures was Alecos?'

Dimitra nodded miserably. 'He must have made an error.'

'The only error he made was thinking he could get away with it.'

'But why should he wish to falsify our accounts?' asked Vasilis.

Vasi shook his head. 'I'll talk to you about it later, Pappa. I'd really like to speak to Alecos and ask for his explanation before I go to the bank on Monday and ask for an enquiry. Dimitra, you obviously have his mobile number. Will you read it out to me, please?'

'I'm not getting any reply from him.'

'There could be a fault on your 'phone.'

Dimitra gave him a scathing look and read out Alecos's telephone number. Vasi wrote it down and then keyed the numbers into his own mobile. The line was completely dead. Vasi frowned and tried again with the same result. He shrugged.

'I can only think he dropped it somewhere and it's damaged. He probably hasn't realised.' Vasi shuffled the papers together and pocketed the disk Dimitra had lent to Alecos. 'There's nothing more we can do here today. We'll give you a lift home, Dimitra, and when

Alecos does contact you please tell him we wish to speak with him urgently. I'm sure it's no good asking you not to tell him that we've checked the disk and that I'm planning to visit the Head Office first thing on Monday morning. If he has any sense he'll ask to meet with my father and myself before then and give us an explanation.'

As they made their way out of the hotel Vasi stopped at the reception desk and asked for the room to be made ready for occupation, along with another suite.

'I shall be returning this evening with a friend,' he explained. 'I only expect us to be here the one night, but if my plans change I will let you know.'

'Of course, sir. That will be no problem.' The receptionist smiled and looked at Vasi curiously. The man had never asked for two suites to be reserved in his name before. If he was planning to stay in Heraklion for the night why wasn't he staying with his father?

'Saffie, I am so sorry. I know Cathy will have looked after you, but your plans for the day were ruined.'

Saffron shrugged. 'Provided I'm not sitting in that police station I'm quite happy. Cathy has been a marvellous hostess. We haven't stopped talking all afternoon. How did you get on?'

'We've found where the discrepancy lies. I think Alecos did some imaginative accounting.'

Saffron frowned. 'What's that?'

'Where you put in false figures to try to disguise a problem. No one minds if it's a small amount where ninety cents has been entered as nine which makes the balance eighty one cents out, but we are talking about far larger sums than that.'

'You were going to tell me why you thought Alecos had altered the figures,' Vasilis reminded his son.

'I didn't want to say anything in front of Dimitra. For all I know Alecos has changed his 'phone number and she gave us the old one. If that was the case she could be talking to him now and he will have a plausible story ready for the Head Office. I really would like to speak to him first and see if there has been some genuine mistake on his part, but somehow I doubt it.'

'So why do you think he asked Dimitra for the copy disk and changed the figures?'

'When I asked him for a loan to buy the Imperia he wanted to know all about my plans for the hotel. He then went behind my back and bought it himself. I wasn't sure if he was going to have a heart attack or pass out when I told him I was no longer interested in the property. I think, and it is only a thought, that Alecos 'borrowed' the money from our account to purchase the hotel. He expected to sell it back to me for far more than he paid. That would have meant he could replace the money into our accounts before we realised it was missing and make a handsome profit for himself. We would never have known if Mr Palamakis hadn't warned me about the problems with the hotel and I hadn't changed my mind about investing.'

'Surely that's totally illegal,' frowned Saffron.

'Of course,' agreed Vasi, 'But manipulation of the accounts by the banks have been known to take place. Whoever is responsible is given the sack. Unfortunately there is always someone else willing to take the risk and hope not to be discovered.'

'So what will you do?' asked Cathy.

Vasi shrugged. 'There's nothing we can do until the bank opens on Monday. I'm going to hire a car and drive Saffie back to Elounda. We'll spend tomorrow down there and I'll try to make up to her for today.'

'I have to take my passport in to the police station,' Saffron reminded him.

'We'll do that first thing. I also have to report to the police station. It should only be a formality. Then the rest of the day can be spent however you wish.'

'What about your car?'

'I'll call at the police station on Monday after I've been to the bank and see when they're prepared to release it. I wish I knew who it was who vandalised it. I'd be sending them the bill for car hire and the repairs.'

Vasilis frowned. 'Maybe someone planned to break into the house and realised when they saw your car that you were staying there. It could be a good idea if you asked Lambros to leave the dogs up there over night in case they come back.'

Vasi nodded. 'I'll have a word with him when we're down there.' He frowned. 'It must have been someone pretty local who knew the dogs were not there. I can't see a stranger to the area taking a chance when there are notices saying there are guard dogs patrolling.'

'Maybe they didn't see them as it was dark.'

Vasi smiled. 'In that case it was even more of a shame the dogs weren't there. Imagine being pinned up against the wall by those two.'

'They would probably have tried to sue us for keeping dangerous dogs! Are you staying for a meal or do you want me to drive you to a car hire?' asked Vasilis.

'We ought to leave now. I'll call a taxi. The driver is bound to know of a hire place that's open. We could drive around for hours before we found one.'

Saffron picked up her mobile. 'I ought to phone Marianne to let her know what's happening.'

Vasi shook his head. 'Wait until we've hired the car or we won't know what time we'll be back in Elounda.'

Saffron opened her mouth to say that Marianne would not be concerned about the time of her arrival and Vasi shook his head again. 'We don't want her to be expecting you in a couple of hours and then wondering what has happened when we are later.'

Vasi drove the car he had hired to the Central hotel. He smiled at Saffron as he drew into an unmarked parking space.

'I've booked us in here for the night.'

'So that's why you didn't want me to 'phone Marianne?'

'Exactly. I knew if I told my father I planned to stay in Heraklion for the night he would offer us the spare bedroom. I prefer to be alone with you. I arranged for two suites to be ready for us this evening.'

'Two?'

'I have a reputation to protect.' Vasi grinned at her. 'We need only use one.'

'What about my reputation?' asked Saffron.

'They do not know you, whereas I am the owner. I cannot be seen to be bringing young ladies to the hotel to spend the night with me.' Vasi looked at her with mock seriousness.

Saffron gave a little giggle. 'I haven't even got a toothbrush with me.'

'Nor have I. That is no problem. We will go out for a meal and there's bound to be a pharmacy open where we can buy one. You can call Marianne and say we have decided to stay in Heraklion for the night and will drive down tomorrow morning.'

Vasi and Saffron entered the suite he had booked for Saffron and rumpled the bedding, left the basin and the shower wet as if they had been used and a damp towel draped over the rail, before retiring to the room two doors further along the corridor.

Vasi switched on the television. 'I want to see the local news,' he explained. 'There may be something about the accident.'

The television cameras had taken shots of the accident site from all angles, showing the track marks and trail of broken bushes where the car had slid sideways down the ravine finally come to rest at an angle up against a large boulder with the bonnet a mass of twisted metal. With a sombre face the newscaster asked for anyone who may have been in the vicinity between the hours of eleven at night and five that morning to contact them. They were trying to determine the exact time of the accident and hoped someone would have noticed the broken barrier as they drove past. The name of the victim was given as Alecos Vikelakis, the manager of the bank in Aghios Nikolaos. The reporter added that the registration number of a car believed to have been the cause of the accident had been telephoned anonymously to the police and they were requesting the informant to come forwards as he could be a vital witness.

Vasi drew in his breath. 'So that was why they wanted to charge me.'

Saffron looked at him in surprise. 'What do you mean?'

'The accident victim was Alecos Vikelakis, the bank manager.'

'Why should that make any difference?'

'I told the police I was going to the bank in Heraklion to ask for an investigation into the reason why Alecos had refused the loan I had requested. They obviously think I pushed him off the road in retaliation and that was how my car was damaged.'

Saffron looked at Vasi, her eyes wide. 'But that's impossible. The damage was done to your car when you were parked outside your house.'

'We know that is the truth, but they do not. I would not be so stupid as to try to drive him off the road and over the side. If the car wheels locked both cars could go over the edge. I was in the maintenance division in the air force. I know how engines work. If I had wanted to cause Alecos to have a car accident I could have tampered with his vehicle and that would have been far safer for me.'

Saffron shuddered. 'It doesn't bear thinking about. His car looked such a mess.'

'The rocks and trees would have caused that when it slid down the side of the ravine.'

'So why do they think someone forced him over the edge? Why couldn't he just have been driving too fast and misjudged the corner?'

'They've come to that conclusion due to the damage on the driver's side of the car.'

Saffron looked at him dubiously. 'I don't see how they can tell the difference between the damage on one side from the other.'

'They have specialists who understand the effects of impact damage. If he drove over the edge accidentally it is likely he would have ended up nose first in a tree or possibly somersaulted and landed on the roof. It appears that he travelled down the ravine sideways which would indicate that his car had been rammed and forced over.' Vasi frowned. 'I ought to 'phone Dimitra. She was trying to contact him this afternoon and couldn't understand why she couldn't get through on his mobile. It will have been an awful shock to her if she heard about it through the news.'

'Did they say how badly Alecos was hurt?'

'He's in a critical condition, multiple fractures and concussion.'

Saffron shuddered and waited whilst Vasi keyed in Dimitra's number.

'Hello.' Her voice was tremulous.

'Dimitra, it's Vasi here. I've just seen the news?'

'Yes.'

'I'm very sorry. Is there anything I can do to help?'

'No.'

'Take whatever time you need off work. My father will understand.'

Dimitra did not answer him. She closed her mobile and curled back up on her sofa, overwhelmed in a cocoon of misery. It was all Vasi's fault. If there had not been a mistake somewhere in the accounts Alecos would not have borrowed the disk in the first place. He would not have been driving back to Elounda on a Friday night and would not have had the accident.

Sunday 23rd September

'So,' Vasi said, 'I have explained to Giovanni how I came to be arrested yesterday and thanked him for his help. You have collected your passport. We will visit the police station and speak to Mr Christos. When I have seen Lambros about the dogs what would you like to do?'

Saffron sighed. 'I think a lazy day beside your pool would suit me. We could take the dogs for a walk when it cools down.'

Vasi smiled at her. 'I too, would like that. Yesterday was a very bad day. I would like to relax and try to forget.'

'Could we give John a ride into Aghios Nikolaos? Uncle Yannis 'phoned and said he would really appreciate his help with cleaning the top shelves in the shop. Giovanni said he would take him in later, but I'm sure he has other jobs he'd like to be getting on with.'

'No problem. Find John and say we will take him in with us. He can return with Uncle Yannis when the shop closes.'

Saffron smiled and went inside the house to speak to John. She had already suggested the idea to him when Yannis had telephoned with his request.

Saffron found the police at Aghios Nikolaos far more pleasant than those in Heraklion. Inspector Christostofferakis greeted Vasi as a friend and wanted to hear about his car being vandalised.

'You are quite sure it happened whilst you were in the house?' he asked.

'Certain.'

'Superintendent Solomakis asked me to go up and look for any signs of paint chippings on your drive. I didn't find any.'

Vasi frowned. 'There were flakes of paint on the drive when we left that evening. I'd planned to sweep them up in the morning, but they must have blown away during the night. Did you ask Lambros if he had noticed any?'

The Inspector shook his head. 'He was cleaning the windows when I arrived. Took his time about answering the gates to me; then had to go and shut the dogs in. I asked him to show me where you usually parked your car and if he'd noticed anything unusual that morning. He said the dogs had been a bit excited and restless when he arrived, but nothing else.'

Vasi looked at the policeman earnestly. 'I didn't run Alecos off the road, Mr Christos.'

Christos shrugged. 'I have to keep an open mind. I'll 'phone through to Heraklion and say you've been in and also that I've seen the lady's passport and all is in order. Don't forget you have to report to a station every day whilst you're on bail.'

Vasi pulled a face. 'I feel like a criminal. Do you need to know my movements?'

'Not unless you plan to leave the country,' Christos smiled. 'Then I have to arrest you.'

Vasi smiled back. 'We're planning to spend the day at the house, lounging around the pool, take the dogs for a walk later and then go out for dinner. I don't think that will give you grounds for arresting me.'

'Enjoy your day.' Christos held out his hand to Saffron. 'My pleasure to meet you,' he said in Greek and Saffron smiled back, having no idea what he had said to her.

'Tell me,' said Saffron as they left the station, 'Why do you call that policeman Mr? I thought you had to address them using their rank.'

Vasi smiled at her. 'His surname is Christostofferakis. It is easier to shorten it to Christos, which happens to be his first name anyway. He has been the policeman in Aghios Nikolaos since I was at school here. Everyone calls him Mr Christos. Now, there is one other thing I would like to do whilst we are in Aghios Nikolaos. I would like to see if my friend Yiorgo is at home.'

Saffron nodded. 'Do you want me with you or shall I go for a wander around the shops?'

Vasi hesitated. 'I would like you to meet Yiorgo, but he does not speak English well. I need to talk to him. I want to tell him about Alecos and my car.'

'Then I'm sure it's better if you visit him without me. Why don't I go for a wander around and meet you back at the car in an hour?'

'You would not mind doing that?'

'Of course not. Would you like me to make it two hours?'

Vasi smiled. 'You begin to understand the Greek ways. An hour only gives us time to say hello to each other.'

Saffron squeezed Vasi's arm. 'Two hours it is. If you don't arrive I shall be calling you on your mobile.'

Vasi knocked on the door of Yiorgo's house and Barbara glared at him. 'Just because you're in town doesn't mean Yiorgo can spend the day with you. He's finally putting a cupboard door back on for me and he has to look after the boys this afternoon whilst I'm working.'

'I'll not keep him more than two hours. I'll even stay here and talk to him if it's more convenient for you.'

Barbara scowled. 'Provided he's back here by three thirty. My shift is four 'til ten and they don't like it if I'm late.'

'I'll make sure he's here by then, Barbara. Where are you working?'

'Wendys. It's good money during the season.' Barbara turned away from him. 'Yiorgo,' she called. 'Vasi is here.'

'Vasi?' Yiorgo was delighted. 'Come in, come in.' He emerged from the kitchen a screwdriver in his hand. He clasped Vasi to him, the screwdriver waving dangerously towards Vasi's neck. 'So, what brings you down here? Pappa told me you were very busy keeping an English girl entertained. Has she gone back to England or is she just tired of you?'

'Neither,' smiled Vasi. 'If you'd like to come with me you can meet her. She only speaks English, but I'm sure your smile will say a hundred complimentary words.'

'Let me finish putting a screw in this cupboard door. Young Stavros swung on it and pulled it loose. Barbara has been on at me for days to repair it.'

Vasi followed Yiorgo into the kitchen and waited whilst he fixed the last screw in place and checked the door closed properly. He replaced the screwdriver into his tool box and turned to Vasi.

'So, where are we going?'

'Anywhere reasonably quiet where we can sit and talk. I've got a problem.'

Yiorgo raised his eyebrows. 'She won't let you or she's let you and you've created a problem?'

'Nothing like that,' Vasi assured him. 'It's to do with Alecos.'

'It said on the news he was in hospital,' frowned Yiorgo. 'You're not planning to visit him, are you?'

Vasi shook his head. 'The police think I pushed him off the road.'

Yiorgo stopped drying his hands and looked at Vasi in amazement. 'That's ridiculous. You didn't, did you?' he added.

'Of course not. Let's find somewhere to have a beer and I'll tell you exactly what happened.'

Yiorgo listened attentively as Vasi related the events of Friday and Saturday. Yiorgo let out a long whistle when he finished. 'So you think Alecos has tampered with your accounts to stop you from buying the hotel you wanted and the police think you pushed him over the edge in retaliation?'

Vasi nodded. 'I'd like to know who vandalised my car, though. It's a bit of a coincidence that happened the same night.'

'There's no problem,' Yiorgo sat back and drained his beer. 'I'll tell the police I was working late up at your house. I'd had a couple of drinks with you and as I left I stumbled against your car with my tool box. I didn't realise at the time that I'd done any damage. Or I could say that after you took your girl home we went out together to a number of local bars and didn't get in until about five.'

Vasi shook his head. 'Thank you, Yiorgo, but no thank you. I can't start making up stories to tell the police. Once they checked them out and found they were lies I'd be in worse trouble.'

'So what do you want me to do?'

'Nothing, really. I just wanted to talk to you. See if you had any ideas.'

'There must be a way to prove you were nowhere near that road,' frowned Yiorgo. 'They were asking for a witness to come forwards. There must be any number of dark saloon cars with some numbers the same as your registration.'

Vasi nodded. 'I'm sure there are, but how many have damage to the passenger side?'

'Have you spoken to Lambros and asked him if he saw any paint chips? If he did see some and told the police that would bear out your story.'

'I'll ask him when I collect the dogs. I'm planning to keep them up at the house all the time. I don't like to think of anyone prowling around up there, particularly at night. I think my father's probably right. He reckoned someone had planned to break in and when they saw my car outside they changed their mind and scraped it out of spite or frustration. Do you want another beer or shall we go to meet Saffron? I've promised Barbara you'll be back in time to look after your boys when she goes to work.'

Yiorgo pulled a face. 'If she hadn't insisted I came out of the navy she wouldn't have to go out to work.'

'If you hadn't left the navy Barbara would have left you,' Vasi reminded him.

Yiorgo shrugged. 'I should have called her bluff. At least I was happy then.'

Vasi raised his eyebrows. 'You're not happy now?'

'I've always hated working for my father and I'm no good at building. He only gives me the menial jobs, which to be fair are the only ones I'm capable of doing.' Yiorgo sighed heavily. 'I do miss being out at sea.'

'Why don't you become a fisherman?'

'I know even less about fish than I do about building.' Yiorgo shook his head. 'My problems are of my own making. If I hadn't got Barbara pregnant I doubt if I would have married her.'

'Then you wouldn't have three lovely boys.'

'That's true.' Yiorgo nodded gravely. 'I certainly wouldn't want to be without them. Come on, take me to meet this English girl. I know you want my approval. How old is she?'

'A bit older than me.'

Yiorgo stopped. 'Older than you? Are you dating a grandmother?'

Saffron was waiting by the car when Vasi and Yiorgo arrived. She had walked up the hill to the Square and then wandered back down to the pool area and sat at a taverna. Thoroughly bored she decided to visit Yannis and Ourania in their shop. She took the first turning up the hill and then realised she should have walked further on. Their shop was in the next road. Berating herself for her stupidity she stood in the shade and considered. If she returned to the pool she would have to climb up the next hill and she was already feeling hot and uncomfortable; surely there would be a road where she could cut across.

Shrugging her shoulders she decided to walk on rather than retrace her steps and as she reached a bend in the road she saw there was indeed a road that intersected the hill. She walked along it anxiously, hoping she would see the turning that would lead down to Ourania's and not find it was a dead end and she would have to turn back.

Saffron took a left turn that led back down the hill towards the pool and recognised it as the side road where Ourania had her shop. She slowed as she drew nearer. If she entered the shop she would be expected to stay and have a cold drink or piece of fruit, whilst trying to make conversation. Yannis would probably think she needed a ride back to their house and it could be difficult making him understand that she was meeting Vasi. Did she really want to struggle with Yannis's limited English whilst Ourania and Marisa sat there smiling at her?

She retreated to the top of the hill and continued to walk along the road, sure the next turn would take her back down to the pool and from there she would make her way back to where Vasi had parked the car. The buildings appeared to be offices, with names on brass plaques attached to the walls. She wished Vasi was with her so he could tell her the profession of the occupants.

If the vehicles that were parked along the road were owned by the workers behind the closed doors their occupations did not lead to affluence. All the cars were dusty, some of them looking as if they had sat there for a number of weeks, and one was sprayed with red paint. She wondered why anyone would have picked on just one car if they had been out spray painting and not attacked all of them. As she walked past she noticed the wing mirror was missing on the passenger side, the lights were smashed and beneath the red paint were dents and scratches.

Intrigued she looked at the car more closely, wishing she had her camera with her. As she stood there she realised how foolish she was. If she went down to Ourania's shop she would see John there and would be able to talk to her relatives with him acting as an interpreter. She would also be offered a cold drink. He was bound to have his camera with him and if she told him about the car he would no doubt be only too willing to walk up the hill and take a photograph.

John looked down at her from the top of a tall pair of steps as she entered the shop. 'Have you been abandoned?' he asked.

Saffron shook her head. 'Vasi wanted to meet his friend Yiorgo and tell him about the car incident. Apparently Yiorgo only speaks Greek, so I said I would go for a walk.'

Ourania mopped her forehead to indicate that it was hot and Marisa produced a glass of lemonade from the fridge in the stock room which Saffron accepted gratefully.

'I should have bought some water when I was down by the pool. I'd had a drink down there but I didn't realise how hot and thirsty I would get walking up the hill.'

'Why didn't you walk on the shady side?' asked John.

'I did, but I'd taken the wrong turning and then had to walk along the top road where there wasn't any shade.'

'So what are you planning to do until you meet Vasi?'

Saffron looked at her watch. 'I said I'd be back in the car park in a couple of hours. I've walked up to the square and around the pool and I still have over half an hour before Vasi is due to meet me. That was why I thought I would come up here to see you and Uncle Yannis, of course.'

'An exciting way to spend your Sunday afternoon,' grinned John.

'We're going to collect the dogs and go for a swim and a walk later. I don't mind Vasi spending some time with his friend, and it's easier for him if I'm not there so he doesn't have to continually interpret.'

'You really must learn Greek, Saff.' John shook his head at her.

'Maybe it's as well that I can't or I'd know what you were saying about me behind my back.'

'As if we would! We might *speculate* about you and Vasi, but....'

Saffron placed her hand on the steps. 'How do you fancy a quick trip to the ground, John?'

'I'll hang on to the shelf and bring all the ornaments down with me,' threatened John. 'Ourania will have a fit, Marisa will have hysterics and Yannis will beat you.'

'I'm sure he wouldn't.'

'He would beat you black and blue for destroying his stock. I'd take a photograph of you so that you would always remember how wicked you had been.'

'Have you got your camera, John?' Saffron looked around. John's camera was usually hung around his neck.

'Of course. I put it in the stock room.'

'Would you come and take a photo for me?'

'What do you want? The family outside the shop with you?'

Saffron shook her head. 'I saw a car when I was walking along the top road. It's in a terrible state and has been sprayed with red paint. If I'd had my camera with me I would have taken a photo to show Vasi. His damage is nothing by comparison.'

'Really?' John frowned. 'Our cars get bumped and scraped but no one usually takes spray paint to them.'

'Someone went to town on this one.'

John climbed down the steps and walked into the stock room to collect his camera. Saffron placed her empty glass on the counter and thanked Marisa, whilst John assured Yannis he would be back to finish cleaning the shelves and replacing the items under Ourania's instruction in a short while.

It was hot in the small car park and Saffron was relieved when she saw Vasi and Yiorgo approaching. The attendant, who insisted on parking all the cars himself, had nearly run into her twice and she was convinced it was a deliberate act on his part. She shook hands with Yiorgo and wished she could understand the swift interchange that took place between them, where Vasi had grinned and threatened Yiorgo with his fist in response. She had only caught the Greek word for grandmother.

Vasi backed the car carefully out of the narrow space that had been allotted to him and Yiorgo held the door open for Saffron before he climbed in the back.

'Had you been waiting long?' asked Vasi.

'Only a few minutes,' Saffron smiled. 'I took my time as I expected you to be late.'

Vasi raised his eyebrows at her. 'Never. Where did you go?'

'Up to the Square, then round the pool. I walked up to Uncle Yannis's shop and went in and asked John to take a photo for me.'

'What of?'

'There's a car parked up there that's in a far worse state than yours and it's been sprayed with red paint.'

Vasi relayed the information to Yiorgo. 'You ought to go and have a look at it,' advised Yiorgo. 'If the damage is the same as on yours it may have been done by the same person.'

Vasi shrugged. 'That still doesn't tell me who did it.' He edged his way carefully out into the oncoming traffic on the main road. 'This town is becoming a nightmare to drive in when the tourists are here. They ought to be given driving lessons before they are allowed to hire a car.'

'Then they'd hire scooters and be even more of a menace. Drop me off here. If you drive round you'll get caught in the one way system.'

Vasi drew in to the side of the road and Yiorgo tapped Saffron on the shoulder as he opened the door. 'Good man, good friend,' he said in English and pointed to Vasi through the window. Saffron nodded and smiled, unsure what she was supposed to reply.

Vasi watched his friend walk away and shook his head. 'Poor Yiorgo.'

'Why do you say 'poor Yiorgo'?'

'He is very unhappy. He married far too young, a baby on the way. He enjoyed his life in the navy and at first Barbara did not seem to mind. When they had three children she decided he should be at home, being a full time father.'

'And?'

'She gave him an ultimatum. Either he left the navy or she left him.'

'So what did he do?'

'He left the navy and is working for his father. He does not enjoy it. I offered to employ him as a waiter and he said that would be even worse. He could not bear to be inside every day. Now, whereabouts was that car you saw?' asked Vasi.

'In the road that runs across the hill behind the turning to Uncle Yannis's shop.'

'We'll avoid the town and drive up that way.'

Saffron raised her eyebrows. 'What's the point of that?'

'Yiorgo said I ought to see if the damage looked the same as mine. If it does and I report it to Inspector Christos it adds a bit more weight to my claim that my car was vandalised.'

'I'd say it was a good deal worse. That was why I asked John to take a photo. At least spray paint wasn't used on yours.'

Vasi drove carefully through the narrow streets where vehicles were parked on both sides of the road. He did not want to cause any damage to the car he had hired as he knew he would be charged excessively by the company for repairs. He drew up alongside the damaged car and looked at it carefully.

'There's no actual damage on it, just the paint,' he observed.

'Get out and have a look at the passenger side,' Saffron advised him. 'You'll see what I mean then.'

Vasi looked in his mirror and opened his door carefully. He walked on to the pavement and looked at the passenger side where it was dented and scraped, wherever the worst damage appeared the paint seemed to have been applied most heavily. He returned to the driver's side, pleased to see there was a current tax disk displayed. The car had obviously not been abandoned and the driver could be traced.

He climbed back into his car and smiled apologetically at Saffron. 'I'm sorry; I think I should go back into Aghios Nikolaos to tell Mr Christos about this.'

'You think the same person vandalised this car as well as yours?'

'I'm puzzled. People in Crete do not vandalise cars.'

Saffron shrugged. 'It could have been damaged at any time, possibly by a tourist.'

'If they damaged this one why not damage any of the others

that would have been parked along here? Why drive to my house and attack mine and why didn't they spray mine with red paint?'

'This car could have been sitting here for days.'

Vasi shook his head. 'I don't think so. All the cars are dusty, but the windscreen on this one is considerably cleaner. You wouldn't bother to clean your windscreen unless you planned to drive your car.'

'Maybe they cleaned it before they realised it had been damaged.'

'I am sure you would notice immediately if your car had been spray painted. You would certainly look at both sides to see the extent of the damage.'

A delivery van behind them sounded his horn. Vasi raised his hand in apology and started his engine. 'So, we return to see Mr Christos again. We will then have a late lunch and collect the dogs.' He squeezed Saffron's hand. 'There will still be time for a swim this afternoon.'

Superintendent Christos listened to Vasi's description of the car and frowned. 'What do you expect me to do about it?'

'I thought you might be able to trace the owner. See if he knows how the damage occurred. He might have interrupted the vandal and that's why only the one side has been scraped. He might be able to identify him and then you could ask the culprit if he damaged my car also.'

Christos sighed. 'I'll drive past on my way home and take down the details – if the car is still there,' he added.

'Thank you, Mr Christos. Will you let me know if you find out anything?'

'Give me your mobile number.'

Vasi relayed the number to Christos who wrote it down on his pad. 'I don't hold out much hope, but if anything comes of it I'll let you know.'

Vasi drove to Lambros's house where the two dogs greeted him effusively. He tickled their ears as Lambros restrained them by their collars.

'I didn't think you were around, Mr Vasi.'

Vasi raised his eyebrows. 'Where did you think I was spending the weekend? In jail?'

Lambros shook his head. 'Of course not,' he replied scornfully. 'I thought you were up in Heraklion.'

'Did you know I had been arrested yesterday?'

'No. Whatever for?' Lambros was incredulous.

'The police think I caused the accident that involved Alecos Vikelakis.'

'So that's why Mr Christos came up to the house yesterday and wanted to look around.'

Vasi nodded. 'Someone damaged my car when it was parked outside the previous evening. Did you see any paint chippings lying around when you went up in the morning?'

'I swept them up and put them in the garden bin.'

'Did you tell Mr Christos you'd done that?'

'He didn't ask me. He wanted to know where you usually parked your car and I showed him. He asked if I'd noticed anything unusual when I arrived earlier and I thought he meant at the house. The dogs were restless and I looked all over the house before I started work just in case there was anyone inside.'

Vasi pulled out his mobile 'phone. 'I'm calling Mr Christos. Will you tell him what you have just told me about clearing up the chippings?'

Christos listened patiently as Lambros stammered his apologies for not informing him about sweeping up the flakes of paint and putting them in the bin.

'Are they still there?' asked Christos eventually.

'They should be. I only put the bin out when it's full.'

'Very well. Tell Mr Vasi to wait for me at your house until I arrive and we'll go up together and you can show me.'

Lambros handed Vasi back his 'phone. 'Mr Christos is coming

up and we have to wait here for him.'

Vasi clicked his tongue in annoyance. By the time they had been up to the house and answered Christos's questions the afternoon would be over.

'I have a friend in the car. May she come in and wait in your house?'

'Of course. She'd probably prefer to sit outside where the wife is. There's a bit of shade and it's cooler there. We weren't expecting visitors.'

'Wherever suits you.' Vasi guessed that Lambros's wife had not cleaned inside that day and she would be horrified and embarrassed if she spotted a cobweb or some dust whilst Vasi and Saffron were there.

Despina shuffled her feet back into her shoes and collected a jug of iced water and two bottles of beer from the kitchen. She hoped she was not going to be asked to offer hospitality to Christos when he arrived as there was no more beer in the fridge and she did not fancy walking down to the shop until later in the day when it would be cooler. The dogs lay down, one each side of Vasi and he glanced at them fondly.

'Tell me about the dogs' behaviour that morning. What made you think there could be an intruder around?'

'Well,' Lambros considered whilst he took a mouthful of beer. 'They were excited when we arrived, so I thought you might be there. I expected them to go tearing up the drive as soon as I opened the gates and let them off their leads. Instead they went over to the wall and began to sniff around, then in the shrubbery. It may have been a hedgehog or a cat they had scented, but they usually seem to realise an animal has just passed through and the scent isn't worth following. Today they were persistent. When I reached that mess of paint they were sniffing around that as well. Once I took them to the back they just wandered about as usual, but it made me wonder if there was anyone inside.'

'How did they behave when Mr Christos arrived?'

'Barked their heads off and frightened him half to death,' grinned Lambros. 'He refused to come in until I had them shut in.'

'They didn't start sniffing around the shrubbery again?'

Lambros shrugged. 'They may have done. I let them out after Mr Christos left and went back to cleaning the windows.'

'In future I'd like the dogs left up at the house all the time. If someone is thinking of breaking in they'll soon be deterred by these two. It was Cathy's idea for you to bring them back here. She thought it would be easier for you and they wouldn't be lonely.' Vasi shook his head. 'There's not much point in having guard dogs unless they're up at the house.'

Saffron listened uncomprehendingly to the interchange between the two men whilst sipping her glass of water. She felt hot and dirty. This was not how she had envisioned spending her day. All she wanted now was to have a swim or a cool shower to feel refreshed. She glanced surreptitiously at her watch. In another hour the sun would be off the pool and the temperature of the water would drop dramatically.

Stelios had walked up the hill to Vasi's house and seen no sign of him or his car, despite climbing the wall and sitting there for half an hour watching the front of the house. The dogs were not in evidence, another sign that Vasi was not at home. Stelios smiled. He hoped he would hear on the next news bulletin that a man had been arrested for causing Alecos's accident.

He had lowered himself carefully down the wall, not wanting to snag his trousers or scuff the toes of his shoes too badly and retraced his steps down to Elounda. It was then that he realised he had misjudged the time badly. The buses were on a Sunday timetable and he would have four hours to wait for the next one to return him to Aghios Nikolaos. He had debated upon taking a taxi and decided against it. There was no rush for him to return to the town. He decided to have a meal in one of the tavernas and catch the bus later in the afternoon. He chose a seat at the front of the taverna just before the turn off up the hill to Vasi's house. From that vantage point he would certainly see Vasi's car if the man did return to his home.

Various hire cars passed by, some going up the hill and returning a short while later after their occupants had walked around Pano Elounda and Kato Elounda, taking photographs of the villagers' houses and commenting on some of the primitive aspects they encountered. Stelios took no notice of any of them. He would only be interested if Vasi's dark saloon car drove by.

He was surprised when he saw Superintendent Christos in his marked police car take the turn up the hill; then smiled complacently. Obviously Vasi had been arrested and the police were now going to search his house. How he wished now that he had bought a small quantity of drugs from a dealer he knew and placed them in Vasi's car. That would have guaranteed he would have been charged and the taint of peddling or taking drugs would stick to him forever.

Stelios ordered another beer, pleased he had decided to stay in Elounda. He would remain in the taverna until he saw the policeman return, even if it meant he missed the next bus and had to have a taxi back to Aghios Nikolaos.

Christos knocked on Lambros's door; the barking of the dogs had alerted Vasi to his imminent arrival. He hoped the dogs were restrained in some way. He didn't trust guard dogs. If they weren't chained they could attack before their owner had a chance to call them to heel.

Lambros opened the door and ushered Christos out to the patio. The dogs were standing on each side of Vasi, ready to attack if he gave them the command.

'Could you put the dogs somewhere else,' he asked. 'They make me nervous.'

'They'll not hurt you. Let them have a sniff at you and give them a pat and you'll have nothing to worry about.'

Dubiously Christos extended his hand and allowed both dogs to sniff him. 'Good dogs,' he managed to say, but did not risk lifting his hand to pat them.

'Lay,' commanded Vasi and both dogs obeyed him immediately whilst keeping a watchful eye on Christos.

'Now, Vasi, tell me more about this paint that you say was in your drive.'

Vasi sighed. How many more times did he have to repeat the story? 'Lambros swept it up when he went up to the house on Saturday morning and put it in the bin.'

Christos nodded. 'That's what Lambros told me over the 'phone. How do I know you haven't placed it there yourself?'

Vasi looked at Christos in amazement. 'Don't you believe me?'

Christos shook his head. 'It isn't a question of whether I believe you. If I had to give evidence in court I wouldn't want to find out later that I'd been duped and committed perjury.'

'After we left the police station this morning Miss Bartlett wandered around the town and I met up with my friend Yiorgo. His wife will confirm that I went to their house and we left together on foot. The car park attendant can confirm that my car didn't leave the car park until I returned with Yiorgo to where Miss Bartlett was waiting for me. She told me about the car she had seen that had been sprayed with paint and after I dropped Yiorgo near his house I drove up there with her to have a look for myself. You know I then returned to the station and reported it to you.

'Miss Bartlett and I had lunch,' Vasi dug in his pocket, 'There's the bill. We then drove straight up here to collect the dogs from Lambros. That was when he told me he'd swept up the paint and I asked him to 'phone and tell you. You said we were to stay here,' Vasi spread his hands, 'so here we are.'

Christos nodded. 'Hold on to that bill for the time being. I may want it later as proof that you stayed in the town. Now, can we go up to your house? I'll have a look in the bin and then you'll be free to spend what remains of the day as you please.'

'Would Lambros be able to ride in your car?' asked Vasi. 'I

want to take the dogs up and he won't want them leaping all over him in the back. Unless you're willing to have them in the police car,' he added.

'They can't ride in my car,' Christos replied firmly. 'I'll take Lambros. He'll have to sit in the back and his neighbours will probably think he's been arrested.'

Lambros shrugged. He had never ridden in a police car and the neighbours could think what they liked. With luck Mr Christos would also give him a ride back.

Vasi keyed in the code for the gates and drove a short distance up the drive, closing the gates once Christos had drawn up behind him.

Saffron looked at him in surprise. He did not usually park this far down the drive.

'I want to let the dogs out,' he explained. 'I want to see if they go to the wall or the shrubbery again.'

Vasi opened the back door of the car and both dogs leapt out and began to sniff at the ground.

'Is that how they behaved with you, Lambros?'

'Pretty much, most of the way up the drive they were scenting something.'

'We'll leave the cars here,' announced Vasi. 'We can watch their behaviour as we walk.'

Christos opened the trunk of the police car and took out a canvas holdall. If he needed any of the equipment inside it would save him walking back down the drive.

The dogs, noses close to the grass, sniffed and snuffled, sometimes travelling in a straight line and then stopping to sniff at a shrub before moving on. They had almost reached the top of the drive where Vasi parked his car when both of them began to jump at the wall and bark.

Vasi looked at the Inspector. 'I would say I had an intruder who came in over the wall about there.'

Lambros shook his head. 'They didn't do that on Saturday. They only seemed interested in the wall lower down.'

'Then maybe our intruder has returned. Search.'

Vasi gave the command to the dogs and pointed towards the house. Saffron felt the hairs on the back of her neck stand up as both dogs raced up the drive. They stopped briefly at the spot where Vasi usually parked his car, then continued to run around to the rear of the house, returning swiftly from the other side and back to the wall where they sat looking up at the wall and back at Vasi intermittently.

'Good dogs. Leave.' Vasi looked at Christos. 'I would say from the dogs' behaviour that someone climbed over the wall at that spot and not very long ago. By their reaction the scent there was much fresher than lower down by the gates. I'll certainly keep them up here in future.'

Saffron gave a little shiver. She could not understand the conversation but she was disconcerted by the uncharacteristic behaviour shown by the dogs. When Vasi had rescued a hedgehog from them their bark had been different, more of an excited yap. Their bark now was deep and menacing, interspersed with low growls.

Reluctantly the dogs left the wall and sniffed at the grass, before disappearing into the shrubbery and one emerged carrying something in her mouth that the other kept trying to seize.

'Drop,' ordered Vasi and a long piece of chrome trim was laid at his feet.

'Don't touch that,' warned Christos. 'Let me look at it. Keep the dogs away.'

Vasi clicked his fingers and the dogs trotted obediently to his side. Christos bent and examined the strip of metal that lay on the grass. He straightened up and sighed. Thranassis was not going to be happy that he had not made a more thorough search of the grounds on his previous visit. This looked like the trim from the side of a car and if the break at the end matched the break on Vasi's car it certainly bore out his story that his car was vandalised whilst on his own property.

'I'll need to take that with me.' Christos opened the holdall and selected a large brown paper bag. Carefully he wrote on the bag the approximate location where the trim had been found, the date and the time, before lifting it up by one end and slipping it inside. 'Doubt if we'll get any prints from it, but I'll take it anyway. If your dogs find anything else let me know. Now, where's this bin with the paint, Lambros?'

Christos peered inside the garden rubbish bin. He took a torch from the holdall and shone it inside the container. 'I can't see a thing in there. It will have to be tipped out.'

'Wheel it over to the drive. I don't want that mess all over the lawn. If it's on the tarmac it can be swept up afterwards.' Lambros could envisage spending the remainder of his afternoon being spent picking up debris.

Between them Lambros and Vasi tipped the container up allowing the contents to dribble out.

'Stop,' ordered Christos. He bent down and began to examine the mixture of grass, leaves and weeds that lay on the path. Mixed in with them were pieces of metallic paint of various sizes. He stood up and wiped his brow. 'I'll take some samples with me. You won't be able to use it for a while and make sure you don't put it out for collection.' From the holdall he took another paper bag and knelt to place the painted scraps inside. Finally satisfied that he had enough he stood up and mopped his brow again. Ideally the paint flakes should have been photographed in situ before being swept up. He wished he had questioned the conscientious gardener more closely on his previous visit.

'You can put that lot back in, but remember you can't use it again until I say.'

Lambros glared at him. He had heard him the first time and understood. Did the policeman think him stupid?

Vasi looked at Christos anxiously. 'Can I tell my lawyer you've been here and taken some paint samples and piece of car trim away?'

Christos shrugged. 'No reason why not.'

'And you'll tell Superintendent Solomakis in Heraklion?'

Christos nodded. He did not relish the thought of making that 'phone call and admitting to failing to find the trim and not asking the gardener about paint chips. It all added credence to Vasi Iliopolakis's statement that his car had been vandalised whilst sitting outside his house. On his return to the station in Aghios Nikolaos he would have a look at the car that Mr Vasi had reported as being vandalised there. If the tax disk was in place as Vasi said he should be able to trace the owner and he could offer that piece of information to Thranassis and hope his own short comings would be overlooked.

'I'll be off, then. Don't forget to report to the station tomorrow, Mr Vasi.'

Vasi sighed. 'How long do I have to do that for?'

'Until all the charges against you are formally dropped.'

Christos began to walk down the drive to his car, Lambros hurrying after him in the hope of being offered a ride in exchange for opening the gates.

Vasi looked at Saffron apologetically. 'I'm sorry, Saffie. This has been another ruined day and your holiday is nearly at an end.'

'We have the remainder of the afternoon and this evening and I don't leave until Wednesday.'

'Tomorrow I have to go up to Heraklion again and try to sort out the problems at the bank with my father,' frowned Vasi.

Saffron took his hand and squeezed it. 'I understand, besides, I really ought to spend some more time with my grandmother and the rest of my family. I have neglected them terribly.'

Christos left Lambros at his house and drove back to Aghios Nikolaos deep in thought. Why would anyone deliberately damage Mr Vasi's car and then try to implicate him in causing a serious accident? Had Mr Vasi deliberately run Alecos Vikelakis off the road and when he returned to his house done further damage to his own car to support his story of vandalism? Christos shook his head. Mr Vasi had never caused any trouble as a youngster, he had not been involved in any fights or been stopped whilst driving his car after he had been drinking. It didn't make sense and it certainly did not explain the behaviour of the dogs.

So deep in thought was Christos that he nearly missed the turn off that would take him to where he understood the vandalised car was parked. He stopped beside it and examined it carefully, noting the dent in the front wing, broken lights and loss of wing mirror and finally taking down the number on the tax disk. He would arrange to have the vehicle taken into a garage until the owner had been traced. Despite being parked on a back road it was an eyesore.

Stelios watched Inspector Christos drive back through Elounda. He wished he knew for certain if Vasi had been arrested. He looked at the bar tender.

'Any chance of seeing the news?' He nodded towards the large television set.

The bar tender scowled. He had been watching the motor cycle racing and the final race of the day was just about to start.

'What's so urgent? The last race will be over in fifteen minutes.'

'I want to know if anyone has been arrested for that accident. The victim is a friend of mine. Once I've heard an update you can go back to the racing.'

Grudgingly the bar tender changed channels and Stelios sat and listened intently. To his disgust and frustration there was no mention of the accident. As the weather forecast began he placed his money on the table and walked out. 'Thanks,' he called over his shoulder.

Quickly the bar man turned back to the racing, just in time to hear the winner announced. He clenched his fists. The next time a customer asked for the channel to be changed he would ignore him.

Dimitra decided she would have to go to the hospital and visit

Alecos. She wanted to ask if he had made any alterations to the disk she had lent to him and alert him to the fact that both Vasi and his father knew there was a discrepancy. There had been no further updates about the accident on the news during the day so she assumed Alecos had regained consciousness and was beginning to recover from his injuries.

She chose her wardrobe carefully. She certainly could not wear black. That would mean she thought Alecos was dead, but nor should she wear her usual bright colours which would look uncaring. Finally she settled for a blue skirt and white blouse. She belted the blouse tightly and looked at herself in the mirror. Eminently suitable, smart, but restrained. She applied the minimum amount of makeup; she might have to shed a few tears for Alecos's benefit and she would not want her mascara to run.

Dimitra entered the hospital and enquired at the reception where she should go to visit Alecos Vikelakis. To her surprise within a few moments a doctor arrived and took her aside to a private room.

'Are you a relative, miss?'

Dimitra shook her head. Should she say she was engaged to Alecos? That could make her look stupid when he denied it.

'We are very good friends,' she smiled up at the doctor noting that he was extremely good looking.

'I'm sorry; I'm only allowed to give information to the family.'

'He isn't dead, is he?' she asked in a stricken voice.

'No, but he is still unconscious.'

'Am I able to see him?'

'There would be little point in you visiting him today. As I said, he is still unconscious.'

'What about tomorrow? I could come tomorrow.'

'I really cannot speculate on his medical condition in advance.'

'I do need to see him.' Dimitra batted her eye lashes at the doctor. 'I'm sure he would be pleased to know that I had come and I have some important business that I need to tell him about.'

'I don't think Mr Vikelakis will be interested in business for a while, however important it may seem. I suggest you telephone and ask after him in a couple of days. He may well have recovered consciousness by then and you would be able to visit him briefly at the end of the week.'

Dimitra thought rapidly. 'I'll call in tomorrow. I pass the hospital on my way home from work. What time will you be on duty?'

'There will be no need to see me. The reception can advise you regarding Mr Vikelakis's condition.'

'I'd rather see you. No doubt reception deal with numerous requests and they could get the information confused between patients.'

'That's very unlikely,' replied the doctor dryly. 'Now, if you will excuse me. I do have patients that need my attention.'

'I'll see you tomorrow.' Dimitra nodded firmly and held out her hand. 'Thank you for your time.'

The doctor looked after her as she left. She was a striking looking woman with exceedingly attractive long legs. He might well make time to see her again the following day.

Monday 24th September

Christos arranged to have Stelios's car moved from the side of the road into a secure garage. He inspected the car again whilst he waited for the driver with the hoist and flatbed truck to arrive. He could not impound every vehicle that had a few dents and scratches but this one looked as if it had been involved in an accident that should certainly have been reported. It could be wise to have the car safely locked away until he had traced the owner and been given an explanation for the damage.

'Where shall I dump it?' asked Andreas as he lowered the ramp to the flatbed. 'In the pound or at the tip?'

'Neither,' replied Christos. 'I'd like it locked in a garage. There's a chance it may have been used in a crime. Wear gloves whilst you deal with it in case it has to be tested for fingerprints.'

'I always wear gloves when I move a car,' Andreas remonstrated. 'I don't want to be accused of scratching the paintwork.'

'I don't think anyone will accuse you of that in this case,' remarked Christos dryly. 'I don't want any possible prints smudged. I'll follow you down to the garage and as soon as it's safely locked inside I'll have the key. I don't want anyone doing any repair work on it.'

'Who's the owner?'

'I don't know yet.'

'Then we're not likely to do any repairs. We'll want to know who's going to pay for them before we start.'

The driver slung the straps from the hoist beneath the car and attached a wire tow rope to the rear chassis. Christos watched as the car was slowly pulled backwards up the ramp to the bed of the flat back, the tension in the straps keeping it central. Christos examined the space where the car had been parked; there was red paint on the ground, but no paint chippings. The damage to the body work had obviously taken place elsewhere.

Vasi drove to the police station in Heraklion and reported to Superintendent Thranassis Solomakis. The man glowered at him; still certain that if he had kept him behind bars for the weekend he would have elicited a confession. Now Christos was interfering and said paint flakes had been found in a rubbish bin at the man's house and also a piece of chrome trim. A badly damaged car had been impounded on Christos Christothorassanakis's instructions and Christos had informed him that he was tracing the owner and would want to know where he had been when Alecos had been forced off the road.

'It's my case,' he informed Christos tersely. 'You have no right to interfere.'

'I'm not interfering. The car was parked in my prefecture and Mr Vikelakis and Mr Iliopolakis live locally. I could ask to have the case transferred down here to me.'

'The incident took place on the main highway. That comes under my jurisdiction.' Thranassis bristled with indignation.

'So why are we arguing? We should be working together. When I have found out who owns this car I will let you know. If he lives in Heraklion you can question him; if he lives locally it makes sense that I interview him.'

Thranassis could feel his blood pressure rising. The car had been found in Aghios Nikolaos and it was more than likely that the owner lived in the area. Christos was taking the case away from him and would eventually get all the credit if he succeeded in finding the culprit and bringing him to justice.

'Let me know when you have a name,' growled Thranassis and was about to slam the receiver down when he heard Christos speak to him again.

'You'll no doubt send me through a full report of the accident scene and the damage to the victim's car as soon as you receive it?'

Thranassis was speechless with annoyance. He had had no intention of sending the report through to Christos.

'Thranassis – Thranassis – are you there?'

'Yes.'

'I'll look forward to receiving the report as soon as it is completed, along with the photographs. If anything comes of my enquiries this end I'll let you know.'

The telephone line went dead and Thranassis's rage increased further. The man had even managed to have the last word!

Vasi drove to the Central hotel and met his father as arranged. He related to him that Lambros had confirmed sweeping up the chippings from the drive and Christos had collected samples.

'We took the dogs up and they rooted around in the shrubbery and found a piece of trim. I'm sure it belongs to my car. Mr Christos took that away also.'

Vasilis nodded. 'I'll 'phone Lakkis and let him know.'

'Did Mr Christos take a photograph of the trim or paint chippings before he took them?' asked Lakkis.

'I don't know,' replied Vasilis. 'I'll ask Vasi to speak to you. He was there.'

Lakkis repeated his question to Vasi.

Vasi shook his head. 'Mr Christos didn't take any photos and it didn't occur to me to do so.'

'So if Mr Christos loses them you have no evidence that they were removed from your property and in all probability came from your car. Is there any way you can get some photographs of the bits of paint you say are still in the bin? Mr Christos could come and remove the bin or it could be emptied by accident. At least then if the samples are lost you'll have proof that is where they came from.'

Vasi frowned. 'I'll try to arrange it.'

'I suggest you make it a priority to arrange it. If the case should go to court I won't be able to say that your car was vandalised whilst outside your house if we have no proof at all to substantiate the claim. Hand me back to your father.'

'Yes, Mr Tsilikadis.' Vasi raised his eyes heavenwards as he handed his father back his mobile 'phone.

Vasilis listened to the instructions the solicitor was giving him replying 'Yes, Lakkis,' at intervals. Finally Vasilis turned to his son.

'Do you think John would be willing to go up and take some photos of the paint in the bin?'

'I'm sure he would,' nodded Vasi.

'You call him and then I'll call Lambros and tell him to expect him to expect John and what he's going to do. Are the dogs there? If so I'll ask Lambros to look after them. I wouldn't want them to think John was an intruder and pin him into a corner.'

'They need controlling,' affirmed Vasi. 'They became rather excited over a section of the wall. I think someone had been up there earlier. If they're planning a robbery they'll get a nasty shock.'

'There's little of value in the house.'

'Because it's a large house and you are known to have won the lottery many years ago they probably think you have a fortune stashed away in there.'

'Then if they do get in they'll have a big disappointment. Do you want to have another look at the accounts before we go to the bank?'

Vasi shook his head. 'They won't have changed overnight. I've collected the bank receipts for the last fortnight from the Katerina and the Elounda hotel and I called in at Hersonissos for theirs. We'll take in these from the Central and if necessary I can ask Aristo to bring in the ones from the beach hotel. Has Dimitra come in to work?'

'Not yet.'

'I did tell her she could have some time off if she needed to be with Alecos. She's probably planning to go into the hospital. I'll give her a call.'

'I'm not sure I trust that girl.'

Vasi shrugged. 'I think Alecos used his relationship with her to persuade her to give him the disk. She would have had no reason to mistrust him.'

Stavros Tanakis had arrived at the bank considerably earlier than usual and examined the accounts for the hotels. He looked back over the previous months. There had been the usual excess of income over expenditure and the pattern continued until the previous week. The expenditure for wages showed a slight increase, no doubt accounted for by someone doing extra hours and invoices had been paid up to date, but there had been no income recorded and when he tried to agree the balance manually he was unsuccessful. Not only had credits not been entered, the balance carried forward from the previous week was incorrect.

He could feel himself sweating, despite the air conditioning. If the discrepancy was due to a malfunction of the bank's computers how many more customers were going to complain that their accounts were showing incorrect balances? Customers would lose faith in the bank's integrity. No doubt there would be an enquiry and the bank could be sued. He accessed accounts at random, requesting large withdrawals and on each occasion his request was granted and he was given permission to proceed. It appeared the problem was only with Mr Iliopolakis's accounts, which he found puzzling, but some consolation.

Vasi shook Stavros by the hand and smiled. 'Thank you. I understand you were very accommodating to my father on Saturday. I would have spent the weekend languishing in the local jail without your help.'

Vasilis took a seat and opened his briefcase. 'We need to get these accounts sorted out as quickly as possible. I want to relieve Mr Pirenzi of the burden of being a guarantor and the person responsible for misappropriating our funds to be prosecuted.'

Stavros spread his hands. 'We have no evidence that anyone has acted improperly. I am sure it is a simple computer malfunction and we will be able to rectify the situation immediately.' He spoke far more confidently than he felt.

Vasi shook his head. 'We have here the bank receipts for the previous week from the hotels. All of them have the date stamped on them showing the day the deposit was made. We have also brought a copy of the back-up disk from my computer. This shows there is more than enough money in the account for you to have accessed my bail money and given my father a promissory note.'

'As I say, it has to be a computer malfunction.' Stavros could feel himself beginning to sweat again.

'I disagree. I approached your branch in Aghios Nikolaos last week and asked for a loan to purchase a property. I was told that I did not have enough collateral, my father would have to agree to guarantee me and approval would have to be gained from you. I subsequently discovered that the owners of the property had been told by Mr Vikelakis that I could not afford the purchase and he had made the purchase himself. When I spoke to him about this he was most insistent that I should buy the property from him immediately. I refused.'

Stavros swallowed. Alecos Vikelakis had not approached him for his approval of a loan for Vasi Iliopolakis. There would have been more than enough collateral with the hotels the young man owned outright and no reason to consult his father.

Vasi leaned forward. 'When my father requested bail money the discrepancies on our accounts came to light. I spoke to the employee who has overall responsibility for agreeing the accounts each week and making a copy that is locked in the safe. She admitted that she had also taken a copy for herself each week without telling us. I believe her when she said she had done this with the best of intentions. Mr Vikelakis, who I understand to be a good friend to her, said there had been a computer problem at the bank whilst transferring money between our accounts. Neither my father nor I had asked for any transfer to be made.

'Mr Vikelakis asked to borrow her back-up disk to rectify the matter and thinking she was helping everyone she agreed. Mr Vikelakis returned the disk to her and his unfortunate accident occurred as he drove back to Aghios Nikolaos. Dimitra, my father and I looked at the disk yesterday and compared it with the master disk that had been in the safe. I have paper copies of the information on both disks here and you will see there are discrepancies.'

Vasi placed the separate folders of papers on Mr Tanakis's desk.

Stavros breathed a sigh of relief. 'If the computer in Aghios Nikolaos failed that explains the problems we encountered.'

Vasi shook his head. 'It does not. The back-up disk that Mr Vikelakis borrowed should still be identical with the master copy and it is not. If the problem was at Aghios Nikolaos why are the credits that were paid in to the banks at Heraklion, Hersonissos and Elounda not showing?'

Stavros frowned. 'There must be a simple solution. It's quite possible that the back-up disk failed.'

Vasi sat back in his chair. 'Then please prove that to us.'

Stavros could feel the sweat trickling down between his shoulder blades. 'I will have to check the cashiers' records for the transactions. It could take a considerable amount of time.'

'We will leave the paper copies with you. In the meantime I know the total that was paid in to the bank last week and I would like that amount added immediately to our accounts. The balance carried forward from the previous week also needs to be rectified.' Vasilis placed the copy of the back-up disk and the total sum of the missing credits on Stavros's desk beside the folders.

Stavros shook his head. 'I cannot do that. I have to be able to take the money from somewhere to put it to your account and we do not know where it is at present.'

'All the more reason for you to find the error rapidly. We will return when you re-open this afternoon and I expect to find our accounts showing the correct balance.' Vasilis closed his briefcase and rose. 'I appreciate the help you gave me at the weekend, but unless this situation is rectified without delay I may well have to consider taking my business elsewhere. I hope there has not been any manipulation of our accounts by Mr Vikelakis. Unfortunately he is not in a position to explain his actions When you find where our money has been credited I may make a formal request to have the bank accounts audited. I would not want to think that other customers had suffered similar problems.'

Stavros Tanakis's hands were clammy with sweat as he turned his attention back to the computer.

Saffron sat with her grandmother. 'I have neglected you. I intended to spend every morning with you.'

'I can't see why you would want to spend time with an old lady like me. I'm sure Vasi has a good deal more to offer.'

Saffron blushed. 'I was supposed to be helping him to look for a new apartment, then he saw a hotel he thought he would like to buy. It was the one where Churchill and Gandhi stayed and he asked me to do some research about them both. One thing led to another,' Saffron shrugged, 'and the time just flew by.'

'So did you find a suitable apartment?'

Saffron shook her head. 'Once he began to make plans for the hotel he was no longer interested in apartments. At the moment he's staying at his father's house.'

Annita shuddered. 'That's a great big lonely place. I can't think whatever possessed Vasilis to build up there.'

'They have a marvellous view.'

'And no neighbours nearby. Who do you call on if you need some help?'

'The village is only a short way down the hill.'

'Hmm. A short way down and long way up, particularly when you're no longer young.'

'Vasi has a car.'

'I hear he had an accident. All the years I drove in New Orleans I never even had a parking ticket.'

'Vasi didn't have an accident,' Saffron answered somewhat indignantly. 'Someone damaged his car deliberately and the police thought he may have been involved in an accident.'

'Why would anyone want to do that?'

'I don't know. Vasi thought maybe someone had planned to break into the house and when they saw his car was there they scraped it in spite.'

'Seems a far-fetched idea to me.' Annita sniffed derisively. 'If you plan to break in somewhere and realise the house is occupied you usually want to get away as quickly as possible. You don't risk hanging around to damage a car. Who has Vasi upset recently?'

'Upset?' Saffron looked at her grandmother. 'Why should he have upset any one?'

'How do I know! I'm only giving you my opinion. I think Vasi has probably fired someone from one of the hotels or refused to give someone a job and they had a grudge against him; so they decided to take their resentment out by scratching his car.'

'I'll mention your idea to Vasi this evening,' Saffron promised.

Annita raised her eyebrows. 'Why aren't you meeting him until then? You don't have to spend hours with me.'

'He has to go to the bank with his father. There's some problem with the accounts. A bank computer went wrong and they need to get it sorted out.'

'It was much easier when the tellers wrote it all in their books. You knew where you were then. If you had a query they could look it up and give you the answer straight away.'

'It is much the same now. Everything is still recorded and if necessary it can be printed off.'

'Yannis keeps his own books. He won't go near Giovanni's computer. He says he doesn't trust it and he never has a problem getting his accounts to agree.'

Saffron smiled to herself, remembering her conversation with

Marcus the previous year about accounting. She was quite sure the end of year accounts Yannis presented for his tax would agree and probably show he had made a loss rather than a healthy profit.

'Whatever suits him,' she said and changed the subject adroitly. 'I'm sure I haven't seen all your photographs, yet, Grandma. Did you ask Bryony if she had another album ready?'

Annita sniffed. 'She says she's putting them all on the computer. I told her I wanted them left in the albums. They'll get lost otherwise.'

Saffron sighed. 'They'll still be in your albums, but they'll be copied on to the computer. That way they'll never fade or get damaged. Shall I ask her to bring an album in and you can tell me who everyone is.'

'If you want. I would have thought by now you would be able to recognise everyone.'

'Not without your help, Grandma.' Saffron rose and escaped thankfully to find Bryony.

'I need your help, Bryony. Can you bring a photo album in to Grandma, please? Any one will do. I just want to distract her from computers. She's convinced her photos will be lost if you put them on to a disk.'

Bryony giggled. 'I'll tell you what, I'll bring the lap top in with the disk and the album. That way I can show her on the screen and she will see she still has the photo.'

'She seems a bit cantankerous today.'

'She's waiting for the results of her monthly medical tests to come back. She always gets a bit edgy and up tight then.'

'Is she ill?'

Bryony shrugged. 'I very much doubt it. I've never known her to be ill apart from flu or a common cold, but she has a horror of being sent into hospital with something nasty wrong with her. Marianne would only do that if she was totally incapable of nursing her here.'

'She's not likely to be ill now. She's far too old. At her age she's been exposed to just about every germ going around and has built up immunity.'

'That doesn't stop her worrying. She'll be back to normal tomorrow when I've collected the result from the doctor and she knows she has nothing to worry over. I often wish they didn't insist on doing these tests for the elderly. It would save a good deal of stress. You take the coffee in and I'll be along in a minute or two.'

Annita sat with the photograph album open on her lap. She looked at the screen on the lap top and had to admit the pictures were exactly the same except that Bryony had typed beneath each one the names of the people and when and where the photograph had been taken.

'See, Grandma,' explained Bryony, 'I have only copied them and typed in the information you gave me. That way I don't have to try to remember everything. I'm going to give Saffron a copy to take back to England with her.'

Annita sighed and closed the album. 'You don't need me to go through it with you, then, Saffron. There's no point spending time looking at old photos when Bryony is going to give you a copy of your own.'

'Then tell me more about your life in Aghios Nikolaos when you were a girl, or what it was like when you first went to America.'

'I've told you as much as I can remember,' replied Annita irritably. 'Why don't you got for a walk or a swim?'

Saffron looked at Bryony for guidance and she nodded. 'That's a good idea, Grandma. Saffie can talk to you later. She's been so busy rushing around with Vasi that she's had no time for swimming.'

Saffron blushed. Apart from the previous weekend, she and Vasi had found plenty of time to go swimming together, usually as a prelude to passionate love making.

Dimitra lay in bed and considered. Should she behave as the conscientious employee and go in to work as usual or would it be better to stay away until Vasi and his father had reconciled the accounts with the bank? She was sure Alecos had made some very simple error and he would be able to explain everything once he had regained consciousness. She was equally sure that if Mr Iliopolakis had left the disk with her she would have been able to find the mistake Alecos had made and put it right.

Thinking of Alecos recovering brought to her mind the doctor she had spoken to the previous day. If she made a discreet 'phone call she could probably find out at what time his duties finished. It would then be a case of using her charm to try to ascertain the extent of Alecos's injuries. Broken bones could be mended, but she did not want to find herself with a brain damaged man who needed continual care. It could be in her own interest to begin to distance herself from their relationship now.

She propped herself up on one elbow and reached for her mobile and pressed the numbers for the hospital, waiting for some minutes before her call was finally answered.

'I'm enquiring about Mr Alecos Vikelakis. Can you tell me how he is he today?'

'Hold and I'll put you through.'

There was another frustrating delay whilst Dimitra waited to be connected to the ward, but she was relieved when she found she was speaking to a nurse.

'Mr Vikelakis has shown a slight improvement.'

'Oh, that is good news. There is just one more thing I'd like to ask. Doctor Melanakis asked me to call in and speak to him again today. What time does he go off duty?'

The nurse on the end of the line frowned. It was unusual for the doctor who was the head of the trauma unit to ask a relative to come in to speak to him unless their condition was life threatening. She looked down again at the notes she had that related to Alecos. The man was still unconscious. That could be why the doctor wanted to speak to the woman.

'He's due to leave at five today.'

'Thank you. I'll arrive shortly before then and wait. I wouldn't want to interrupt him. Thank you for your help.' Dimitra closed her mobile and smiled triumphantly. Unless the doctor had some urgent prior engagement she was sure she would be able to persuade him to spend some time with her, ostensibly to discuss Alecos.

Stelios walked briskly up the hill in Aghios Nikolaos to where he had parked his car. He would drive it in to a garage on the outskirts of town and claim the damage had taken place over the weekend. He stopped in consternation when he saw it was no longer where he had parked it. He walked a short distance along the road to make quite certain that his memory was not playing him tricks and he had not left the car further down. Returning to where he was certain he had parked he could see dribbles and splashes of red paint on the road.

Why would it have been taken away? He was not infringing any parking regulations by leaving the car there. He could only assume he had unwittingly used a parking space that was habitually used by one of the local office staff and they had requested its removal, probably claiming the car had been there for weeks and had been abandoned.

He would go down to the police station and ask if the car had been towed away. As he walked back down the hill he began to plan his story in his head. He would say he had parked his car there a few days earlier and had not had occasion to use it since then. If the police decided to ask the workers in the local area how long the car had actually been there they would probably only have noticed it after it had been sprayed. He stopped and lit a cigarette, sucking in the smoke greedily. This needed thinking about. He lived the other side of town so why should he park his car so far away from where he lived?

Stelios shook his head. He would go to the police station and say his car had been stolen. He had only just realised it was missing as he had not used it since he had returned from work on Friday afternoon. He would be irate that it had been stolen, but when they told him it had been vandalised as well he would be furious. He ground out his cigarette with his heel and walked on. Maybe the car having been moved was to his advantage after all. He could claim for the damage on his insurance and the police would corroborate his story.

Inspector Christos Christostofferakis looked up as Stelios entered and approached his desk.

'How can I help you, sir?'

'I want to report that my car has been stolen,' said Stelios in a loud voice, making sure the other officers heard him.

'Please have a seat,' Christos waved his hand. 'I'll need to have some details from you.'

Christos took a form from beneath his desk. It certainly made a difference to his paper work having printed forms for lost or stolen items. He simply had to check the boxes that had been filled in and get the complainant to sign it as correct before he transferred the information to the computer. Previously he had been forced to type out long descriptions of goods or articles and was held liable for any discrepancies.

'If you would be good enough to complete this form, sir. We will then make a search in our computerised records and see if we have any reports of a car being abandoned. If we don't have any luck there we can ask our officers to look out for it.'

Stelios scowled. 'Don't you want to know where it was parked?'

'That's all on the form, sir. Do you need a pen?' Christos pushed a ballpoint across his desk.

Stelios entered his name, address, car registration, make and colour. When he was asked to complete the question *'Where was the car parked when last seen?'* he hesitated and finally wrote in the name of a road a short distance from his lodgings.

Christos accepted the form back and scrutinised it carefully. 'You're quite happy that you have given us all the details, sir?'

Stelios nodded. 'It's disgraceful that you can't leave your car for a couple of days without someone driving off in it,' he complained.

'I quite agree,' Christos sympathised with him. 'If you will just bear with me a moment I'll get our records checked.' He rose and went to a desk at the back of the room. If his memory was correct he certainly did not want the man to see the details that would come up on the screen.

Christos read them carefully. Everything matched except for the location where the man claimed the car had been parked. There was no reason to disbelieve his story, but he had no intention of releasing the vehicle until it had been thoroughly checked over and eliminated from their enquiries into the accident on the Heraklion highway.

Christos shook his head as he returned to his desk. 'No reports at the moment, sir. You can be contacted on this 'phone number?' He pointed to the number of a mobile that Stelios had inserted.

'Any time. How long do you think it will take to find my car?'

'I really cannot speculate, sir. It could have been driven anywhere. I'm sure it will be located very soon.'

Stelios nodded. 'I'll wait to hear from you.' He rose and walked out of the police station feeling pleased that he had shown just the right level of annoyance and compliance. It was not until he had walked almost back to his lodging that it occurred to him that anyone seen driving his car anywhere in Crete would have been stopped and questioned. The knowledge gave him an uneasy feeling.

Christos telephoned Thranassis for a second time that day.

'I just wondered how the examination of Mr Iliopolakis's car was progressing. Do you have a report yet?'

'No. I said I would inform you when it was ready,' replied Thranassis curtly.

'Any idea how much longer they'll be spending on it?'

'How would I know?' Thranassis could feel his blood pressure rising.

'I just wondered if they wanted me to bring those paint samples up to Heraklion.'

'I'm sure they have more important evidence than a few flakes of paint. The man probably did additional damage to his car to add credence to his story.'

'I think that's unlikely and I would like them to have a look at the car I impounded,' Christos continued patiently. 'Do you know if they photographed the area, particularly any paint flakes that may have been lying around?'

'I'm not in forensics. I expect they carried out their examination of the site as usual. I'm expecting the report to say that any paint found came from Mr Iliopolakis's car.'

'Personally I think it more likely any paint would have come from the car I have locked up down here. I'll arrange to have it brought up for examination.'

'They still have to examine the victim's car. A vandalised car will have to wait. This is more important.'

'Quite. I'll telephone Babbis tomorrow and see if he can give me any kind of time frame.'

Thranassis replaced the receiver, deliberately cutting off their conversation. Christos smiled to himself. Had Thranassis been more polite he would have informed him that he now knew the name of the owner of the sprayed car.

Stavros Tanakis sat in his office awaiting the return of Vasilis and his son with trepidation. He had examined the daily printouts from the cashiers and each one confirmed that the amount recorded on the hotel accounts had been paid in. He had totalled them and if he added them to the discrepancy between the balance of the previous week and the one that had been carried forward, the accounts then agreed exactly with the back-up disk belonging to Mr Iliopolakis. He would have to credit the man's account, but he still needed to know where the money had been allocated.

Bearing in mind the suspicion that had been thrown on his employee, Alecos Vikelakis; he had looked at the man's account and could find nothing irregular. His salary was credited each month and an amount transferred to a savings account. He had a second savings account that had been opened two years earlier. It had shown a very healthy balance, large amounts having been paid in during the previous two years, up until the previous week, when most of it had been withdrawn. He surmised that was the money that had been used to buy the hotel that Mr Vasi had mentioned. He wondered idly where the man had obtained the sums, certainly he had not been paid enough to make such large deposits, and decided he must have been gambling successfully.

He tapped his pen on the table. He would telephone Alecos Vikelakis's father and ask after the condition of his son, as a concerned employer should. He would then ask if any paperwork that could relate to bank transactions had been found on his person.

In the meantime he had no choice but to credit Mr Iliopolakis's accounts with the missing payments from a Suspense Account and correct the balance that had been brought forward from the previous week. He would leave the loan guaranteed by Mr Pirenzi showing as an unpaid debt on the Bank Loans Account and would certainly not charge him interest. He hoped that once Mr Iliopolakis saw his accounts showing the correct balance the loan would be conveniently forgotten and he would have time to make a more thorough investigation and find out where the discrepancy lay.

He certainly did not want to have to report to Athens that he had an insoluble problem, nor did he want Mr Iliopolakis to request a complete audit of the bank. That would bring a team of inspectors down on the bank and who knew what else they might uncover in the way of irregularities. He was only five years away from retirement and did not want to do anything to jeopardise his pension.

Stavros telephoned Mr Vikelakis, relieved when the man finally answered the 'phone.

'Nikos, this is Stavros here. I just thought I'd 'phone to ask if you have any news of your boy.'

'I thought you were the hospital calling.' Nikos Vikelakis sounded exhausted.

'I'm sorry. Are you expecting them to call?'

'They said they would when he recovered consciousness. We spent two days sitting up there with him and we're trying to catch up on our sleep.'

'Then I'll only keep you talking for a few minutes. With Alecos in hospital we've got a few problems in the branch. You know what it's like when the manager is out of action for a few days. He seems to be the only one with the answers. I just wondered if the hospital had given you any papers he had with him at the time of the accident.'

'Should he have had any with him?'

'I don't know, but we can't lay our hands on some information that we need and I thought it worth my while to 'phone and ask if Alecos had it with him.'

'What kind of information?'

Stavros rubbed his hand over his forehead. He didn't remember the ex-manager as being quite so dense when he had been working, but then he hadn't received the shock that his son had been badly injured in an accident. He must be patient with him.

'I can't be specific. I'm not sure myself exactly what they are looking for. If there's anything amongst his belongings that are not obviously personal they could be relevant.'

'I put a bag in his room. I'll have a look at it later when I've had some rest. My ulcer's playing me up.'

'I'm not surprised,' sympathised Stavros.

'If there's anything relevant there I'll drop it in to the bank tomorrow.'

'Thank you, Nikos. I hope the hospital 'phone you soon with some good news.'

Stavros heard Nikos sigh deeply. 'I expect they will.'

Vasilis studied the accounts that Mr Tanakis had printed off whilst he and Vasi sat in his office.

'You'll find everything is quite correct now, Mr Iliopolakis. I can only apologise that such an error occurred and for the inconvenience it gave you.'

'So where had my money gone?'

'I believe it was credited to another account in error.'

Vasilis raised his eyebrows. 'I trust such an error will not happen again.'

'I will personally supervise your account. Rest assured there will be no more problems.'

'And the loan that you granted me at the weekend? I presume I am able to tell Mr Pirenzi that he is no longer bound by his guarantee?'

Stavros licked his lips. 'Certainly. I have placed the loan on a separate account and once the bail conditions have been lifted it will be forgotten.' How he hoped that he would be able to trace the Iliopolakis money and clear the outstanding debit he had placed on the Bank Loans Account before the bank had to complete an annual return. That could cause some very awkward questions being asked.

Vasi leaned forward. 'So if I requested a loan in the future it would be granted?'

Stavros tried to smile confidently. 'That would obviously depend upon the credit rating on your account and the collateral available at the time of your request. If you asked for one today I would have no hesitation in complying.' Stavros sincerely hoped the man was not going to request any such thing.

Vasi nodded. 'I trust you will enquire why my request was refused by Mr Vikelakis.'

'Naturally. As soon as he is released from the hospital I will make it a priority.'

Vasi shook his head. 'I would feel happier if you started to make some enquiries now. Mr Vikelakis could be in hospital for a considerable amount of time. I understand he has concussion. His memory could be impaired.'

Stavros crossed himself. 'I sincerely hope not.'

'I hope not also. I will expect to hear from you within the week.' Vasi spoke firmly, giving Stavros no option but to nod in acquiescence.

'What are your plans now, Vasi?' asked Vasilis.

'I'm going to call in to the garage briefly and see what new cars they have available, then I'll drive down to Elounda. I promised Saffie I'd take her out for dinner tonight.'

'You're going to get a new car, then?'

'I've thought about it. I had planned just to get my old one re-sprayed, but goodness knows how long the police plan to keep it and what state it will be in when they finally release it. I decided it could be more sensible to put the price of a re-spray and the cost of hiring towards buying a new one.'

Vasilis nodded. His son's decision regarding a new car made financial sense. 'Make sure you keep a close eye on the accounts this week.'

'I shall take a back up every night. I'll also come in and have a look at the Central accounts on Wednesday. I'm planning to bring Saffie up to the airport.' To Vasi's annoyance he felt himself blush as he imparted the information to his father. 'She wants to say goodbye to Cathy,' he added as an excuse.

'I would have thought her family would have brought her up so they could see her off.'

'Oh, they'll drive up as well. It's just easier if we split up and use two cars rather than their mini-bus. It means I can go about my own business afterwards.'

Vasilis nodded. 'I'll tell Cathy to expect you.'

'It will only be a brief visit,' Vasi warned him. 'She has to be at the airport by two thirty.' He did not want Cathy to have a lunch prepared and expect them to stay for the afternoon.

Vasi drove away. There was something niggling at the back of his mind and he hoped that during the drive back to Elounda he would remember what it was. He called at two garages on his way out of town and had a cursory look at the cars they were offering for sale. He accepted the details of three vehicles and promised to consider them over the next couple of days and return on Wednesday.

He did not really want to think about Wednesday. Saffron would be returning to England and he realised she was going to leave a space in his life that was going to be difficult for anyone else to fill. He tried to cheer himself with the thought that he was going to visit her in London in November and that was only two months away; then he remembered, he was unable to leave Crete until he had been cleared of having anything to do with Alecos's accident. With a heavy heart he took the turn on to the highway that led from Heraklion to Aghios Nikolaos.

There were still signs in place restricting the speed limit before and after the place where Alecos had plunged through the barrier and over the side into the gorge. Alecos. Alecos had borrowed the back-up disk. Alecos had advised Dimitra to make a copy and keep it for herself in case there should be a computer failure. The bank made a copy every day in case of such an eventuality. *Every day.* That was what had been troubling him. If the bank made a back up every day there should be evidence on a disk that the money from the hotels had been paid in and also the account where it had been credited. There would have been no need for Alecos to borrow the back-up from Dimitra to rectify the situation.

He needed to 'phone Stavros Tanakis. He looked at the road ahead in frustration. There were very few places where he could safely pull over and make a telephone call. He was certainly not going to take a chance and end up the same way as Alecos. Maybe that was what the man was doing when he had been hit. If he had been foolish enough to stop on the bend to make or answer a call another car could easily have run into him.

Half an hour later Vasi was able to stop in an area by that had been created for people to take photographs of the gorge and, if they were fortunate, of the eagles soaring high above on the thermal currents.

Stavros listened to Vasi asking about the back-up disks the branches sent to the head office each day. He cursed himself. He should have thought of that first, rather than sit there trying to work out figures and spending hours checking the paper copies with Mr Iliopolakis and his son.

'You realise, Mr Vasi, that we have hundreds of thousands of disks stored here. We have to keep each of them for a year until the bank has made an annual return and it has been agreed.'

'They must also be labelled. All I'm suggesting is that you look at the back-ups covering the last month for the branches where we do our banking.'

'That would mean looking at about a thousand back-ups!'

'Then just look at the last two weeks.'

'You're still asking me to look through five hundred.'

Vasi sighed in exasperation. 'Mr Tanakis, you only have to look at our hotel accounts; not everyone's. Start with last week and see if any anomaly shows up. You've already looked at the tellers' receipts so you know the money was paid in and the amount. Just check to see if it was credited to our account and if it wasn't ask the computer to search. I very much doubt that anyone else paid in exactly the same amount as us on the same day.'

'It will take me a long time. I do have other duties and appointments with customers.'

'Then make it a priority. Hand your other duties on to an under manager. I'll call in on Wednesday to see if you have had any success.' Vasi closed his mobile. How he wished he had access to the back-ups that were sitting in the bank.

Over lunch Saffron regaled her relatives with her encounter with the Cretan police and Vasi's arrest a second time.

'I still cannot understand why they think Vasi would do something so awful?' said Marianne.

'It was because his car had been vandalised. The policeman in Heraklion was convinced the damage was where Vasi had run Alecos through the barrier. I was so relieved when we went up to collect the dogs yesterday that Lambros said he had found paint chippings. It proved Vasi was telling the truth.'

Monday 24th September

Marcus shook his head. 'It doesn't, Saffron. He could have knocked off a few chips himself.'

'Marcus!' Saffron was horrified. 'Vasi wouldn't do anything like that; besides, I was with him all evening and we found the damage when he was about to bring me home.'

Marcus smiled at her outrage. 'I used to be in insurance, remember. It's given me a suspicious mind. You'd be amazed the things people do to try to cheat an insurance company, so why not try to cover up a crime you've committed?' Marcus held up his hand. 'I don't think for one minute that Vasi damaged his car further, but look at it from the point of view of the police. A car forced off the road, a damaged car apprehended and the driver says the damage took place whilst he was parked in his private grounds. His only alibi is that of his companion who insists she was with him the whole time. An anonymous caller says he saw a car fitting the description of the one Vasi drives and with three numbers on the registration plate the same as Vasi's. Add to that the fact that he had a disagreement with the victim only a day or so earlier and the police think they have a pretty strong case.'

Saffron was forced to smile. 'When you put it like that I suppose it does sound suspicious.'

'How long has Vasi got to report to the police for?' asked Marianne.

'I don't know. Until they're satisfied that he had nothing to do with it, I suppose.'

'Will that stop him from visiting you in England?' asked John.

'I hope not. He's not coming until November.'

'If he can't come I will,' offered John.

'You came earlier with Nicola,' Saffron reminded him.

John shrugged. 'So I could always come again, besides, it would be shame to waste his ticket. Is he coming to collect you later? I'll ask him if he'll pass his ticket on to me if he can't go.'

'You most certainly will not,' Giovanni told him sternly in Italian. 'Manners for a start. You do not invite yourself anywhere, you wait to be asked. Think how hurt Vasi would be if you suggested you had his ticket. He would think you didn't believe him.'

'Sorry, Pappa. I didn't mean it to sound like that.' John lowered his eyes. 'I was only joking, Saff,' he added in English. 'I'm sure the police will let him visit England. November's ages away. Whoever caused the accident will have been caught by then.'

'I do hope so. Vasi is looking forward to coming to England so much.'

John raised his eyebrow at her. 'No doubt you are also looking forward to him being there?'

Saffron let the tip of her tongue appear between her teeth as she looked at John. 'I hope he will enjoy himself.'

John grinned and raised his eyebrows. 'What are your plans for today until Vasi arrives?'

'Nothing much. Maybe another swim, then wash my hair.'

'Fancy coming up to Vasi's house with me? He's asked me to take some photos of the paint chips. It's his solicitor's idea, just in case Mr Christos loses the samples he took away with him. You can have a swim in the pool whilst you're there.'

John pressed the bell at the gates of Vasi's house to alert Lambros of their arrival. Both dogs raced down the drive barking frantically. Saffron looked at them nervously.

'I'm quite happy with those two when Vasi is here, but do you think it will be safe without him?'

'Lambros will control them. If you're really worried I can ask him to shut them in.'

Lambros appeared at the top of the drive and called the dogs to heel, telling them to stay before he approached the gates and entered the code to open them. John drove slowly up the drive, Lambros walking beside him. When they reached the dogs he slipped a hand through the collar of each one and they stood tensely at his side.

'I'll hold them whilst you put the bike over there. Then come and let them sniff you. They should be happy enough with the lady.

They know her.'

John nodded, set the bike against a tree and held out his hands to the dogs as he walked slowly towards them. They strained at their collars until he had petted them, then they relaxed and as Saffron approached they both wagged their tails. She lowered her hands to fondle their ears and found her hands being licked.

'Hmm,' she said. 'I'm glad they're friendly towards me, but that is a bit much. My hands are all wet and slimy from their spittle.'

'Can't be as bad as when they're covered in blood and muck when you operate.'

'I have gloves on then. Can you open the door for me? I don't want to get the handle dirty and I'll have to wash before I do anything else.'

John swung the door of the kitchen open. 'Do you want to go down and swim whilst I take these photos?'

Saffron shook her head. 'No, wait for me. I'm quite interested to see what you are going to do. When I get bored I'll go for a swim.'

Lambros wheeled the garden bin up to the patio. 'It's all messed up with grass and weed,' he apologised to John.

John opened the lid and looked inside. 'That's impossible,' he declared. 'Even with a flash I'll not be able to get a decent photograph of anything. It will have to be emptied out.'

'Where do you want me to empty it? Here?' asked Lambros.

John shook his head. 'It will have to be emptied inside. There's too much breeze out here.'

John helped Lambros pull the bin into the kitchen and the two men were just about to up-end the bin when Saffron reappeared.

'Whatever are you doing?'

'We've got to empty it and it's too breezy to do it outside.'

'You can't just tip it up on the floor. You need to put something down first.'

'What do you suggest?'

Saffron frowned. Had she been at home in England they always kept some old sheets to use to protect the carpet or furniture if necessary. 'Ask Lambros if there are any old cloths around.'

Lambros disappeared and returned a few moments later with an armful of old rags that he used to clean the garden tools. Saffron shook her head.

'They're not quite what I had in mind. I'll have a look upstairs and see if I can find where Vasi keeps his sheets. We can always take it back with us and send it to the laundry with those from the chalets.'

John waited patiently until Saffron returned and spread a large white sheet out on the kitchen floor and folded it in half. John photographed the bin and then the contents. He waited whilst Lambros tipped up the bin and the miscellany of garden rubbish and paint chippings fell out. John looked at the collection perplexed.

'How am I going to photograph that lot? It's just a heap of rubbish.'

'You'll have to sort it out. I'll help,' offered Saffron. 'Take a photo as it is now and then you can take another later.'

John took half a dozen shots from different angles and then joined Saffron on his knees. He began to pull leaves and grass out of the pile and push it to one side.

'This is silly,' declared Saffron. 'Don't do any more until I've found a bucket. We can put the rubbish in there and then tip it straight back into the bin. We'll have to do it carefully or the paint chips will just crumble up to nothing.'

John sighed. This was going to take a good deal longer than he had envisaged.

They worked slowly and methodically for nearly two hours, John taking another photo each time the pile diminished considerably. Finally he and Saffron straightened up.

'Now what?' she asked.

'I'll photograph the pile of chips and then I'll lie some of the larger ones out and take photos of those. You can go and swim if you want, Saff. You've done more than your share.'

Saffron rose to her feet gratefully. 'I'll see you down there in a little while. It shouldn't take you very long and then it can all be dumped back in the bin and Lambros can put it back outside.'

John spread the paint chippings out on the sheet. He wished he had asked Saffron to stay to help him. Her fingers were far more nimble than his. He pushed a couple closer to each other and realised they fitted. By pure coincidence he had placed them together. He photographed them, zooming in to show the edges, and then again when he fitted them together. He wondered if any more would fit and before he placed a new one down he tried to fit it against those already there. He became intrigued by the puzzle, moving the pieces around and each time he thought he had a match he took a photograph.

'What are you up to, John? I thought you were going to join me for a swim.' Saffron stood in the kitchen with her towel around her.

'Come and look at this.' John pointed to the selection of pieces where the broken edges fitted together.

Saffron crouched down and looked where he indicated. 'Surely they should match. If you broke a plate the broken edges would fit back together.'

'I wasn't expecting so many to fit.' John frowned. 'Has Vasi got a computer here?'

'Of course.'

'Can you show me where it is? I want to look something up if it will let me in.'

Saffron looked dubious. 'Should you? I mean, after the problems at the bank it might not be a good idea to try to use Vasi's computer. He might think you were trying to break in to the accounts.'

John smiled at her. 'Provided I can get on to the main screen I will use my password. I only want to look at the Internet. I won't go near anything of Vasi's. You can watch me to make sure.'

Hesitantly Saffron followed John in the room where Vasilis had kept his computer and watched whilst John waited for the screen to flicker into life. John typed in his password and was allowed to proceed.

John went straight to the Internet and typed in the name of a site in America that dealt with crime.

'What are you looking for?' she asked curiously.

'I'm sure I watched a programme about a hit and run accident in the States. The police examined the paint chips and matched them to the vehicle. It was used as proof to convict the driver.'

'What good is that? We know Vasi didn't do it and they won't find any of his paint on the wrecked car.'

'No, but suppose there are paint chips that can be matched to another car?'

Saffron frowned. 'What are you suggesting?'

'That car in Aghios Nikolaos that was badly damaged; suppose that was the one that caused the accident? There should be paint chips at the crash site that would match. That would prove that Vasi was innocent.'

'But if there's no paint there belonging to Vasi's car it must mean he's innocent.'

'The police could say it had blown away or they couldn't find it amongst all the other rubbish there was around. Got it!'

John pointed the cursor at the site and requested that the programme was played. He fast forwarded the description of the accident until he reached the part where the chips of paint were discussed, examined and matched to the vehicle. He pointed at the screen triumphantly. 'That's the answer.'

Saffron sighed. 'It may be the answer, but you will have to get the police to agree with you. I imagine work like that is very expensive to carry out. They may not think it worth their while.'

'It would be worth it to Vasi to prove his innocence.' John frowned. 'I wonder if Vasi has photos of the damage to his car? If so I could enlarge those and then superimpose these over the top. Provided they matched I could take them to the police to prove that the system works. I'll 'phone Vasi now and ask him if he has any photos.'

Saffron nodded. She had little faith that the police would bother with the procedure John had described.

Nikos Vikelakis began to empty the carrier bag. He had only examined the contents cursorily when he had been asked to sign to take possession of them at the hospital. Alecos's wallet appeared to be intact with both money and credit cards, along with his bank book. His watch had been wrapped in a handkerchief, despite the fact that it was obviously broken along with his mobile. There were no keys in the bag belonging to him; no doubt they were still with the wrecked car. With reluctance Nikos inserted a hand into the empty pockets of the torn trousers; then tossed them on to the bed. He wondered if he was allowed to throw them away or whether the police expected him to keep them along with the blood stained shirt. At the bottom of the carrier were Alecos's shoes. In one was a wad of folded paper, obviously torn from a note book and inside the folds was a flash drive. In the other was some loose change.

He looked at the sheets of notepaper, there were names and amounts listed and he wondered if this was the information Stavros wanted. Maybe Alecos had intended to deliver the papers and memory stick to the man in person and arrived after the bank had closed. That could account for him being in the area. He would probably have stopped in Heraklion for a meal and he might even have visited the cinema before commencing his drive back to Aghios Nikolaos. That could be the reason why he was driving back at that late hour.

Nikos returned downstairs and took an envelope and sheet of writing paper from the stock he had purloined from the bank before retiring. He wrote a brief note to Stavros saying he had found the notes and memory stick amongst Alecos's belongings. If they were nothing to do with the bank he would be grateful for their return. He wrote 'FOR THE ATTENTION OF STAVROS TANAKIS' on the outside of the envelope, placed the items inside and sealed it. He would deliver it to the local bank in the morning and they could send it up to the Head office in their Courier Bag.

Tuesday 25ᵗʰ September

Dimitra decided she must go in to work at the Central. She had not received a telephone call from Mr Iliopolakis to say she was fired, but nor had he enquired why she had not been in to work the previous day. If she stayed away any longer Vasi and his father might well begin to think that she did have something to do with the discrepancies in the hotel accounts.

How she wished Alecos would regain consciousness and be able to explain how the mistake had happened. She would telephone the hospital when she returned from work and ask a nurse on the ward if Alecos had made any progress. She might even be able to speak to Doctor Melanakis.

'Stavros, I'm going down to the bank this morning to leave an envelope to be delivered to you. I don't know if any of it is relevant.'

'What's in there?'

'Some papers with notes made by Alecos and a memory stick. They were amongst his belongings. It could all be private, of course, and nothing to do with the bank.'

'If it's private I'll return it to you immediately,' promised Stavros. 'Are you coming to visit your son today?'

'I hadn't planned to. There's not much point in driving all that way and just looking at him attached to wires and machinery. Why?'

'I just thought it could be quicker for you to drop the items in to me in Heraklion than wait for the courier bag to arrive.'

Nikos shook his head, although he knew Stavros could not see him. He had disapproved of the fast car that Alecos had bought after he had been made manager of the Aghios Nikolaos branch. Now look what had happened; he had probably been driving too fast around the steep bends of the highway and contributed to his accident.

'I may be up at the end of the week. I'll see what the doctor has to say.'

'Yes, of course, I understand.' Stavros bit back his annoyance. He knew if it was his son lying injured in hospital he and his wife would have spent every minute of their day with him. 'I hope you'll soon hear some good news.'

Stavros replaced the receiver and cursed silently. He needed to see the papers and memory sticks as quickly as possible in the hope of finding the cause of the error that had somehow occurred on Mr Iliopolakis's account. If he waited for the courier bag to arrive he would not receive it until Wednesday afternoon.

He picked up the telephone keyed in Nikos's 'phone number again. It rang a number of times before Nikos finally answered it, breathing heavily.

'Yes?'

'Nikos, it's Stavros again. There's no need to take that envelope down to the bank. One of the trainees has to come up to Heraklion today. He can collect it from you and bring it with him. Save you the journey.'

'Why didn't you think of that earlier? I'd just gone upstairs when you 'phoned again.'

'I'm sorry. I only remembered after we finished our call.'

'When's he coming?'

'In about half an hour. Is that .....'

The line went dead as Nikos replaced the receiver. Stavros shrugged. He must now 'phone the bank at Aghios Nikolaos and ask them to release one of their assistants for the day to collect the envelope and deliver it to him.

Vasi drove down to Yannis's house to collect Saffron. He had spoken to Mr Tsilikadis at John's request and collected copies of the photographs of his car that the police had taken before driving back from Heraklion. He was not sure why John wanted them, despite the young man trying to explain to him about superimposing and matching when they had talked.

Vasi handed over the envelope and John grinned delightedly. 'These are not perfect, but I'll be able to give you an idea of what needs to be done. Come along to my dark room and I'll show you. You come too, Saff. You'll see exactly what I mean then.'

John showed Vasi the photographs he had taken of the paint chippings earlier in the day. They looked enormous where he had enlarged them. 'I've only just started because it takes time to do this sort of thing. I've made copies of each one and I'm going to enlarge your photos of the car damage. I've cut round my copy photos so all I have is the paint chip, no background.' John worked as he talked.

Saffron and Vasi waited patiently until John laid the enlarged photograph of part of the passenger door on the table. Using a pair of tweezers he picked up one of the cut outs and began to place it on the damage, turning it slowly and finally discarding it. John repeated the procedure four times until he finally pronounced himself satisfied that a chip fitted, the edges of the paint remaining on the car fitting perfectly with the cut out that he laid on top.

'That's amazing,' remarked Vasi. 'Where did you learn about that?'

'Watching a television programme,' grinned John. 'I just happened to remember it when I saw a couple of chips fitted together. I looked the programme up on the Internet to refresh my memory and I found out a couple of other interesting facts.'

Vasi raised his eyebrows. 'Tell me.'

'Wing mirrors have numbers on the back relating to the make of vehicle and year of manufacture. You haven't lost a wing mirror, but if one belonging to another car has been found it could well have come from the vehicle that caused Mr Vikelakis's accident.'

'You have to replace your wing mirror if it's damaged,' remonstrated Vasi. 'You're not likely to find any vehicles driving around without one.'

With the air of a conjuror John produced the photograph he had taken of Stelios's car at Saffron's request and pointed. 'No wing mirror.'

Vasi shrugged. 'That doesn't prove anything. He could have lost his wing mirror at any time. Whoever sprayed the car could have broken it off at the same time.'

'So why didn't they leave it lying in the gutter? It could be used as proof if one with a matching number was found at the crash site.'

'The police will have cleared the area.'

John nodded. 'I'm sure they have, but why should they take any notice of an odd wing mirror? They probably didn't even bother to pick it up.'

Vasi sighed. 'John, I know you're trying to be helpful, and I'm grateful to you for taking the photos for me, but I don't see any point in pursuing your ideas. The police would probably say such a procedure would be too time consuming and expensive.'

John set his mouth in a determined line. 'The man in America was convicted on the evidence of the wing mirror and the paint chips that fitted with the damage on his vehicle. Our police ought to examine any paint chips found at the site and check any wing mirrors they may have found.'

Saffron frowned. 'Can I make a suggestion?'

The two men looked at her.

'Why doesn't Vasi speak to his solicitor? If he thinks John's ideas are feasible then he could approach the police. Surely they would take notice of him.'

John drove into Aghios Nikolaos with Vasi and Saffron. It had taken a considerable amount of time before Vasi had been able to speak to his solicitor and request that paint samples found at the crash site should be sent to the forensic department for testing to prove they did not come from his car.

Mr Tsilikadis had sounded puzzled by Vasi's request. 'That should be undertaken as a matter of course, but I'll telephone the police in Heraklion to remind them,' he promised. 'It will no doubt take some time for the results to come through. Of course, if the driver who caused the accident is found in the meantime you could be accused of wasting police time and resources.'

'I'll take that chance,' replied Vasi. 'They can always use whatever they find as additional evidence when they prosecute the culprit. I'll speak to our local police and ask him to ensure that the samples he collected from my bin are not discarded as rubbish.'

John walked confidently into the police station with Vasi. 'Good morning, Mr Christos. Can you spare us a few minutes of your time, please?'

'Good morning, Mr John, Mr Vasi. Have you come to report in?'

Vasi nodded. 'If you could make a note that you've seen me I'd be grateful, but we really came to speak to you about the investigation.'

Christos shook his head. 'I'm not allowed to discuss that with you.'

'I'm not asking you for any details. John has taken photographs of the paint chippings that were in the rubbish bin and.....'

Christos held up his hand. 'You should not have touched that Mr Vasi or you Mr John. That's regarded as police evidence.'

Vasi shook his head. 'There is nothing on the bin to say it should not be touched. As far as I am aware you only told Lambros he was not to use the bin or empty it until you gave permission.'

'Because it is police evidence.'

Vasi waved his hand. 'I was acting on the instructions of my solicitor. He said I should have insisted you took photographs of the trim and paint chippings before you removed them. I asked John to take photos of those that remained and whilst he was doing so he realised that many of the edges matched each other. He's brought along his photographs to show you.'

Christos sighed. He should have thought to ask for a police photographer to come and take photographs before he had emptied the bin and removed anything. He could even be accused of tampering with evidence if Mr Vasi's solicitor felt it would help prove his client was innocent.

John spread the photos out on the desk and began to place the cut out chips on top to show how they matched up.

Christos shrugged. 'Some of them probably would match up, Mr John.'

'Has anyone collected paint chips from around Mr Vikelakis's car to see if any of them match with Mr Vasi's car?'

'I'm sure the local police have scoured the area.'

'Has Mr Vikelakis's car been checked to see if there is any paint on the body work that matches that of Mr Vasi's car? Have they found any wing mirrors?'

Christos frowned. 'What exactly do you want to know, Mr John?'

John leaned forwards and began to explain about the television programme he had seen that had subsequently given him the idea of matching up the paint chips with the damage.

Christos shook his head. 'That was a television programme, Mr John. You cannot believe everything you see and hear on the television.'

John sighed in exasperation. 'I've shown you how these match up. Vasi has spoken to his solicitor and he agrees that any paint chips found on the site should be sent to the forensic department for examination. Even if they are the same colour as Vasi's car the constituency of the paint won't match his.'

Still Christos shook his head. 'The kind of investigation you are suggesting takes a good deal of time and is therefore expensive. It's very unlikely the police would be able to spare so much from their budget on one case.'

'I think it could be cheaper for the police in the long run. If they refuse to consult with forensics then I shall instruct my solicitor to conduct an enquiry and they could well be sued for withholding evidence that would prove me innocent.'

'And another thing,' John hurried on, not wishing to give Christos time to interrupt. 'Wing mirrors have numbers on the back relating to the make of the vehicle and year of manufacture. Vasi hasn't lost a wing mirror, but if one belonging to another car has been found it could well have come from the vehicle that caused Mr Vikelakis's accident. I don't expect to be given access to that or the information, but could you ask the police in Heraklion to check?'

Christos smiled at the intense young man. 'Thank you, Mr John, I'll bear all your information in mind and speak to the police in Heraklion. I am not in charge of the investigation, you understand.'

John sighed, looked at Vasi in despair and spread his hands. 'I've done my best, Vasi.'

Christos watched as the two men left the station and joined Saffron where she was waiting in the car. Maybe there was some value in the information the young man had given him and looking at the photographs had certainly been impressive. He wished he was younger and knew more about these modern techniques that were used. He began to write down some notes on his pad. *Check for paint on Vikelakis car. Check for mirrors – details on back?* Mr Papandrakis's car had a broken front light and also a wing mirror was missing. He would put in a call to Heraklion and see if they could give him any further information, but first he would speak to Andreas and ask if there was a number on the back of the wing mirror that was still in situ on the vandalised vehicle.

Vasi sat in his hired car with Saffron beside him. 'So, it is the last day of your holiday. What would you like to do?'

'We ought to look for an apartment for you.'

Vasi shrugged. 'That can wait. Now I have reported to Christos, we will do whatever you like.'

Saffron hesitated. 'Do you really not want to live in your father's house?'

Vasi shook his head. 'It is far too big. It has always been too big. I know when Pappa built it he envisaged having more children. It would have been more practical to have built a smaller house and added rooms if they were needed, as Yannis has done with his house.'

'Suppose you turned it into a hotel?' she suggested tentatively.

'It is not large enough to be a hotel.'

'Think of the Imperia; you said you wanted ten rooms upstairs that you could make into bedrooms with bathrooms en suite.'

'There are only three rooms upstairs at my father's house.'

'That's true, but they are enormous rooms. If you made them smaller you would have at least six bedrooms.'

Vasi shook his head. 'Six rooms do not make a viable hotel. The only reason I was prepared to invest in the Imperia was because Churchill and Ghandi had stayed there. You suggested that people would want to stay so they could claim they had slept in the same room as one of them and I thought it was a good idea that would make money. Without that association I would not have considered purchasing such a small property.'

'Marjorie made a suggestion, but I'm not sure if it would be practical.'

Vasi raised his eyebrows. 'So tell me. You gave me good ideas for the gymnasium and also for my apartment. Ideas are always worth considering.'

'This is Marjorie's idea, not mine.'

'So? She can have good ideas also.'

'She thought the house could be used as a specialist holiday centre. You could advertise it as an ideal location for artists. The views are wonderful and the light changes as the sun moves round during the day. Or you could offer it as a centre for visitors to learn how to make authentic Greek food, or be shown how to do weaving or embroidery.'

Vasi sat silently, contemplating Saffron's suggestions. Finally he started the engine of the car and smiled at her. 'We will look at the house and you can tell me more of your ideas. We can consider if it would be practical.'

Saffron smiled. So much for spending the day however she wished. She should not have mentioned Marjorie's idea to him on her last day. Once Vasi began to think about the possibilities of a hotel he became totally obsessed.

Christos telephoned Thranassis and asked if he had any further information regarding the examination of the site where Alecos's car had been found.

'What's your rush?' asked Thranassis. 'I'll send the report through to you when I have it.'

'I just wanted to ask about something that may have been found there. I didn't want to disturb Babbis unnecessarily.'

Thranassis felt his anger building up. There was no reason why any relevant information should be withheld from him.

'What do you want to know? I may have the answer, save you troubling them.'

'It's only a query. If you've not had the report back yet you won't know,' replied Christos smugly. He was not going to disclose that he was in possession of the serial number from the back of the wing mirror on Stelios's car and wished to check if one with a matching number had been found in the vicinity.

'What is it you want to ask them?' persisted Thranassis.

'If it's relevant I'll let you know what they say.' Christos ignored the question and replaced the receiver. He chuckled to himself. He could imagine just how furious Thranassis was with him for not divulging the information.

'Babbis, this is Christos from Aghios Nikolaos. I'm enquiring about that car that was wrecked on the highway. No, I know you haven't sent your report to Thranassis yet, I've just been speaking to him. I need to ask you something that could be important to the investigation.'

Christos heard Babbis give a deep sigh. 'What?' he asked in a bored voice.

'I presume you scoured the immediate area?'

'Of course,' Babbis's voice was scornful. He and his men knew their job. They didn't need a local policeman telling them procedure.

'Amongst your findings was there a wing mirror that didn't belong to the wrecked car?'

'A wing mirror?'

'Yes. You should have found two belonging to the wrecked car. Did you find any more than that?'

'Hold on. I'll have to have a look.'

Christos waited until Babbis returned to the 'phone. 'According to our listings we found enough pieces of broken lamp and window glass to fill a sack, three bumpers, various lengths of trim, seven tyres, one car seat, a suitcase, two number plates, five wing mirrors, an exhaust pipe,......'

'Five!' Christos interrupted him.

'So it says. Obviously this lot didn't all come from the car we have here. We have to check everything then we can discard the rubbish that people have thrown over the side.'

'Don't throw away the wing mirrors,' insisted Christos.

'They don't all belong to this car.'

'You should have two that belong to the car, either still attached or loose amongst the debris. One of the others could belong to the car that forced him over. Behind the glass there should be a serial number and the make and model of the car the mirror came from.'

'We know that. We're not novices.'

'Babbis, listen a moment, please. I have a car impounded here. It has considerable damage on the passenger side and a wing mirror is missing. Can you give me the serial numbers from the mirrors you have and I'll check them against the car we're holding.'

'We have the car here that forced the vehicle off the road.'

'I know Thranassis thinks that's the correct vehicle, but I'm not sure. The car he impounded has both wing mirrors intact and the glass on the lights isn't broken.'

'These other mirrors are just throwaways.'

'Very likely, but just as a favour to me, would you give me the numbers so I can check them out? If there's a match I'll let you know.'

'I suppose so,' Babbis agreed grudgingly.

'And another thing; could you let me know the colour and length of the trim you've collected?'

'You wouldn't like the shape of each piece of glass whilst you're at it?' replied Babbis sarcastically.

'No, but don't throw anything away yet; direct instructions from the suspect's solicitor.' Christos felt the sweat coming out on his forehead as he said the words. He could imagine how annoyed Thranassis would be when he heard. 'I'll expect a call from you, in, say, half an hour?'

'My report should be ready by tomorrow, can't it wait until then?'

'If my suspicions about the wing mirror are correct you'd have to be re-writing your report. If I'm wrong there's nothing lost except a few minutes of your time,' replied Christos dryly and heard Babbis replace the receiver loudly.

'So what do you wish to do?' asked Vasi as he ran his finger lightly down Saffron's ribs.

Saffron wriggled out of his reach. 'I can't concentrate if you do that,' she said laughingly. 'I think we should talk about the house first, bearing Marjorie's ideas in mind. You know you won't be able to settle until you've decided whether it would be feasible or not.'

'I thought you might like to swim first.' Vasi raised his eyebrows at her.

Saffron hesitated. She would indeed like to have a swim and then spend the remainder of the morning enfolded in Vasi's arms. She shook her head firmly. 'Business first, pleasure afterwards.' She kissed him lightly on his lips and stepped away quickly before he could take hold of her.

With an exaggerated sigh and spread of his hands Vasi unlocked the front door.

'Why are we going in this way?' asked Saffron. 'We always go round to the patio?'

'You are a visitor. You have come to stay at my select hotel for a week to learn how to cook properly.'

Saffron shook her head. 'No, I have not come to learn how to cook properly. I have come to be taught how to cook Greek food.'

Vasi raised his eyebrows. 'There is a difference?'

'There certainly is,' replied Saffron firmly. 'And you haven't told me why we are entering here.'

'I was explaining when you interrupted me.' Vasi spoke in a hurt tone. 'I do not expect my visitors to interrupt me when I am giving them important information.'

Saffron giggled. 'Go on, then. I'm a visitor.'

Vasi nodded. 'I open the door and welcome you. What is your first impression?'

'How large the hall is.'

'So it could be made smaller?'

'I think so. If you removed the cloakroom you could bring the wall over to where the stairs begin.'

'And what would you do with the space you have created?'

'I would take down the internal walls and make three bedrooms, each with a bathroom en suite. Now you have nine bedrooms.'

Vasi nodded. 'Here is your room, madam. There is no separate toilet on this floor so you will have to return to your room whenever you need it.' Vasi saw Saffron frown. 'It is the same for everyone, Madam. The guests have to return to their rooms whenever they need toilet facilities, whichever floor they are staying on.'

'That's not practical, Vasi.'

'It was your idea,' he protested.

'You would have to provide a cloakroom somewhere else. You have to think about the staff. You could have two bedrooms on this side and two cloakrooms next to them.'

'And on the other side of the hallway? What would you expect to see there?'

'The lounge, with a bar in the corner and the dining room.'

Vasi nodded. 'That leaves just the kitchen.' He shook his head. 'I do not think the house is large enough for Marjorie's idea.'

'We've just made eight bedrooms.' Saffron smiled at him mischievously.

Vasi raised his eyebrows suggestively to her. 'Which one would you like to occupy?'

Saffron shook her head. 'Not yet, we need to talk some more and see if a conversion is practical.'

Vasi sighed dramatically. 'So, we have enough bedrooms for sixteen guests. If all the sixteen wanted to learn to cook there would not be enough equipment in the kitchen and certainly not enough space. Then we have to consider their evening meal. I do not think the dining room is large enough for eight tables of a comfortable size.'

Saffron smiled. 'Vasi, you are thinking in terms of a conventional hotel. Let's go and sit on the patio and I'll explain Marjorie's idea more fully.'

Vasi followed Saffron through to the patio, collecting two bottles of beer from the fridge as he passed. 'Now,' he said, 'Explain, please.'

'Have you got a pen and paper? You may want to write some of my suggestions down.'

Dutifully Vasi rose, went through to the room Vasilis had called his office and collected a pad of plain paper. He sat back down at the table, took a mouthful of his beer and looked at her expectantly.

'The conversion of the bedrooms has been completed, so we know we have eight rooms giving enough accommodation for sixteen people. When people book they will have to say which activities they would like to enjoy.' Saffron pulled the pad of paper towards her. 'We will say that six couples have booked. Three of the men wish to go walking and explore the area. Three men are artists. You could provide an easel and stool for the artists but they have to bring their own materials. The six women with them wish to cook.' Saffron divided the paper into columns and headed each column with the activity and the projected number of participants. 'Four more people book and three want to cook and one is an artist. That gives you nine people in the kitchen and whoever is helping them. You have to decide if the kitchen is large enough and has enough equipment for six people.'

Saffron held up her hand as Vasi was about to interrupt. 'You are also offering traditional weaving and embroidery classes. Four people are weaving whilst five are cooking. Two days later five people are weaving and four are cooking. Instead of having eight separate tables in the dining room you have two large ones. The dishes the women have cooked during the day are served as the evening meal so there is no wastage.'

Vasi shook his head. 'It will not work. If sixteen people said they wished to cook all week and nothing else we could not accommodate them. They would only have two opportunities if we divided them into groups of five, and there would still be one person left over. What would they do on the other days?'

'Vasi, these are only ideas. You would have to make it quite clear in your advertisement that the kitchen can only have a maximum of six people working in there at any one time. You tell them that the days when they are not cooking they can lay by the pool, try their hand at painting, join in with the weaving and embroidery classes, go walking, visit Elounda and Spinalonga or go to Aghios Nikolaos. When they book they also have to fill in a form so you know what is expected of you. Provided they know exactly what is on offer they can decide how they want to spend their time before they come. Some of them may not want to join in with anything, but prefer to be in a small hotel and please themselves each day. You may get some single people booking and for them it would be a way of making friends and having some company.'

Vasi looked at Saffron doubtfully. 'We offer weaving, so where do we place the loom? It is a large item of furniture. Also we will need someone who knows how to weave and how to instruct. We will need staff for cleaning, where do we find them? Someone will have to live here to cover for any emergency in the night and also to prepare the breakfast. That is one bedroom that cannot be rented out. We will have to employ someone who is qualified to teach cookery. I cannot see that the idea will make any money.'

Saffron leant her elbows on the table. 'You are not offering Cordon Bleu cookery courses. You are offering an experience. There must be some women in the village who are good cooks. Would they be willing for a couple of women to use their kitchen under their supervision and tuition? That way their dishes would be more authentic. The same with the weaving; does anyone already have a loom in their house? You would have to pay them to teach the visitors, of course, but it could work out cheaper than you employing teachers.'

'I'm not sure, Saffie. I would have to think about it carefully and talk to my father. It is his house.'

'Of course. I am only telling you some of the ideas that Marjorie had. It is a way of making use of the house if you are not planning to live here.' Saffron smiled. 'You might even find that you had visitors in the winter months who wished to help harvest the olives.'

'Why would they want to do that?'

'For the experience.'

'Yes? You really think so?' asked Vasi dubiously,

Saffron laughed. 'Vasi, English people enjoy doing the strangest things. They like being called eccentric.'

Vasi frowned. 'Why should they be called e-central if they do strange things?'

'Not e-central, eccentric. It means doing unconventional things, being different from other people.'

'So I could advertise this as a centre for eccentric people?'

Saffron shook her head. 'I wouldn't advise it. It could be

misconstrued as a holiday retreat for people suffering from dementia or Alzheimer's.'

'Explain, please.'

'They are a form of illnesses. People begin to act out of character and they forget how to complete the simple basic tasks they have done since childhood. They tend to behave irrationally and finally withdraw into their own world and need to have specialist care.'

'We do not have that in Greece,' Vasi replied firmly.

'I'm sure you do, but in Greece the elderly are kept within the family unit and looked after. The family do not say their grandmother or grandfather has dementia, they say they have become very forgetful recently due to their advanced age.'

Vasi looked at Saffron in surprise. 'How do you know the people say that when you do not speak Greek?'

'It is what we used to say in England before it became a recognised medical condition. The longer we live the more likely we are to suffer from it. The brain cells die and do not reproduce.'

'So you and I will have this dementia?'

Saffron shrugged. 'Maybe. My grandmother doesn't suffer from it and look how old she is.'

Vasi shivered. 'This is not a nice thing to contemplate. Why are we talking about our old age?'

'We were talking about people being eccentric,' Saffron reminded him. 'I merely told you it was not a good idea to say you catered for them.'

Vasi hit his forehead with the flat of his hand. 'You see – already my brain cells are dying and I do not remember.'

Saffron shook her head in mock solemnity. 'That is so sad. You obviously do not remember how we have been swimming and enjoying ourselves.'

'That I could not forget.' Vasi drained the last of his beer and reached for Saffron's hand, 'But maybe my memory needs to be refreshed.'

Christos waited impatiently for Babbis to return his call. He was beginning to wonder if the man had spoken to Thranassis and been told not to give him the information when the telephone finally rang.

Christos listened intently to the numbers Babbis read out from the wing mirrors that had been found and copied them down carefully, certain that one of them was the same as Andreas had given him earlier. 'And the measurements of the chrome trims that you collected?'

Again Christos wrote down the figures he was given. 'Are all trims the same width?' he asked.

'Near enough.'

Christos sighed. 'I may have to get back to you for an exact measurement. In the meantime please keep everything. I'll let you know later if any of the wing mirror numbers are the same as the one on the car I have here. I have another question for you, Babbis, whilst we're talking. Have you taken paint samples from the body work?'

'Thranassis told me to take samples from the car he's holding.'

'I suggest you take some from the wrecked car also.'

'What for?'

'It could be a useful addition to the evidence if you find paint transferred from one car to another and make certain you preserve any flakes or chips that were found in the area.'

'Are you suggesting involving forensics? I'll need permission from Thranassis before I'm allowed to send them to the lab for analysis. It all costs money.'

'No need to send them at this stage. Just make sure you have samples.'

'Anything else?'

'Not that I can think of at the moment. Thanks for your help.'

Christos heard Babbis grunt as he replaced the receiver. Samples of paint from the bodies of both cars should have been taken as a matter of routine. It was a painstaking procedure and Babbis had obviously tried to avoid the extra work and expense it would involve.

'I need to go out,' Christos announced to his two companion officers. 'I'll take my own car and I doubt if I'll be that long.'

The officers exchanged looks and one patted his pocket. With Christos out of the station for a while they would be able to sneak round to the back and have a cigarette.

Christos drove to the garage on the outskirts of Aghios Nikolaos where Stelios's car had been taken. He knocked on the door and entered the dark building. 'Andreas, are you in there?' he called.

'Out the back,' came the answer from a mechanic, his head just showing above the level of the pit, a van jacked up precariously above him.

'I'll go through.' Picking his way carefully between oil stains and tools that were strewn around Christos made his way to the rear of the building. The door to the yard stood open and he walked back out into the bright sunshine.

'Andreas?'

A man wearing greasy overalls rose to his feet from behind a car. He spat the screws he had been holding in his mouth into his hand and grinned at Christos.

'What have you done to your car?'

'Nothing. I want to speak to you about the one you brought in for me yesterday.'

'The red paint job? It's a mess. I haven't touched it,' Andreas hastened to reassure Christos as he saw the look of alarm on the policeman's face. 'I only removed the glass from the wing mirror to give you the number and I've put that back now.'

'I'm going to ask you to take it out again.'

'Why didn't you say you wanted it left out,' grumbled Andreas. 'I put the car into the lock up and there's hardly any space between the wall and the car.'

'I need to check that number for myself.'

'Don't you trust me to know my numbers?'

'Police business, Andreas. I have to be able to say that I have seen it.'

Andreas pulled out his bunch of key and picked up the screwdriver he had been using when Christos arrived.

'Did you wear gloves when you removed the mirror?'

Andreas glanced at him scornfully. 'You can't work in gloves.'

'In that case I'll have to get you to come in so I can take your prints.'

A look of alarm crossed Andreas's face. 'What do you want those for?'

'Just to eliminate you. If we find prints on the mirror we need to know who they belong to. Here, wear these.' Christos handed the mechanic a pair of latex gloves.

Christos stood and watched as Andreas deftly unscrewed the mirror from its base and then carried it over to a work bench. Having pried the glass from the holder he held it up for Christos to see the numbers that were engraved into the metal.

'Put a light on, Andreas. It's too dark in here to see anything. I don't know how your men manage to work.'

'We do most of it outside unless we need the pit.' He reached out and pressed a switch, flooding the work bench with light, making Christos blink.

Christos peered at the faint numbers. 'You're sure that's a three not a five or eight?'

'Certain.'

Christos consulted his notebook. The numbers definitely matched those belonging to one of the mirrors that Babbis had read to him over the 'phone. 'You replace it on the car now. When you come down to the station to give your prints I'd like to have a statement from you as well.'

Andreas raised his eyebrows. 'Why do I need to make a statement?'

'Just to say that you removed and examined the wing mirror in my presence at my request so I could record the numbers. We don't need to mention that I had asked you to take it off earlier.'

Andreas shrugged. Provided he was not going to be charged with any wrong doing he would suffer the indignity of visiting the police station and having his prints taken.

'I want to have a look at the damage to the passenger side. We'll need more light and a rule.'

'Will a torch do?'

'Provided you can see properly. Leave your gloves on. I want you to do some measuring for me.' Christos walked back to where the car was parked. 'I'll hold the torch whilst you measure the length of the trim that has been ripped off.'

Andreas bent down and ran the rule along the car. 'Near enough one hundred and twenty five centimetres.'

'Near enough is not good enough. I need it to the last centimetre.'

Andreas frowned and ran the rule along the side of the car again. 'One hundred and twenty seven point three centimetres.'

'Exactly?'

'Exactly,' nodded Andreas. 'Do you want me to measure it again?'

'What's the width?'

'Six centimetres.'

'Is it the same width on all cars?'

'Not always. It can vary between five and eight. Six is pretty standard.'

Christos nodded. 'Thanks, you've been very helpful. Off the record, from your experience, how do you think the damage to the body work happened?'

'At a guess I'd say someone ran into him.'

'So there should be another car around with similar damage?'

Andreas shrugged. 'That would depend. If a lorry backed into him they might have nothing more than a broken light or bent bumper to show for it.'

'Well, we can't stop every lorry that has a bent bumper. We'd have a traffic jam in no time and they'd all claim that the damage had happened whilst they were parked and nothing to do with them. I'll be in touch, Andreas, and let you know what has to be done with the vehicle.'

'If it was mine I'd scrap it. It's old and hardly worth repairing.'

'Andreas, I think you should be very grateful that it is not your vehicle,' Christos replied gravely. 'Just leave it locked in there untouched until I speak to you again. If anyone should come asking about it tell them you haven't set eyes on it. Tell your men to say the same and warn them not to touch it under any circumstances or they'll be giving me their fingerprints.'

Andreas raised his eyebrows. He would love to know why the vandalised car was of such interest to the local police.

Christos returned to the police station. He was going to enjoy telling Thranassis that he was in possession of the car that had probably forced Mr Vikelakis off the highway.

'You can't be certain that you have the vehicle,' argued Thranassis. 'Our men have not examined the car. You've only a local mechanic's word for the damage.'

'The serial numbers on the wing mirror matches that of one found at the crash site. The length of missing trim measures near enough the same as one of the pieces that was collected from the area. If I arrange to have it transported up to Heraklion can you ensure that Babbis and his team check it over thoroughly? It will need to be fingerprinted. The owner reported the car as stolen and I doubt if the thieves took the precaution of wearing gloves.'

'Babbis hasn't finished examining the other car that we brought in.'

'I think you'll find the vandalism on that one was pure coincidence and has nothing to do with the accident. I'll also send up the trim and some of the flakes of paint that were found in Mr Iliopolakis's garden. I'm pretty sure they'll match up with his car. By the way, Mr Iliopolakis's solicitor is insisting that the paint flakes found at the crash site are sent to forensics for examination. I've told Babbis and he said he would need your permission. You will obviously tell him to proceed.'

With great satisfaction Christos replaced the receiver before Thranassis could reply.

Stavros waited anxiously for the arrival of the young man from Aghios Nikolaos. Yannis handed over the envelope Nikos had given him with a quizzical look.

'What is so important about it that I had to drive up?' he asked.

'Just an investigation into some investments that his son had been working on. I needed his copy so I can report back to a customer.'

'If they're good investments will they be open to employees?' asked Yannis eagerly.

'I won't know how profitable they could be until I've examined Mr Vikelakis's findings,' smiled Stavros. 'I'm sure you'll be advised if they would be to your advantage. Have you filled in your expenses claim form? I'll initial it and you can take it to one of the cashiers for reimbursement.'

Stavros returned hurriedly to his office and opened the envelope. He read the names, with amounts listed beside them on the sheets of paper and frowned. Had Alecos been doing some private investments for customers without adhering to the appropriate bank procedure? Presumably the flash drive would have details of the companies where these people had trusted their money and no doubt Alecos would have claimed a percentage of their return.

He inserted the memory stick in the machine and frowned in consternation. It appeared to contain only another copy of Mr Iliopolakis's hotel accounts. Why would Alecos Vikelakis have a copy of those in his possession? He scrolled down carefully, none of the amounts paid in to the various accounts and verified by the cashiers were listed. To make doubly certain he took out the folders Vasilis had left with him containing the paper copies of the accounts and checked them against the figures on the screen.

He unfolded the papers that had accompanied the flash drives and smoothed them out. There was a list of names and account numbers with an amount and date beside each one. On a separate page the amounts had been added together and a further sum added to them. Stavros scratched his head; surely that amount was the same as had been paid in from the hotel in Hersonissos? He checked again with the screen and was about to place a tick on the paper when it occurred to him that he should not add any marks of his own. Feeling foolish, doing work that was usually delegated to the most junior member of staff, he went out into the banking hall and photocopied the pages from the notebook.

He returned to his desk, placed the pages from the notebook back into the envelope and into his drawer to ensure their safety. Slowly he checked each amount on the photocopied page with that on the screen and on the paper printout Mr Iliopolakis had left with him. He did not want to make a mistake. Half an hour later he had to admit that accounts had been credited with funds to which they were not entitled. One error could be excused as a manual error; the incorrect account number having been entered. A second error smacked of carelessness, but for all of the entries to be wrong indicated that someone had deliberately falsified the accounts. Had Alecos Vikelakis discovered this and been planning to bring his evidence to the bank to show him and expose the culprit?

Stavros closed the document on the memory stick and replaced it in the envelope. Using the photocopied list he returned to the master programme for all the accounts held for the branches in the Prefecture. Each time he entered a number he was told it did not exist. After five unsuccessful entries he cursed himself for a fool and changed his search to the Lassithi area. The first number he tapped in brought up an account and he studied the details carefully.

Once a year for the last thirty years a deposit had been made. The amounts ranged from seventy three drachmas to one thousand two hundred drachmas and after that the deposits were credited in Euros. At no time had a deposit been larger than four hundred and thirty six Euros until the last one which amounted to four thousand three hundred and twenty five Euros. Following the large deposit almost the full amount had been withdrawn. According to the date the credit had been made eighteen months earlier and the account had been returned to its original balance the following day. A credit of eighty two drachmas had been entered at a later date, appearing to be the usual annual deposit.

Stavros wiped the sweat from his brow. Obviously the error had been found and rectified. It had to be coincidence that the amount agreed with the money that had been paid in from the Hersonissos hotel. He entered the next number on the list and found almost a replica of the previous account. A small amount paid in annually, then a large deposit that had been withdrawn again immediately. Once again the total agreed with a credit from the Katerina hotel that should have been showing on Mr Iliopolakis's accounts. Assiduously Stavros entered the numbers for all the accounts, checking the totals that had been deposited and subsequently withdrawn. They could not all be excused as errors. There was a definite pattern, but where had the money been credited if it had not gone to Mr Iliopolakis's account? He tapped his lips with his pen.

He did not want to think that one of the bank's employees had been deliberately falsifying the accounts for his own benefit, but the signs certainly indicated that had happened. Reluctantly Stavros entered the account number for Alecos Vikelakis and scrutinized the deposit account in his name a second time. According to the dates all the deposits had been made during the previous two years. The last amount credited agreed with the discrepancy between the balance of the previous week on Mr Iliopolakis's copy of the accounts and the one showing on the bank computer. Alecos's account showed most of the money to have been withdrawn and transferred to another bank a few days earlier.

Feeling guilty for mistrusting the manager, Stavros ran off a paper copy and began to compare the account details with the pages from the note book. Finally Stavros sat with his head in his hands. Mr Vasi appeared to be correct when he had voiced his suspicions about the bank manager. Mr Vikelakis had obviously moved money from the Iliopolakis hotel accounts to others.

Once Mr Vikelakis had regained consciousness he would have to be questioned. If he did not have satisfactory answers, the matter would have to be referred to the head office of the bank in Athens.

Wednesday 26th September

Saffron had packed the last of her belongings and looked around the room she had used at Yannis's house for the previous fortnight. She stood by the window and looked out across the bay to Spinalonga feeling thoroughly miserable. If she did not have Marjorie to consider she might well contemplate seriously returning to Crete and to Vasi.

At the thought of Vasi her heart constricted. The previous year he had asked her to stay so they could get to know each other. He had not made that suggestion this year, despite their relationship becoming intimate. Had she been deceived yet again by an attractive man?

With a deep sigh she made her way to Annita's room. 'May I come in, Grandma? I've come to say goodbye.'

'So, you are returning to London.' Anita shook her head sadly. 'We will miss you, Saffie. Vasi will miss you also.'

Saffron shrugged, trying to pretend that she was not unhappy about returning home. 'I'm sure he will have plenty to occupy him.'

'He's a good man, Saffie.'

'I know.' Saffron felt a lump in her throat.

'I took a big risk when I went to America with Elias. I never regretted it.'

'Are you trying to say I should stay here with Vasi?'

'Why not? If you love someone it is only right that you should be with them, not hundreds of miles away.'

Saffron shook her head. 'Vasi hasn't asked me to stay.'

'Then he's a fool! If he asked would you stay?'

'I don't know.' Saffron shook her head unhappily. 'It would mean I could no longer work as a doctor.'

'Your work means more to you than Vasi?'

Saffron ignored the question. 'I have to think about Marjorie. I couldn't leave her alone in England.'

'You are putting obstacles in your way that do not have to exist. What happens when Marjorie is no longer there for you to care for? I wish Father Lambros was still with us. He would be able to explain to you the questions you need to answer in your heart.'

'Who was Father Lambros?'

'Elias's uncle. You've seen a photograph of him. I met him by chance and he made me realise that I was the cause of my unhappiness. He made me examine my head and my heart honestly. Had I not met him I would not have married Elias.' Annita smiled at the memory of how she had avoided the young man whose attentions she had felt certain she did not want. 'I would probably have spent the rest of my life living in one room in Athens. I felt I had been hurt so badly that I could never love again. You have been hurt, Saffie, but you have to put that hurt behind you and learn to love and trust again.'

Saffron felt the tears running down her cheeks. Did Annita know about her disastrous marriage to Ranjit? Bryony had assured her she would keep the information about him murdering his first wife to herself.

'I want to stay, but part of me is frightened,' she admitted.

'So at last you are being honest with yourself. Why are you frightened?'

'I don't want to make a mistake. I don't want to be hurt again.'

'Why should it be a mistake? You have been happy to spend the last two weeks almost exclusively in his company. Why should you not be happy to spend the rest of your life with him?'

'Two weeks is not a very long time to get to know anyone. It would be such a big step to take and I don't speak Greek.'

Annita snorted in derision. 'Stop making excuses to yourself. Cathy has never learnt to speak Greek, despite the number of years she has lived here. You could go to classes and learn. You have to decide what is more important in your life – being a doctor or being happy with Vasi.' Annita patted Saffron's hand and handed her a tissue.

Vasi arrived as arranged and placed Saffron's luggage into the boot of his hired car.

'Giovanni was going to take that,' remarked Saffron.

'And if, for some reason, Giovanni is delayed, you will be at the airport and your luggage will not be with you. That would not be sensible.'

'I'm sure it could be sent on to me later. Provided I have my handbag with me I know I have my passport and some money.'

'You have said goodbye to everyone?'

Saffron nodded. 'I saw Yannis, Ourania and Marisa before they went to the shop. I've spent some time with Grandma and I've seen John.'

'So we will now drive to Heraklion and you can say farewell to Cathy.'

Saffron nodded mutely. She was not enjoying saying goodbye and dreaded the moment when she would have to give a final wave and walk through passport control alone.

Saffron stood hesitantly at the barrier. Everyone had hugged and kissed her, but she felt a reluctance to take that final step. Vasi placed his arm around her.

'If you do not go through now you will miss your flight.'

Saffron nodded, still unwilling to leave.

'We will have much to talk about when I come to London.' Vasi squeezed her to him one last time. 'Go now,' he urged.

Saffron nodded again. She lifted her head and tried to smile. 'Goodbye, everyone. Thank you all so much.' Without looking back she walked through the passport control and began to hurry towards the departure lounge where late comers for her flight were being paged.

'What are you planning now, Vasi?' asked Giovanni.

'I have to go to the Central and meet my father. We will then go to the bank and see if they have finally sorted out the problems with the accounts. If they have not,' Vasi's mouth set in a grim line, 'my father plans to move everything to another bank.'

'Let me know what happens. If Vasilis moves his accounts I'll move ours. We can't afford for them to make a mistake on ours. We don't have the same sort of collateral as you and it could leave us in an embarrassing position for a few days.'

'I was very thankful that all the employees and outstanding invoices had been paid up to date. Can you imagine what would have happened if the staff had tried to cash their wage cheques and been refused?'

'You still think Alecos Vikelakis had something to do with it?'

Vasi nodded. 'I'm sure he had. I just wish he hadn't had that accident so he could be questioned.'

'Did you tell the bank manager of your suspicions?'

'I did, but I can't force him to make an enquiry into Alecos's account without starting court proceedings. I know I would be told to wait until Alecos had recovered sufficiently to be able to make a statement and that could be weeks. Even if he is guilty of manipulating our accounts for his own benefit I'm not convinced the bank wouldn't cover it up for the sake of their reputation.'

Dimitra showered, washed her hair and styled it carefully. She shaped her finger nails, wishing she had not broken one the previous day, and painted them a pale pink. She was uncertain whether Mr Iliopolakis would expect her to go into work or stay away and be at the hospital with Alecos. She had taken two days off and was now thoroughly bored. She was not sure if she was still employed. Neither Mr Iliopolakis nor Vasi had actually fired her, but neither of them had they said when they would expect her in at work. She would arrive as usual, she decided, apologise for her absence and say she had been so shocked she would have been quite unable to perform her duties. It was quite likely that whatever the error had been on the accounts it would have been found and reconciled by now. She felt secure in the knowledge that she had not made a mistake.

She would ask to leave early and say she was going to the hospital. She hoped the attractive doctor would be there and she would be able to speak to him. She looked in her wardrobe. Again she did not want to dress in her customary flamboyant colours. She pulled out a lilac coloured cotton suit and then replaced it; the sandals she wore with it pinched ever so slightly. The coffee coloured dress had been a bad purchase; the colour made her skin look sallow so she could not wear that. Cream would not look right with pink nail varnish and she did not want to have to paint them again.

Half an hour later, with most of her clothes lying on her bed; she decided she would wear her blue skirt again, but this time with a pink blouse. That solved the problem of her nail varnish, she knew her white sandals were comfortable and both blouse and skirt were suitable for wearing to work.

Christos arranged for Andreas to transport the car that had been sprayed with red paint up to Heraklion. 'I want it covered with a tarpaulin,' he said firmly.

'It's not going to rain,' remarked Andreas. 'Even if it did it wouldn't wash that muck off.'

'It isn't the paint that I'm worried about. I don't want to lose any prints that could be on there. They could be vital. You're sure your men haven't touched it?'

Andreas shrugged. 'No reason to do so. I locked it in the garage and apart from me you're the only person who's been in there. What's so important about it anyway?'

'It was reported stolen.' Christos was not prepared to give the garage owner any further information.

'Any number of people could have touched it whilst it was parked and before it was stolen.'

'Very true, but inside I would only expect to find the prints of the lawful owner and the thief. I'm also hoping that whoever sprayed it put his hand on the car at some point.'

'I don't see why a car thief would bother to spray it. That's only going to draw attention to it.'

'I agree. I think there could be quite a few questions for this car to answer. Make sure you see Babbis and get him to sign your delivery docket.'

Andreas pulled the last strap tight to hold the car in place on the truck. 'Anything else?' he asked.

'Just plead ignorance if Babbis asks you any questions. You're just the driver.'

Christos decided he would drive up to Heraklion. He really should speak to Thranassis. They were, after all, supposed to be colleagues and it really was only right that he passed on the information he had regarding Stelios's car. It was supposed to be his day off, a day he usually spent at home, pottering in his garden or completing the odd jobs his wife was always able to find for him. She would not be pleased that he was going up to the city and he hoped that the offer to take her with him would mollify her.

Aspasia shook her head. 'What would I want to go up there for? If I need anything I'll get it from the town here. I wanted to visit my sister.'

'I can take you there before I go to Heraklion,' offered Christos. 'There's no urgency for me to get there.'

'Why are you going up?' she asked suspiciously.

'I want to have a chat with Thranassis.'

'You could do that over the 'phone.'

Christos nodded. 'I can talk to him, but I also want to show him a few things and to do that I need to be there. I should be back by late afternoon and I can collect you from Delphine's.'

'It's supposed to be your day off.'

Christos shrugged. 'Police business has no respect for your day off.' He was relieved that he would not have to spend the day with his wife's sister. The women would gossip happily and he would be expected to be sociable to his brother-in-law whom he disliked intensely.

'Alecos, Alecos, can you hear me? If you can hear me blink your eyes.' The nurse spoke to him gently as she did every half an hour to see if he had regained some semblance of consciousness. She repeated the message again, watching his eyes closely. Had he made some attempt to open them or was it her imagination? Should she alert the doctor or wait until she had a definite response to report?

She leaned forwards in her chair and watched his face carefully. Beneath his eyelids she could see his eyes were moving from side to side. 'Alecos, open your eyes,' she tried again, but the movement stopped.

The voice that appeared to be coming from far away penetrated Alecos's consciousness dimly. His head was pounding. He must have drunk far too much the previous night. He struggled to remember where he had been and how he had spent the evening. He would have to get up when the pain in his head lessened and telephone the bank and plead illness.

Thranassis was surprised when Christos walked into the Heraklion police station.

'What brings you up here?' he asked.

'A number of things; but primarily to see you and pass on some information that I thought you might find useful in the accident investigation,' smiled Christos.

'I haven't had Babbis's report through yet, if that's what you're after.'

Christos shook his head. 'That isn't why I'm here, although I'll be interested to read it as soon as possible. I've had that car that has been sprayed with red paint brought up. I authorised Andreas to remove the glass from the wing mirror that is still in situ and check the numbers. To the best of my knowledge they match those of a wing mirror found at the crash site. The owner of the car reported it stolen and there's considerable damage on the passenger side. I've asked Babbis to arrange to have it fingerprinted. If the prints belong to any of our known joy riders we should be able to pick them up and it will be pretty certain they caused the accident.'

Thranassis glowered at him. 'What about the number plate? Are any of the numbers a match for the ones we were given?'

Christos shook his head. 'Nothing like, and it's a different model from Mr Iliopolakis's car.'

'I don't see why you're so interested in it then.'

'I'm certain Mr Iliopolakis is not involved. He and his friend ate at a local restaurant that evening and the owner has confirmed they were there.'

'Mr Iliopolakis could have driven up to the highway after they had eaten.'

Christos smiled. 'I'm pretty sure he didn't. Apparently he and his companion returned to his father's house and he took the young lady home in the early hours of the morning.'

'We don't know what time the accident happened,' announced Thranassis triumphantly.

'That's true,' agreed Christos, 'but I'd like to put out another appeal on the television news and ask anyone who was travelling on the road between nine that night and six in the morning to contact us. One of the drivers must have seen if the barrier was broken and that could narrow down the time scale.'

'So why didn't they report the accident?'

'They may not have realised how recently it had happened. It would have been dark and they would have been travelling at speed. Makes me wonder how our anonymous caller could be so certain of the numbers he gave us from the registration plate.' Christos raised his eyebrows speculatively at Thranassis.

'And you came all the way up here to tell me this? You could have 'phoned.'

'I wanted to have a look at Mr Iliopolakis's car for myself.'

Christos drove from the station over to the garage that was used solely by the police. Babbis greeted him with a resigned sigh.

'I haven't had a chance to finish my report yet.'

'I'm not here for that, although I'm as anxious as Thranassis to read it. I'll not hold you up for very long. I'd just like to have a look at Mr Iliopolakis's car and the other car that went over the edge. Personally I think it more likely the one covered in red paint ran him off the road.'

Babbis shrugged. 'Even when I've finished my examination I may not be able to state categorically which car it was. I'll judge the damage on each and I will be able to say which one was more likely to have been the cause, but unless you can produce a witness or the driver confesses I can only give my opinion.'

'I understand that. I know Mr Iliopolakis is convinced that forensics won't have found any traces of paint from his car at the crash site. He claims he was nowhere near the road that night and that his car was vandalised whilst it was in his own driveway. I'm inclined to believe he's telling the truth. I haven't questioned the owner of the other car yet. He reported his car stolen. Of course, the damage to the body work could have been done some time ago and he's not bothered to have it repaired.'

'Hope he's insured because it's going to cost him.'

'Are you able to tell how recently it was damaged?'

'Not to any degree of certainty. If it was done a couple of years ago rust will have begun to set in. After a while the damaged metal begins to dull down, but I wouldn't want to put an exact time frame on it.'

'If he's been driving it around with a broken front light and no wing mirror we should have picked him up,' frowned Christos.

'That could have happened whilst he was parked up. There's nothing to say you can't drive around with your car dented. Now, do you want a quick look at these cars? I need to get my initial report finished and no doubt you're going to be breathing down my neck for this other one.'

'Any idea when the print boys will have finished?'

'No idea. There's bound to be prints just about everywhere and they'll have to take all of them. It could be a couple of day's work, maybe more. Then they'll need to be checked. Have you got prints from the owner?'

'Not yet. I'll wait until Friday and ask him to come in. I'll explain why we need his prints, and tell him about the damage he can expect to see when he gets his vehicle back. I don't think he'll be a very happy man.'

Christos looked at Alecos's car. The number plate was hanging off, both front lights were smashed, a hub cap was missing, the radiator grill was buckled and the windscreen shattered. The wing mirror on the driver's side was hanging loosely down by the door, the door itself was so distorted that it would not close and the back door looked little better. Slowly Christos walked around to the passenger side. The paintwork was dented and scratched, but not so badly.

'By the way this looks he was pushed off sideways through the barrier.'

Babbis shrugged. 'Could be, or it could have been two separate impacts. If the driver was out of control he would have swung the steering wheel away from this car and then tried to right his own and in doing so collided a second time. Judging by the marks down the side of the hill I would say he travelled most of the way sideways, then hit a rock that caused him to jack knife. Up until then he was probably still expecting to get out of the car and walk away.'

Christos raised his eyebrows.

'I understand the man is concussed along with some broken bones. If the car had stayed sideways on he would have been unlikely to hit his head on the windscreen,' explained Babbis.

'As soon as he regains consciousness the police will get a statement from him. There's just a chance he might be able to describe the driver. If it was Mr Iliopolakis they went to school together and had actually met on business during the week. He would certainly be able to recognise him.'

Babbis nodded. 'The other car is over here.' Christos followed the man to the next garage where Babbis inserted a key, opened the door and switched on the light.

Christos looked at Vasi's car. The only visible damage was to the passenger side where a length of trim was missing and there were scrapes and gouges; both wing mirrors were intact and also the lights.

'Comparing the damage here with that on the victim's car, I would find it hard to believe this one was involved.'

Babbis shrugged. 'Can't say.'

'I've sent you up a piece of trim that was found in the shrubbery at Mr Iliopolakis's house. I'd like you to see if it's the missing piece.'

'Trim is trim.'

'Quite, but now I have seen the car for myself I think you will find it fits virtually perfectly. The wing mirrors are in place and one you found at the crash site matches numerically with the red painted car. I've also sent up some paint samples from Mr Iliopolakis's car and I'm sure there will have been some paint transference from one car to the other. Mr Iliopolakis's car is black; the other car is a very dark blue.'

'It will all be checked.' Babbis sounded bored. Was this policeman trying to tell him his job? He stood with his hands on his hips waiting for Christos to leave.

Christos took a last look at Vasi's car and walked out of the garage.

Stelios had a dilemma. He had planned to claim on his insurance for the cost of having his car repaired and re-sprayed due to vandalism, but now he had no idea where his car was. Until the police had found whoever had stolen it from where he had left it parked he could do nothing. He was puzzled that there had been no sighting of it reported. With the red paint daubed all over the body it was certainly distinctive. He decided he would go to the police again and complain about their lack of progress rather than wait until they contacted him.

He was annoyed when he was told that Inspector Christos would not be in the station again until Friday and no one else could help him. Mr Christos had not left any instructions for him to be telephoned so it had to be presumed that the car had not yet been found. With a sympathetic smile and shrug of the shoulders Spiro assured him they would let him know as soon as they had any news and he was welcome to return on Friday to speak to the Inspector.

'Hello, Dimitra. How is Alecos? Have you heard?'

Dimitra nodded. 'Progressing satisfactorily, according to the doctor.'

'I'm pleased to hear it. You'll be glad to know that the bank has sorted out whatever the problem was on the accounts.'

'Your father told me.' Dimitra compressed her lips.

'Dimitra, I am truly sorry about Alecos's accident and I assure you I had nothing to do with it.' Vasi spoke earnestly.

Dimitra shrugged. She did not really know how to reply to Vasi. She found it hard to believe that the mild mannered man would do something so aggressive and out of character simply because Alecos had refused to give him a loan. On the other hand if Vasi thought Alecos had altered the hotel accounts deliberately he might well feel justified in taking his revenge physically.

'If you need to take some time off we'll understand; either now or a bit later as Alecos recovers.'

'Thank you.'

Vasi sighed. The girl appeared to be keeping a tight rein on her emotions. 'Do you have some friends you can spend time with?' he asked.

Dimitra looked at him scornfully. 'Of course.'

'That's good.' Vasi nodded. 'I wouldn't want to think you were sitting home alone feeling miserable and worried.'

Dimitra looked at him from under her lashes. What was this sudden concern that Vasi was showing for her? Was he hoping to take Alecos's place? She would certainly not bother with the hotelier a second time. Dr Melanakis was a much more interesting proposition. She would ask to leave work early and call in at the hospital and ask if there was any news of Alecos and hope to see the good looking and charming doctor.

'Actually I would like to leave early today so I can speak to the doctor at the hospital.'

Dimitra strolled down the road and entered the hospital just before five. She approached the reception desk and smiled at the bored and miserable looking woman who sat there. 'I have an appointment with Dr Melanakis at five. Please could you let him know that I have arrived.'

'Dr Melanakis does not make appointments to see patients.'

'I'm not a patient. I have come to speak to the doctor about a friend who was in a car accident. I saw the doctor yesterday and he asked me to come again today so he could discuss the extent of my friend's injuries with me. I took time off work so I could be here at the time he said,' Dimitra spoke petulantly.

'You'll have to wait.'

'But you will let him know that I'm here, won't you?' Dimitra was suddenly alarmed that the doctor could leave by a rear exit and she would be none the wiser.

'Name?'

'I'm not sure if I told him my name.' Dimitra gave a shaky little laugh. 'I'm a friend of Mr Vikelakis.'

'Doctor Melanakis, please come to reception when you are free.' The bored looking receptionist began to gather her belongings together. She also left the hospital at five and if she was late she would miss the bus. She did not want to stand for a further half an hour until the next one arrived.

Dimitra sat in a chair, her legs carefully slanted to one side and her skirt pulled up as high as she dared. She hoped none of the patients who were milling around waiting for their turn at the reception desk would obstruct his view of her. She held a magazine in her hands, but was using it as an excuse to watch the door without making her actions obvious. When she saw Dr Melanakis looking at her through the glass panel she pretended not to notice him, turning the page of the magazine and smiling, as if at something she was reading.

Dr Melanakis looked at Dimitra's legs. He wished her skirt was pulled up even higher so he could see more of her thighs. He had a longing to squeeze the firm flesh that was within his view, feeling his heart race and the blood pulsing through his veins. He took a deep breath. He was a doctor. He was used to seeing females' legs, although they were not usually in such attractive and provocative poses, inviting him to place his hands on them. He walked across and stood over her.

'Doctor,' Dimitra positively purred at him. 'How good of you to give me some time. How is Mr Vikelakis today?'

'He has shown a small improvement.'

'You mean he has regained consciousness?'

Doctor Melanakis shook his head. 'Sometimes it can take weeks or even months for a patient to recover full consciousness. There was some movement of his eyes behind the lids today.'

Dimitra frowned. 'You probably think me very silly, but how do you know he was moving his eyes?'

'It was noted on his chart by the nurse who is monitoring him. I didn't witness it myself.'

'So it isn't happening all the time?'

'We hope there will be an increase of movement tomorrow. Until Mr Vikelakis regains consciousness we will not be able to ascertain if he has suffered any brain damage.'

'Brain damage? What kind of brain damage?'

Doctor Melanakis licked his lips. 'It can be rather involved to explain and at this stage we have no evidence either way.'

Dimitra opened her eyes wide and gazed at him. 'I would like you to explain to me. I know I am very ignorant of medical matters, but I'll concentrate hard and do my best to understand.'

'Maybe if we went somewhere quieter it would be easier to talk,' suggested the doctor. 'I am off duty, but sooner or later I will be called if I am still on the premises.'

Dimitra smiled. 'Wherever you suggest, doctor.' She stood and smoothed her skirt down to a more decorous length. She gave a little giggle. 'I realised earlier when I asked to speak to you that I had not told you my name. I'm Dimitra.'

Doctor Melanakis inclined his head towards her. 'I'm pleased to meet you, Dimitra. There is a coffee shop a short distance away. It would probably be more suitable if we sat in there and talked.'

The doctor walked to the main door and held it open for her to pass through. If he had her somewhere more private there might be a chance for him to touch that inviting flesh. He took her elbow and steered her across the car park to the main road.

'Have you just finished work?' he asked, wanting to know more about her and wishing to avoid the medical details regarding his patient.

'I left a little early. I have a very understanding employer.'

'What do you do?'

'I am in charge of the finance for a number of hotels.'

Doctor Melanakis raised his eyebrows. 'Really? That is a very responsible job.'

'I have been in charge for over a year now. I tried to explain to the manager how to use the computer, but he was a poor learner and not very interested.'

'So where are you based?'

'At the Central, but Mr Iliopolakis has five hotels in all.'

'And you have to manage the finance for all of them?'

Dimitra hesitated. 'Not exactly. Each hotel sends the figures for the income and outgoings each day and I make sure they are entered correctly. At the end of the week the wages are calculated for the employees and that is usually where a problem arises. Some have worked overtime and the calculation is not always correct. I have to find the error and rectify it so the books balance.' Dimitra exaggerated wildly. If there was a disagreement over a figure she would telephone the hotel and demand that the receptionist should find the mistake and call her back.

Doctor Melanakis held the door of the coffee shop open for her and pointed to an empty table. 'You have a seat and I'll go up to the counter. What would you like?'

'A frappe, please.'

Dimitra looked at the table he had indicated where there was only a bench seat set against the wall. She settled herself comfortably, making sure her skirt was pulled higher than ever. So far everything was working out perfectly.

Doctor Melanakis carried her frappe and a coffee for himself back carefully. 'Would you like a pastry to accompany your drink?' he asked.

Dimitra shook her head. She did not want to make crumbs or end up with a piece of nut stuck in between her teeth. 'Thank you, no. Just a frappe will be fine, but you have something if you wish.'

'I'm not hungry,' he smiled. 'I had a rather late lunch.'

'Dealing with a patient, no doubt.' Dimitra looked at him from beneath her eyelashes and waited for him to take his seat.

As Dimitra reached for her frappe she managed to move a little closer so her thigh was touching his. Dr Melanakis caught his breath. Was she inviting him?

Dr Melanakis cleared his throat. 'You wished to know more about the medical condition of your friend.'

Dimitra nodded. 'Yes, you were going to explain to me about possible brain damage.'

The doctor looked at the calm young woman next to him. He certainly did not expect any histrionics from her, but it would be better if he did not give her too many details. 'The extent of the damage depends very much on which part of the cranium has taken the force of the impact. If a part of the skull is depressed it will either press on a nerve or obstruct the blood flow. If the blood is unable to flow around as normal the brain is starved of oxygen and brain damage in varying degrees is the result depending on the length of deprivation.'

'And Alecos is unconscious due to a blow on the head,' observed Dimitra.

Dr Melanakis nodded. 'His head impacted on the windscreen of the car. Obviously we have taken x-rays and scans. Despite having a skull fracture he doesn't appear to have any other signs of damage, no depressions or internal bleeding, but until he regains consciousness we are unable to fully assess him.'

Dimitra let out a sigh. 'So not having any other signs of damage apart from a fracture is a good sign?'

'It is a positive sign, along with the movement of his eyes.'

'Do you have any idea how long it will be before he regains consciousness?

Doctor Melanakis shook his head. 'Every patient is different. I cannot begin to guess. He will be monitored constantly and have the best of care I assure you.'

Dimitra frowned. 'If he does suffer from brain damage what form would it take?'

'I cannot possibly speculate at this stage.'

'Who would know?'

'At present no one would be able to give you a definitive answer. You would need to speak to a neurosurgeon. I am only the trauma specialist. I recommend the immediate treatment to alleviate the condition. If the nerve centres have been affected by pressure this can have an effect on mobility, speech, memory,' Dr Melanakis shrugged. 'All the parts of the body are controlled by the brain. A man can walk down the street appearing fit and healthy. If you ask him his address he will be unable to tell you. His memory cells have been starved of oxygen and no longer function correctly. Another man needs to be pushed in a wheelchair as he has no control over his limbs, but he can hold an intelligent conversation. His nerve cells have been damaged, but the mental capacity of his brain has not been diminished.'

'I think I understand.' Dimitra looked up at the doctor. 'Thank you for taking time to explain to me. May I speak to you again? When I have telephoned I have been told he is as comfortable as can be expected and that doesn't tell me anything.'

Doctor Melanakis smiled. He would be only too willing to meet this charming young lady with the attractive legs again. 'Does the hospital have your telephone number? They would be able to contact you with news of his progress.'

Dimitra shook her head. 'I'm not family.'

'Maybe I could have your telephone number?'

'Of course. You can contact me at any time.'

Dimitra reeled off her mobile number and the doctor wrote it down on his serviette. He would transfer that to his private book of telephone numbers later.

'May I have your number, doctor?' she asked.

'Please call me Filippos,' he smiled. 'It is more friendly than calling me doctor.'

'Then may I have your 'phone number, Filippos?'

'It is better that you come to the hospital to contact me. I am often unable to answer my telephone if I am dealing with patients.'

Dimitra nodded understandingly. 'If I called in again at the end of the week would you be able to spend some time with me and tell me how Alecos is progressing?'

'I'd be delighted. If there is any positive news in the meantime I will telephone you.'

Dimitra smiled contentedly. A doctor was held in far higher esteem than a bank manager or hotelier.

Saffron landed at Gatwick and hauled her case to the train station. She stood at the exit and watched the rain falling steadily as she called Marjorie on her mobile.

'I've just landed. I'll take the tube and get a taxi from the station. I should be home within an hour.' Somehow the words had a hollow ring to them. She talked about going home to Yannis's house and also to Vasi's, both places feeling more welcoming to her than the suburb of London where she had lived for most of her life.

'It's just post holiday blues,' she told herself. 'When I wake up tomorrow and get in to work I'll be back to normal. I shall enjoy seeing the recovery people have made from their injuries or operations. I'll come home to a nice meal cooked by Marjorie and she'll ask about my day. The last two weeks will just fade into oblivion and seem like a dream.' She swallowed hard. 'But I will miss Vasi and everyone,' her subconscious added.

Her conscience aroused she remembered she had promised to text Vasi to say she had arrived safely back in England; she ought to text Marianne also. She pulled her mobile out again and keyed in the letters for the messages and pressed 'send', turned it off and replaced it in her pocket. Once she was back with Marjorie she was sure the hollow, empty feeling she had inside her would go away. After all it was only six weeks before Vasi was due to visit England and she would pass the time arranging outings she thought he would enjoy.

Saffron sat with Marjorie, nursing a cup of hot chocolate in her hands. 'It's good to be home. I hate having to spend so long hanging around in airports.'

'So what did you do whilst you were there? Anything exciting?'

'I can't really say that it was exciting, but it was certainly different. I was arrested.'

'What! Whatever were you arrested for?'

Saffron smiled at Marjorie's outrage. 'I'm exaggerating. I was detained by the police for a while to help with their enquiries. It was Vasi who was arrested.' She was not going to admit to the panic she had felt when being taken into a small room to be interviewed by an interpreter.

'What on earth had he done?'

'Nothing. His car had been vandalised and by coincidence there was a very nasty accident on the highway. The police thought his car was involved and wanted to keep him in prison.'

'How awful. What did you do?'

'I 'phoned Marianne and she 'phoned Vasilis who 'phoned his solicitor and they met me at the police station. Vasilis took me back to spend the afternoon with Cathy whilst he and the solicitor arranged for Vasi's bail money. Then there was a problem there as the bank said Vasilis did not have enough money on his accounts and it seems there was an internal accounting error of some sort.'

'Poor Vasi. It must have been a horrible experience for him. No doubt it's all sorted out now.'

Saffron shook her head. 'The bank account has been sorted, but the police still think Vasi pushed Alecos off the road. They suggested he had driven there and done it after he had taken me home. He still has to report to the police station every day.'

'How long will he have to do that?' frowned Marjorie.

'Until the police realise he's innocent I presume. It was made to look worse for him because the injured man is the local bank manager who had refused to give Vasi a loan a few days earlier. I must tell you about that.'

Saffron related to Marjorie how Vasi had wanted to buy the Imperia hotel. 'Alecos bought it from under Vasi's nose thinking he would want to buy it back, but by then Vasi had changed his mind. He said Alecos tried to insist and looked really ill when Vasi refused. Vasi is sure that Alecos had something to do with the discrepancy in the accounts.'

'Can't the police question him?'

'He's still unconscious. Vasi and his father spent most of Sunday at the hotel checking over the accounts with their back-up disk. They called in the girl who usually does the finance work on the computer and she admitted she had lent Alecos a copy of the accounts. He had driven up to Heraklion to return it to her and his accident happened on his way back to Aghios Nikolaos.'

'Oh, dear, poor Vasi. He must be so worried.'

'I think he's more concerned than he admits.' Saffron yawned. 'I'll have to go to bed, Marjorie. I'm two hours ahead of you, remember. I spoke to Vasi about your ideas for his house being made into a holiday centre. He seemed quite interested and said he would speak to his father.' Saffron yawned again. 'I'll tell you more details tomorrow. I really can't keep awake any longer.'

Friday 28th September

Stelios walked into the police station at Aghios Nikolaos and asked to speak to Inspector Christos.

'Have you found my car yet?'

'I believe we may have done, sir. I'd just like to go over a few details again.'

'There's no need for any more details if you've found it. Tell me where it is and I'll go and collect it.'

'I'm afraid that isn't possible at the moment, sir.'

Stelios frowned. 'Why not?'

Christos scratched his head. 'Can you tell me again exactly where you parked it last?'

'I put that on the form I filled in.' Stelios tried desperately hard to remember in which road he had claimed to have parked his car.

'And you are quite sure that was correct? You couldn't have parked it somewhere else as there was no available space on that occasion?'

Stelios shook his head. 'Of course not. My neighbours know it is the space that I always use.'

'So they would be able to confirm that it was parked there on the Friday night?'

'I doubt if they noticed.'

Christos stroked his chin. 'I was just wondering if a neighbour may have seen a stranger drive it away.'

Stelios shrugged. 'They were probably in bed.'

'That would depend upon the time the car was moved, of course. Do you ever lend your car to anyone else?'

'No.'

'You'd have no objection to giving us your prints, of course. It will only take a few moments and then we will be able to compare them with those that have been found in your car.'

'What's the point of that? My prints will be all over it.'

'So the only fingerprints we should find inside it would be yours and those belonging to whoever removed it without your permission?'

'All I want is my car back.' Stelios felt beads of sweat standing out on his forehead.

'I'm sure you do. Unfortunately we are going to have to keep it for a while longer. It was found abandoned up on the hill and I fear when you do have it returned you will not be very happy with the condition it's in.'

'What do you mean?'

Christos ignored the question. 'When you last saw your car was there any obvious damage to the bodywork, sir?'

Stelios thought rapidly. There was no way he could claim that his car had been in pristine condition. 'A couple of dents in the rear bumper and a scratch beneath the handle on the passenger's side and a few more scratches on the driver's side.'

'I'm afraid there is considerable damage to the passenger side. You're quite sure there was nothing more than a scratch to that side when you parked?'

'Certainly not.' Stelios tried to sound indignant.

'No doubt when we are able to release it you will be able to claim on your insurance.'

'So why can't I have it now?'

'As I said, sir, we wish to examine it to see if there are any fingerprints in the car that do not belong to you.' Christos placed the fingerprinting kit on top of his desk and reached out for Stelios's hand. 'If you would just place your finger there.'

Stelios withdrew his hand swiftly. 'There's no reason to take my prints. It's my car.'

'I have explained, sir, that we wish to see if there are any fingerprints in the car that do not belong to you. The only way we can do that is to have a sample of your prints.'

'That's not necessary. I refuse.'

Christos straightened up. 'I'm afraid I have to insist. We think your car may have been involved in an accident.'

Stelios paled. 'That had nothing to do with me. I was nowhere near the highway.'

Christos raised his eyebrows. 'Why should you assume I am speaking about that accident? Unfortunately there was more than one over the weekend.'

Stelios glared venomously at Christos and hurried towards the door. 'Let me know when I can collect my car,' he called back over his shoulder.

Christos watched him go and wondered if he could have handled the situation more tactfully. Unless the man had a criminal record there should be no reason for his reluctance to give his fingerprints and why should he have immediately concluded that Christos was referring to the highway accident? He would have a look in the police records and see if he could turn up any information about Stelios Papandrakis.

Alecos groaned and the nurse was by his side immediately. She wiped his forehead with a cool cloth and took his pulse.

'Can you hear me, Alecos?' she asked quietly.

A sound that could have been taken for 'yes' came from Alecos.

'I'll give you a drink. I'm sure your throat is very dry.' From a feeding bottle she tipped a minute amount of water into Alecos's mouth and then proceeded to moisten his lips. 'I'll give you a little more in a few minutes. If I pulled down the blind could you try to open your eyes?'

Without waiting to see if Alecos tried to answer she pressed the bell to alert the desk in the main ward that she was requesting someone to come to the room and walked to the window to pull the blind closed.

'Did you call?' a nurse poked her head around the door.

'I believe he's conscious. Can you let the duty doctor know? I expect he'd like to give him a quick check over.'

'Try to open your eyes, Alecos,' the nurse encouraged him.

Alecos tried and succeeded in raising his left eyelid slightly.

'That's very good. I'll give you another sip of water and I'm sure when the doctor has seen you he'll say I can give you as much as you want.' She repeated the procedure with the feeding cup, again moistening his lips, taking care not to break open the fresh skin on the partially healed wounds.

Alecos lay motionless. Where was he? His head hurt intolerably, he had a bad taste in his mouth, his tongue felt swollen to twice its size and there were strange noises in his ears. Through his half open eye he could see someone hovering over him, but could not make out their features. He closed his eye again. If his headache would go he would feel better.

Dimitra walked confidently into the hospital and asked for Doctor Melanakis.

'He's not here today. It's his day off.'

Dimitra shrugged as if unconcerned, but inwardly she was annoyed with herself. She should have telephoned first, now she had had a wasted journey. 'I'm sure someone else will be able to help me, although he did say I was always to ask for him.'

The receptionist raised her eyebrows. 'If you tell me the name of the patient I'll check which ward they are in and ask someone to speak to you.'

'Thank you. I'm enquiring about the progress of Mr Vikelakis.'

The receptionist checked her computer and dialled an extension. The telephone could be heard ringing in the distance and when it was answered the receptionist relayed the request. She listened to the answer and turned to Dimitra.

'I've just spoken to his nurse. She's unable to leave him at the moment. She asked me to tell you she is happy with the way he is progressing.'

'Oh, well, that has to be positive news I suppose. I'll call again next week and see if Doctor Melanakis is able to give me any further information.'

The receptionist nodded and looked at the woman waiting patiently behind Dimitra. 'Can I help you?'

Dimitra felt herself dismissed, but could think of no valid reason to stay at the hospital any longer.

Vasi sent an e-mail to Saffron.

'Thanks for letting me know you arrived home safely. How is Marjorie? I'm sure she has missed you. I am missing you. I want to talk to both of you some more about the ideas you gave me for my father's house. I do not think it is practical to make bedrooms on the ground floor. I have not mentioned any of this to him yet. He is still concerned about the bank discrepancy; although I am sure it was something that Alecos did deliberately and not the fault of the bank. Dimitra visited Alecos after work today, but I will not know how he is until she comes in to work on Monday. Once the doctors say he is well enough I want to ask him about the manipulation of the back-up disks. He will need to have a very good story before I will be convinced that it was a computer error.

I have heard nothing from my solicitor and I still have to report to the police each day. Mr Christos looked very pleased with himself when I went to the station this morning so I hope that is a good sign. They are still keeping my car and I have decided to buy a new one. I have seen two that I like, but they are both larger than mine was. I do not need anything larger. My main requirement is reliability. I have been told that if I place my name on a list for a new car, the same as my original, I should have to wait no longer than three months. That is not practical. I do not want to hire a car for any longer than necessary.

The dogs seem to be happy up at the house all the time. Lambros takes them for a walk in the morning and again in the late afternoon. They have not given any indication that an intruder has been around. It is possible that a couple of boys from the village had climbed the wall, or even a curious tourist, and that is what excited the dogs when Mr Christos was here with us.

I do not lay awake at night and worry about someone breaking in. I do lay awake and think of you. Do you think of me or are you too busy with your work at the hospital? I am so looking forward to November when I will visit you in London.'

Saffron felt tears coming into her eyes as she read Vasi's words. Apart from him saying he missed her and thought of her it was an impersonal communication that could have been sent to anyone.

Stelios listened to the evening news and heard the second appeal that was given out asking for any driver who had used the main Heraklion to Aghios Nikolaos highway on the previous Friday night after nine or during the early hours of the Saturday morning to come forwards. The newscaster added that Mr Vikelakis was still in hospital with multiple injuries, but the doctors were satisfied that he was making a slight improvement each day.

Stelios clenched his fists. Why were they still appealing for witnesses? He had told them the he had seen a car being driven recklessly and passed on three of the numbers that appeared on Vasi's registration plate. He would have to telephone them again and say he was sure he had recognised Vasi Iliopolakis behind the wheel.

He walked into the hotel a short distance from his lodging and dialled the number for the police station.

'I've some information about the accident on the highway,' he whispered into the mouth piece.

'I'm sorry, sir. I'm having a problem hearing you. Could you speak up, please?'

Stelios cleared his throat. 'I have a bad throat,' he whispered again. 'Vasi Iliopolakis was driving the car that caused the highway accident.' He replaced the receiver quickly before the policeman had a chance to ask his name and how he came to be a witness.

Antionis wrote down the message from the anonymous caller and the time he had received it. He dialled the number to ascertain where the call had originated and wrote that down also. He did not want Mr Christos to accuse him of negligence when he passed the message to him the following morning.

He had only just finished writing when the telephone rang again. He lifted the receiver with a sigh. He hated being on night duty over the weekends during the holiday season. It was probably a local bar calling asking for a drunken tourist to be arrested.

'How can I help?' he asked.

'I heard the appeal on the television and my wife said I ought to 'phone you. We were driving on the highway last Friday.'

'Did you witness the accident?'

'No, but something happened that stuck in my mind.'

'What was that, sir?'

'A car tried to drive past us and had to draw back when another car came around the corner. It was going far too fast and I thought for a minute it was going to hit us. Had me really worried; nowhere to go except over the edge.'

'So you are 'phoning to report a speeding car that passed you on the highway last Friday?'

Antionis hoped he was not going to get too many calls of a like nature. Some drivers thought they were immortal and drove the highway recklessly.

'Not just the speeding; although he was obviously driving dangerously. I could see the passenger side was damaged.'

Antionis stiffened. This was more interesting. 'If I could just have some more details, sir. Your name and address to start with.'

The man complied and Antionis wrote the details on a fresh sheet of paper. 'And where were you travelling from?'

'We'd been to the airport; taking my son and his wife up to

catch a flight to Italy. They decided they'd like to spend a week in Florence and then move on to Venice for a further week.'

'And what time would this have been, sir?'

'We had to have them there by six thirty, but their flight didn't take off until eight thirty. We'd left a bit early to make sure we were there in plenty of time and then their flight was late departing.'

'So what time did you leave the airport and regain the highway, sir?'

'We waited with them for a bit, until their flight was called, then the wife said we ought to have something to eat before we drove home. We found a very nice little taverna on the outskirts of Heraklion. The service was a bit slow, but I can certainly recommend their food if you're up that way.'

Antionis sighed. The man would be telling him the menu in a minute. 'So what time did you reach the highway, sir?'

'Must have been nearly ten, I suppose. Yes, must have been about that time because the wife said we'd made good time to be back indoors by eleven fifteen and remarked that Elias and Ariadne would have arrived in Florence before we'd driven back to Aghios Nikolaos. She checked the answering machine and sure enough there was a message from them.'

'And which part of the highway were you on when the incident occurred, sir?'

'Incident? Oh, you mean the overtaking. Well, we'd passed the turn off for Malia but not reached the Neapolis road. I don't use the road that often, just up and down to the airport a couple of times a year. I've no reason to go up to Heraklion for anything else, no relatives living there. The wife's family live in Karterides. Nice little place. Do you know it?'

'I'm afraid not.'

'You should take a drive out there some time, very pleasant village.'

'I'll remember the name, sir. Now, are you able to give me a description of the car that passed you?'

'It was dark.'

'Yes, I understand that, but the colour it appeared in your lights.'

'No, the car was dark. Black, blue, dark green maybe. It certainly wasn't white.'

'You didn't make a note of the registration number, I suppose?'

'No, I was too busy complaining to the wife that the driver had nearly caused an accident. Once he passed us I never saw him again.'

'Well, you've been very helpful, sir. I'll pass this information on to Inspector Christos in the morning and I'm sure he'll be in touch with you. He may ask you to come down to the station to make a statement. You'd have no objection to doing that, would you, sir?'

'Would you want my fingerprints?'

Antionis smiled to himself. 'I don't think that will be necessary, sir.'

'Shame. That would have been something to tell the grandchildren; not that we have any yet. Three years my son's been married now and we're still waiting. The wife keeps asking, and all they say is 'when we're ready'. You'd think they'd want a little one to show off, wouldn't you? Have you got any?'

'I'm not married, sir. Now if you will excuse me, I have a call coming in on the other line.'

'Yes, of course. There's just one more thing, what time would you like me to come down to the station tomorrow?'

'We'll call you, sir.'

'I'll wait by the telephone. Well, I don't mean that literally, but I'll make sure I'm at home all day.'

'Thank you, sir. Goodbye.' Antionis replaced the receiver with a sigh of relief, thankful that he would not have to take a statement from the garrulous man the following day.

Saturday 29th September

Christos read the notes Antionis handed to him with interest. 'Good thinking on your part to find out the 'phone number of our anonymous caller. He's obviously using a public telephone and no doubt it's pretty close to wherever he lives.'

Antionis grinned with pleasure. It was good to receive praise from the Inspector.

'I'll get on to that later. I'm more interested in the man who was driving home from the airport.'

'He has a wife, son and daughter-in-law, but no grandchildren yet. They've been married for three years and have gone to Florence and then plan to visit Venice. Despite the flight being delayed they arrived in Florence before the parents arrived back in Aghios Nikolaos, although Mr Plastirakis said they did stop at a very good taverna for a meal before driving back home.'

'What!'

'It's impossible to stop him talking. He keeps going off at a tangent. It took me well over half an hour to get the facts out of him. Oh, and I forgot – he'd quite like to have his fingerprints taken.'

Christos raised his eyebrows. 'Whatever for?'

'So he can tell the grandchildren, when they finally arrive.'

Christos shook his head sadly. 'I hope he'll have had something more exciting than being fingerprinted happen in his life that he can tell them about. I want to have a look in records and see if there's anything about this man Stelios Papandrakis. When I mentioned taking his prints he couldn't get out of here quickly enough. Makes me suspicious that he could have a record.'

'Is he a local?'

'The address he gave is local. I'll be interested to see if he's moved around frequently.'

Antionis yawned. 'Good luck. I'm off to my bed. I'll be back at eight and you can let me know if there's anything you want me to follow up.'

Christos sat and sipped at a cup of sweet, black coffee thoughtfully. He would try the telephone number that Antionis had left with him first. That would be a job out of the way. The telephone rang unanswered until the line went dead. Christos gazed at the telephone in annoyance. If he had to go through the system to find the number he would not be able to do so until Monday and even then it would be a slow procedure as he was passed from one department to another. He would try it again in ten minutes.

He looked at the address Stelios had written on the form he had completed to report his stolen car. The house either belonged to a relative or he rented a room. He dialled up enquiries at the telephone exchange and was rewarded with a telephone number after he had spent time identifying himself as from the police.

Christos checked the telephone number on the form Stelios had filled in and was pleased to see that it was completely different. It would have been embarrassing to have the man answer the call. He looked at the clock. It was still early. He would try the telephone number the anonymous caller had used and see if anyone answered this time.

He was just about to replace the receiver when he heard a breathless 'Yes?'

'Good morning. I'm sorry to trouble you so early. Who am I speaking to?'

'I'm the porter.'

'Porter?'

'Yes, this is the Palace Hotel.

'Is that reservations?'

'No, you've come through to one of the public 'phones in the foyer. This is the number you need.' The man reeled off a series of digits and Christos wrote them down. They could be useful at a later date.

'Thank you for your help.' Christos replaced the receiver and looked at the number thoughtfully. Anyone who knew that hotels usually had a telephone in the foyer that could be used by the guests could have walked in and used it. It was interesting that it was only a short distance from the house where Mr Papandrakis claimed to live.

Christos wished it was a weekday so he could contact the local employment and tax office. His investigation into Stelios Papandrakis would have to wait until Monday. That left just the man who had telephoned the station the previous evening for him to interview. He glanced at the clock again. He would wait another half an hour before telephoning and asking the man to come to the station.

Dimitra planned her day as she lay in bed. She would go shopping first, then clean her apartment. After lunch she would take a shower and wash her hair before going to the hospital to enquire about the progress Alecos had made and also see Filippos. If she claimed to have hurt her ankle would he offer to drive her home in his car? Once at her apartment she could ask him to help her up the stairs and invite him in. She was sure he was attracted to her and she would encourage him. It would be a good idea to change the sheets on her bed, despite having done so only two days earlier.

Vasi took the dogs for a walk up on the hill behind the house. The last time he had walked them there he had been with Saffron. He felt his chest constrict. The weekend yawned before him and he had no idea how he would pass the time alone. He wished he had been able to purchase the Imperia. Arranging for the refurbishment would have occupied him all his waking hours. He thought about Saffron's suggestion that his father's house was turned into a holiday centre. He was unable to consider the idea seriously until he had spoken to his father and gained his approval. He would telephone him later and ask if he could invite himself for lunch the following day. That would at least take care of Sunday.

He whistled to the dogs and they began to follow him back to the house, knowing they would be fed and petted before being left to their own devices for the day. Vasi wished Monty was still alive. He had been a true companion to him, not just a dog kept to guard the house. Yiorgo had been so envious that he had a dog of his own. Poor Yiorgo. They had been inseparable friends when they were boys. It was sad that Yiorgo's marriage had turned sour. It was an insoluble problem and Vasi wondered if they would stay together once the boys were older.

Vasi's thoughts having turned to Yiorgo, he decided he would call him and see if they could spend the evening together. It would be better than spending the evening alone and he could talk to him about Saffron and her suggestions for his father's house.

Christos dialled the number belonging to the man who had telephoned Antionis the previous evening. The call was answered with alacrity.

'Mr Plastirakis? This is Inspector Christos from the police station. I was....' Before Christos could finish his sentence the man had interrupted.

'Yes. You want me to come down to the station to give you my statement. I told the wife you'd be 'phoning me. I'm ready to come whenever it suits you. I can be with you in about twenty minutes. I'll walk down rather than bring the car. Parking is always difficult in the town. I'll bring the wife with me and you can take a statement from her at the same time. Better make that half an hour. She doesn't walk as quickly as I do. Touch of arthritis. None of us getting any younger, are we? That's what I keep telling my son. We'd like some grandchildren before we get too old to enjoy them, but he seems to think there is plenty of time. We only had the one child so we're relying on him and his wife to produce a couple.'

As the man finally stopped to draw breath Christos interrupted. 'Thank you, Mr Plastirakis. I'll expect you in about thirty minutes.' He replaced the receiver before the man had a chance to reply to him and sighed deeply. He would obviously need to put aside the remainder of the morning to take the statement from the garrulous man.

Mr Plastirakis arrived at the station, evidently having hurried there as he was out of breath and red in the face. His wife, using a stick to aid her walking, had obviously struggled to keep pace with him as she was even more breathless and she wiped her face with her sleeve.

'I'm Mr Plastirakis. I've been asked to come down to the station to give a statement. I came as quickly as I could. Fortunately I was already washed and shaved. I'm a pretty early riser. Comes from long habit. Had to be at work by seven each morning. I used to like to get in a bit earlier so I could get myself organised for the day. Can't abide these workers who slide in through the door at the last minute. They think no one notices....'

'If you would take a seat, please.' Christos cut across the monologue. 'I will be with you in just a few minutes.' Very deliberately Christos turned his back and pretended to busy himself at a table at the side of the room. He frowned fiercely at Stavros who was smirking openly.

'Any more of that and you'll be on traffic duty for a couple of weeks,' he threatened.

'Yes, sir.' Stavros lowered his head, unable to take the smile off his face.

'If you would like to follow me.' Christos walked over to where the couple were sitting. 'Would you care for some refreshment?'

'A glass of water would be welcome. Good for you, water. Glass of wine is all very well with a meal, but it doesn't quench the thirst like water. I've heard recently that unless you drink sufficient water the brain dehydrates and shrivels up. Not a very nice thought to think your brain will look like a walnut just because you didn't drink the odd glass of water.'

'And for you, Mrs Plastirakis? Do take a seat and I'll arrange for some water to be brought in.' Christos closed the door hurriedly after them and returned to the front desk.

'Stavros, please bring in a jug of iced water and three glasses. If I am not out of there within two hours please come and interrupt me. Tell me there's a message requesting me to report to Vrouhas urgently. If Mr Iliopolakis comes in to report just make a note of the time.'

'Yes, sir.' Stavros smirked again and it was noticed by Christos.

'I've warned you about traffic duty. If you forget to come in after two hours you're on traffic duty for a month.' He emphasised his threat by pointing his finger at the junior policeman before returning to the side room.

'Water on the way,' he smiled. 'Now, if I can just take some details from you, please. Your full name and address Mr Plastirakis.'

'I gave that to the officer I spoke to last night. A very pleasant man. He said he would pass all the details on to you. Mind, I only gave my name so I suppose you want the wife's as well. She was with me, of course, so she could be considered a witness also, but naturally she didn't see it as clearly as I did. Sitting in the passenger seat you don't get such a good view as the driver does of these things.'

Mr Plastirakis was interrupted by Stavros entering with the water as requested. He poured three glasses and assured Christos he would be outside if he was needed. Christos nodded and picked up his pen again.

'Now, if I could just have your full names and address to start with.'

Mr Plastirakis picked up his glass of water and drank half of it in one gulp. 'That's better. Nothing like a drop of water.' He reached out and filled his glass to the brim again. 'I always tell the wife I'd rather have water from the tap any day that any of these fancy waters they put into bottles.'

'Your address, Mr Plastirakis,' Christos reminded him.

'We live at twenty four Proteos Street in Aghios Nikolaos. It's a nice quiet area. Do you know it? We don't get any trouble up that way. Not an area that the tourists frequent. No hotels or boarding houses. We're quite an elderly community. We've lived there for how long?' He looked at his wife but answered before she had an opportunity. 'Must be nearly thirty years. Moved there when the boy was about a year and seen no reason to move on since. Decided it was good for a youngster to have a bit of garden to play in rather than just the street. Live in an apartment and you only have a balcony. Not enough space for a boy to run around and use up his energy. I said to the wife, a house with a garden is what we need now he's a growing lad. An apartment was fine when he was just a babe, but we need a bit more space now.'

'I understand you were driving your son and his wife to the airport on the Friday evening when the accident happened. You told my colleague a car tried to overtake you and you saw the side was badly damaged. Is that right?'

Mr Plastirakis shook his head. 'It was on the way back that we saw the car. We'd dropped the son and his wife at the airport. They had a flight booked to Florence so I said we should get to the airport in good time. Of course, when we arrived they announced the flight had been delayed.' He took another mouthful from the glass of water. 'They said we should go on home as they didn't know how long they'd have to wait, but we said we'd stay with them and help to pass the time. As it turned out the delay was no more than a quarter of an hour, was it?' He turned to his wife for confirmation and she nodded.

'We left when they had to go through passport control. We're not allowed to go through there unless we're travelling as well, of course. It took a bit of time to get out of the car park, lot of coaches around and those taxi drivers think they rule the road. Expect everyone else to give way to them. What with the tourists who've just arrived and those who are leaving there's congestion everywhere. No system or organisation. Now, if I were in charge I'd have separate entrances for the coaches and taxis. They all expect to drop or pick up right outside the main entrance and there's just not the space. Causes tail backs and then passengers start to panic that they'll be late and miss their flight.' As Mr Plastirakis paused for breath and another mouthful of water Christos interrupted hurriedly.

'So you were driving on the highway on your return from the airport. Can you describe the car that tried to pass you?'

'The wife suggested we found somewhere to have something to eat before we drove back. We'd left before having an evening meal so both of us were feeling ready for some food. The wife had offered to make some sandwiches to take with us, but I didn't want her to have to go to extra trouble. She'd cooked a lunch for all of us earlier. A very nice piece of chicken. I really enjoyed that. Chicken has always been a favourite of mine and the son is pretty partial to a nice leg when it has been properly cooked. The wife's a good cook.' He beamed at her fondly.

'I'm not that familiar with Heraklion and I certainly wasn't going to take a chance on eating anything in the cafeteria at the airport. You never know how long it's been sitting on the shelf. I said we'd drive into the outskirts of the town and there was bound to be somewhere. We hadn't gone that far when I spotted a small taverna that looked clean and decent. I had a look at the menu they had in the window and the prices looked reasonable, so I said we'd take a chance. It was very good. I said I'd recommend it. Here,' Mr Plastirakis dug into his pocket and pulled out a card. 'I'll leave that one with you. I took a handful with me so I could pass them around. You'll not be disappointed. We had omelette and chips and the salad was complimentary, well, included in the price I expect.'

'So having had a meal what time were you on the highway?' asked Christos patiently.

'We were back indoors about eleven fifteen. The wife remarked on the time as there was a message on the machine from the son to say they had arrived in Florence and the hotel where they were staying was very good. They'd picked it out of a brochure so they were taking a bit of a chance, but they said if it wasn't up to their expectations they would complain and move somewhere else. Always a bit chancy picking somewhere to stay without having it personally recommended.'

'So you were on the highway at what time?' Christos reminded Mr Plastirakis of his original question.

'Must have been about ten, maybe a little earlier. I did think I might have a problem picking up the right road having taken a detour to find the restaurant, but it's well sign posted. Just have to keep your wits about you at the roundabouts to make sure you leave at the correct exit.'

'And where were you on the highway when the car tried to overtake you?'

'Right on a bend. A few more seconds and the driver would have crashed head on into an oncoming car. Brought me out in a sweat, I can tell you. He would probably have knocked us over the side.' Mr Plastirakis mopped his face at the memory. 'That could well have been the end of both of us. Idiots like that shouldn't be allowed on the road. I was just about to shout at him when he saw the headlights of the oncoming car and dropped back behind me.'

Christos held up his hand. 'Now, this is very important, Mr Plastirakis. I need to ask you some questions and I'd be obliged if you would answer them as briefly as possible. I'll ask you for more details if I think they could be relevant.'

Mr Plastirakis sat forward in his chair. 'Concentrate, Stassa.'

'Are you sure it was a man who was driving?'

'Certain,' Mr Plastirakis replied immediately. 'You are too, aren't you, Stassa?'

Mrs Plastirakis nodded her head dutifully.

'Now you only saw the car alongside you for a few moments. Are you able to tell me the colour of the vehicle?'

For the first time Mr Plastirakis hesitated. 'I say it was black, but the wife says it was dark blue.'

'And what damage was visible on the passenger side?'

'The front wing was definitely buckled and dented. There were marks all along the side, looked like someone had scraped something along it.' Mr Plastirakis stretched out his arm and drew his fingernails along it leaving a series of parallel marks. 'Looked like that, only much worse.' He thrust his arm towards Christos. 'Didn't it?' He offered his arm to his wife and she nodded again.

'When the car actually passed you did you see any other damage?'

'The back door was dented, but he drove past too quickly for me to take in too much detail.'

'You didn't manage to see any of the registration numbers, I suppose?'

Mr Plastirakis shook his head dolefully. 'I reckon I would have noticed if it had been a foreign number plate, although he was moving so fast. I decided to slow down a bit. I even drew in to one of the parking spots and sat there for a few minutes. If he continued to drive like a maniac he'd have an accident sooner or later and I didn't want to be going too fast to avoid it. I thought it would be prudent to put a bit of distance between him and myself.'

'Very wise, sir. Now, at any time whilst you were on the highway did you notice a broken barrier?'

Again Mr Plastirakis shook his head.

'And you were approximately where on the highway when the overtaking occurred?'

'We'd passed the turn off for Neapoli, so it would be about a quarter of an hour's drive before we reached the tunnel.' Mr Plastirakis nodded. 'Yes, must have been. I thought about turning off to Keratidia and stopping there and having a brandy, to steady my nerves a bit, you know. The wife advised against it. She said if we met another crazy driver and he hit us I would be accused of drinking whilst under the influence and be blamed. Don't believe in drinking and driving myself. Think those who do should have their cars taken away. That would stop them.'

'Did you get the impression that the driver who tried to overtake you had been drinking?'

Mr Plastirakis shrugged. 'I couldn't say. It's possible, of course. It could account for his recklessness.'

'If I showed you some photographs do you think it likely you would be able to recognise the driver?'

The husband and wife exchanged cautious glances. 'Maybe,' said Mr Plastirakis finally. 'I might be able to say which photo resembled him. I wouldn't want to accuse an innocent man. That's not my nature. He was there one minute and gone the next. No time to take note of any distinguishing features like moles or a broken nose. He definitely wasn't wearing glasses.' He announced triumphantly.

'Were you able to see if he had a beard?'

Mr Plastirakis frowned. 'I certainly didn't notice one and I'm a pretty observant person. He may have had that scruffy unshaven look that seems so popular with the youngsters at the moment. Just makes them look in need of a good wash in my opinion; almost as bad as the current fashion of wearing your trousers without a belt. Must be uncomfortable to have to keep pulling them up; and who wants to see their underwear anyway?'

'So there's nothing more you can tell me about the driver?'

Mr Plastirakis shook his head dolefully. 'If he'd drawn up alongside us at the traffic lights I could have had a proper look at him.'

'When the car passed you did you notice anything unusual about it apart from the damage?'

Again Mr Plastirakis shook his head. 'It was a dark saloon. Definitely not one of those large four wheel vehicles or a van and it wasn't a hire car. They usually have the name of the firm plastered all over it. Free advertising, that's all that is.'

'If you looked at some photographs of cars would you be able to pick out the model?'

'Sure to. I've always been interested in cars. Hobby of mine. Everyone needs a hobby they can enjoy in their spare time. Not that I ever seem to have much of that. Always something to do around the house. Bit of decorating to keep it presentable or the garden needs attention. I've a couple of fruit trees and the wife makes jam. I could bring you in a pot, couldn't I, Stassa?'

Mrs Plastirakis duly nodded her head in acquiescence.

Christos rose. 'I'll have your statement typed up. If you agree it's accurate I'll ask you to sign it. You could look at the car photographs whilst you're waiting.'

'You don't want my fingerprints?' asked Mr Plastirakis hopefully.

'That won't be necessary, sir. I'll only keep you a short while longer.' Christos escaped from the room thankfully, sending Stavros in with the folder of car photographs. He had spent over an hour with the couple eliciting their scanty evidence. If the car that had passed them had been involved the most valuable piece of information was the approximate time that it did so. Vasi Iliopolakis claimed to have been in a restaurant in Elounda between ten and eleven that night and could certainly not have been driving along the highway.

Mr Plastirakis read the statement through carefully, his index finger moving from word to word slowly. 'Mustn't make a mistake,' he declared. 'Could be accused of perverting the course of justice. Wouldn't want to do that. I'm a law abiding citizen. Always have been and always will be.'

'Were you able to identify the car from the photographs?' asked Christos as Mr Plastirakis finally signed the statement with an almost unreadable signature.

Mr Plastirakis frowned. 'As I said, it was a dark saloon. I picked out three and it could have been any one of them. These new cars all look the same. Twenty years ago you could tell a car by the shape. You didn't have to look for a name on the back. Now they're all so similar. Individuality has gone from cars as it has from so many other things. They call it progress and modernisation.' He shook his head sadly. 'Give me the old days. You knew where you were then. Now everyone is in such a rush they hardly pass the time of day with you.'

Christos looked pointedly at his watch. 'Unfortunately the police suffer from the same complaint – lack of time. I am very grateful to you for coming in and being such a help, but I do have another appointment that I need to keep.'

Mr Plastirakis nodded. 'Of course, of course. Just doing my duty as a conscientious citizen. Come along Stassa, we mustn't take up any more of this good man's time. I'm sure he has more than enough to do. It's a sad state of affairs that the police are always so busy. Shows just how many criminals we have in our midst. Must rub shoulders with them every day of the week and not know what nefarious activities they've been up to. Wish I'd joined the police force when I was a young man. I'm all for justice and meting out punishment when it's deserved.'

As Mr and Mrs Plastirakis exited the police station Vasi entered and held the door for them. Neither of them gave him a second glance, but Mr Plastirakis could be heard telling his wife that it was nice to meet someone who had some manners. Christos sighed and shook his head. He wondered if Mrs Plastirakis was ever allowed to voice her opinion about anything.

Christos looked at the map of Aghios Nikolaos. The Palace Hotel was literally at the end of the road where Stelios Palamakis claimed to live. He hoped someone would have been working in the reception area on Friday evening and noticed a man coming in to use the call box. It could be worth his while to walk around there and ask a few questions.

He must also send a copy of the statement given by Mr Plastirakis to Thranassis. He had read it through a number of times, but the only salient points he was able to elicit was the approximate time when the car had passed them and that it was a dark coloured saloon driven by a man. The damage the couple reported seeing corresponded roughly to that on Stelios Papandrakis's car, but they had made no mention of red paint.

It did not make sense. Why would anyone who had borrowed the car to make a journey that necessitated driving on the highway spray the car with red paint when they parked it back in Aghios Nikolaos? He felt certain it was Stelios Papandrakis's car that had been seen. The number on the wing mirror that had been found at the crash site matched the one that was still in situ on Stelios Papandrakis's car. Had any of the other cars in the area been sprayed with paint he would have classed the vandalism as a separate incident. There had to be something obvious here, staring him in the face, but he was totally unable to see what it was.

Vasi entered the taverna on the waterfront at Aghios Nikolaos where Yiorgo was waiting for him. He was drinking a beer and Vasi signalled for two more bottles to be brought over to the table.

'Hope you don't mind meeting here, but it's close to where I'm working today.'

'We could have met this evening if it was more convenient.'

Yiorgo shook his head. 'Barbara's working. I'm supposed to be plastering a couple of walls so they are ready for painting on Monday. It's a lousy job. Once you've started you have to finish or the plaster mix goes off and you have to start all over again.'

'Is it alright for you to leave it?' asked Vasi anxiously.

'I've done one wall so I deserve a break. You said you wanted to talk to me. What about?'

'Well,' Vasi shifted uncomfortably in his chair. 'I don't know what to do.'

Yiorgo raised his eyebrows, but did not interrupt.

'You know I was seeing Saffie and I'm going to England in November?'

Yiorgo nodded.

'If I asked her to marry me do you think she'd come back with me?'

Yiorgo looked at his friend in disbelief, then let out a peal of laughter. 'How do I know? I only met her once. If she married you she'd obviously come back here with you.'

'It's not as easy as that. She's a doctor.'

'So? She gives up being a doctor.'

'Suppose she doesn't want to?'

'Then she either refuses to marry you, or you get married and she stays in England.'

'That wouldn't be very satisfactory,' frowned Vasi.

'Then you go and live in England.'

'I can't do that. My business is here. She also has her stepmother to consider. She made a suggestion the day before she left and I've been wondering if there was something more behind it.'

Yiorgo raised his eyebrows.

'We were talking about my father's house,' continued Vasi. 'I don't want to live there and it's not big enough for a hotel. She said Marjorie, her stepmother, had suggested it was turned into a specialist holiday centre. It would cater for people who wanted to paint, or learn to cook or weave. Apparently these holidays are quite popular in England. I said I would talk to my father about it, but then I wondered if it was her way of telling me that Marjorie would be willing to come over here if I asked her to organise it.'

Yiorgo shook his head. 'How old is her stepmother?'

Vasi frowned. 'I don't really know. Not as old as Rebecca, but older than Cathy.'

'Does she go out to work now?'

'I don't think so, no, I'm sure she doesn't.'

'So why would she want to now?'

'It wouldn't be like going out to work. It would be more like supervising.'

Yiorgo shrugged. 'So if we disregard her stepmother and the

fact that she's a doctor what makes you think she would agree to marry you? You could have been a holiday romance in her eyes and she has someone else back in England.'

Vasi shook his head. 'She's a widow. I know there's no one else in England. She's been badly hurt in the past. Suppose she gave up being a doctor to return here with me and then she wasn't happy? She would be hurt again and this time it would be my fault.'

'You're sure she isn't just a holiday romance for you?'

Vasi sighed. 'There's something very special about Saffie. I didn't realise how much I was going to miss her.'

'I suggest you wait until you've been over to England. You may have cooled off by then. Don't act hastily or you could regret it.' Yiorgo pointed to himself. 'Do you want another beer?'

Vasi shook his head. 'One's enough for me at mid-day.'

Yiorgo called for another bottle. 'Plastering is thirsty work,' he grinned. 'Have you spoken to your father about turning his house into a holiday centre of some sort?'

'I'm driving up to Heraklion for lunch tomorrow. I'll speak to him then and see how he feels. If he says an outright no then I'll forget the idea. He'll probably want me to get details of conversion costs. Would your father be interested in doing the work?'

Yiorgo shrugged. 'It would depend how much work was involved and how quickly you wanted it done.'

'If we did go ahead I'd want it up and running by the start of next season.'

'As I said, it depends exactly upon what you have in mind. Let me know the position when you've spoken to your father. Have you had your car returned to you yet?'

Vasi shook his head. 'I'm considering buying a new one. The police could hold on to mine for weeks. I still have to report to them each day.'

'Have you heard how Alecos is getting on?'

'I asked Dimitra and she said the hospital is pleased with his progress. I still want to know what he was up to with the accounts for the hotels.'

'I wonder if he saw whoever it was who pushed him over the side,' mused Yiorgo.

'He may have done, but would he ever recognise them again? He's been unconscious and it's over a week now since the accident happened.'

'Unless his assailant was someone he knew.'

Vasi looked at Yiorgo in horror. 'I did not push him over the side.'

'I'm not suggesting you did, Vasi. It has to be a pretty hard impact at speed to break those barriers. It isn't often a car actually goes over. It usually gets tangled up in the barrier and more often than not if another car is involved that one is still sitting there as well.'

'Why would anyone want to push Alecos over deliberately?'

'I should imagine quite a number of people would. He wasn't popular at the bank with the customers. He had such a supercilious and condescending attitude.'

Vasi considered the remark. 'I thought he was just unpleasant to me, but that wouldn't be a reason for me to push him off the highway.'

'Someone obviously thought they had a good excuse.' Yiorgo looked at his watch and scraped a piece of plaster from the face. 'I must go or I'll not have that wall finished by the time Barbara has to go to work.' Yiorgo drained his beer and placed his hand in his pocket for some change.

Vasi shook his head. 'I'll get these. Do you want a ride?'

'No, thanks. I'm only round the corner. Let me know what your father says about his house.' Yiorgo pushed back his chair and walked out of the taverna. Vasi watched him go with a heavy heart. He wished he was able to do something that would make his friend happier.

Dimitra had invested in a pair of very tight black trousers and an equally tight T-shirt. She studied her appearance critically in her bedroom mirror. Were the trousers a mistake? She had struggled to get into them and they were certainly uncomfortable. She would wear them that afternoon and then return them to the shop and get her money back. She thrust out her ample bosom and decided to remove her bra. To see her breasts unfettered was sure to be an added attraction to the doctor and he could only interpret it as an invitation. She smiled to herself. She would enjoy teasing him until she was ready to give him the satisfaction that she knew he was beginning to crave.

Filippos Melanakis considered telephoning Dimitra. She would want to know that Alecos had regained consciousness. He resisted the urge. He really must telephone his patient's father first, besides, if he called her just before his duty ended for the day he could offer to spend some time explaining Alecos's progress to her. He wondered what her reaction would be if he sank his fingers into the delicious looking flesh on her thighs and decided his experiment should be in private. He felt himself becoming aroused and licked his lips in anticipation. If she came to the hospital he would offer to drive her home. He could suggest a private chat in her apartment, knowing they would not be interrupted. He began to enjoy imagining how those plump thighs would feel and looked at his pager in annoyance when it broke into his reverie.

Mr Vikelakis entered the small hospital room where his son was being cared for. The nurse in attendance smiled at him and rose from her chair.

'I'll give you a few minutes alone with your son, but don't expect too much response from him. No doubt he's still suffering from a very bad headache.'

Mr Vikelakis nodded and looked at the damaged body that lay on the bed. Alecos's head was bandaged, he had purple bruises on his face and his eyes were swollen. Machinery monitoring his vital signs was clicking gently in the background, a television screen showing graphs of his heart beat and pulse and a drip was inserted in his arm.

'Alecos, can you hear me?'

Alecos attempted to open his eyes. 'Hello, Pappa,' he managed to say.

'You've been banged about a bit, but the Doctor tells me you're making good progress.'

'Yes.'

'How did the accident happen?'

Alecos did not answer his father. He had no clear recollection of anything at the moment. His body hurt all over and he remembered hitting his head on something very hard. The doctor had told him he had been in a car accident so he must have been hit as he crossed the road. Why was he crossing the road? Surely he would have looked to see if there was a vehicle coming and not just stepped out.

'Drink,' he said thickly.

'I hope you hadn't been drinking,' said Mr Vikelakis. 'That could invalidate your insurance claim for your car. It's costing enough to have you in here as it is. Can't afford to lose that as well. I've filled in the forms to be reimbursed for the hospital care and private nursing, but it all takes time. The bank is being very good. They say your full salary will be paid for three months. It will be reduced if you're unable to go back to work after that. I can't touch it, of course, so we'll have to sort out what you owe me later.'

Alecos closed his eyes again. His father was not making sense. All he wanted was a drink of water.

Dimitra crept into the hospital room, unsure how she would find Alecos. She had been told by reception that she could visit for a few moments, but must not tire the patient out. She had been insistent that she needed to see Dr Melanakis before he left the hospital for the day and promised to return to reception to wait for him after her brief visit.

She was disconcerted when she saw Alecos's father was already there. She had never met the man, but the likeness between father and son was remarkable.

'Hello,' she smiled. 'You must be Alecos's father. I just called in to see how he was.'

At the sound of her voice Alecos opened his eyes. 'Dimitra. Drink.'

Dimitra looked around until she spied the feeding cup. She held it and tipped a little into Alecos's mouth. Mr Vikelakis felt stupid. That was what his son had asked him for. The word 'drink' had not referred to his car accident at all.

'I'm only allowed to stay for a minute or two,' Dimitra bent over Alecos. 'I just wanted to see how you were for myself. All the hospital keep telling me is that you're progressing.' She placed a light kiss on his cheek and straightened up. 'Now you're on the mend I'll call in again. I'll leave you with your father today.'

Relieved to have such a good excuse to return to reception and wait for Dr Melanakis, Dimitra left the room. She could feel Mr Vikelakis's disapproving eyes on her as she closed the door.

Dimitra stood at the side of reception with her back to the desk, pretending to read the various notices that were pinned on the board.

'Dimitra,' Dr Melanakis walked towards her with a pleased smile. She looked good in trousers, despite the fact that they covered the flesh on her legs, but her tight T-shirt, showing the curves of her breasts and the outline of her nipples, was a direct invitation to his hands. 'I was going to telephone you when I came off duty to tell you the progress Mr Vikelakis has made.'

'How very kind of you to think of me. I came by on the chance that I would be able to speak to you and I was allowed to visit Alecos for a few minutes. His poor face.' Dimitra shook her head sadly. 'No doubt all his injuries will heal in time.' She smiled brightly at the doctor. 'I do hope you will be able to reassure me about that.'

'I am sure I will. A few scars may remain of course, but there should be no lasting damage.'

'And his brain, Doctor? Do you know yet if he will have any

detrimental effects from the accident?'

Dr Melanakis shook his head. 'It is still too early to say with any certainty. The signs are good. He is showing a response to stimuli and able to make his basic needs known. I am just finishing my duty if you would care to have coffee with me I could tell you a few more details.'

Dimitra appeared to hesitate and looked at her watch. 'That is very kind of you. I must not be too late home. The lady downstairs relies on me to keep an eye on her granddaughter for half an hour. She looks after her during the day whilst her mother works. There is a time gap between her mother coming to collect her and her grandmother going to work.' She fabricated the excuse swiftly. She must not let the doctor think she was too anxious for his attentions, besides, it amused her to see the way he was ogling her breasts.

'And you care for her during this time?'

Dimitra shrugged, her breasts straining at the fabric of her T-shirt. 'Hardly care for her. She is nearly nine, not a baby, but they both like to know there is an adult in the house.'

Doctor Melanakis clenched his hands. He wanted to reach out and feel those tantalising orbs of flesh. I am sure I could drive you home so that you will be there in good time.' The doctor smiled. She had given him a good excuse to have her alone in his car.

Dimitra smiled happily. She was sure she would be able to manufacture a little foreplay in the car and the next time she saw the doctor he would be only too willing to take her home. She could always claim her commitment to the lady downstairs prevented her from asking him in if she wished to delay his intentions a little longer.

Doctor Melanakis took her elbow and was about to steer her out of the hospital when his pager sounded. He stared at the message in annoyance and disbelief. 'Excuse me, one moment.'

He strode over to the reception desk. 'I have just been paged. There must be a mistake. I'm off duty.'

The receptionist shook her head. 'Sorry, Doctor. Coach and a van have tangled with each other. We're expecting multiple casualties. Everyone is on standby.'

Trying to smile, but inwardly furious, Doctor Melanakis returned to Dimitra. 'I am so sorry. We will have to delay our chat. We have some emergencies arriving and I have been asked to stay to deal with them. I have no idea how long I will be here.'

'No problem, Doctor. I understand. Your work has to come before pleasure. I will call in next week some time and see how Alecos is progressing. We may be able to have a coffee together then.'

'I certainly hope so.' Doctor Melanakis watched Dimitra walk to the door. The first time in over six weeks that he had been asked to stay to deal with emergencies and it had to be today!

Sunday 30th September

Vasi lay in bed, his hands clasped behind his head, thinking of the best way he could approach his father with Saffron's proposal. She had suggested dividing up the bedrooms and bathrooms upstairs to double the number. That was practical, but he did not think that making bedrooms on the ground floor would be at all suitable. The cost would be exorbitant. It could be cheaper to build a small annex in the grounds. There would have to be someone living on the premises to provide a breakfast and deal with any queries or emergencies the guests had, so there would only be five bedrooms available. That person would also have to be capable of dealing with the bookings and organisation of the events in which the guests wished to participate.

If everyone who came was an artist there was no problem. They could either sit up on the roof, in the grounds or go off into the hills as they fancied. Walkers again could be left to their own devices. It was the cookery and weaving that he was having difficulty with. He should have made some enquiries in the villages and seen if a woman there had a working loom and would be willing to allow clumsy, inexpert novices to handle her precious piece of equipment. He frowned again. To the best of his knowledge few people in the villages spoke more than a few words of any language other than Greek.

He would talk to his father about it; maybe Cathy would have some ideas, but he could not see the scheme being practical. Vasi threw back the sheet that had been covering him. He would shower, take the dogs for a walk and then look around the house and try to visualise it the way Saffron obviously could, as a visitors' centre.

Alecos lay in the hospital bed. The nurse no longer sat at his side monitoring the machines his body was attached to and trying to raise him from his stupor. He tried to recall exactly what had happened. He remembered leaving Dimitra, despite her urging him to stay the night with her. Something to do with papers. Papers and Vasi. Why should he think of Vasi? He had papers and a back-up disk in his jacket pocket and they were something to do with Vasi Iliopolakis. What had happened to them?

Mr Vikelakis opened the door quietly. 'Are you awake, Alecos?'

Alecos opened his eyes as far as he could. 'Yes.'

'That's good. We've come up to see you again. You do look better than yesterday. The doctor said he was very pleased with you. If you continue to progress like this he said you could probably be transferred to the hospital at Aghios Nikolaos at the end of the week. That would save us having to make the journey.'

'Good.'

Mrs Vikelakis elbowed her husband out of the way. 'Let me look at him. Oh, Alecos, your poor face, it's still all bruised and cut and your nose is crooked. It's a miracle you survived.' She crossed herself fervently and raised her eyes heavenwards.

'Belongings.' To speak Alecos had to remove the oxygen mask that was helping him to breathe without putting too much pressure on his damaged ribs, but to do so hurt his shoulder.

'No problem there. The hospital gave me your clothes and possessions. I have them at home.'

'Do you know who did this to you?' asked his mother.

'Vasi, pa...'

'Vasi!' Mrs Vikelakis turned horrified eyes on her husband. 'Vasi Iliopolakis always was a vicious little boy. Remember how he assaulted Alecos when he went up to their house to play? He's a thoroughly nasty character. We'll have to tell Inspector Christos as soon as we return to Aghios Nikolaos and no doubt he'll arrest him. Good thing too. No one's safe in their beds with someone like him around.'

Alecos tried to make sense of his mother's words and gave up. His father had told him he had his possessions and that must include the papers and the disk. What was so important about them? He wished he could remember.

'Sleep,' said Alecos and closed his eyes. It was such an effort to talk and trying to concentrate on the words his father and mother were saying had brought a return of his headache. At least if he feigned sleep he would not be expected to answer any of their questions and he might also be able to remember the importance of the papers.

Mr Vikelakis put a hand on his wife's shoulder. 'I suggest we leave him be for a while. We'll go and have a drink in the coffee shop along the road and come back when he's had a rest.'

Mrs Vikelakis nodded. She bent over Alecos and kissed his cheek, oblivious to the wince of pain he gave.

'Don't you worry,' she assured him. 'Your father will speak to Inspector Christos when we get back home, won't you Nikos? That Vasi will soon be behind bars and not able to hurt you ever again.'

Mr Vikelakis nodded soberly. Once his son had been transferred to the local hospital he did not plan to ever drive along the highway again. Every twist and turn alarmed him and he had a desire to close his eyes when he reached the place where Alecos had been forced over the side. He pressed his hand to his stomach. Just thinking about the road made his ulcer hurt.

'Pappa, it's only an idea and you may not like it. In that case I'll forget all about it.'

Vasilis frowned at his son. 'Is it to do with the accident?'

Vasi shook his head. 'Nothing at all to do with that. It's just frustrating to have to remember to report to a police station each day. Twice I've nearly forgotten and I don't want to forfeit the bail

185

money just because of a slip of the memory.'

'Surely you wouldn't have to do that?'

'I don't know, but I don't want to take the chance. No, this is about your house. You know I don't want to live there all alone. It's far too big for me.'

'You should get married and have a family. It wouldn't be too big then.'

Vasi shrugged. 'One day, maybe. Saffie said Marjorie had given her an idea. In England it has become popular for people to go somewhere and learn the local crafts. She thought it could work in Elounda.'

'What do you mean?'

'We could offer holidays where visitors learn how to do authentic Greek cookery and weaving. Saffie said they might even like to come and pick our olives in the season.'

'So you're suggesting turning the house into an industrial centre?'

Vasi smiled. 'Not at all. Saffie suggested that we divided up the bedrooms so that we doubled the number. One would have to be used by the manager. That would mean that ten people could stay at a time. Before they arrive they say what they want to do and we arrange it.'

Vasilis shook his head. 'That's not practical. You'll need chambermaids, a chef, waiters; all the staff that you have at the hotel and just for ten people. It would never pay.'

'It wouldn't be like a hotel. The guests would be responsible for keeping their rooms clean whilst they were there and we would have the rooms thoroughly cleaned when they left. If they were learning Greek cookery the food they had cooked would be served as their evening meal. We would only offer breakfast and they would have to make a sandwich for their lunch. All we would need to do is have the ingredients available.'

'People don't want to look after themselves when they're on holiday.'

'Giovanni doesn't cater for any of his guests. If they can't be bothered to make a meal they go over to the taverna.'

'So who would teach them how to cook Greek food?'

'There are two options there. Either someone is employed or we ask some of the village women to allow them into their kitchens.'

Vasilis looked sceptical. 'Some of them still have a traditional oven.'

'Exactly. That would make their cooking really authentic. Then there's the weaving. I don't know if anyone has a working loom in the village. I'd have to ask around.'

'There wouldn't be enough room in their cottages for ten people and a loom!'

'Not all ten would go there at once. Two or three at a time for a couple of days whilst the others were cooking and then they would swap over. If no one has a loom I thought we might put one in the small lounge, but that would mean employing someone to teach them how to use it.'

'Do you really think you'd have enough interested people to make it work?' asked Vasilis.

'I don't see why not. We could also say that it was an ideal location for artists and walkers, or just to have a lazy week by the pool and soak up the sun. Photographs! I've just thought. I'm sure John would come up and talk about photography. He could show them how to take really good photos. A competition for the best one at the end of the week. And Greek. We could offer lessons in basic Greek.'

Vasilis shook his head. 'Vasi, you're getting completely carried away. I'm not saying the idea doesn't have potential, but I think it needs a good deal more thought and planning than you've put into it at the moment.'

Vasi's face fell. 'I'm sure it could work.'

'Probably, but the finance needs to be looked at. How much will it cost to make six bedrooms from the original three? How much would a loom cost if you had to buy one? How much would you have to pay any of the local women if they agreed to have total strangers in their homes? All that needs to be found out before you can decide how much to charge these guests. No one expects to make a profit from a new venture in the first couple of years, but how long do you estimate it will take to recoup your expenses?'

'I haven't worked any of that out. I wanted to know how you felt about the idea before I went any further. You could have turned it down out of hand and been adamant that the house stayed exactly as it is. I know I don't want to live there, Pappa, but I would hate to see it become derelict.'

Mr Vikelakis drove slowly back to Aghios Nikolaos. There really had been little point in making the journey. Alecos was still unable to hold a conversation with them. The boy had said no more than a dozen words the whole time they had been there. Having left him to sleep, they had returned after their visit to the coffee shop and found him still uncommunicative and sleepy. The nurse had assured them that this was quite normal and sleeping would help his healing process, but Mrs Vikelakis was not so sure.

'He's been in there a week. He should be sitting up by now.'

'He only regained consciousness on Friday. You can't expect too much from him after a week of being concussed. The doctor says he's recovering well.'

'At least he remembers who caused his accident. We'll go straight to the police station and tell them. No doubt they'll send a policeman to the hospital to take his statement. Then that stuck up Vasi Iliopolakis will get what he deserves.' Mrs Vikelakis spoke vituperatively. 'Once our Alecos knows he's safe from that monster he'll make a far quicker recovery. I'm sure of that.'

'I expect you're right, dear.' Mr Vikelakis had learned long ago that it was easiest to agree with his wife's opinions.

Inspector Christos listened to Mr Vikelakis with consternation. According to Mrs Vikelakis Alecos had been quite definite about identifying Vasi as the cause of his accident.

'I asked him if he knew who had hit his car and he said 'Vasi' quite clearly. That Vasi always picked on him when they were at school together. He used to keep a vicious dog and when my Alecos tried to defend himself against it Vasi punched him. The poor boy was in pain for days. We never let him go up there again to visit.'

Mr Vikelakis sat silently. The incident his wife was referring to was not exactly as she described it, but he could not deny that when she had asked their son who had caused his accident he had said the name 'Vasi'.

'I'm pleased to hear that Mr Alecos is recovering. I'll certainly contact the police in Heraklion and I'll go along and interview Mr Vasi again,' promised Christos.

'Aren't you going to arrest Vasi Iliopolakis?'

Christos shook his head. 'I need a sworn statement from Mr Alecos before I can do that. I assure you Mr Vasi has already been questioned, but we have no grounds to arrest him at the moment. Mr Vasi has to report to a police station every day so he will not disappear from Crete.'

Christos watched the couple leave and shook his head sadly. Had he made a bad error of judgement believing Vasi was innocent?

Vasi sat down and wrote an e-mail to Saffron.

'I spoke to my father today about your idea to turn his house into a specialist holiday centre. He does not think it will make money. He reminded me that I have not found out the cost of converting the bedrooms, the price of a loom, the wages I would need to pay for instruction in cooking and weaving. I did think of two other good ideas whilst we were talking. I suggested John showed people how to take excellent photographs and we also taught the visitors a little Greek.

My father said I was getting carried away with the idea and maybe I am. I wish you were here so we could discuss it properly. I did not tell him about your idea to make more bedrooms on the ground floor as I do not think that is practical and it would be very expensive. If I had to install a loom in the house I would have to use one of those rooms. My father's office would be needed for the administration work, so the best place to put it would be in the small lounge.

I will speak to Lambros on Monday and ask if any of the women in the village still weave. If they do I could ask them if they would be willing to teach visitors and how much they would charge. We would have to pay for the wool and I do not know how much that costs.

My father says you need to have more than ten guests staying to make a profit each week. How much do people pay in England to stay at one of these centres? Would it be possible for you to contact one of them and find out for me?'

Saffron smiled to herself. This was the gymnasium and the redecoration of Vasi's apartment all over again. He was quite capable of finding out the answers to these questions without involving her.

Monday 1st October

Christos kept eyeing the clock anxiously, waiting for a reply from Heraklion regarding Alecos giving a statement that accused Vasi Iliopolakis of causing his accident. Thranassis had sounded so smug and self satisfied over the telephone when Christos had requested a police officer visit the hospital.

'I knew I was right,' Thranassis said. 'We'll have him in by the end of the day.'

The accusation against Vasi did not sit easily on him and having seen the damage on both the cars in question Christos was inclined to think the one he had impounded was more likely to be the one involved. It was possible, but rather far-fetched, that Vasi would have stolen a car, run the man off the road and then returned and vandalised his own car. What would have been the point in doing that? It would have been far more sensible to leave his own car undamaged if he was going to deny all knowledge of the incident.

He wondered if he should telephone both the Unemployment Office and the Tax Office to make enquiries about Stelios Papandrakis or was he wasting his time? There was something about the man that he did not trust, or was that another error of judgement on his part? Why had the man refused to give his fingerprints if he had nothing in his past to hide? It would do no harm to check the man out.

Christos decided he would walk around to the address the man had given as his lodgings. He would have a word with either the owner of the property or another tenant and see what information he could elicit about the man. From there he could walk around the corner and speak to reception at the Palace Hotel. There was just a chance they had noticed a man making a call on the Friday evening and might be able to identify him.

'I'm going out for a short while,' he announced to Stavros. 'If Thranassis calls from Heraklion let me know immediately.'

Stavros nodded. He had no wish to be put back on traffic duty and knew Christos was quite capable of carrying out his threat if he did not obey his superior's instructions.

Christos walked leisurely along the roads leading to Stelios Papandrakis's residence. It was good to have an excuse to get out of the office for a while. He might even treat himself to a chicken and mushroom pie to take back for his lunch, although his wife had made him a sandwich as usual. He could always eat that later in the day.

He scrutinized the house from the opposite side of the road. Someone was making an effort to keep it in good repair. The front door had been painted recently, but the facade was certainly showing signs of wear. The net at the ground floor window was clean, but the upstairs window had the shutters firmly closed.

Christos knocked and waited. He hoped he was not going to wake anyone up and he also hoped that it would not be Stelios Papandrakis who answered the door. To his relief an unknown man opened the door and looked at him in surprise.

Christos smiled and showed his identification. 'Would I be able to come in and have a few words with you, please? It's just a general enquiry; you're not in any trouble.'

'Glad to hear it, although what trouble I would be in I can't imagine.' The door was opened wider and Christos walked into the room that doubled as both a lounge and dining room. 'Have a seat. Would you like me to call my wife? She's in the kitchen.'

'If it's no trouble.' Christos eased himself into a chair. He looked around. The room was spotless, despite being full of furniture and every available surface had either a photograph or ornament displayed.

A woman emerged from the kitchen, wiping her hands on her apron as she came. She looked anxiously at her husband.

'Is it about our lodger?' she asked.

'Why should you assume that, madam?'

'Well,' she twisted her hands nervously. 'We haven't told the landlord that we have a lodger. He might insist on charging us more rent.'

'I'm not here on behalf of your landlord.' Christos was surprised. He would expect the elderly couple to have owned the house. 'If your lodger is Stelios Papandrakis I'd just like to ask you a few questions about him, but nothing for you to be alarmed about.'

'Is he in trouble?'

Christos shook his head. 'He came in to the station to report his car had been stolen. I thought I would ask if you happened to have seen anyone tampering with it.'

'When was it stolen?'

'About ten days ago. He said he parked it as usual and it was gone when he went to use it.'

The man shook his head. 'He doesn't always park it outside. Sometimes all the spaces have gone.'

'Do you know where he would park then?'

'No idea.'

'Does he use his car for work?'

'I wouldn't expect him to. He works at the California Bar in town. Easier to walk there than look for a parking space.'

'Has he worked there long?'

'As far as I know he started there this season.'

'Is that when he came to lodge with you?' asked Christos.

The man nodded. 'He said he'd been working in Hersonissos at a hotel, but it had closed down. Pleasant man; he's been no trouble. He pays his rent regularly and never makes a noise when he comes in at night.'

Christos rose. 'Thank you for your time. There's just one other thing about the car – was it damaged in any way?'

The man and woman looked at each other and she shrugged. 'Damaged? Not that I ever noticed, what about you, Elias?'

The man shook his head. 'Odd dent and scratch, but nothing that would make you look at it twice.'

Christos shook hands with both of them and moved carefully through the furniture to the door. He hoped his visit would only be remembered for the questions he had asked about the car as he was sure Stelios would be told he had called.

Christos studied the facade of the hotel. It would probably describe itself as 'unpretentious' but in his mind it was decidedly scruffy. The door slid open for him as he approached and he advanced across a marble floor that had been carelessly mopped earlier in the day. He showed his credentials to the receptionist and looked around the foyer. On the far wall stood two pay 'phones.

The receptionist frowned. It would not be the first time the police had called asking to speak to one of their guests and that usually meant the visitor departed hurriedly without paying their bill.

'Yes?' she asked in a bored voice.

'Would you have been on duty on Friday evening?' asked Christos.

She shook her head. 'I only work days. Finish at six.'

'Who would have been on duty after you left?'

'Stefanos I expect. He usually does Tuesday to Saturday.'

'Would it be possible for me to have a very quick word with him?'

'He's over there.' She indicated a man sitting with an empty coffee cup before him and the newspaper spread out on the table. No doubt he had been watching and listening to their conversation.

Christos walked over to him and the man continued to look down at the newspaper.

'Excuse me, are you Stefanos?'

'Who wants to know?'

Again Christos showed his credentials.

'I wasn't here and I don't know anything about it.' He returned his eyes to the paper.

Christos sat down opposite. 'Rather a sweeping statement when you don't know what I am going to ask you.'

Stefanos shrugged. 'Ask away. You'll still get the same answer.'

'I understand you were on duty as receptionist on Friday night.'

'Could have been.'

'Would you have noticed a man coming in to use a pay 'phone?'

'No.'

'Surely if you were at the reception desk you would have seen anyone using them to make a call.'

Stefanos shrugged again. ''Phone calls aren't my business.'

'So you didn't see any one using the 'phone on Friday?'

'I've told you. No.' Stefanos scowled and looked back down at the newspaper.

Christos rose. 'Thank you for your time.'

Stefanos did not answer him and Christos nodded to the girl behind reception as he left. That had been a total waste of his time. Disconsolately he made his way back to the police station, forgetting to buy himself the promised pie and further disheartened when Stavros said there had been no message from Thranassis.

Christos mulled over the scant information he had been given by the couple where Stelios lodged. According to them he was a model tenant and Christos had no reason to doubt them. It was just something in Stelios's attitude that niggled away at him. He would give the Benefit Office a quick ring and see if the man had claimed when his previous employment ended and before he commenced his work at the California Bar. It was possible the man was still claiming benefits that he was not entitled to and that could account for his uncooperative attitude.

Christos listened to the message from the Benefit Office, telling him which extension he would need to certain claims. Finally it told him to hold if he wished to speak to someone. He sat there patiently listening to the ringing until the line went dead. He sighed in exasperation and dialled the number again, listened to the message and waited whilst the 'phone rang interminably and finally cut off. He would have to pay them a visit if he wanted an answer.

As always the office was busy, crammed with people, either queuing or lounging against the walls clutching a numbered ticket. Their eyes were fixed on the automatic system which would tell them when their number could approach the desk and an arrow would show over the appropriate station. This was one time when Christos was not prepared to be patient. He pushed his way to the front of the queue, ignoring the complaints from those already waiting, and showed the girl his badge.

'I'd like to speak to someone about unemployment benefit,' he said.

'Take a number,' she said without looking up.

'This is police business, not personal,' Christos snapped back. A ripple of comment went back through the people. Police. Who were they checking up on?

'You'll have to make an appointment.'

'How do I do that?'

'By telephone.'

Christos shook his head. 'I have tried to telephone, but no one answers. I am here in my official capacity and I would like to speak to someone *now*.'

'You'll need to go upstairs.' The girl had hardly looked up from the papers she was studying.

Christos looked around and could see no sign directing him to the stairs. He was just about to interrupt the girl again when a woman touched his arm. 'The stairs are in the corner.'

'Thank you.' As he turned to go the crowd parted for him. They would certainly not stop anyone from leaving; it would make their turn arrive a little more speedily.

Christos was out of breath by the time he had climbed the two flights of stairs to the top floor. It was certainly less crowded up there and one girl was sitting at a desk in the far corner with no one queuing in front of her. Relieved that he would be able to see someone immediately, Christos walked over to her.

'Name?' she asked before he had a chance to open his mouth.

'Christos Christostofferakis.'

'How do you spell it?'

'That's not relevant. I'm here on official business.'

'I cannot fill out a form and give you an appointment unless I can fill in your name.'

'I'm known as Mr Christos. I'm from the police. I'm making some enquiries and would be grateful for a few minutes with someone who can help me.'

The girl looked at him steadily. 'We're busy. The form has to be filled out with your full name and initialled by me before you can hand it in downstairs. They will make you an appointment.'

Christos took out his credentials and laid them on the desk before her. 'I would not want to have to arrest you for obstructing an officer of the law in his enquiries. I would like to see someone *now* to answer some questions.'

The girl threw her pen down on the table, gave a loud 'tut' and picked up the telephone. She turned her back on Christos and held a very quiet conversation with someone on the other end.

'Mr Balibasakis can see you in about fifteen minutes,' she announced.

'Thank you. Where shall I wait?'

She shrugged. 'Over there.'

Christos moved a short distance away from her desk. He was not going to be lost amongst the other people who were waiting and the girl think he had left.

Mr Balibasakis took his time leaving his office and it was nearer to half an hour before he opened his door and stood there looking at the people who were waiting resignedly for their turn. Christos strode over.

'Mr Balibasakis? I'm Inspector Christos Christotothorassanakis from the Aghios Nikolaos police and I would like just a few minutes of your time to ask you some questions.'

Mr Balibasakis frowned. He knew who the man was. He had seen him at the police station when he had been in to complain about receiving a parking ticket. The man had been most unhelpful and sent him to the Traffic Police where he had spent most of the day lodging an unsuccessful appeal.

'I'm not allowed to divulge personal information unless the person has been involved in criminal activities,' he said pompously.

'I'm sure you'll have no such problem with my queries,' smiled Christos. 'If we could go into your office?'

Reluctantly Mr Balibasakis held the door open and allowed Christos through. He waved Christos to an upright wooden chair and took the padded seat behind the desk for himself.

'What is it you want to know?'

'Mr Stelios Papandrakis, currently lodging at,' Christos read off the address. 'I understand he was working at a hotel in Hersonissos until the establishment closed. If you are able to give me the name and address of the hotel I would be grateful.'

'Why don't you ask Mr Papandrakis?'

'This is a confidential police matter. I am not able to approach him for the information at the moment.'

'When did he leave?'

'I don't know exactly, probably about seven months ago.'

'Did he draw unemployment benefit in Hersonissos?'

'I have no idea, but I would expect so. He may have moved straight to Aghios Nikolaos, of course.'

'Is he working now?'

'I understand he works at the California Bar.'

'And still draws unemployment benefit?'

Christos shrugged. 'If he is that would be for you to deal with. I would just like the name and address of the hotel where he was previously employed.'

Mr Balibasakis pulled back his cuffs and began to press keys on his computer. He would finish his game of chess; the policeman would not know he was not searching various sites for the man's records. He frowned, if he moved his Queen he was going to leave his King exposed to an attack by both a pawn and a Knight. If he moved his Knight the Queen was still in danger from a Bishop. He sighed. It was impossible to concentrate properly with the policeman sitting opposite him. He saved and closed his game and entered a search for Stelios Papandrakis.

'Here we are,' he said. 'I've managed to find him. He worked at the Kronos. One of Mr Iliopolakis's hotels.'

Christos tried to hide his surprise. 'You wouldn't have a telephone number, I suppose?'

'Won't be much good to you if the place is closed down.' Mr Balibasakis wrote a number on a sheet of paper and passed it across to Christos.

'It may have re-opened under new ownership. I can give it a try, nothing to lose.' Christos rose. 'Thank you for your time. I suggest you move your Rook; that would save your Queen temporarily.'

Mr Balibasakis looked at the policeman in disbelief. How had he known he was playing chess rather than looking up the details of Stelios Papandrakis?

Christos smiled. 'Your screen is reflected in the window. I suggest you pull down your blind in future.'

Mr Balibasakis's face reddened, then purpled with annoyance, whilst Christos let himself out, feeling decidedly pleased that he had embarrassed the pompous official.

Once back in the station Christos telephoned the Kronos Hotel in Hersonissos. His call was answered with alacrity by a young man.

'Kronos Hotel. How may I help you?'

'Are you open?'

'Yes, sir. We will be open until the last week in October. Would you like to make a booking?'

'I was told you had closed down.'

'You were misinformed, sir. We have been open all season.'

Christos felt confused. 'I'll let my friend know,' he said and replaced the receiver. He sat looking at the instrument until Stavros knocked on the door to his office.

'Superintendent Solomakis on the line for you, sir.'

'I'll take it here.' Christos waited for the ring tone before lifting the receiver. 'Thranassis?'

'My officer has just returned from the hospital,' he said without preamble. 'Mr Vikelakis is not well enough to make a statement at the moment.'

'I see. Have you any idea when he may be?'

'The doctor wouldn't commit himself. Have you re-interviewed Mr Iliopolakis?'

'Not yet. I was waiting for your call before I asked him to come in.'

'Hmmh.' The line went dead and Christos smiled to himself. He knew that Thranassis had been hoping to arrest Vasi Iliopolakis that day on the evidence of a statement made by Alecos Vikelakis and his ambition had been thwarted. He would telephone Vasi and ask him to come down for a chat. He could ask him about the Kronos hotel at the same time.

Vasi sat in Christos's office and appeared completely relaxed. 'I did come in this morning and report, Mr Christos. You weren't here at the time.'

Christos smiled. 'The information was passed on to me. I just wanted to have a discussion with you, off the record, so to speak.'

Vasi raised his eyebrows and Christos continued.

'I'd like you to put yourself in my position for a moment. I'm a police officer and as such I have to keep an open mind about a case until the guilty party is apprehended. I also have to look at the evidence from all angles. I am not accusing you of anything, Mr Vasi, but suppose, just suppose you are guilty of running Mr

Vikelakis off the road.' Christos watched Vasi's reaction closely.

Vasi shook his head. 'I swear the accident was nothing to do with me.'

Christos continued as if he had not spoken. 'Suppose you returned your young lady home and then, having had a little too much to drink, you decided to borrow a car, and drove up to the highway in the early hours. Maybe it was just bad luck for Mr Vikelakis that his was the car that you hit. You hadn't intended to cause an accident to anyone.'

Vasi looked at him blankly. 'Why would I use someone else's car and then deliberately damage mine?'

'Yes, I admit that is something that I find rather puzzling.'

'I was never anywhere near the highway at any time that day or that night and I certainly had not had too much to drink.'

'Unfortunately we only have your word for that, Mr Vasi. Oh, I don't disbelieve you, but I do wish you had a reliable alibi.'

Vasi frowned. 'Should I be contacting my solicitor?'

Christos shook his head. 'This is only an informal chat. I really wanted to ask you about the Kronos hotel in Hersonissos.'

'The Kronos? What has that got to do with the accident?'

'The name just happened to come up whilst I was pursuing another enquiry.' Christos ignored Vasi's question. 'I was told the hotel had closed, but when I telephoned to check it is up and running; has been all season.'

Vasi nodded. 'That's correct. I closed and refurbished before the season started and it's doing well now.'

'You have a reliable manager?'

'He's excellent.'

'How long has he been there?'

'Only since the season started.'

'The previous manager did not wish to stay on?'

Vasi's lips compressed into a thin line. 'I'm afraid I had to sack him.'

'Really? Hand in the till?'

'He was using the hotel as a brothel out of season.' Vasi spoke bitterly; he was still ashamed of being associated with such an activity.

Christos raised his eyebrows. 'And you had no knowledge of this?'

'He told me he was letting rooms to young people who were looking for work. Once they had found some they would move on to permanent accommodation. It seemed like a good idea to cover the winter running expenses. He paid me the rent and then pocketed a percentage of the girls' earnings.'

'How did you find out?'

'Alecos told my father I was running a brothel.'

'Really? How would he know?'

Vasi shrugged. 'I don't know. He may have used it.'

'Just as a matter of interest, what was the name of the manager?'

'Stelios Papandrakis. Came with good references. Said he needed to move from Sitia to be near his mother in Hersonissos.'

'Is he still in Hersonissos?'

'I have no idea. Once I'd sacked him I had no further interest in the man.'

'You didn't consider prosecuting?'

Vasi spread his hands. 'What was the use? It would have been his word against mine. He would have said I had agreed to the arrangement and there was no way I could prove that I had not.' Vasi shook his head. 'I gave him a minute's notice, told him to pack his belongings and leave. I gave the girls a couple of hours and refunded their week's rent so they could go to a hotel. I wished I hadn't after I saw the mess and damage they had left behind. I called Mr Palamakis up to change the locks and board up the ground floor. I didn't want any of them getting back in when I wasn't there.'

'So rather than covering your costs over the winter season you ended up with a considerable amount of extra expenditure?'

'I certainly did. My fault, I suppose, for not going down unexpectedly during the winter months to check up on it.' Vasi shrugged. 'I'm more careful now.'

Alecos lay in his hospital bed. He was sure when he had opened his eyes earlier there had been a policeman sitting in the chair. The police probably wanted a statement from him regarding his car accident. He remembered now; he had been driving along the highway when a car had run into the side of him. The impact had shocked him and he had felt his front wheel grazing the metal barrier. He had twisted the steering wheel in an effort to get all four wheels back on the road and the car had deliberately run into him a second time, sending him through the safety barrier and sliding down the hillside. After that all he remembered was pain.

Dimitra considered whether she should visit the hospital after work that day and decided she would not. She did not want to give the doctor the impression that she was chasing after him. It was annoying that he had been paged the previous day just when he had asked her to go for coffee and promised to drive her home for her fictitious child care duty. She had seen the hungry way in which he looked at her and she was sure he would have made an amorous advance and suggested meeting her somewhere other than at the hospital to further their acquaintance. She would enjoy teasing him a little longer with an implied promise of spending enjoyable and intimate moments with her and when the time was right she would ensure that she gave him the ultimate pleasure he sought.

She envisioned him caressing her gently, pleading and begging her to allow him to remove her clothing, whilst she pretended to hesitate to encourage his desperation. She would finally stand there, naked, before him, and he would kiss her from top to toe, his ardour increasing visibly until she finally took pity on him and led him into her bedroom.

Dimitra gave a little shiver of anticipation and pressed 'delete' in mistake for 'insert' and watched in horror as the file she had spent an hour compiling disappeared from the computer screen.

Saffron opened up her e-mails, hoping to see one from Vasi telling her about his father's opinion of the idea to turn his house into a holiday centre. There was nothing. She shrugged. There was plenty of time for him to send one through during the evening. From an envelope she removed her credit card receipts. Her salary would be through on the last day of the month, and a large bill to her credit card company had already arrived. She must check to see that the payment they were requesting was correct.

She spread them out on the desk before her and began to tick them off. The one for her flight was the largest, followed by some shopping she had done at the local supermarket and then refused to let Marianne reimburse her. They would not hear of her paying anything towards her stay with them and she had insisted that she must make a contribution. She looked at them. The goods were itemised in Greek, but quite clearly at the top of each bill was the date and the time.

Carefully she ticked each one off. Once the conversion from Euros to sterling had been made they still amounted to considerably more than she had realised at the time. It was being with Vasi that had made her careless. He never glanced twice at a bill before he paid it. She wondered how much his credit card bill would have amounted to over the time she had been in Crete. He had always insisted that he paid for their restaurant meals and used his credit card to do so. Credit card receipts; they had a date and time; provided Vasi had kept his he could prove what time they left the restaurant on the Friday evening.

Saffron picked up her mobile 'phone and called his number, relieved when he answered immediately.

'Vasi, this is very important.'

'What has happened?'

'Nothing, everything is fine here. Listen to me. Do you have your credit card receipts for our restaurant meals?'

'They are around.'

Saffron breathed a sigh of relief. 'They have the date and time on them. Find the one for our meal on that Friday night and it will prove what time we left the restaurant.'

There was silence from the other end of the 'phone.

'You do have it, don't you, Vasi?'

'It is somewhere around. I will have to look for it.'

'If you can't find it the restaurant should have their copy.'

'They will have sent it to the bank by now for payment.'

'Then the bank will have a record of it, or the credit company.' Saffron felt frustrated that he seemed so unconcerned. 'We should have thought and asked the police to check it out earlier. Ask Mr Christos to take a copy of it and give a copy to your solicitor. It proves you were not on the highway.'

Saffron heard Vasi give a deep sigh. 'Mr Christos suggested today that I drove to the highway after I had taken you home. A restaurant receipt will only prove that I did not do so during the evening.'

'Do they still not know what time the accident happened?'

'Dimitra says Alecos has only just regained consciousness. I'm sure the police will take a statement from him as soon as possible. He may remember the time he was driving there.'

'You will look for it, won't you, Vasi?'

'Yes, I promise. Thank you. It was a good idea you had.'

'Was Mr Christos serious?'

'I am not sure.'

'What did he say exactly?' Saffron frowned. She had liked the policeman and Vasi had been of the impression that Mr Christos had believed him when he said he had nothing to do with Alecos's accident.

'He said I could have taken you home then stolen a car and driven to the highway and caused the accident.'

'Why would you steal a car?'

'So that I would not be suspected.'

Saffron shook her head. 'That doesn't make sense. You steal a

ALECOS

car and have an accident and then you go home and damage your own which immediately makes you a suspect. That's just stupid.'

'He said it was just an informal chat. He said he really wanted to ask me about the Kronos hotel in Hersonissos.'

'What was that about?' asked Saffron curiously.

'He said it was to do with another enquiry. He just wanted to check with me to see if it was still open.'

Saffron frowned. 'He could have 'phoned you or the hotel to find that out.'

'It was no inconvenience to go in. I was at the Katerina. What have you been doing today? Operations or consultations?'

'Eight operations were scheduled and then the last one had to be cancelled for an emergency.' Saffron sighed. She did not want to discuss her day. Vasi's problems were uppermost in her mind. 'Vasi, you won't forget to look for that restaurant receipt, will you?'

'I will do it now. When I have found it I will mail you.'

'And you will copy it and take it in to Mr Christos?'

'I promise. Do not worry, Saffie.'

Tuesday 2nd October

Alecos felt better. His head ache had diminished to a dull throb and his breathing was less painful. The oxygen mask had been removed from his face and he had spent an hour without its assistance. He wished the nurse would come in and replace it. He needed to think and the effort of remembering to take shallow breaths took all his concentration. What was so important about some papers and their connection to Vasi? He drifted off to sleep; awakening suddenly as a stab of pain shot through him as he inadvertently took a deep breath.

He fumbled for the bell to summon the nurse, who appeared with alacrity.

'Breathing – hurts,' he gasped.

Quickly the nurse placed the oxygen mask over his mouth and nose and turned it on to allow a small amount of the oxygen to flow through and assist his breathing. Immediately Alecos relaxed. He could now fill his lungs again without the excruciating pain. He closed his eyes again. He must try to think.

He had visited Dimitra, but it was not his usual weekend visit or he would have stayed there over night. He had to return to Aghios Nikolaos. He needed to go into the bank on Saturday morning to do something important; something to do with some papers and a back-up disk. Back-up disk. A back-up disk of Vasi's hotel accounts. Why did he have that with him? Had Dimitra given it to him?

Slowly the memory came back to him. He had bought the

Imperia hotel from under Vasi's nose. To raise the capital he needed for the purchase he had moved money from Vasi's hotel accounts into semi-dormant bank accounts and then into a new account in his name. He had been sure that Vasi would buy the hotel back from him at an inflated price, enabling him to transfer the money he had borrowed back to the rightful owner.

Vasi had refused. He felt a white hot anger go through him. His scheme had been so simple and fool proof. The papers with the details of the accounts he had used along with a copy of the back-up showing the transactions on Vasi's hotel accounts had been in his jacket pocket. He groaned. He had planned to go into the bank on the Saturday and replace the money into the hotel accounts. There were bound to be other semi-dormant accounts where he could access more cash to replace the amount he had paid for the Imperia. It was unlikely that any of the customers who used their accounts so rarely would realise for a considerable amount of time, if ever that the balance was incorrect. Should the errors be drawn to the attention of the bank it would appear there had been a computer malfunction.

He had never intended to steal the money. If Vasi had paid up as he should have done then he would have put all the money back into the various accounts where it belonged. He wondered if that was why the policeman had been in his room the previous day. Had Vasi reported him for misappropriating funds?

He groaned again. At least if the papers and back-up disk were safely in his father's keeping he could tell the bank he had discovered and was investigating the problem. Rather than dreading the difficult visit he was expecting from his parents he was now longing for them to arrive.

Vasi found the credit card slip relating to the meal he and Saffron had shared on the Friday evening. He had stuffed it into an envelope along with other credit card slips and put it in his bedside drawer. He never bothered to look at them until his statement arrived. He would then count the number of slips and provided they matched the number of transactions recorded he did not check the individual amounts. He had never noticed there was a date and time on any of them.

Vasi placed the receipt carefully into his wallet. He would copy it and then take it in to Mr Christos when he made his daily visit to the police station. If the time of the accident could be ascertained and it had occurred whilst he was in the restaurant or shortly afterwards the rather large bill would prove he could not have been involved.

Christos studied the slip of paper intently. It was clearly dated for the Friday evening and the time was eleven thirty seven when it had passed through the computerised credit card machine. If Mr Plastirakis's information about the damaged car passing him between ten thirty and eleven was correct there was no way it could have been Vasi Iliopolakis driving it.

Various other people had reported seeing the barrier broken, but at a later time during the evening and early hours as they drove along the highway. Many others must have driven past and never noticed. That was not surprising. They would have been concentrating on the road and on that particular stretch there were no lights. It was unfortunate that the accident had not been reported until the early hours of the morning by a curious tourist who had stopped to look at the barrier and seen the car down in the ravine.

He scratched his head. This was an enigma. The damage described by Mr Plastirakis matched the damage on the car belonging to Stelios Papandrakis, but Mrs Vikelakis had been adamant that her son had accused Vasi of pushing him off the road. If Stelios Papandrakis had been sacked from his position as hotel manager by Vasi Iliopolakis he might well hold a grudge against the man. He could have vandalised Vasi's car from spite, but it was a coincidence that it should have taken place on the same night as the accident.

There were also the anonymous telephone calls, one giving

part of Vasi's car registration number and the second accusing him of being the driver. That could also have been a vengeful act by Stelios Papandrakis, but how would he have known that Vasi was under suspicion? All his enquiries seemed to lead back to Stelios Papandrakis, but apart from a damaged car he had no evidence against him. Why should the man have drawn attention to himself by reporting his car stolen unless he was genuinely innocent?

It could be worth making a telephone call to Babbis to see if his report on the cars was completed. That might shed some light on the problem.

Mr and Mrs Vikelakis entered Alecos's room quietly. Alecos's eyes flickered open.

'Hello,' he greeted them weakly.

Mrs Vikelakis hurried to his side. 'Are you feeling better? What has the doctor said? We haven't spoken to him yet. Do you know when you're being transferred?"

Alecos ignored her questions. 'Pappa, papers – in my – jacket.'

Mr Vikelakis beamed. 'I handed them in at the bank. Stavros Tanakis 'phoned and asked if any papers you had relating to bank affairs could be sent up to him in Heraklion. I wasn't sure what he wanted, but there were some papers and one of those new fangled memory sticks in with your clothes. I took them into the branch at Aghios Nikolaos and they said they would send them up to him. He promised to return anything that was personal. I haven't heard from him so they must have been the ones he wanted. Good job they were safely in your coat pocket. If they'd been lying loose on the seat they would probably have been blown away.'

Alecos groaned. If the papers were in Heraklion it must mean that Vasi had discovered his manipulations and asked for an enquiry. He wished now they had been lying loose in the car and blown away.

'He's hurting, Nikos. Ring his bell and get the nurse to come and give him something to ease his pain,' ordered Mrs Vikelakis.

Alecos glared at his mother as best he could through his swollen eyelids. He was not groaning with physical pain. Having been anxious to see his parents and ascertain if his father had the papers he was now ready for them to leave. If the papers were in the hands of the manager of the bank in Heraklion he was certain that was why there had been a policeman in his room the previous day. If he appeared again he would claim loss of memory of any events before the accident.

'Babbis, is there any chance you have finished the reports on the accident vehicles?' asked Christos.

'Should be ready in about another half an hour. I'll send a copy through to you.'

'Tell me what forensics came up with regarding the paint samples.'

'They haven't done any work on them. Thranassis said there was no need. The accident victim has identified the driver who forced him off the road.'

Christos clicked his tongue in annoyance. 'The victim's mother claimed he had told her the name of the person. When the police tried to interview him he was hardly conscious and the doctor forbade any questioning. Until he's made a formal statement I don't think we should discount any evidence.'

'So what am I supposed to do?' asked Babbis sulkily. 'You tell me one thing and Thranassis tells me another.'

Christos sighed. 'I still think those paint samples should be checked out with forensics, but another week won't make any difference. Just make sure they don't get lost. What about the prints on the other car?'

'They're still working on it. It's smothered.'

'Inside is more important than out. Any passerby could have put their hand on the outside. I'll have a look at the records Athens holds and see if the prints of the owner are on record. I asked him to give me a sample and he refused. I had no grounds to insist, but I get the feeling we may find something recorded under his name,' explained Christos patiently.

'If you know the name of the owner what's so important about the prints?'

'He claims his car was stolen. If it was, there should be prints other than his own inside. I'd like to know who they belong to.'

'We're not likely to have the prints of a joy-rider on file.'

'I agree, but there's just a chance that the vehicle was stolen by a professional thief. He may have used it whilst committing a crime and abandoned it afterwards.'

Christos telephoned Athens and requested they conducted a search for any information they might have on Stelios Papandrakis.

'I'm particularly interested to know if you have his prints on record. I asked him to give them last week and he immediately refused. Made me suspicious. What is he hiding?'

'What are you holding him for?'

'I'm not. I have no reason to suspect him of any crime at the moment. He reported his car stolen. It's been found, damaged and vandalised. I just wanted his prints to eliminate his from any others that might be found inside.'

'I'll 'phone you back if I find anything.'

By late afternoon Christos had decided the search he had requested had been fruitless when the telephone rang and the officer from Athens informed him he had a match.

'Picked up for possession. A few grams, said it was for his own use. First offence so he was let off with a caution, but printed nonetheless. Do you want me to send them through?'

Christos nodded. 'Please. Could you send a copy to forensics in Heraklion and another to me down here?'

'No problem. I'll do it now.'

Dimitra had brushed her hair and renewed her make-up before leaving the Central hotel. She would visit Alecos and hope that she would be able to see Dr Melanakis. She was sure he would invite her out for coffee if he was free today. She had seen the way he had looked at her when she was wearing her tight trousers and T-shirt and wished she could have worn them to work that day, rather than a skirt. Mr Iliopolakis did not like her wearing trousers. She attributed this to the fact that he liked to look at her legs, rather than his insistence that all the female staff wore a skirt and blouse and the men must wear a formal shirt, as a matter of principle, although they were allowed to leave off their ties when it was very hot.

As she entered Alecos's room she was disconcerted to see both of his parents in attendance and was thankful that she had not worn her tight trousers. She had sensed his father's disapproval of her on her previous visit. She gave them a bright smile.

'How is Alecos today?' she asked quietly.

'He seems a little better, but he's still in pain. We had to call the nurse to ask her to get him something to ease it.' Mrs Vikelakis answered her and looked Dimitra up and down critically. The girl could do with an extra few inches on her skirt and the top buttons on her blouse needed fastening.

'I'll not stop,' smiled Dimitra. 'I was passing on my way home from work and thought I would just call in to ask after his progress. Alecos,' she bent over the bed, 'Are you awake, Alecos? It's me, Dimitra.'

Alecos opened his eyes as far as he was able. 'Disk,' he muttered.

'You returned it to me. It was a good job you did as there had been some error on the accounts and it was needed to sort everything out.'

Alecos felt alarmed. 'Who?' he asked.

'Mr Iliopolakis and Mr Vasi sorted it. Something to do with the bank computer. Nothing for you to worry about.' Dimitra smiled at him brightly. 'You do look better than when I saw you last,' she observed. 'I was so worried when I first saw you. I spoke to the doctor the other day and he says you're progressing very well. I'm not going to stop as you have your parents here. I'll call again in a

ALECOS

few days and I'm sure I'll see even more of an improvement in you.'

She bent and kissed his cheek lightly, smiled farewell to Mr and Mrs Vikelakis and left the room hurriedly. Now for the real purpose of her visit.

Doctor Melanakis eyed Dimitra through the glass panel of the door. She was wearing a skirt again and her long and shapely legs looked more attractive than ever. He clenched and unclenched his fists. How he longed to have a handful of that succulent, firm flesh. He wiped his sweating hands down his trousers and walked towards her.

'Hello, Dimitra. Have you just finished work?'

Dimitra smiled up at him. 'I just popped in on my way home to visit Alecos. He seems considerably better. Are you able to tell me about his progress?'

'Would you consider joining me for coffee again? It is so much easier to talk away from my work environment.'

'I would be delighted.'

Dimitra accompanied the doctor across the road from the hospital and into the coffee shop they had patronised before. Dimitra immediately made her way to the bench seat and settled herself comfortably. Whilst Dr Melanakis busied himself up at the counter purchasing a frappe and a black coffee Dimitra took the opportunity to pull her skirt up a little higher.

'I cannot tempt you with a pastry on this occasion?'

Dimitra shook her head and glanced at him coyly from under her eyelashes. 'I was always told a girl should resist temptation.'

Dr Melanakis raised his eyebrows. 'And do you?'

'Sometimes it is very difficult. Do you give in to temptation, Filippos?'

The doctor swallowed. If he gave in to temptation at this moment he would be arrested. 'It can be impossible on occasions not to do so.'

If her skirt rode up any higher he would be able to have a tantalizing glimpse of the soft hair between her legs. Was she inviting him? Dare he place his hand on her bare thigh? He lifted his coffee cup with a shaking hand and wiped his mouth with a paper napkin after taking a mouthful. He deliberately dropped the napkin into his lap and as he retrieved it he had the perfect opportunity to run his hand along her thigh.

Dimitra gave a little wriggle of pleasure. He wished now he had suggested they had sat in his car. He was sure he would have been able to insert his hand into her panties and grasp that desirable, plump mound. Filippos Melanakis took a chance and squeezed the inside of her thigh. Dimitra gave a little giggle and placed her hand on his, as if to restrain him.

Dimitra leaned towards him. 'I understand Alecos is making good progress?'

Filippos nodded. He could almost see her breasts down the unbuttoned neck of her blouse and the feel of her thigh beneath his hand was exciting him almost unbearably. Reluctantly he withdrew his hand from her leg. He must control himself.

'Yes, he has regained consciousness and spoken a few words. He is still in considerable pain from his injuries, of course, but there has been a marked improvement in his condition.'

'And there is no sign of brain damage?'

'It is still rather too early to tell. He may have some memory loss. That is often the way the mind deals with traumatic events. It will not surprise me if he has no recollection at all of the accident.'

Dimitra nodded solemnly. 'I understand. Will that be a problem to him?'

'If it is only the accident he cannot recall it will be no problem. It is when the memory is affected by the loss of customary mundane events that the patient experiences distress.'

Dimitra frowned. 'How do you mean?'

'He may not remember how to cut up his food, to use a knife and fork. That is when the patient goes to therapy and he has to be educated again as if he was a child.'

'How long do people who suffer like that spend having therapy?'

Doctor Melanakis shrugged. 'They all differ. Some people find they can cope after just a few sessions, others never regain the ability to truly look after themselves again.'

'How sad,' murmured Dimitra. 'I do hope Alecos will not be badly affected in any way.'

'The next few weeks will give an indication. The nurses monitor his conversation with them. They are the ones who usually notice a problem. Visitors can also be helpful if they notice anything untoward in the patient's speech.'

Dimitra raised her eyebrows. 'In what way?'

'Well, he may well ask for a 'dunk' when he means a drink. The word is similar, but he cannot remember it.'

'Oh, dear, that could cause some embarrassing problems if someone did not know him! Alecos asked for a drink the other day when I was there, so at least he knows that word.'

Doctor Melanakis was just about to put his hand on Dimitra's leg again and suggest that he drove her home when his pager went off. He fumbled in his jacket pocket and drew it out. He had completely forgotten the weekly meeting to discuss which patients the doctors considered well enough to be discharged or transferred to their local hospital within the next few days. He debated whether he could claim to have a prior appointment, but that could lead to some very awkward questions having to be answered.

'Unfortunately I will have to leave you,' he smiled, his regret genuine. 'I am due to attend a meeting at six this evening and I am unable to miss it.' Doctor Melanakis stood and moved the table out a short way to assist Dimitra to stand.

'Would you have the time to speak to me next week if I called in?'

'Certainly. Shall we make that definite date for Monday?'

Dimitra gave a little giggle. 'That makes it sound like quite a romantic meeting.'

'I will see you over here in the coffee shop. Then if I am delayed you will not have to hang around in the reception area.'

'I hope nothing will delay you, but I do understand that your patients have to come first.'

Doctor Melanakis smiled. He would ensure that he was able to take her home on that occasion and he knew exactly how he would enjoy every second of his time with her if his plans came to fruition.

Alecos ignored the presence of his parents. He wished they had not been there when Dimitra had visited. He would have liked to be able to ask her if Vasi and his father knew he had tampered with their accounts and also if the knowledge had been passed on to the bank. Until he knew the situation and was capable of thinking carefully and planning he would feign loss of memory. No one would be able to prove otherwise. Once he could talk and concentrate more easily he might well ask Dimitra to visit him so he could question her and then he would be able to formulate a plan.

If he could get his hands on the back-up disk again and access the bank accounts he could change the name on his bank account to that of Dimitra. That would show him as the innocent victim of a manipulative and scheming woman. She worked for the Iliopolakis chain of hotels and she had been tempted. Alecos was sure he would be able to alter the accounts to exonerate himself and implicate her. He would be able to work out the details when he was once again able to concentrate properly.

'Thranassis, I am not prepared to charge Vasi Iliopolakis until I have made some more enquiries or until Mr Vikelakis has made a statement under oath.'

'He's already accused Vasi Iliopolakis. You told me yourself that Mrs Vikelakis had been in to the station and said her son had said Vasi pushed him off the road,' Thranassis replied angrily.

Christos sighed. 'I know, but when you sent your officer to take his statement he was barely conscious. He could have just said the first name that came into his head. I have a bill here which shows the time Mr Vasi left the restaurant and a statement by Mr Plastirakis about a damaged car driving recklessly and trying to pass him between ten thirty and eleven.'

'The statement from Mr Plastirakis means nothing. That could have been any car.'

'That is why I have asked for paint samples to be analysed by forensics. If those found at the crash site prove to belong to Mr Vasi's car I'll agree you have a case against him.'

'We've been told part of the registration number and it's the same as Mr Vasi's. A witness says he saw Mr Vasi driving and causing the accident. We already have a case,' insisted Thranassis.

'I'm not prepared to consider that evidence until we know the identity of the anonymous caller. I think that could be someone who has a grudge against Mr Vasi and has taken advantage of the situation to implicate him,' explained Christos patiently. 'I think the car that took Mr Vikelakis off the road is more likely the vandalised one that I sent up. The number on the wing mirror found at the site matches that still in situ on the car.'

'That could have been tossed there by whoever stole the car.'

'Quite true, but rather a coincidence for it to land where it did. Another reason for forensics to test the paint samples. See if any of them match up with Mr Papandrakis's car. I'm sure if we tried to charge Mr Vasi at this stage his solicitor would be able to discount all the evidence you say we have against him. I'd rather wait until we're a hundred per cent certain that he's guilty. You don't want to end up being sued for wrongful arrest.'

'Me!'

'You're the one who is trying to press charges. I'm not prepared to sign an arrest warrant.'

Christos smiled to himself as the receiver was slammed down forcefully, ending their conversation.

Thursday 4th October

'Vasi, I've just been told that Flora has died.'

'What!' Vasi could hardly believe the news Yiorgo was imparting to him. 'When did it happen?'

'Last night.'

'How?'

'I don't know any details. Makkis saw that Manolis had not come down to his boat so he asked Andreas where he was. Andreas didn't know and he asked Dimitris to go up to the house and see if anything was amiss with Manolis. He's getting on a bit and they thought he might be ill.'

'And they found it was Flora. Poor Manolis. Is there anything we can do?'

'I'll go up later and have a word with him, but I doubt it. What can you do when that happens?'

'I was thinking of funeral arrangements. If there's any problem, you know, financially, give me a call.'

Yiorgo was silent for a moment. 'Manolis is a very proud man.'

'I wouldn't make it obvious; just have a quiet word with him. I could even say that my grandfather had left him something in his Will and the funds had only just been released.'

'I doubt if he'd believe you after all this time. I'm sure the other boatmen would contribute if he's short of money.'

'I'll let my father know. I'll also 'phone Giovanni and tell him. I'll come in to town tonight and you can tell me the arrangements for her funeral.'

'You'll have to come to the house. Barbara's working.'

'No problem. What time does her shift start?'

'She's on seven 'til eleven.'

'I'll be there about eight. Do you want me to pick up a pizza?'
Vasi heard Yiorgo hesitate. 'No, I'll have fed the boys by then.'

'I'll come earlier and bring enough for all of us.'

'They'd enjoy that.' Yiorgo accepted gratefully, knowing that
Vasi would bring far more than enough for one meal. The remaining
slices could go into the fridge and make a meal for the boys the
following day, even if Barbara said it wasn't healthy to eat pizza.

'There's enough here to feed an army,' declared Yiorgo as Vasi
placed the boxes into his outstretched hands and returned to the
car for more.

Vasi grinned at him. 'Don't you remember how we could eat
when we were their age? It was like a contest to see which one of
us could manage more than the other. Cathy used to make triple
the amount on the days when you were eating with us.'

Yiorgo smiled guiltily. He knew he had overeaten when he was
at Vasi's. Yiorgo had learnt at an early age that if there was a large
bowl of salad and more than one loaf of bread on the table there
would be very little else for his supper that night.

'We'll feed the boys, then they can go out to play whilst we
talk.' Yiorgo placed plates on the table and sent his sons to wash
their hands, sending the older one back a second time. 'That one
just hates washing.' He shook his head in despair. 'I dread to think
what kind of a dirty scruffy individual he'll turn into.'

'He's so like you,' declared Vasi.

'I'm not dirty or scruffy,' replied Yiorgo indignantly.

'I meant to look at.' Vasi would not have dreamt of mentioning
that Yiorgo's trousers were fraying at the hems and his shoes
needed to be repaired. He would have a look in his wardrobe when
he returned home and turn out some of his old trousers to give to

Yiorgo, ostensibly for work.

'I'm going to put two of these pizzas in the fridge now otherwise they'll stuff themselves silly and be up all night with stomach ache.'

'Can you put the ice cream in the fridge at the same time? I hope it hasn't started to melt already. If the boys know there's ice cream to follow they won't risk eating too much and not having any room left.'

'I'll bring some beer, or would you rather have wine?'

'Not with pizza. Beer is fine.'

Vasi divided the pizzas into portions and placed a plate in front of each boy.

'He's got a bigger piece than me,' complained Andreas.

'That's because I can't cut straight,' Vasi informed him. 'You can have another piece when you've eaten that.'

'You wouldn't like to take this trio back with you for a week or two, I suppose?' suggested Yiorgo. 'You deal with them better than I do. I would have cut another slice and given it to him to keep him quiet.'

'It's called the novelty factor,' replied Vasi. 'I would have no idea how to keep them amused and out of mischief all day.'

'They're not bad boys. I just find it a bit trying when I get back from work and have to be responsible for them rather than sitting down to relax.'

'No doubt Barbara finds it the same, having to go out to work in the evening when she should be relaxing.'

'She wouldn't have to go out to work if she hadn't insisted I leave the navy,' grumbled Yiorgo.

Vasi wagged his finger at him. 'You had to make a choice, remember, and you chose these three.'

'I just made the wrong choice years ago.'

'You could have made a far worse one. Be thankful for what you do have.' Vasi raised his bottle of beer. 'Cheers.'

The boys finished their meal, scraping the ice cream bowls clean, and Andreas still insisting he had been given less pizza than his brothers. Yiorgo threatened to clip his ear if he continued to complain, but Vasi smiled.

'If Andreas is still hungry I will take a pizza out of the fridge and he can sit there and eat it all if he wishes.' Vasi shook his head sorrowfully. 'It will be a shame if there is not enough left for him to have some more tomorrow and he will have to watch his brothers eating theirs. No doubt his mother will be able to find him some bread to eat.'

Andreas looked at Vasi doubtfully. He finally decided it was not worth risking having to go without pizza the following day. 'Can we go out and play, Pappa?'

Yiorgo nodded. 'Not too much noise,' he warned them.

'We'll only be playing football.'

Yiorgo sighed. He knew exactly how noisy that would become when they were joined by the neighbours' children and the game took place up and down the street accompanied by shouts, yells and cheers.

'So,' said Vasi, leaning back in his chair, 'What did you find out about Flora's funeral?'

Yiorgo frowned and shook his head. 'I didn't really find out anything. I went up to see Manolis and he was just sitting there. He kept saying she wasn't to go into the tower and had to stay here.'

Vasi caught his breath. 'He obviously thinks she'll be taken over to Spinalonga and placed in the tower there.'

'But he knows that hasn't happened since the island was closed.'

'He's probably in shock and not thinking straight. Had Flora been ill?'

'Dimitris said Manolis hadn't mentioned her being ill, but he had looked very tired some mornings, as though he hadn't slept well.'

'I wonder what he'll do? As far as I know he hasn't any relatives to go to live with.'

Yiorgo gave Vasi a horrified look. 'You're not suggesting I ask him to come and live here? Barbara would never stand for it.'

Vasi shook his head. 'Certainly not. I was just speculating.'

'Did you tell Cathy?'

'She wants me to telephone her as soon as I know when Flora's funeral is to be held. She and Vasilis will drive down and bring Rebecca with them. I spoke to Giovanni and he said he would tell Yannis. I imagine they'll all come as well. Is there anyone else we ought to notify?'

'I shouldn't think so. The fishermen will spread the word between themselves and there's no one else left who was connected with the island. Flora was the last and now she's dead.'

'The end of an era.' Vasi shook his head sadly and drained his beer. 'Any more where that came from?'

Manolis sat and looked at the empty bed where Flora had spent her last hours. The doctor had insisted that she be taken away and placed in the morgue until her funeral. He was numb. Yannis had taken to drink after Phaedra had died and Basil had left Crete planning never to return after the death of Katerina. Now he truly knew how both men must have felt.

He gave a deep sigh. He had to get his affairs in order. He had no family and he saw no need to make a present to the government. With an effort he rose and walked along the road to the church. As he entered he removed his old cap with the two bullet holes and held it between his hands.

'Father, may I speak with you?'

The priest looked at him with compassion. No doubt the man had come to seek solace for his loss. 'Of course, my son. Come through.' He led the way to his parlour and indicated that Manolis should take a seat.

'How can I give you comfort? We both know that your beloved wife is in a better place now, free from pain and living with the angels.'

Manolis looked at him sceptically. 'I'd like you to conduct the burial service for her. She has to be buried in the local church yard.'

'Of course. All the inhabitants of Aghios Nikolaos are taken there as a matter of course unless their relatives wish them to return to the town of their birth.'

'You must make sure she is buried there; nowhere else.' Manolis gazed at him intently.

'Certainly. I guarantee that is where she will rest so you can visit her frequently.'

'When can you do it and how much will it cost?'

The priest looked at him. He was not used to his parishioners being so direct when they had so recently been bereaved. 'Would Saturday suit you?'

Manolis shrugged. The day was immaterial to him.

'Would that give you enough time to notify relatives and friends?'

'I have no relatives.'

'Saturday it is then. I'll make the necessary arrangements. Just let me know if there is anything personal you would like added to the service. You don't have to do it now. You have a couple of days to think about it.'

'I'd like you to write a letter for me. My hands are not as good as they were.' Manolis flexed a gnarled and scarred hand.

The priest nodded. 'Certainly. Do you wish to do that now?'

Manolis gave a deep sigh. 'Yes. Get it over with.'

The priest pulled a sheet of paper towards him. 'Who is it to be addressed to?'

'I don't know her name.'

The priest gave the fisherman a puzzled look. 'How am I to write a letter to someone if you do not know their name?'

'It's to the old lady who lives with Mr Andronicatis.'

'So shall I address the letter to him and ask him to give it to her?'

'I can deliver it.' Manolis frowned. 'Address it to Father Andreas's sister.'

'And what would you like me to say in this letter?' The priest was beginning to think that the death of his wife had definitely affected the fisherman's brain.

Manolis closed his eyes. 'I spent the war years with the resistance.' He was still proud of the memory.

'Is that what you would like me to write?'

'No. I'm just telling you something,' Manolis spoke impatiently. 'I sailed with an Englishman and we helped wherever we could, delivering supplies and taking people to safety until the Germans smashed my boat. It lay on the beach in splinters.' Manolis felt another lump coming into his throat as he remembered his beloved boat. 'After that we went to the mountains and fought with the resistance. When the war ended I came back here. My English friend entrusted me with a mission on his behalf. I visited Father Andreas in Heraklion and he gave me his father's fishing boat. He had no use for it.'

The priest looked at Manolis dubiously. This sounded like the ramblings of an old man.

'I have to give it back. I shall not be using it any more. Father Andreas is dead, but his sister is alive. She is very old. She will know who to give the boat to, or she may wish to sell it. Whatever she does with it is no concern of mine. This is what I want you to write. To tell her that I have given her back her father's boat.'

The priest raised his eyebrows. It was the strangest request that had ever been made of him. 'If you no longer have your boat how will you make your living?'

Manolis shook his head sadly. 'I shall never go to Spinalonga again.' He wiped a tear from his eye and spoke gruffly. 'Are you going to write it?'

The priest bent his head and wrote a few lines. 'Do you wish me to read it to you?'

'I can read,' Manolis informed him stiffly. 'It is writing I find difficult.' Manolis took the sheet of paper and read the words slowly.

After the war Father Andreas made me a present of his father's boat. I have no further use for it so I am returning it to his sister.

He nodded. 'If I sign it will you witness my signature? I want it to be official.'

Father Constantine was not at all sure that the letter would be a legal document if challenged in a court of law, but that would not be his concern. He watched whilst Manolis scrawled his name across the bottom, then added his own and the date.

'Could you write *'To Father Andreas's sister'* on the envelope?'

The priest complied and watched as Manolis folded the paper carefully and placed it inside the envelope along with two keys. 'The padlock and the engine,' he explained. 'Thank you, Father. How much do I owe you? I'll pay you for the funeral service now.' With a heavy sigh he added. 'It is another duty done.'

From the church Manolis walked to the outskirts of the town to the stone mason and ordered a simple cross to be made from granite with Flora's name and the date of her death inscribed. Again he paid in cash and left instructions that Father Constantine was to be informed when the monument was completed and it could be placed at the head of the grave.

Christos looked at the notes he had made. Stelios Papandrakis had been employed by Vasi Iliopolakis and given the sack earlier in the year. He could easily have damaged Vasi's car as an act of revenge, but why wait so long? Christos scratched his head. If Stelios Papandrakis had been the culprit it was a strange coincidence that the accident on the highway had taken place the same night. The other coincidence was the theft of Stelios Papandrakis's car at the same time. He dismissed the anonymous telephone calls as evidence, feeling certain they had been made out of spite by Stelios.

He read again the statement by Mr Plastirakis. If the car he saw had caused the accident there was no way Vasi Iliopolakis could have been driving. The receipt from the restaurant proved he had been in there at the time he claimed. Christos had interviewed the owner and he confirmed that Vasi and Saffron had eaten there that night, but he had been busy and could not say at what time they had left.

Christos sighed heavily. He really could do nothing more until forensics returned their report.

Vasi e-mailed Saffron with the news of Flora's death. He reminded her that Flora had originally lived on Spinalonga and after the restrictions were lifted on the island Manolis had married her and brought her to the mainland.

'She was never truly accepted. Had they not known that she had lived on Spinalonga they would have ignored her amputation. Despite her having been given a clean bill of health, along with so many of the others, people were still afraid that she might infect them. She tried to ignore the attitude of the local people and attempted to get to know her neighbours. It took a number of years before they eventually accepted her.

My grandfather visited their house on many occasions, and sometimes Rebecca went with him. They had no children and it was Flora who tended their garden. According to Rebecca, Manolis was not interested. He enjoyed sitting out there in the evenings and was always willing to move a pot of flowers for her, but he never planted anything himself.

I met Flora a few times when I went to church in Aghios Nikolaos rather than in Elounda. She and Manolis always sat at the back and no one was sitting next to them. When I did so people stared at me and whispered amongst themselves. Manolis asked me back to their house on every occasion and I had no hesitation in accepting to join them in their meal that Flora had cooked.

Flora was an excellent cook and considering she had only one arm she managed amazingly well, rarely asking Manolis to help her. I don't know what he will do now. He is really getting too old to be able to manage his boat safely on his own. If he gives up taking visitors to Spinalonga he will only have fishing to provide him with an income and how will he spend his time when he is not at sea?

We will all go to the funeral, of course. Giovanni and Marianne have said they will come to the service, and I am sure Yannis and

Ourania will be there. Some of the fishermen are bound to come, along with his immediate neighbours.

I felt very sad when Yiorgo told me. To the best of my knowledge Flora was the last person alive who had lived on Spinalonga.'

Saturday 6th October

Manolis walked slowly along behind the black draped coffin as it was carried through the street to the church. He had expected to be the only mourner and was surprised to see the other boatmen had given up their day to join him in his grief. He was even more surprised when he noticed Basil's widow dapping at her eyes surreptitiously and accompanied by her daughter and son in law. Vasi and Yiorgo stood close to them and he realised he had another duty to attend to.

The church was nearly full, but Manolis thought bitterly that many of the congregation were not there to mourn the loss of Flora, but to see for themselves that the leper woman was no longer in their midst. He saw them crossing themselves devoutly and murmuring prayers, finally exorcising the town of her presence.

The number that followed him to the graveyard was less and he averted his eyes as Flora's tiny coffin was placed into the ground. He would wait until they had completely filled her grave with earth before he left. He had to ensure she was not removed and taken over to Spinalonga to be placed in the tower as soon as he turned his back.

The priest touched his arm. 'It is over, my son. You can leave now.'

Manolis shook his head. 'I shall stay here.'

'Then I have to ask you to excuse me.'

Manolis shrugged and did not try to stop the priest as he walked away. Gradually those who had walked to the cemetery chose to follow the priest's example until only Vasi and Yiorgo were left standing there with him watching the earth land on her coffin, gradually covering it and filling the hole.

'I think we should see him home,' said Yiorgo quietly. 'He seems to be in a daze.'

Vasi nodded. 'I wonder if a neighbour who would sit with him, or maybe one of the boatmen.'

Yiorgo took Manolis's arm. 'Time to go, my friend.'

Manolis let out a deep sigh and allowed himself to be led away. He did not look back. There was no need. He would be returning soon enough.

They walked in silence to his cottage and were wondering if they should approach a neighbour when Manolis spoke to them for the first time.

'You need to come in. I have to give you something.'

Yiorgo and Vasi exchanged looks. They were not sure if they wanted to go inside and possibly have to try to comfort the broken man.

From the table he picked up the envelope with the letter and the keys to his boat. 'I'd like you to deliver this for me. You know the family. Make sure it gets to the right person.' He pushed it into Vasi's hands. Written on the envelope was 'For Father Andreas's sister.'

Vasi looked at it in surprise. Why was Manolis sending a letter to Annita? 'You want me to give this to Giovanni's grandmother?'

Manolis shrugged. 'If that's who she is. Make sure she reads it.' He reached up and removed his old hat with the bullet holes from the peg on the wall and passed that to Vasi also. 'Look after my hat.' He walked over to the door and held it open. 'Goodbye,' he said and waited for them to pass through.

Vasi looked at the hat in his hands almost reverently. 'Why do you think Manolis gave me his hat? I thought he treasured it.'

'Seeing you probably reminded him of the time he spent with

your grandfather. He's probably planning to have a good turn out and throw away a lot of rubbish.'

'Well I'm certainly glad he didn't throw this out. It's, well, symbolic.'

'Why do you think he's written a letter to Giovanni's grandmother? He didn't even seem to know her name.'

'Maybe it was something Flora asked him to do. It was her husband who helped Yannis to get the islanders declared free from infection, remember. It's probably just a letter to say thank you. I'll drive back that way and deliver it on my way home. It's the least I can do to say thank you for his hat.'

'Time for a beer?' asked Yiorgo.

'I could certainly do with one. I mustn't stay too long. Pappa, Cathy and Rebecca are staying at the house tonight. It's all ready for them, but I ought to put in an appearance at a reasonable time and be sociable.'

Annita turned the letter over in her hands. 'Why on earth should the man write to me? I don't know him.'

'I have no idea,' smiled Vasi, 'but he was most insistent that I delivered it to you and ensured you read it.'

'Oh well, open it for me. If it requires an answer I'll ask Marianne to write to him and Yannis can deliver it on his way to the shop tomorrow. What are those keys?'

Vasi placed them on the table beside Annita. 'They were in the envelope.' He handed her the sheet of folded paper.'

'Oh!' Annita read the few words again. 'Well, well, that's a surprise. I had no idea.'

Vasi looked at her curiously.

'My brother gave Manolis our father's fishing boat. Did you know that?'

Vasi shook his head. 'I know the Germans smashed his boat, but I never thought to ask him where he bought his new one.'

'He didn't buy it.' Annita shook her head in disbelief. 'Andreas *gave* it to him and now he's giving it back to me! What am I going to do with it? I'm rather too old to go out fishing now.'

Vasi smiled at the thought of the old lady hauling on the sails or rowing. 'Maybe he thought you could give it to John.'

'What would John do with it? It's a big fishing boat, nothing like the little craft he runs around in. It would be no good to him unless he was going to be a fisherman.'

'He probably means you to sell it. I'll put the keys back in the envelope so they don't get lost. They must be something to do with the boat or he wouldn't have sent them.'

Annita nodded absently. What was she going to do with a fishing boat?

Once Vasi had left Annita picked up Elias's photograph. 'Elias, life is still full of surprises. Fancy Andreas giving Pappa's boat away! I thought my Pappa had sold it when he left Crete and came to us in America. I wonder if he thought he would come back one day and that was why he kept it?' She frowned. 'What am I going to do with it? I don't know any fishermen nowadays and I wouldn't want to think that it just sat in the harbour and rotted. Maybe Yannis or Giovanni will think of a use for it or know someone who would want to buy it. Why didn't Manolis sell it? Did he consider that would be dishonest as the boat had been given to him? Selling it would certainly have been the sensible thing to do. I'll ask Giovanni to speak to him and tell him I don't want the boat. He can sell it and use the money to keep him comfortable in his old age. Do you think that's the right thing for me to do, Elias?'

Nodding in answer to her question, Annita replaced Elias's photo on the table next to her bed.

Dimitra walked into Alecos's room at the hospital and was surprised to see him propped up in a sitting position.

'You do look better,' she observed. His face was still bruised and one eye was only half open, but he was able to smile at her.

'I feel better than I did.' It was quite difficult to make out his speech where his front teeth were missing. Both legs were encased in plaster, whilst his right arm was plastered and in a sling. 'I'm being transferred down to Aghios Nikolaos next week.'

'When will you be out of plaster?'

'They say about four more weeks.'

'Then will you be discharged?'

'I expect so. Now I feel better it's boring lying here.'

'Alecos,' Dimitra felt embarrassed at having to ask him about the accounts for the hotels. 'Do you remember you asked me to lend you the back-up disk for the Iliopolakis hotels?'

'Have you still got it?' asked Alecos.

Dimitra shook her head. 'I had to give it to Mr Vasi. There was a problem at the bank and they needed it to try to sort things out. Did you alter anything on it?'

'Why?'

'The back-up you returned to me didn't agree with the one I had given to Mr Iliopolakis. The balance was wrong and the credits for the week were missing.'

'I don't remember anything about it,' replied Alecos as firmly as he was able.

'You've just asked if I still had it,' said Dimitra in surprise.

'I don't know what you're talking about.'

'Are you trying to say the mistakes were my fault?' asked Dimitra.

'I don't remember,' repeated Alecos.

Dimitra glared at him. 'Mr Iliopolakis and Vasi spent a whole day in the bank until it had been sorted out.'

'Then it was a bank error.'

'Is that what you were trying to sort out when you asked me to lend you the disk? Did you take a back up of the incorrect bank account and then get the disks muddled up?'

'Maybe. I don't remember.'

Dimitra looked at him in exasperation. She had hoped Alecos

would have some reasonable explanation for her regarding the discrepancies that had been found. 'What do you remember, Alecos?'

'That my head hurt. I could hardly breathe.'

'Do you remember how your accident happened?'

'Why?'

Dimitra shrugged. 'I thought you may have seen whoever pushed you off the road. The police think Mr Vasi may have done it.'

Alecos closed his eyes. That was interesting. So far he had claimed to have no recollection of how the accident had happened, but if Vasi was being accused that could definitely be to his advantage. He needed to think carefully.

'I'm tired,' he said.

Dimitra smiled at him. 'I understand. Would you like me to go so that you can go to sleep?'

'Yes.'

'I'll come in and see you again before you're transferred,' she promised.

Alecos lay motionless in the hospital bed, thinking over Dimitra's words about Vasi being suspected of causing his accident. If the police charged Vasi he would end up in prison and there would be no way the man would be able to bring any charges against Alecos for the illegal manipulation of his bank accounts. He smiled inwardly. His accident had been quite fortuitous. He would claim to have no recollection of events leading up to it.

Manolis counted out the money that was in his battered old cash box. There was more than enough. He wrapped a piece of paper around the notes and tied it with string and wrote a few explanatory words on the wrapper. He would deliver it later. He poured a glass of raki and saluted the sketch he had of Yannis. It was due to him that he had finally been able to bring Flora to the mainland and be legally married to her.

'Thank you, Yannis,' he said as he filled his glass a second time.

It was quite dark by the time Manolis had emptied the bottle and he rose unsteadily to his feet and picked up the bundle of money, placing it in the deep pocket of his trousers. Leaving the door to his cottage open he made his way unsteadily to the church and pushed the bundle of money through the opening of the offertory box that stood inside behind the door. Father Constantine would find that tomorrow.

Picking his way carefully along the road, he walked into the cemetery and across to the newly dug grave that he had watched the men fill up with earth earlier that day. From his belt he removed his fishing knife from the sheath, lay down on the fresh earth and very deliberately slit his wrists.

Sunday 7th October

Vasi answered his mobile 'phone reluctantly. He had drunk more wine that usual last night in the company of his family and secure in the knowledge that he did not have to drive anywhere. His head was aching and his tongue felt thick in his mouth. Two cups of black coffee had improved his head ache, but he definitely felt out of sorts.

'Yes?'

'Vasi, it's Yiorgo. I have terrible news.'

Vasi heard Yiorgo's voice breaking with emotion. 'What is it? Barbara? One of the boys?'

'No, it's Manolis. They found him this morning. He's dead.'

'What!' Vasi sat down heavily on the kitchen chair.

'It's true. The whole of the waterfront is talking about it. Father Constantine found a bundle of money in the offertory box early this morning. Manolis had put it there. He went round to his house to ask for an explanation and there was no sign of him. He thought he may have gone to the cemetery and that was where he found him.'

'Was it his heart?' asked Vasi.

'He'd cut his wrists.'

Vasi swallowed hard. Words would not come to him. He felt wracked with guilt. They should have stayed with him or at least made certain he had a companion for the evening.

'Vasi, are you still there?'

'Yes,' he managed to whisper. 'Why didn't I stay with him?'

'No one was to know that was what he would do. If he hadn't done it yesterday he could have done it tonight,' argued Yiorgo reasonably. 'We weren't really friends of his.'

Vasi sighed. 'When we were youngsters we were only too willing to spend time talking with him, wanting to know all his war time stories. Once he'd satisfied our curiosity we no longer bothered with him. Poor old man.'

Yiorgo felt his own conscience pricking at him. 'I always used to speak to him if I saw him on the waterfront. I was never sure if he really remembered who I was.'

Vasi ran a hand across his throbbing head. 'I'll have to let my father know. He'll have to tell Rebecca.'

'Did you deliver that letter to the old lady?'

'Of course.'

'Then you ought to go and tell them the news.'

Vasi telephoned his father before washing his face for a third time that morning, hoping that when he arrived at Yannis's house whoever was there would not know he had shed tears over the death of the old boatman.

Bryony greeted him with a smile. 'What brings you down here, Vasi? Since Saffie went home we've hardly seen you.'

Vasi ignored her gibe. 'Is Giovanni around? I need to speak to him.'

'What's wrong?' For the first time Bryony noticed Vasi's pallor and moist eyes. 'Your father? Is he alright?'

'It's nothing to do with them. They're all fine.' Vasi tried to smile.

'Not Saffie?'

Vasi shook his head. 'I'm sure Marjorie would 'phone you immediately if there was any problem.'

Bryony nodded. 'Go on out to the patio. I think Giovanni is in his room, probably making a start on the end of season accounts. Would you like a drink?'

'Just a coffee, please. I had a bit too much last night and I'm suffering.'

'I didn't know Manolis had arranged a gathering.' Bryony

sounded quite hurt that the men from the most notable local family had not been invited.

'He didn't. I was with my family.' Vasi felt the lump returning to his throat. He had enjoyed his evening whilst Manolis had been wrapped in such a cloak of misery that the only solution he could envisage was to take his own life.

Bryony cast a wary glance at Vasi. He looked as if he might burst into tears at any minute. 'I'll find Giovanni,' she said, 'and put the coffee on.'

It was some minutes before Giovanni appeared. 'You know about Manolis?' he asked immediately.

Vasi nodded. 'I came to tell you.'

'Uncle Yannis has just telephoned me from the shop.' He shook his head. 'It's a bad business. How did you hear?'

'Yiorgo called me. We walked back to Manolis's house with him after the funeral. He asked us to come in and that was when he gave me his old hat with the bullet holes and asked me to deliver the letter to your grandmother.'

'Did you know what was in the letter?'

'Not until she opened it and told me. It seemed very strange at the time, but now we know why he returned his boat. He obviously thought that was the honourable thing to do if he was not going to use it anymore.'

'That's all very well, and I appreciate the thought behind it, but what use is it to Grandma?'

'She could sell it.'

'It might not be worth selling. Who knows what work is needed on it. In the meantime we're paying mooring fees. It would probably be better to send it to the scrap yard tomorrow.'

'You can't do that.' Vasi looked at Giovanni in horror.

'Why not?'

'It's Manolis's boat.'

Giovanni shook his head. 'It's Grandmother's boat now and she certainly doesn't want it. No, I'll see how much I'm offered for scrap. They'll probably charge for towing it round to their yard,' he added morosely.

'Are you serious?' asked Vasi.

Giovanni nodded. 'By the time I've paid mooring fees and the cost of having it towed I'll probably be out of pocket, whatever they pay me for salvage. Better to get rid of it as soon as possible.'

'You wouldn't have to pay mooring fees if you brought it round here to your jetty.'

'Not much point in doing that. It would just sit there until it had rotted away and I'd still have to pay to have it cleared. I'm sure Grandma will agree and not want to keep it out of sentiment.'

'How much do you want for it?' asked Vasi.

Giovanni shrugged. 'I've no idea how much boats sell for. Why? Are you interested?'

'I could be.' Vasi leaned forward. 'I know someone who would be capable of sailing it round. If you could moor it here for a few days we could see what condition it's in. At least you'd know if it was worth selling and be able to put a price on it.'

'And if it's a wreck?'

'Then I ask my friend to sail it to the scrap yard for you.'

'How much will he charge?' frowned Giovanni.

'He'll do it as a favour for me. You've nothing to lose.'

Giovanni considered the offer. It was true he had nothing to lose, but what was Vasi hoping to gain? He was a business man and would no doubt be expecting to make a profit somewhere.

Vasi drove back to Aghios Nikolaos hoping Yiorgo would be as enthusiastic about his idea as he felt. He found his friend shovelling rubble on a building site whilst his father and brother were busily painting the outside.

'Can you spare a moment, Yiorgo?'

Yiorgo straightened up and wiped his sweating hands down his trousers, leaving streaks of dirt. 'Glad of a break,' he muttered. 'I can paint a wall as well as either of them. Wouldn't hurt them to take a turn at clearing up the mess and loading the dumper.'

Vasi smiled sympathetically, remembering how willingly and enthusiastically Yiorgo had worked when they had cleared the rubble from the wall around the swimming pool. The work had been a novelty then to both of them, but Vasi had to admit that he would have no inclination to do the manual labour now.

'I've just come from Giovanni's.'

'Did you tell him about Manolis?'

'His Uncle Yannis had just telephoned him. You know Manolis asked me to deliver a letter to their grandmother?'

Yiorgo nodded and Vasi was forced to smile as he imparted the contents to his friend. 'He returned his boat to her.'

Yiorgo looked at him in amazement. 'What do you mean? Returned his boat to her?'

'Apparently it originally belonged to her father. After the war her brother gave it to him. He'd obviously decided even before Flora's funeral that he was going to end his own life. Father Constantine had written the letter and witnessed Manolis's signature to make it legal.'

'Who would dispute it anyway? Manolis had no relatives to lay claim to it.'

'I think he just wanted to feel he had done the right thing rather than leaving it in the harbour to rot.'

'So what's Giovanni planning to do with it?'

'Well, he's a bit aggrieved that he'll have to pay mooring fees and eventually have to pay to have it towed to the scrap yard.'

Yiorgo looked at Vasi in horror. 'He can't do that! I'm sure Manolis didn't leave it to the old lady with that in mind. He could have sailed it round to the scrap yard himself.'

Vasi smiled delightedly. 'That's what I thought. I told Giovanni that if it was brought round to his own private jetty he wouldn't have to pay mooring fees to the harbour master.'

'Good idea, but if he's planning to scrap it he'll have to pay more to have it taken back to Aghios Nikolaos.'

'That's where you come in.'

'Me? I don't know what would be useful to salvage from a fishing boat.'

'You sail it round to Giovanni's. You could do that, couldn't you?'

Yiorgo hesitated. He had not handled a small craft since he had managed to persuade Manolis to take him out with him some weekends before he had joined the navy. He was not even sure if he had ever truly been in charge of the boat or if Manolis had always kept control.

'I suppose so,' he frowned.

Vasi nodded. 'You look it over and let me know if you consider it worth selling as a seaworthy craft.'

'It's bound to be sound. Manolis had to get a certificate each year to enable him to take tourists out to Spinalonga.'

'I'd forgotten that. There was no certificate in the envelope with the letter, just a couple of keys.'

'It has to be displayed on the boat so the inspectors can descend on you at any time and check it. No good saying you've got it somewhere at home. If they can't see it on view you're chained to the side until it's produced. If it's out of date you get a hefty fine.'

'How do you know?'

Yiorgo smiled. 'Manolis got caught one year. His certificate was two days out of date and he had a boat load of passengers when the inspectors walked on board. He was furious.'

'So you don't think there would be any reason to send it to the scrap yard?'

'I wouldn't think so. Coat of paint to smarten it up if Giovanni's plans to sell it; polish up any brass fittings. Make it look good.'

'So when can you take it round to Giovanni's?'

Yiorgo shrugged. 'I could do it at the weekend.'

'I'll let Giovanni know to expect you on Saturday.'

'Are you coming with me as my crew?'

Vasi looked at Yiorgo in horror and Yiorgo broke into a peal of laughter.

'I like boats as much as you like aeroplanes,' replied Vasi.

'You're safer in a boat. Not so far to fall if you go over the side.'

Vasi shuddered at the mere thought. 'Let me know what time you plan to leave here and I'll meet you at Giovanni's and drive you back. I'll tell Giovanni to expect you.'

Yiorgo nodded, his eyes gleaming. He would make a leisurely journey sailing from Aghios Nikolaos to Elounda and enjoy every minute of his time back on the water.

Vasi had sent a brief e-mail to Saffron telling her that Flora had died. She had replied promptly saying that although she did not know Manolis she was sad on his behalf and hoped the funeral would not be too much of an ordeal for him.

He now sent her a much longer mail, describing the funeral and how he and Yiorgo had returned with Manolis to his house.

'He seemed so 'lost' somehow. He asked us to go inside his house and both Yiorgo and I were reluctant. We thought it would be more suitable if we found a neighbour to stay with him. He gave me a letter to take to your grandmother and he also gave me his old hat with the bullet holes in, then he told us to go. It seemed a bit strange, but we did as he asked. This morning I had a telephone call from Yiorgo to say that Manolis had committed suicide that night. Apparently he had gone up to the churchyard and cut his wrists.

I felt very bad that we had not stayed with him, but Yiorgo insisted that if that was his intent he would have killed himself when we did finally leave him. I delivered the letter to your grandmother on my return home and it was such a surprise. Manolis had returned his boat to her. Apparently the boat had originally belonged to her father and her brother, Father Andreas, had given it to Manolis after the war.

Giovanni was not pleased to think he would have to pay mooring fees before having it towed to the boat yard to be scrapped. I could not bear to think of that happening and I have arranged for Yiorgo to sail it around to moor at their jetty. I have also agreed to buy the boat from your grandmother. Giovanni is going to find out a fair price for me.

I know I hate the water and boats, but I have had ideas. Provided the water is deep enough I plan to build a jetty at the hotel in Elounda and offer trips to Spinalonga from the hotel. It will save the people who are staying down there from having to walk up to the Square.

If I cannot build a jetty then I will continue to pay the mooring fees in Aghios Nikolaos or see if I can arrange a berth in Elounda marina. I am going to ask Yiorgo to be in charge of sailing the boat out to Spinalonga with the tourists each day. He does not know this. I am going to meet him on Saturday when he sails the boat round to your family's house and talk to him about it.

Do you think this is a good idea?'

Saffron felt her eyes fill with tears as she read the mail. Poor old Manolis. She wiped them away with her fingers; then felt them coming again. Vasi was such a good, kind man. He had no interest at all in possessing a boat, but he was willing to spend unlimited money hoping to make his friend happy.

Monday 8th October

Alecos lay with his eyes closed feigning sleep whenever anyone entered his room. If only the nurse would leave him alone and stop fussing around. He needed to think carefully. He must ensure that if he was interviewed by the police his story was the same each time. He would claim to have no recollection of anything to do with the bank accounts, but he would assure the police, despite the gaps in his memory, that he quite clearly recalled seeing Vasi's face as his car had hurtled over the side of the ravine. As he congratulated himself again on his scheme a thought struck him. He had also altered the accounts for the hotels that belonged to Mr Iliopolakis. Vasi might be in prison and unable to take any action against him, but he realised Vasi's father would not hesitate to press charges.

The thought made him sweat. Even claiming that he had lost his memory would not prevent an ignominious dismissal from the bank and the loss of his pension. Word would get around in Aghios Nikolaos. He would no longer have the sympathy of the townspeople for having been injured; they would turn their backs and shun him.

He needed to think of another way to prevent his name from being besmirched.

Vasi telephoned his father and told him he had bought the old fishing boat that had belonged to Manolis.

'Whatever for? You don't like being out on the sea.'

Patiently Vasi explained the ideas he had for running trips to Spinalonga.

'I would have thought there were more than enough boats going out there.'

'Pappa, you haven't been down here to see the crowds who want to go over. Since that book came out people are falling over themselves to get there. The travel companies organise excursions over there and monopolise the boats for the coach loads of people they bring from all over Crete. The business is good for the locals.'

'We're in the hotel business, not excursions.' Vasilis sighed. 'How much are you going to need from the bank to get this project under way?'

'No more than the loan I needed to purchase the Imperia. I've arranged to have an echo sounding of the bay tomorrow. I thought it could be feasible to have a jetty built out from the hotel. That way we have a monopoly on the visitors who are staying with us.'

'How much will that cost?'

'I've no idea. It depends upon the results of the soundings. I obviously can't extend too far out or I'll be accused of causing an obstruction. Once I know the results from the echo company I can get some estimates. If it isn't practical or too expensive I'll forget the idea and just keep a mooring berth up at the Square or in Aghios Nikolaos.'

'If it's such a good business proposition why didn't Giovanni keep the boat? He's already got a jetty.'

'I think I took him by surprise when I offered to buy it and he agreed to the sale before he realised the potential.' Vasi smiled to himself, remembering how readily Giovanni had agreed to the purchase.

Dimitra studied her wardrobe carefully. She was convinced Filippos Melanakis was attracted to her. Should she encourage him further, making it obvious that his attentions were welcome or keep him in suspense a little longer? She frowned. Once Alecos had been transferred to Aghios Nikolaos she would have no further excuse to visit the hospital and meet Filippos. She would tease him one more time, making sure the man was so inflamed with passion for her that he would agree to visit her apartment the following day. The lady downstairs always seemed to know who had visited the upstairs apartment but on a Tuesday she visited her daughter. She smiled to herself, imagining him down on his knees, begging her for her favours, which she would finally grant.

She knew just what she would wear today. She had the ideal item. The cheesecloth blouse was decorous enough to wear to work with her bra and camisole beneath, but if she removed her underwear her breasts were clearly visible.

She gave a little giggle. She wondered what his reaction would be. She remembered the first time she had worn it when meeting Alecos. He could not wait to return to her apartment and had parked off the main road behind some trees and taken her with an urgency he had never shown before. She would not allow Filippos back to her apartment on this occasion. She would make him wait. Whilst he was collecting their coffee she would have a fictitious 'phone call, asking her to return to the Central as there was a problem with the accounts. He would no doubt offer to take her in his car and she might allow his hands to stray from the steering wheel. He could have just a small sample of her attractions to wet his appetite.

She slipped into the ladies cloakroom in the coffee shop and removed the camisole and her bra. She cupped her breasts in her hands, then rubbed her nipples vigorously until they were hard and erect. She slipped her blouse back on, left the top three buttons undone and leaned towards the mirror. The doctor would have an almost unrestricted view of her breasts if he sat next to her. She smiled to herself. His reaction could be interesting.

As she left the cloakroom she saw Doctor Melanakis arriving and looking around for her. She smiled brightly, thrust out her chest and walked over to him.

'Have I kept you waiting? I'm so sorry.'

Doctor Melanakis swallowed. Her breasts were just begging to be squeezed.

'Not at all. I have only just arrived. Have a seat. Would you like your usual frappe?'

Dimitra nodded and walked over to the bench seat that was so convenient for a little discreet foreplay. The doctor joined her and seemed uncertain whether to sit opposite where he could drink in the view of her tantalizing breasts or next to her where he would be able to touch her legs. As he sat beside her, Dimitra moved so she was sitting slightly sideways on the seat. She wriggled her shoulders, as if relaxing them, and knew by the sharp intake of the doctor's breath that she had presented him a view of her body that he appreciated.

Filippos placed his hand on her leg, his fingers feeling the soft flesh of her inner thigh and his erection grew alarmingly in response. Dimitra looked down at the doctor's crotch. She knew exactly the effect she was having on the uncomfortable man as she squeezed her thighs together trapping his hand. She leaned towards him, ensuring that her blouse gaped and he had an unrestricted view of her naked breasts.

Doctor Melanakis passed a trembling hand over his forehead. He moved his hand from between her legs and gave a strangled gasp.

'If you will excuse me for a moment.' He rose hurriedly and made his way as quickly as he was able to the toilet. He needed immediate relief.

He washed his hands and leaned his head against the cool mirror. He must exercise more control over his hands and body or the result could be disastrously embarrassing. He knew exactly what he wanted to do, but a coffee shop was not the place to indulge his desires. She was bound to invite him back to her apartment today and then he would have free reign to his appetite.

He returned to the table and Dimitra noted with inner amusement that his trousers now lay flat and he was having no trouble walking.

She was sure she knew how he had spent his time in the privacy of the toilet and was convinced that would only make him more anxious to be somewhere alone with her so they could enjoy each other. He would no doubt seize the opportunity of visiting her on Tuesday.

Dimitra removed her mobile 'phone from her handbag and frowned. 'Excuse me a moment.' She read the message she had sent to herself whilst Filippos had been occupied in the toilet. She turned it round so he could read it.

'computer problem. need u at central a s a p vasi.'

'I'm so sorry, Filippos. I have to return to work. I expect Mr Vasi has done something stupid on the computer and he really has very little idea of how they function. I will probably press a key and all his problems will be solved.'

'You have to go now?'

'Unfortunately.' Dimitra leaned towards him, giving him another long look at her unfettered breasts. She shrugged and they almost jumped out of her blouse. It was all Filippos could do to restrain himself from touching them. 'It is part of my contract that if a computer problem arises I have to go in to help to rectify the situation, whatever the time of day or night.' Dimitra placed her hand on his leg. 'I will call for a taxi.'

'Certainly not. I will take you to the hotel.'

Dimitra smiled. 'That's so kind of you, Filippos. I would certainly appreciate you driving me there. I wish I had turned my 'phone off; then Mr Vasi would not have been able to contact me.'

Filippos also wished she had turned off her 'phone. 'Hopefully the next time we meet you will do so. Would you like me to wait for you? I could take you home afterwards.'

Dimitra shook her head. 'I may be five minutes or five hours. I could not ask you to wait.' She glanced at him coyly. 'If you are free tomorrow when you finish your duties you could always visit me at my apartment and we could share a glass of wine.'

Filippos nodded eagerly. 'I would be delighted. Give me your address.'

Dimitra delved into her handbag and handed the doctor the card advertising the Central hotel that she had written her details on. As he took from her he could resist no longer. His hand fastened around her breast and he drew in his breath sharply as he felt her softness beneath his fingers.

'Filippos,' Dimitra murmured, 'Not here, in public. Suppose someone saw you doing that?'

Reluctantly Filippos withdrew his hand. 'You should not wear such a revealing blouse, my dear. It is an invitation no man could refuse.'

'Oh, dear,' Dimitra pretended to be embarrassed. 'My bra fastening broke and I had to take it off as it was so uncomfortable. I did not realise my blouse could be seen through. It is a good job you are taking me to the Central. If I had used a taxi the driver may have had the wrong impression. I'm sure when I reach the hotel I shall be able to find a safety pin so I can make myself respectable again.'

Dimitra stood and clutching her handbag to her chest she walked with Filippos to the coffee shop door.

'If you wait here I will fetch the car.'

'Oh, dear, I have embarrassed you as well as myself.'

'Not at all,' Filippos was not prepared to admit that his groping had excited him again and he wanted a few moments alone to regain his composure.

Filippos drove sedately through the town, whilst Dimitra sat with her arms crossed hiding her breasts from his view, but she had ensured that her skirt had ridden up as high as possible. He drew up a short distance away from the hotel and placed his hand on her thigh again. She reached her arms up around his neck and pulled his head down towards her bare breasts. 'I can't wait for tomorrow,' she whispered in his ear.

'Dimitra....' His hands were up beneath her skirt.

'No.' Dimitra pushed him away. 'I have to go. I will see you tomorrow.' She opened the car door and stepped out, again holding her handbag close to her chest, as she walked the few yards to the hotel entrance.

Filippos leaned his head down on the steering wheel and groaned. He had been so ready to take her today.

Dimitra slipped inside the toilet in the entrance to the hotel and quickly replaced her bra and camisole top. Once more decently dressed she approached the revolving door to leave the hotel and nearly bumped into Vasi.

'Hallo, Dimitra. I didn't realise you were still here. Have you been working late?'

Dimitra shook her head. 'No, I forgot something I had left in my drawer so I just came back to collect it.'

'We both of us have a problem with our memory,' he smiled. 'I also have returned to do something I had forgotten. If you care to wait a moment or two I will be able to take you home. It's on my way back to Elounda.'

Filippos was still sitting in his car outside the hotel when he saw Dimitra leaving with Vasi. He ground his teeth with rage. She had not been called back to work at all. She had returned to meet the manager and now no doubt she was going to spend the evening allowing him to participate in the delights she had to offer.

He waited until Vasi had drawn away from the kerb and began to follow them.

Filippos was surprised when Vasi drew up outside an apartment building, the couple exchanged a few words and Dimitra climbed out of the car. She gave a little wave of her hand as she ran up the steps and inserted her key into the lock. Vasi drew away and Filippos searched for a convenient parking space. He was not prepared to wait any longer.

Dimitra opened the door of her apartment when the bell rang, expecting to see the lady who lived below. She looked surprised when she saw Filippos standing there.

Before she had a chance to greet him he strode inside. 'You

were not called back to work,' he growled.

'Oh, I was, but by the time I arrived Mr Vasi said he had sorted everything out. He felt so guilty at calling me back that he drove me home.' Dimitra hoped Filippos would believe her story. She laid her hand on his arm. 'Sit down and make yourself at home. I'll just slip into something more comfortable; then I'll make some coffee, unless you'd prefer a glass of wine.'

Dimitra knew she would not be able to postpone Filippos's intentions any longer. She was not sure she wanted to. She walked into her bedroom, making sure she left the door open wide enough for Filippos to see her reflection in the full length mirror. As she removed her blouse and camisole, throwing them to one side, Filippos entered.

He seized her shoulders and shook her vigorously. 'There will be no excuses from you this time.'

Dimitra tried to smile at him, although her head was spinning from his treatment. 'I have not made excuses, Filippos.'

Filippos ignored her words. He placed one hand in the waistband of her skirt and tugged vigorously. The button popped off and the zip teeth parted, allowing her skirt to fall to her ankles. Still holding her firmly, he ripped off her bra followed by her panties so she stood naked before him.

Dimitra felt her head clearing. 'There is no need to be so rough, Filippos. Let me undress you and then we can enjoy each other.' She began to undo the buttons on his shirt and he shrugged his arms free. As she turned her attention to his trousers she could feel his erection and her own excited anticipation of the impending encounter grew.

His trousers fell to the floor and Dimitra pulled down his underwear. She gave a gasp of surprise when she saw the size of his exposed member. She had never seen a man with such a large organ before and she wondered if she would be able to accommodate him, particularly if he grew any larger. He almost filled her hand as she closed her fingers around him.

'Stop that,' he ordered and pushed her hand away. He seized her buttocks and pulled her closer to him, managing to knead them to his satisfaction whilst he closed his eyes and let out a long sigh of satisfaction. Dimitra placed her hands on his shoulders and pushed herself forwards towards him, feeling his hardness against her body.

He knelt and began to lick, suck and nibble at her inner thighs, his hair and sometimes his forehead, brushing her provocatively whilst he continued to knead her flesh like dough. This was a new form of foreplay and she was enjoying herself. She hoped Filippos would be able to contain himself long enough to satisfy her. Dimitra found she was becoming unaccountably excited although her skin was becoming tender where Filippos was grasping her with his hard fingers. She could feel herself quivering with anticipation as the pressure inside her mounted uncontrollably and Filippos seemed to grow even harder and larger. He rose to his feet, his hands continuing to explore and squeeze the soft flesh of her legs and buttocks whilst his sharp teeth nipped her breasts unmercifully.

Just as she felt she could stand there no longer without fulfilment Filippos released her pushed her back on her bed.

Filippos grasped her thighs, pulling her legs apart and entered her with a force that left her breathless. She wondered if she was going to faint as pain flooded through her.

'Filippos,' she gasped. 'Stop. You're hurting me.'

Totally oblivious to her plea, Filippos controlled her movements, holding her thighs, and moving up and down at his will. His hard fingers continually dug into her soft flesh, alternating between her thighs and her breasts as she squirmed to try to get away from him as the pain became more intense. She gave a little sob that turned into a scream as Filippos forced himself even deeper inside her to accomplish his own relief. He grunted and groaned, squeezing her breasts so tightly she thought they would burst, until he finally let out a roar of accomplishment as he reached his own climax, and subsided rapidly.

He pushed himself off Dimitra. 'I may use your shower?'

Dimitra nodded. This was not how she had envisaged their love making. She had planned for them to share a bottle of wine, and whilst doing so they would explore each other's bodies until they finally retired to her bedroom. She had anticipated gentle foreplay and lying contentedly in each other's arms afterwards before she offered to cook a meal for him. They would return to her bedroom again after they had eaten to tease and excite each other until both of them were satisfied, when they would finally sleep, wrapped in each other's arms, until further desire woke one of them.

Tentatively she rose from the bed, feeling decidedly unsafe as her legs almost buckled beneath her. She could hear the water running and slowly she made her way across the room, holding on to the furniture for support. She was unsure if she would be able to stand in the shower unaided, but that could be a good excuse for Filippos to hold her. She turned the handle of the bathroom door and was surprised to find that Filippos had locked it. He was obviously not expecting her to join him.

She staggered back into her bedroom, picked up a T-shirt and slipped it over her head. She would sit in the lounge and wait for him to finish his ablutions. Her legs and breasts were so sore where he had dug his fingers cruelly into her. She shivered slightly at the memory of the pain he had inflicted on her.

The water stopped running and shortly afterwards Filippos re-entered her lounge. Dimitra could not help but gaze admiringly at his naked body. Did he plan to take her again? He looked ready. Now his first overpowering desire had been satisfied he would probably be more considerate towards her. Without a word he began to replace his clothes. Dimitra watched as he finally knotted his tie. It was with a feeling of relief that she realised he was not planning stay any longer with her. She swallowed hard.

'Would you care to stay for a meal, Filippos?'

His gaze raked up and down her T-shirt. He pulled her to her feet and inserted his hands beneath her T-shirt, lifting it and looking at her naked body. He bent forward and bit each of her nipples hard, before squeezing her breasts, making her draw in her breath sharply with pain. He moved his hands down to her thighs where he stroked her gently before turning the action into a vice-like grip. 'I will see you tomorrow.'

Dimitra looked at him, her eyes wide with foreboding. Her earlier desire for the doctor had completely abated and now all she felt was fear of the powerful man. She shook her head, not trusting herself to speak.

Filippos picked up his jacket and let himself out of her apartment.

Slowly Dimitra walked into her bathroom. How she wished she had a bath rather than just a shower. She wanted to lie down in warm, healing water to soothe her bruised body. She gave a little sob. Maybe, if she had not teased him for so long he would have been gentler. He had been so rough with her that she had not had time to appreciate how he had filled her. He was magnificent. Even after his shower he had looked ready to take her again.

Dimitra looked at her naked body in the mirror. She was covered in bruises and red welts where Filippos had bitten her. She shuddered. The man was an animal. She could certainly not go in to work tomorrow looking as she did. Everyone would want to know what had happened to her and she did not want to admit to the truth.

As she stood there a dribble of blood ran down her leg. She bit her lip in consternation. This was not right. This had never happened to her before, however prolonged and passionate a session of love making had been. Had Filippos been so large and rough that he had torn her internally?

She wiped the blood away with a cloth and looked at the shower again. She did not have the strength to stand in there at the moment. She would rest a while and have a shower to clean her body later.

Tuesday 9th October

Vasi was surprised when his father telephoned to say that Dimitra had not arrived for work at the Central hotel as usual.

'I've tried telephoning her and I'm not getting any answer.'

'I expect she's been held up somewhere.'

'Why hasn't she 'phoned to say she would be late?'

'Perhaps she left her mobile at home. Give me a call later if she hasn't arrived by mid-day and I'll pass by her apartment on my way up and check that she isn't ill or anything.'

'Why don't you come up now? If she doesn't arrive you'll need to complete her work. It will save you having to stay late in town.'

'I've the echo sounding taking place today,' Vasi reminded his father. 'If I have to stay very late I'll beg a bed for the night, if I may.'

'Why don't you stay over anyway?' suggested Vasilis. 'Then if Dimitra isn't well and can't come in tomorrow you'll be on the spot. Save you having to drive up again.'

'That makes sense, provided Cathy doesn't mind.'

'Of course she won't mind,' replied his father scornfully. 'That's arranged then. Even if Dimitra does come in you come over to us for a meal and stay the night. You can let me know more about this boat and jetty idea.'

Vasi declined the offer to go out on the boat that was going to do the echo sounding, despite the bay being calm, hardly a ripple disturbing the surface.

'I need to get on with my work here,' he explained. 'We have a member of staff off sick and I will have to go to Heraklion later. How long do you think the sounding will take?'

The man shrugged. 'Probably the rest of the day. We know the channel in the centre is pretty deep. We just have to sound out the area where you say you want a jetty. I thought if we made a sixty square metres grid it would be sufficient.'

Vasi nodded. He only intended to build the jetty as far out into the sea as necessary. Testing sixty metres for deep water should be more than sufficient.

'When will you be able to let me know the result?'

'I should be able to Fax it to you by the end of the week. I'll send my bill at the same time.'

'Could you send it through on the computer?' asked Vasi. 'I'm never sure if I will be down here or up in Heraklion. Here's my business card.' Vasi withdrew the card from his wallet and underlined his e-mail address. 'I will be able to access that wherever I am.'

For a while Vasi watched as the small boat tacked backwards and forwards in the bay outside his hotel, then went inside to check with the manager that there were no problems that needed his immediate attention.

'I'm going into Aghios Nikolaos now and then on to Hersonissos. Then I shall drive up to Heraklion and be staying there overnight if you need me for anything urgent.'

The manager nodded. He very much doubted that any problem would arise that needed the attention of Mr Vasi.

Vasi telephoned his father as he entered the outskirts of Heraklion. 'Any call from Dimitra?'

'Nothing,' replied Vasilis. 'I've tried her mobile number a couple of times and no one answers.'

'I'll stop by her apartment and see if I she's there. I'm sure the woman downstairs has a key and I could ask her to come in with me. I'm beginning to get a bit concerned that she may have had an accident. It isn't like her to be unreliable.'

Vasi drew up outside Dimitra's apartment, ran up the steps and rang the bell. He waited patiently; then knocked on the door. Her bell might not be working. Still receiving no answer he took out his mobile 'phone and pressed her number. He could hear the telephone ringing very faintly. Vasi bent down and peered through the letter box, unable to see more than a small area.

'Dimitra. Dimitra, are you there? It's me, Vasi.'

He placed his ear to the opening and listened, sure he had heard a sound from inside.

'Dimitra,' he called again. 'If you're there answer me.'

This time he was certain he had heard a sound. There was definitely something amiss. He tried to look through the window, but the curtain obstructed any view he might have had of the living room.

'What do you think you're doing?'

The voice from below made him turn round and he saw the woman who lived beneath Dimitra standing outside glaring at him.

Vasi smiled in relief. 'I'm trying to contact Dimitra. She hasn't come in to work today and she's not answering her mobile. I'm concerned that she may have had an accident. Do you have a spare key to her apartment?'

Slowly the woman nodded. 'I'll not give it to you. How do I know you haven't come to rob the place?'

'I assure you I have not. I'd just be grateful if you would go in and check that all is well with her.'

Giving Vasi another dubious glance the woman returned inside her own apartment and re-emerged with a young man at her side.

'My son will come in with you,' she announced.

Vasi nodded. 'That's fine by me.'

Vasi followed the youth back up the stairs, his mother following them. He unlocked the door and stood back to allow Vasi to enter.

'Dimitra, are you there? It's Vasi,' Vasi called again.

The youth shrugged. 'She's obviously not in.'

'I want to make certain.' Vasi walked into the lounge and looked around. Nothing appeared out of place. 'Dimitra,' he called again and walked to the open bedroom door, stopping aghast as he saw the figure on the bed.

'Get your mother,' he ordered the young man. 'She's ill.'

'Mamma, come here,' he called.

Vasi moved to the side of the bed as the woman entered. 'I don't know what's wrong with her, but I think I should call an ambulance.'

The woman pulled back the sheet and replaced it hurriedly. Dimitra was naked, curled up into a foetal position, her legs and chest covered in welts and bruises, and the bed was soaked in blood.

'Tell them to hurry,' she ordered and took Dimitra's limp hand in her own. 'You'll be alright now, dear,' she assured her.

'What's happened to her?' asked Vasi. 'She was fine when I brought her home last night.'

The woman cast him a suspicious glance. 'It's not up to me to say.'

'Can you stay with her until the ambulance arrives?' asked Vasi.

'Where are you off to?'

'I was going into the lounge to call my father. I'll stay here if you want and do that later.'

The woman did not reply and Vasi walked back into the lounge. He noticed that the woman's son was very effectively blocking the doorway.

'Pappa, I'm at Dimitra's. I've sent for an ambulance. No, I don't know what is wrong. She's covered in bruises and seems to have been bleeding. The lady from downstairs is with her. I'll follow the ambulance to the hospital and telephone you again as soon as I have any news.'

Vasi closed his 'phone and stood in the bedroom doorway. He saw Dimitra's ripped clothing lying on the floor and drew in his breath sharply. Had she been attacked and raped? He would wait for the medical services to arrive, ask their opinion, and if necessary report the matter to the police. His heart dropped. It would no doubt be Superintendent Solomakis he would have to speak to.

He heard the siren as the ambulance drew closer and joined the youth at the door, beckoning to the crew as they climbed out. 'You'll need a stretcher,' he called, but they ignored him and proceeded to climb the steps to Dimitra's apartment.

The woman released Dimitra's hand and retired to join the two men in the lounge. Her face was grim as she looked at Vasi. He certainly did not look the kind of man who would force himself roughly on a woman, but he had admitted bringing her home. No doubt Dimitra had then refused his overtures and he had turned nasty. She had seen Dimitra's ripped clothing and decided she would telephone the police once the poor girl had been removed to the hospital.

Vasi waited. One of the crew went back down to the ambulance and brought up a metal stand and pack of saline solution, returning again to collect a stretcher. Whilst one attended to Dimitra the other entered the lounge.

'Can someone give me some details about the young lady?'

Both the woman and Vasi nodded. The man turned to the woman. 'Does she live here with you?'

'I live in the apartment below. This man came and asked me to use my spare key to let him in. He said he was worried she had had an accident. My son and I came up with him; just to make sure he wasn't up to anything.'

The man turned to Vasi. 'Who are you?'

'Vasilis Iliopolakis.'

'What made you think the lady may have met with an accident?'

'My father telephoned me to say she had not arrived for work and was not answering her 'phone. I was driving up to Heraklion and said I would call in at her apartment just to check that all was well. I tried ringing and knocking, and I thought I heard a movement, so I asked the lady downstairs to give me access. What's happened to her? Will she be alright?'

'Not up to me to speculate on the cause. Once we get her into the hospital she'll be well looked after. If you can just give me the lady's full name and her date of birth. We have the address.'

'Dimitra Artimatakis. I can't remember her date of birth offhand. I can ask my father to look it up in our files.' Vasi pulled his mobile from his pocket.

'You can let us know that later. It's more important that we get her some treatment as soon as possible.'

'Ready,' came a shout from the bedroom and the man nodded and returned to join his colleague. In a matter of minutes they were carrying Dimitra on a stretcher with a drip attached to her arm down to the waiting ambulance.

Vasi passed a shaky hand across his forehead. 'Poor Dimitra,' he murmured. He turned to the neighbour. 'Can I rely on you to lock up, please? I'm going to follow the ambulance up to the hospital. I'll come back this way later and let you know how she is.' Vasi handed her his card. 'If you need to contact me for any reason I suggest you try my mobile.' He underlined the number. 'I tend to move around between the hotels during the day.'

The woman handed Vasi's card to her son and after glancing at it he placed it in his pocket. Neither of them spoke to Vasi and he stepped out of the apartment and hurried down the stairs just as the driver began to pull away in the ambulance.

Vasi paced up and down outside the hospital and telephoned his father. 'Pappa, listen. I went to Dimitra's apartment. She didn't answer the door, but I felt sure she was in there. I asked her neighbour if she could let me in and she and her son came up with me. She's in a terrible state. No, not the neighbour, Dimitra. I don't know what happened to her, but she looks as if someone has beaten her.' Vasi dropped his voice. 'I think she may have been violently raped. Her torn clothes were lying on the floor of the bedroom and there was a lot of blood in her bed. Once I've spoken to the doctor I'm going to the police.'

Vasi frowned as he listened to the answer from his father. 'I don't know how long it will be before Dimitra's able to make a statement. She can always withdraw the complaint. Whoever did this to her deserves to be caught. No woman should be treated the way she has been. Physically she's a mess, Pappa, and what will it have done to her mentally?'

Vasi sighed. 'I've no idea how long I'll be here. I'll call you again when I've spoken to the doctor. Can you look up her date of birth for me on our files? I was asked for it. I think it's in August but I can't remember exactly.'

Vasi waited until his father gave him Dimitra's date of birth and then re-entered the hospital. He approached reception and waited his turn. 'The lady who was admitted a short while ago, Dimitra Artimatakis. I have her date of birth for you.'

'Who are you?'

'I'm her employer, Vasi Iliopolakis.'

'Wait over there. I'll let the doctor know.'

Vasi nodded and found an empty chair. He hoped he would not have to wait too long before someone came to speak to him and he felt able to leave the hospital.

Doctor Tsakonakis examined Dimitra gently. She would need surgery to repair the internal damage that had been inflicted upon her, but her most immediate need was a blood transfusion to replace the amount she had lost.

'Take swabs,' he ordered the nurse, as he filled a syringe with blood from Dimitra's arm. 'You can take them up to the lab with the blood sample. I'll start transfusing her with 'O' until we know her blood group.' The doctor hoped Dimitra would fall into the commonest category. 'If she's 'O' Positive you can get her prepped ready for surgery when she's had that unit. Any local relatives we can ask to donate?' he asked.

The nurse shook her head. 'Very little information, just her name and address. According to the crew the man who called them said he was her employer. They reckon they saw him following them up to the hospital in his car.'

'I'll see if he's outside.' The doctor peeled off his gloves, removed his coat and washed his hands.

Vasi watched as two policemen entered the building and approached reception. The receptionist pointed in his direction and they walked over to him.

'Mr Vasi Iliopolakis?'

Vasi nodded. 'That's me.'

'We'd like you to come along with us, sir.'

'I'm waiting to speak to a doctor about an employee who has been admitted. Could I come along after I've seen him?'

'I'm afraid we're not able to wait, sir. We'd like you to come now.'

Vasi sighed deeply. 'Very well. Just let me tell the receptionist I'm leaving.'

'I'm sure the receptionist is aware that you are leaving the premises, sir.'

Vasi looked over at the reception desk. The receptionist was looking at him as were all the other people who were waiting in the area. 'What about my car?' he asked.

'I'm sure that will be quite safe where it is.'

Vasi felt thoroughly annoyed with himself. He had been so occupied with the impending echo sounding and then finding Dimitra that he had not reported to the police station yet that day. No doubt once he had shown his face there he would be able to have a taxi back to the hospital.

Superintendent Solomakis regarded Vasi with a smirk on his face. Let Vasi Iliopolakis try to talk himself out of this accusation against him.

'I'm sorry,' Vasi apologised immediately. 'I've had rather a busy day and I'd planned to report to you when I left the hospital. It really wasn't necessary for you to send your men to ask me to come in. A telephone call would have been sufficient to remind me. May I go now?'

The Superintendent shook his head. 'I have a few questions I would like to ask you.'

'I've answered all your questions about Mr Vikelakis's accident.' Vasi sighed resignedly. 'I'm not prepared to answer any more without my lawyer being present.'

'This is concerning a different matter. I understand you visited an apartment belonging to a young lady who is in your employ.'

Vasi nodded. 'My father said she had not arrived for work and was not answering her 'phone. I was near her area when I drove up from Elounda and said I would call on her to see there was nothing amiss.'

'But you knew there was something very amiss, didn't you, Mr Iliopolakis?'

Vasi shook his head. 'I thought she may have had an accident and been unable to reach her mobile to call for help.'

'I don't think we could describe your treatment of the young lady as an accident, could we?'

Vasi looked at the Superintendent open mouthed. 'I didn't lay a finger on her. The neighbour from downstairs was with me. She'll confirm that we found her together.'

Thranassis nodded. 'Quite so. You also admitted that you brought her back to her apartment last night. I suggest you went in with her, she may have invited you, and you read more into the invitation than you should have done. When the lady refused your attentions you viciously assaulted her.'

Vasi shook his head slowly. 'That is completely untrue. I didn't even get out of the car.'

'I suggest you parked your car a short distance away and then returned. The lady downstairs is adamant that she heard the lady go in and shortly afterwards someone went up the stairs.'

'It was definitely not me. I said goodbye to Dimitra and drove down to Elounda.'

'I'm sure you drove down to Elounda, but that would have been some time later; *after* you had inflicted yourself on the young lady.' Thranassis sat back and glared at Vasi triumphantly.

Vasi shook his head. 'I'm not saying anything more until my lawyer is present. I take it I may make a 'phone call? That is my right.'

Doctor Melanakis stopped at Alecos's bed and scrutinized his chart. The man had appeared to be progressing so well at first but now he seemed to be content to lay with his eyes closed all day and refused to help himself, relying on his nurse. More brain scans had been taken and there was no sign of any permanent damage.

Alecos knew the doctor was standing there and feigned sleep as usual. He did not want to be considered well enough for the police to question him about the accident until he had worked out the final details of his plan. At first he had intended to say he had seen Vasi driving the car that had pushed him into the gorge. Now he had a better idea.

The doctor replaced the chart at the foot of the bed. He would have a word with the man's parents when they visited and see if they knew if anything was troubling him that would hinder his recovery. His patient certainly no longer needed the services of the trauma unit. A transfer to the hospital at Aghios Nikolaos could be beneficial to him.

Maybe he would ask Dimitra when he paid her a visit later today. He could hardly wait to take her again. At the thought he licked his lips. He had certainly made her pay for encouraging him. He would be apologetic, kind and gentle on his next visit and when she had regained her trust and confidence in him he would take her even more violently than before. That was how he enjoyed his sex.

Thinking about the pleasure he intended to have caused the start of an erection that he tried to push down ineffectually with his hands. He walked over to the toilet cubicle in Alecos's room and locked the door behind him. Immediate relief was needed and he began to picture Dimitra's plump thighs and generous breasts to help him accomplish his desire.

Alecos listened to the doctor grunting and panting. Was he ill? Should he ring his bell and alert someone? He was just about to raise the alarm when he heard a strangled gasp followed by a sigh of contentment. Alecos smiled to himself. So that was what the doctor was up to! He hoped the doctor had been groping a nurse and it was not due to him that the doctor had found a hasty retreat to the bathroom a necessity.

Vasi waited an hour before his father and Mr Tsilikadis arrived.

'Some time to speak to my client privately,' snapped Mr Tsilikadis and the sergeant unlocked the door of the cell where Vasi had been detained and escorted both men to an interview room.

Mr Tsilikadis took a pad of paper from his briefcase and laid it on the table. 'So, Mr Vasi, why have you been detained this time?'

'A girl who works for us appears to have been attacked. I answered their questions at first, thinking it was just routine as I had taken her home the previous evening. Then Superintendent Solomakis accused me of being responsible. I refused to answer any more questions until you were present.'

Mr Tsilikadis sighed. 'So tell me exactly why the police should suspect you.'

'I've done absolutely nothing wrong,' Vasi spoke earnestly. 'I was just about to drive back to Elounda last night when I realised I had forgotten to lock my drawer. I keep the outstanding invoices in there along with the bank receipts. I went back into the Central to do so and met Dimitra Artimatakis coming out. She does the computer balancing for us. She said she had also forgotten something and returned to collect it. As I pass very close to her apartment on the way to Elounda I offered to take her home.

'I left her outside her apartment. I didn't go in. I drove straight back down to Elounda. I'm involved in some business there and that took my attention this morning. I admit I forgot to go into the police station at Aghios Nikolaos to report to Inspector Christos. I had a 'phone call from my father to say that Dimitra had not shown up for work. That wasn't like her. She's reliable. I said I would call at her apartment when I drove up to Heraklion, just to check she hadn't had an accident.

'She didn't answer her 'phone or the door, but I was sure I had heard a sound from inside. I called through her letterbox and she still didn't answer. The woman who lives downstairs came out and asked what I was doing, so I asked her if she would use her spare key to open the door. I went in with her son and when he saw Dimitra he called his mother. She was lying on the bed and there was blood everywhere. I called an ambulance and whilst we were waiting I looked around the room and her clothes were lying on the floor. I didn't touch them, but I could see they were torn. I'm sure someone attacked her.

'I called my father to tell him and then followed the ambulance to the hospital. I wanted to speak to the doctor and then I planned to report the incident to the police. That was when the police arrived and asked me to accompany them here.'

Mr Tsilikadis nodded. 'Have you any witnesses who saw you leave the young lady at her apartment and drive off?'

Vasi shrugged. 'I've no idea. Someone may have seen me, but I doubt if they took any notice. The woman downstairs says she heard Dimitra go in and shortly afterwards someone went up the stairs. It wasn't me.'

Mr Tsilikadis shook his head dolefully. 'You seem to be making a habit of getting into trouble recently! I'll have a word with the Superintendent. You're still on bail so that should hold good for this occasion as well. Once you're released I'll come back to the hospital with you and see if we can speak to the doctor who treated the young lady when she was admitted. He may be able to clarify the situation regarding her injuries.'

Superintendent Solomakis shook his head as Mr Tsilikadis requested that Vasi be released to accompany him to the hospital.

'I've spoken to the doctor. He's convinced the young lady was assaulted. Even if it was with her consent she may wish to press charges for the physical damage that was inflicted on her. The doctor has requested that your client stays in custody until he has given a DNA sample and we also know his blood type.'

'I'm sure Mr Iliopolakis will not object to either. He assures me he had nothing to do with the incident.'

The Superintendent raised his eyebrows. 'We'll see.'

Mr Tsilikadis sighed in exasperation. 'Can these samples be taken immediately?'

Very slowly Superintendent Solomakis raised his eyes and looked at the clock. 'That will depend whether the police doctor is free.'

'Please telephone him and ask him to come as soon as he is available.' Mr Tsilikadis knew it was no use trying to persuade the Superintendent to allow Vasi to leave the police station on bail until the tests had been completed. 'Whilst we wait Mr Vasi will make a sworn statement so he is able to leave as soon as he has fulfilled your requirements.'

Vasi shrugged as Mr Tsilikadis told him he had to give samples and also make a statement. 'Will I be able to leave then?'

'They'll probably want to go through your statement with you, but they should have no reason to hold you any longer.'

Superintendent Solomakis read through Vasi's statement and also that of the downstairs tenant from the apartments where Dimitra lived. The woman had not seen the person she claimed had visited Dimitra's apartment the previous evening. Until the results of the samples supplied voluntarily by Vasi, had been analysed and compared with those taken from Dimitra he had no valid reason to detain the man any longer.

Thranassis had sent two officers to Dimitra's apartment and they had returned with the blood soaked sheet, her torn clothing and a soiled towel they had found on the bathroom floor. The forensic team had taken prints from the front door and also the bathroom taps. He had sent the sheet and towel to the forensic analyst hoping that evidence would be found on them that would link Vasi Iliopolakis conclusively to the crime. As an afterthought he had sent an officer back to take prints from the front door and also the bathroom taps.

'Am I allowed to go to the hospital?' asked Vasi as he left the police station accompanied by his father and the lawyer.

Mr Tsilikadis shook his head. 'It would not be wise for you to visit the young lady until you have been officially informed that you are no longer under suspicion. Such a visit could be construed as intimidation.'

Vasi sighed in exasperation. 'I would like to know how she is, and there's also a question of someone to nurse her. As far as I know she has no family locally and as she's employed by my father and myself we must be responsible for nursing provision, even if it's only temporary.'

Vasilis nodded. 'She may have insurance, of course, but until we know we'll pay for a nurse to be in attendance. That will be in order, won't it?'

'I see no reason why you should not pay for her nursing care. As her employer it is a generous gesture. If Mr Vasi should be found responsible for her injuries then it is only right that his family should pay for her nursing.'

Vasi looked at the lawyer indignantly. 'I've told you. I didn't lay a finger on her. Don't you believe me?'

'It is not a question of what I believe,' replied Mr Tsilikadis dryly. 'It is a question of what Superintendent Solomakis believes. It could be interpreted as a sign that Mr Vasi is guilty.'

Vasi shook his head. 'I don't care what that Superintendent believes. I know I'm innocent and I also know that when the results come back they will prove my innocence. I'm sure when Dimitra is well enough to be questioned she will confirm that I didn't enter her apartment yesterday evening.'

Mr Tsilikadis approached the reception desk and produced his card. 'It is quite urgent that we see the doctor who treated Miss Artimatakis when she was admitted. I appreciate he could be busy. We're willing to wait until it is convenient.'

The woman looked at the card, giving the lawyer's name and address. This obviously had something to do with the police coming earlier and escorting the young man off the premises. She cast a glance over at Vasi. He looked respectable enough, but that didn't always mean anything.

'Is that the man who called the ambulance?'

Mr Tsilikadis nodded. 'Mr Vasi Iliopolakis.'

The receptionist frowned. 'I believe the doctor wanted some details from him. I'll page the doctor. Take a seat.'

It was a quarter of an hour before Doctor Tsakonakis entered the reception area and was directed to where the three men sat patiently. They rose as he approached and he introduced himself.

'I am Doctor Tsakonakis. What can I do for you?'

'Would we be able to go somewhere more private to talk?' asked Mr Tsilikadis.

'Follow me.' The doctor led them into a cubicle where he drew the curtain to give them a degree of privacy. 'I'm sorry, this is the best I can do.'

Mr Tsilikadis nodded. 'I'm sure we'll not keep you long, Doctor. I understand that Miss Artimatakis was admitted earlier. Firstly, how is the young lady?'

'As well as can be expected after her ordeal.'

Mr Tsilikadis pursed his lips. 'Doctor, I appreciate that you cannot give me any confidential information about her condition, but I do need to ask a few pertinent questions.'

'Are you a relative?'

'I am Mr Vasi Iliopolakis's lawyer. Whilst he was waiting to speak to you he was asked to go to the police station. It has been intimated that he assaulted the young lady. A charge that my client vigorously denies. He was the person who telephoned for an ambulance and he had planned to alert the police himself to a possible crime. His father,' Mr Tsilikadis waved his hand in the direction of Vasilis, 'wishes to cover the costs of a nurse temporarily. She is an employee of his and as such feels it is his duty.'

The doctor eyed Vasi speculatively. 'You found her?'

Vasi nodded and explained Dimitra's absence from work and his concern that led to him visiting her apartment. 'I told the woman from downstairs who let me in that Dimitra had been fine when I gave her a lift home the previous evening. I didn't get out of my car and I certainly did not go into her apartment. I expect the neighbour also saw Dimitra's torn clothing lying on the floor and thought she had been attacked as I did. I imagine she was the person who alerted the police.'

Doctor Tsakonakis nodded. 'The police did contact me and advised me they had a suspect in custody. Did you refuse to give a DNA sample, Mr Iliopolakis?'

Vasi shook his head. 'Of course not. I gave one voluntarily, along with some blood, a couple of hairs and' Vasi blushed, 'also a sperm sample.'

Mr Tsilikadis frowned at Vasi. The man should have told him a sperm sample had been requested. 'I assume that means the she was raped?'

'Until I have been able to speak to the young lady about her ordeal I am unable to say whether she was raped or whether the act was consensual and turned violent. We have taken some samples that will be sent for analysis.'

'Has Dimitra said who did this to her?'

'The lady has not yet recovered from her visit to the operating theatre. The police are hoping that she may be well enough to make a statement tomorrow. In the meantime, if you would like to complete the necessary forms at reception, we will see about arranging for a nurse. Now, if you will excuse me.'

Ariadne Viverakis sat in her apartment looking out of the window, watching for her son to return. After what had happened to Dimitra he had insisted that he returned and stayed the night with her. He argued that had she gone upstairs with the man whilst alone he may have turned violent towards her.

Her son had convinced her she must report the incident to the police and the nice Superintendent had assured her she had nothing to worry about, but still Costas had been adamant that he would stay at her apartment that night. Despite his wife's protests he continued to place his shaving kit and a change of underwear ready for the morning in a bag.

'This man who you went up to the apartment with saw you as well as your mother. Suppose he comes here looking for you and you're staying with her?' argued Litza.

'He has no idea where we live. You're quite safe, Litza. For all we know the police have him in custody. You know how old people get. She's trying to put on a brave face and appear unconcerned, but I'm sure she's frightened.'

Litza sniffed. Costas's mother could hardly be called old; she was not yet fifty, and she had never appeared to be a nervous type.

From her position at the window Ariadne saw the man begin to mount the stairs to the upper apartment. He did not look like a policeman. She opened her window a crack and heard him ring the doorbell. After a few moments he rang again; then his heavy tread could be heard coming back down the steps when he did not receive an answer.

Ariadne stiffened. They sounded like the footsteps she had heard the previous evening. The young man who had come earlier in the day had run lightly up the steps and she had not known he was there until he began to bang on Dimitra's door and call her name through the letter box.

She saw him quite clearly as he stood and looked up at Dimitra's windows for a few minutes before opening the door of a white car and sitting in the driver's seat. He continued to look at the apartment block and held something to his ear that she assumed was his mobile 'phone, finally he banged a hand on the steering wheel and drove away.

Ariadne took a deep breath. She would speak to Costas when he arrived and see if he thought she should telephone the police and let them know about the visitor.

The sergeant who took the telephone call from Mrs Viverakis promised to pass the information on to Superintendent Solomakis. He felt doubtful that Thranassis would place any importance on it. The woman said she did not know the man, but would be able to recognise him again. She gave a description of him that would have fitted many men in the town and could only say the car he had driven away in was a white Peugeot.

Wednesday 10th October

On the advice of Mr Tsilikadis Vasi had spent the night at the apartment with his father and Cathy. He had agreed that it made sense for him to be in the town as his father would need him at the Central to complete the work that Dimitra usually undertook and he would also be available if either the lawyer or the police wished to speak to him again.

Having made a detour as he drove to the hotel and reported to Superintendent Solomakis at the police station Vasi now sat in front of the computer. He needed to enter the outstanding work for Monday, but before he commenced he wanted to see if the report from the echo sounding company had been mailed to him.

He scanned the report of the area of the bay outside his hotel and then ran a printed copy off so he could study it more carefully. His idea to build a jetty looked feasible. Armed with this information he would be able to approach construction companies and ask for an estimate. Even if Yiorgo was not prepared to accept his offer there was no reason why he should not employ someone else as a boatman.

Vasi pressed his fingers to his temples. Should he e-mail Saffron and tell her he had been accused of assaulting Dimitra? He would not want her to think he had not told her because he was guilty. Sighing deeply he decided he would do that later. When his father arrived he would ask him to contact the hospital, check there was a nurse to attend to Dimitra and ask after her condition. It was quite possible she had named her attacker by now and Vasi knew he was innocent.

Dimitra gradually regained consciousness. Her body ached intolerably, but she must get up and shower. She tried to sit up and a hand pressed down on her. Her eyes opened wide and she gasped in fear. Surely Filippos had not returned as he had threatened.

She looked at the woman whose hand had restrained her. 'Who are you?' she asked thickly.

'I've been asked to look after you for a few days until you're feeling better.'

'Where am I?' Dimitra frowned as her eyes swivelled around the room. This was not her apartment.

'You're in hospital. You'll be fine now. The doctor will be along later to have a look at you.'

'No!' Dimitra struggled again to sit up. 'I don't want to see him. Let me go.'

The nurse shook her head. 'I'm not allowed to let you out of bed. You had surgery yesterday and you could haemorrhage. Wait until the doctor has been. He'll be able to tell you if you can get out of bed.'

Dimitra shook her head and tears began to course their way down her cheeks. 'I don't want to see him.'

The nurse wiped Dimitra's eyes and offered her a glass of water. 'I'll hold it for you. Not too much or you'll make yourself sick. You'll feel better when your throat is not so dry.'

Dimitra sucked up some of the liquid from the straw, finally turning her head away and closing her eyes. She needed to leave the hospital. She certainly did not want to be there when Filippos Melanakis came to see her. If she did not hurt so much she would insist that she was allowed to dress and leave immediately.

Alecos found the journey down to Aghios Nikolaos hospital arduous. Despite being strapped to a stretcher that was firmly attached to the ambulance he had a horror of falling off as the vehicle negotiated the steep bends on the highway. The continual movement had brought on a return of his headache. The attendant tried to distract him with conversation, but he hardly listened as he longed for the journey to be over.

Ariadne Viverakis telephoned the hospital and enquired about her upstairs neighbour.

'As well as can be expected,' she was told.

She sighed with impatience. 'I wondered if I should bring some clothes and toiletries in for her. She was taken away in an ambulance and had nothing with her.'

'I'm sure she would appreciate the gesture. If you pack a bag and label it with her name you can leave it at reception.'

'I'm not able to see her?'

'I cannot say, madam. When you bring the bag in you could ask again.'

Ariadne looked around her kitchen. She had a cloth bag that would be suitable to place Dimitra's night clothes inside and she could place some toiletries in a plastic bag with them. She could write a message to the girl to say she had sent them and pin it to a nightdress, then tie the handles and ask the receptionist to add a label. She felt virtuous about the neighbourly act she planned, but also hoped it would give her access to Dimitra and she would be able to ascertain exactly what had happened to the girl.

She climbed the stairs to Dimitra's apartment and opened the door, looking around curiously. There were no signs that there had been an intruder. She peered into the kitchen and bathroom before finally entering the bedroom, noticing that the bed had been stripped and the torn clothing removed. She bit at her lips. Should she have asked permission of the police before entering?

She shrugged. She had not been told she could not enter and there was no police tape anywhere in evidence. She would collect the items she thought Dimitra would need and return to her own apartment as quickly as possible. Should the man who had called the previous evening decide to return she did not want him to find her there. For the first time she queried the wisdom of her actions. She should have waited until her son was with her.

Hurriedly she opened drawers and looked for a nightdress or pyjamas, finding only a selection of large T-shirts. Obviously that was what Dimitra wore, if anything, when in bed. She placed a pair of slippers in the bottom of the bag followed by a wrap and the T-shirt. From the dressing table she took a brush and comb and debated whether to add any cosmetics. There was such an array that she had no idea which ones to choose and decided not to bother. From the bathroom she collected a flannel, toothbrush, paste and deodorant, putting them all into the plastic bag and tying the top.

Her duty done she scuttled back down the steps and breathed a sigh of relief when she shut her front door behind her. If she was able to see Dimitra when she delivered the bag she could ask if there was anything else she required and take that in the following day. She would make sure her son was with her if she had to enter Dimitra's apartment a second time.

Inspector Christos studied the report that had been sent through to him from Athens regarding the accident to Alecos Vikelakis. There had been no flakes of paint found at the site that matched Vasi Iliopolakis's car. Christos ringed the information and turned his attention to the second report he had requested regarding the vandalised car belonging to Stelios Papandrakis.

Babbis confirmed that the only prints found inside the car were those of the owner, although there were a considerable number on the exterior. It was confirmed that the number on the wing mirror that had been found at the site matched the number of the one that was still in situ and an analysis of the paint showed that traces of the same paint were present on Alecos's car.

Christos scratched his head. This proved that he was correct when he had surmised that the car belonging to Stelios Papandrakis had been the one involved in the accident, but it was not proof that the owner had been driving it at the time. If, as the anonymous caller claimed, it had been Vasi Iliopolakis, why had the man then deliberately damaged his own car?

He decided he would pay Mr Papandrakis a call and see if he could account for his time on the twenty first of September and if he had any witnesses that could corroborate his story. The California Bar, where he worked, had confirmed that he always had Friday off. It could also be worthwhile visiting Mr Vikelakis now he had been transferred to the local hospital to see whether he had recovered sufficiently to be able to provide him with any relevant information or be able to identify the driver.

Ariadne was just about to leave to catch the bus to the hospital when her daughter-in-law arrived.

'I wish you'd 'phoned. I was just going out,' she remonstrated.

Litza shrugged. 'I thought I'd call in to see how you were. That was a nasty shock you had yesterday. It was a good thing Costas was here at the time. Suppose the man you let in was the one who beat her! He could have done the same to you if you'd been alone.'

Ariadne sighed. She knew the real reason Litza had called was to glean as much information as she could so she could gossip to her neighbours.

'Would you like a coffee?'

Litza nodded and took a seat at the kitchen table. 'Only if it won't hold you up. Where were you going?'

'I was taking some clothes up to the hospital. Dimitra was taken away in an ambulance. She hasn't any night clothes or a wash bag with her.'

'Did you go up to her apartment?' Litza's eyes opened wide. 'Suppose he had still been lurking up there.'

'Don't be silly,' snapped back Ariadne. 'I gave the police a description of the man I saw going up there late yesterday afternoon. No one has been around since. If I saw him here again I'd phone them immediately and I'm sure they'd come out straight away and arrest him.'

'It's a shame Costas wasn't here when he came around. He could have asked him what he was up to.'

'It would have been more sensible for Costas to make a note of the registration number of the car and let the police track him down and ask questions.' Ariadne placed a cup of coffee and a glass of water on the table. 'Do you want a biscuit?'

Litza shook her head; then smiled. 'Well, maybe I will. I'm sure one biscuit won't put any extra weight on me.'

Ariadne placed the tin of homemade biscuits on the table and watched as Litza took two. 'So, tell me, what exactly had happened to the girl? Had she been raped?'

Ariadne shook her head. 'I don't know.'

Litza frowned. 'You must know. You found her; well, Costas says he called you when he found her.'

'All I know is that she was lying on her bed and she was black and blue with bruises.'

'All over?'

'I didn't really look. I just pulled the sheet back over her. She was naked and it wasn't decent for her to be lying there exposed like that before complete strangers. The man who'd come looking for her had called an ambulance and then I just sat and held her hand until it arrived.'

'So you didn't watch them examine her?'

'It wasn't my place to be there,' Ariadne stated primly.

'So you don't know if she was raped or only beaten?' Litza was disappointed that she had been unable to elicit any further information.

'For all I know she had tripped over and hurt herself.' Ariadne placed the lid firmly back on the biscuit tin. 'I really must be off. The bus is only every half an hour and I don't want to miss the next one.'

'Would you like me to come with you?'

Ariadne raised her eyebrows. 'Whatever for? I know my way. The bag isn't heavy and I'm only going to give it to the receptionist to pass on to Dimitra.'

'Aren't you going to see her?'

'She isn't well enough for visitors today.' Ariadne spoke firmly. She was hoping she would be allowed to visit Dimitra, but she did not want Litza with her when she did so.

Inspector Christos drove with Stavros to the lodgings where Stelios Papandrakis lived.

'You wait outside,' he ordered Stavros and knocked on the door. The same man who had opened the door to him before greeted him with a smile.

'Come in. I expect you want to speak to Stelios. Is it good news about his car?'

Christos followed the man through into the cramped living room without answering him. Elias went to the foot of the stairs and called up. Stelios could be heard moving around and then walking down the stairs to the living room. He scowled when he saw who his visitor was.

'You've come to tell me I can collect my car, I gather?'

Christos shook his head. 'I'm afraid we're not able to release it to you just yet. I am here to ask you to accompany me down to the police station. I have a few questions I would like to ask you. Just to clarify the situation, you understand.'

'Are you arresting me?'

'I hope that won't be necessary, sir.'

'Meaning that you will arrest me if I refuse?'

'I would have to ask my officer who is waiting outside to ensure your compliance with my request. Provided I am happy with the answers to my questions you should be free to return home shortly.'

Elias patted Stelios on the back. 'I'm sure you have nothing to worry about. You'll be back in plenty of time to go to work.'

Stelios shrugged. 'I obviously do not have a choice,' he muttered.

Christos sat opposite Stelios in the interview room, whilst Stavros stood by the door. Christos smiled at the uneasy man before him.

'Just a few questions. Nothing for you to worry about.'

'I've never known such a fuss made about returning a stolen car.'

Christos ignored the remark. 'A little bit of background information, first sir. We have your name and address and I believe you work at the California Bar. Before taking up that position you were the manager of the Kronos hotel in Hersonissos. Is that correct?'

Stelios nodded. They had been checking up on him.

'When you visited the station before I asked if you would give us samples of your fingerprints. You refused. Why was that, sir?'

Stelios licked his lips. He would have to tell them about his previous conviction. 'I was picked up once for possession. It was only a small amount and it was for my own use. The police insisted on taking my prints before they released me.'

'Are you in the habit of using substances?' asked Christos.

Stelios shook his head. 'Once, maybe twice a month, just to help me relax.'

'What is it you like to take?'

'Just a pinch of cocaine usually. If I can't get that I'll smoke a couple of joints.',

'And do you remember when you last took something?'

'Probably a week or ten days ago.'

'Would you have taken anything on the evening of the twenty first of September?'

Stelios shrugged. 'I may have done. I don't make a note of the dates.'

Christos leaned forward. 'Tell me, what effect does cocaine have on you?'

'Makes me forget my troubles for a while.'

'And marijuana?'

'The same.'

'They don't make you feel invincible in any way?'

Stelios shook his head.

'Interesting.' Christos smiled. 'I suppose they have different effects on different people. I have heard that some people who have taken cocaine think they can fly and leap out of windows.'

'Probably depends upon how much you take. Is this all you asked me to come down here for? A discussion on drug taking?'

'No, I digressed.' Christos shuffled the papers in front of him. 'According to the form you filled in to say your car had been stolen you had parked it in Athanasiou Street. Are you absolutely certain that was where you left it? You couldn't have made a mistake regarding the location?'

Stelios shook his head. 'Of course not. If I didn't remember where I had parked how would I ever find my car when I needed it?'

'Quite so. Now, you say there was some slight damage to your car. Were both wing mirrors in place when you last saw it?'

'Yes.' Stelios felt some misgivings. Had he lost his wing mirror when he forced Alecos off the road?

'Now, I would like you to think very carefully, Mr Papandrakis. Where were you on the evening of the twenty first of September?'

Stelios shrugged. 'At work, I expect.'

Christos shook his head. 'That was a Friday. Friday is your day off.'

'Then I was probably at my lodgings.'

'Is there anyone who can confirm you were there during the evening and that night?'

'The old couple might be able to. What has this to do with returning my car anyway?'

'We believe your car was involved in an accident that took place during the evening on that date.'

'That wasn't me,' Stelios interrupted hurriedly.

'That is why we would like you to be able to prove where you were during the time in question. You see, you claim your car was stolen, but the only prints we found inside belonged to you.'

'Whoever stole it wore gloves.'

Christos nodded slowly. 'I find it very puzzling. If someone stole your car because they needed to get home to another town they would hardly return it to Aghios Nikolaos afterwards. It is not the winter so they would hardly be wearing gloves as a matter of course. If they just wished to borrow it for a ride and didn't wish you to know they had used your car why didn't they return it to the original parking place?'

'I expect the space had been taken.'

'Quite possibly, but I would have expected them to have been able to find a space relatively close by, rather than the other side of town from your address.' Christos watched Stelios's reactions closely. 'The other thing that I find very strange is why it had been sprayed with red paint.'

Stelios shrugged. 'How would I know? Is there anything else? I'd like to get back and have my meal before I go to work.' He began to rise from the chair.

Christos waved him back down. 'Just a couple more questions. I understand when you worked at the Kronos hotel it was owned by Mr Iliopolakis and he had reason to dispense with your services. Do you hold a grudge against him?'

Stelios clenched his fists beneath the table. 'It was a misunderstanding,' he muttered.

'Are you also acquainted with Mr Alecos Vikelakis?'

'I imagine everyone locally knows him. He's the manager of the bank here.'

'Have you had any dealings with him of a personal nature?'

'Why should I? I've not won the lottery. I don't have a fortune at my fingertips.'

Christos sat back and spoke earnestly. 'I would like you to think very carefully about the twenty first of September, Mr Papandrakis. If anything comes to mind that would prove where you spent the evening, possibly in the company of friends or at a local taverna, please come and tell us.'

'I've told you. I was at my lodgings.'

'You seem very certain of that.'

'I am. Can I go now?'

Christos nodded. 'We may wish to question you further, Mr Papandrakis. I presume we will be able to contact you at your current lodgings?'

'I'm planning to move on at the end of the season.'

'Then please be good enough to leave us your new address.' Christos smiled, knowing full well that Stelios had no intention of advising them of his future whereabouts.

Ariadne sat on the bus taking her to the hospital in Heraklion. Had Litza not called just when she was leaving she could have been on her way home by now. Doubtless the girl would call on her again the following day to see if she had any news of Dimitra that could be passed around amongst her acquaintances. All the girl did was sit with her friends gossiping all day. It was a wonder Costas ever had a meal when he returned after work or a clean shirt to put on his back.

Ariadne walked up to the reception desk and took her turn in the queue of people. She looked at the miserable collection of people who were sitting over at one side, either waiting for medical attention or news of a relative and stiffened, then relaxed. The man in a white coat who was talking to a couple was surely the man who had come to Dimitra's apartment the previous evening. That could explain his presence there. He was a doctor. She would have to call in at the police station on her way home and see that nice Superintendent and explain to him that the man she had described was a doctor at the hospital.

Arriving at the police station Ariadne was told that Superintendent Solomakis was out, but she could leave a message with the sergeant on duty. She hesitated. 'I'll come back tomorrow,' she decided.

Walking back to her apartment Ariadne thought about the doctor she had seen talking solicitously to the relatives. She was certain he was the man she had seen the previous day going up to Dimitra's apartment and ringing the bell, but if he was a doctor he should have known she was in the hospital. Maybe she would speak to Costas and ask his opinion before she troubled the police again.

As she turned the corner into her road she could see a white Peugeot was parked a short distance away from her home. She shook her head. She was becoming paranoid. Many people in Heraklion drove a white Peugeot. Slowly she continued down the road until nearly at her apartment where she stopped and leaned against a neighbour's wall. It certainly looked like the same car as she had seen the previous day.

Filippos Melanakis was furious. He was certain Dimitra was in her apartment and just refusing to answer the door to him. He strode back down the steps and over to his car, slamming the door viciously after him. Ariadne stiffened. Maybe it was not the doctor she had seen at the hospital, but someone who looked incredibly like him, his brother possibly. As the doctor manoeuvred his car from the parking space Ariadne could see the registration plate quite clearly. She would remember those numbers and write them down as soon as she was indoors.

Dimitra received the bag sent to her from reception containing the items Ariadne had selected gratefully. She would be able to wash and brush her hair when she was allowed up and change from the hospital gown into the T-shirt. No doubt she would feel better then, although still bruised and frightened.

She had been relieved when it was Doctor Tsakonakis who entered her room, not Filippos. The doctor had sat beside her and explained that he had needed to give her a blood transfusion and send her to the operating theatre as she had been badly torn internally.

'I've prescribed a course of antibiotics for you. You don't want any sort of infection starting up. We've taken swabs and we'll analyse those to see if there's any other problem we need to treat you for. Rest today and you should be able to get up tomorrow for a short while.'

'Thank you,' murmured Dimitra.

'I understand there is a police woman wanting to ask you a few questions. Do you feel well enough to see her now?'

Dimitra's eyes opened wide. 'Why?'

'The neighbour who found you reported the incident to the police. You may wish to bring charges against your assailant if you did not give consent to intercourse.'

Dimitra shook her head. 'I don't know who it was.'

Doctor Tsakonakis patted her hand. 'I'll ask the police woman to have a word with you. You can explain to her how this happened. It would be better for you to see her now, whilst the incident is fresh in your mind. I'll tell her she can come in.'

Dimitra had insisted she had no idea who her assailant had been. The police woman suggested she might recognise the man from a photograph, but Dimitra shook her head. 'I really did not see him clearly. It happened too quickly.'

'You're certain you would not be able to recognise him?' persisted the police woman. 'We have had a couple of other assaults like yours and do need to apprehend this man. Sooner or later a girl is going to lose her life. You were fortunate to be found when you were or you could have been that girl. Is there anyone you would like us to call who you would feel able to confide in?'

Dimitra felt hot tear coursing their way down her cheeks. She could not tell them that it was the doctor who was the trauma specialist at the hospital who was responsible. They would never believe her. She shook her head.

Thursday 11th October

Dimitra was feeling a little better. Her bruised body still ached and when she moved in the bed there was a dull pain inside her. Surreptitiously she examined her breasts and legs. They were so tender, covered in bruises and red wheals. Filippos had bitten her cruelly, not like the gentle nipping that Alecos had indulged in and she had enjoyed.

With the assistance of the nurse she had been allowed to walk slowly to the bathroom where she had washed herself thoroughly, but she still did not feel clean. She had been promised a shower the following day and was looking forward to allowing the hot water running over her to soothe and cleanse.

Doctor Tsakonakis had visited her again and declared himself pleased with her progress. 'You should be well enough to return home on Monday.'

Dimitra looked at him in alarm. 'I don't want to go back to my apartment.'

'Have you some friends or relatives you could stay with temporarily?'

Dimitra shook her head.

'I'm sorry. We're not able to keep you in hospital once you're well enough to return to your home. In fact after tomorrow you'll not need the attentions of a nurse.'

'How much do I owe her? I haven't any money with me.'

'You don't have to worry about that. I understand that your

employer has covered your expenses.'

'Really? How did he know I was here?'

'I believe he was concerned when you did not turn up for work and asked his son to call on you. He asked your neighbour to let him in with her key and when he saw you he 'phoned for an ambulance.'

Dimitra swallowed. 'I had no idea. I must 'phone him. Did Mrs Viverakis put my mobile in the bag?'

The nurse shook her head. 'Mobiles are not allowed to be used on the wards. I expect she knew and that was why she didn't send it.'

'Now, Miss Artimatakis, unless you give any cause for concern over the weekend I will examine you on Monday and you should be able to return to your home during the afternoon.'

'I haven't got my keys. I won't be able to get in,' protested Dimitra.

'I'm sure you will be able to arrange something with your neighbour. You'd probably like to ask her to bring you in some clothes.'

'How can I contact her without my mobile?'

'There's a pay 'phone in reception. Your nurse can wheel you down there and you can use that.'

Dimitra felt tears coming into her eyes. She did not want to go to the reception area. If she was there it was sure to be the very moment that Filippos came through and he would see her.

Mrs Viverakis saw Litza walking along the road, locked her front door and retired to her kitchen. She did not want her daughter-in-law to visit her today. She knew that once Litza was aware of her intention to go to the hospital she would insist on accompanying her.

All evening she had considered whether she should tell the police that the man she had described to them looked like a doctor at the hospital and that probably accounted for him calling, or should she give them the registration number of the white Peugeot and say the man had been to Dimitra's apartment again. If she was allowed to visit Dimitra she could ask her if he was a friend. She would not want to get an innocent man into trouble.

Superintendent Solomakis was disappointed. The results from the Pathology laboratory where Vasi's blood sample had been sent had been returned, confirming him as type 'O', the same as Dimitra's. Now forensics had declared the sample of his hair that they had compared with the hair that had been found twisted amongst her pubic hair was completely different. He would have to pin his hopes on the DNA results incriminating Vasi, but they would not be available until Monday at the earliest.

He wanted to find this man who seemed able to gain access easily to the apartments of young women and assault them viciously. Earlier in the year two other victims had attended the hospital for treatment, although their injuries had not necessitated admission. They both claimed they had not known their assailant, but there had been no sign that their apartments had been broken into and nothing had been stolen. Finger prints and samples had been taken in both cases and their files searched for a match without success.

Stelios packed his possessions in a holdall. He would go in to work as usual that evening. He needed his wages. The following day he would take the bus up to Heraklion and then catch the ferry to Piraeus. It would be easy enough to disappear into the city and it would not be difficult for him to find employment. Casual workers were not asked for references. He would not be missed until he did not go in to the California Bar on Saturday evening and by then he would make certain he was miles away.

Ariadne was pleased when reception at the hospital said she was able to visit Dimitra. She followed the signs along the maze of corridors until she reached the room where Dimitra lay and knocked timidly on the door. A nurse opened it, asked her name and agreed to ask her patient if she was feeling well enough for a visitor.

Ariadne sat down at the side of Dimitra's bed. 'I'm pleased to see you looking so much better. You gave us a nasty scare.'

'I'm sorry. Thank you for bringing in my washing kit and some night clothes.'

'That was no problem. I realised you had gone off in a rush and had nothing with you. Is there anything else you'd like me to bring in?'

'Well,' Dimitra hesitated. 'The doctor says I could be well enough to be discharged on Monday.'

'So you'd like some proper clothes so you can get dressed,' beamed Ariadne.

Dimitra nodded. 'Yes, please, but I have another favour I want to ask. Would you be able to telephone my employer and ask him if he could visit me?' Dimitra gripped Ariadne's hand and gazed at her earnestly. 'It's very important that I see him before I leave here on Monday and I don't have my mobile with me. I've been told I'm not allowed to use it in here anyway and I don't want to have to go down to reception. I don't feel strong enough yet.'

Ariadne nodded. 'If you can give me his 'phone number I'll call him when I get home. That's no trouble.'

'Promise me.' Ariadne was surprised to see that Dimitra was near to tears.

'I promise.'

'I'll be terribly grateful. And I need some money. Provided I wasn't robbed my wallet should be in my handbag.'

'Would you like me to leave some money with you now?'

Dimitra shook her head. 'Anything I ask my nurse to get for me whilst I'm in here will be added to the bill. It will only be for Monday. I will have to pay for a taxi.'

'I'll bring a bit extra with me when I bring your clothes, just in case.'

'You're very kind,' Dimitra felt the tears welling up in her eyes.

Ariadne patted her hand. 'Don't you worry about anything. Just lay there and get your strength back. I hope you were able to give the police a description of your attacker. We don't want the likes of him around.'

'I didn't get a good look at him,' lied Dimitra.

'I thought it might have been the young man who brought you home.'

Dimitra frowned. 'Do you mean Vasi? It certainly wasn't him. He wouldn't attack anyone. He's the man I've asked you to telephone. You won't forget, will you?' She gazed at Ariadne anxiously.

Ariadne pursed her lips. 'How did he know you were lying in your apartment injured?'

'His father asked him to call when I didn't arrive for work or 'phone in to say I was sick. The doctor told me Mr Iliopolakis is paying my hospital expenses. I need to thank him.'

'I would have thought that could have waited until you were back on your feet.'

Dimitra shook her head. 'It's very urgent that I speak to Mr Iliopolakis or his son as soon as possible. You will 'phone him, won't you?' Dimitra clutched at Ariadne's arm.

'You're quite certain you want me to ask him to visit you here?'

'As soon as he can and certainly before Monday,' affirmed Dimitra. 'It's very important.'

Ariadne looked for the white Peugeot as she walked along her road, but there was no sign of it today. She clicked her tongue in annoyance. She had meant to ask Dimitra if she knew the owner. She would have to remember to do so when she took her in some suitable clothes to wear home, and she must not forget to ask Costas to lend her ten Euros, just in case Dimitra did not have enough money in her purse.

She made a cup of coffee and took the biscuit tin out of the cupboard. She would sit down and watch her favourite television programme. She had missed it the two previous afternoons' episodes and hoped she would be able to pick up the thread of the story. She eased off her shoes and leaned back in her chair, there was something about hospital visiting that made your feet hurt.

The programme she had intended to watch had finished when she opened her eyes. Her coffee sat untouched and cold at her elbow. How long had she been asleep? She looked at her watch. Over an hour! She often dropped off for a few minutes, but she never usually slept as long as that. Guiltily she remembered how insistent Dimitra had been that she should telephone her employer. She should have done that when she first arrived home, rather than sitting down and falling asleep.

Where had she placed the card the man had given her? She remembered him handing it to her and saying she could contact him on his mobile number at any time, but where had she put it? They had been up in Dimitra's apartment at the time, but she was certain she had not left it up there. Ariadne stood in the middle of her lounge and looked around. She was a tidy person and she could see nothing out of place.

Biting her lips in consternation she began to open the drawers of the dresser, looked behind the clock and the mirror, felt down the side of her easy chair and looked into the cupboard where she kept her best linen and glassware. There was no sign of it. Giving a deep sigh she picked up her cup of cold coffee and walked into the kitchen. She would make herself something to eat and whilst she was preparing her meal she might remember where she had put the card for safety.

If she really could not find it she would have to ask Dimitra if she knew his 'phone number when she took her clothes in. She would do that tomorrow. It would be an easier journey on the bus on Friday. On a Saturday they always appeared to be full of youngsters and the Sunday buses were only once an hour. She must 'phone Costas and ask him if he could pass by on his way to work tomorrow and lend her ten Euros. It would be foolish to wait until she had been upstairs and found Dimitra's handbag. There was no guarantee her attacker had not raided her purse before he left.

Litza answered the telephone and Ariadne had to spend a

quarter of an hour answering her questions about Dimitra. Litza was obviously annoyed that her mother-in-law had visited the girl and not asked her to accompany her. Eventually, after the third time that Ariadne asked, she handed the 'phone to Costas.

'I need to ask if you can lend me some money.'

'How much?'

'Only ten Euros. I saw Dimitra today and I'm taking her in some clothes tomorrow. The doctor has said she should be well enough to return home on Monday. She'll probably need to have a taxi. She said there should be enough money in her handbag, but her attacker could have taken it. If it's not convenient I'll have to go to the bank myself, but it's out of my way.'

'Is ten enough?' asked Costas.

'It should be. I have another ten I can leave with her, but I don't want to be short for my weekend shopping. She looks a good deal better than when we saw her last, I'm pleased to say.'

'I'll drop it round on my way to work,' promised Costas. 'If you're not up I'll just put it through the letter box.'

'Of course I'll be up,' replied Ariadne indignantly. 'Oh, another thing, Costas, you know that man who found her, he gave me a business card with his telephone number and I can't find it. Do you remember where I put it?'

'You gave it to me,' replied Costas dryly. 'What do you need it for?'

'Dimitra was most insistent that I telephoned him and asked him to visit her. I promised I would do so, but then I couldn't find his card. Have you still got it?'

Ariadne could hear Costas fumbling in his pockets and finally he declared he had found it.

'Can you read the number out to me? I've got a pen here.'

'There's more than one number. Which one do you want?'

'I don't know. Is there a mobile number?'

Litza leaned over her husband's shoulder. She had managed to hear most of the conversation. 'That looks like a mobile,' she said. 'The others have the names of hotels beside them.' She tapped Costas on the shoulder. 'You offer to 'phone him,' she mouthed.

Costas nodded and read the number out to his mother. 'Are you sure you wouldn't like me to 'phone him?'

'There's absolutely no need for you to trouble. I'll be able to tell him how Dimitra is progressing.' Ariadne guessed the suggestion had come from her daughter-in-law.

'Well, if you're sure.'

'Of course I am. And you'll remember to drop the money in to me tomorrow morning?'

'I won't forget. What time do you plan to go to the hospital?'

Again Ariadne knew Litza was hoping to be able to accompany her. 'I'm not sure. I have a number of jobs to do in the morning, so it will probably be some time in the afternoon.' She would collect the promised clothes and handbag for Dimitra and ensure she caught the ten thirty bus. If Litza came round at lunch time she would find her mother-in-law had already visited the hospital.

Vasi began to type an e-mail to Saffron. He told her how he had found Dimitra and been accused by Superintendent Solomakis of being her attacker.

I can assure you I had nothing to do with it. I happened to say to the woman downstairs that I had given Dimitra a lift home the previous evening and she had told the police. That vindictive Superintendent immediately blamed me. He insisted that I gave him samples of my hair, blood and DNA before he agreed to release me. I know when he gets the results back they will prove me completely innocent.

I just wish he would concentrate on finding whoever pushed Alecos off the highway. When he has found out who did that I will insist that he gives me a full apology. I had planned to sue him for wrongful arrest, but Mr Tsilikadis says as I was released on bail and have not been formally charged it's very unlikely the courts would consider that I had a case.

I am hoping I will get the results of the echo-sounding tomorrow. Yiorgo is going to sail the boat around to Giovanni's jetty on Saturday and I will tell him my plans then. I do hope he will agree. If he refuses ....'

Vasi saved his mail as a draft and answered his mobile 'phone.

'Yes?' he said tersely.

'Mr Iliopolakis?' a woman's voice asked tentatively.

'Yes,' he said again.

'This is Mrs Viverakis. I am Dimitra's neighbour who let you in to her apartment.'

'Yes,' Vasi was suddenly alert. 'How is Dimitra?'

'That was what I wanted to talk to you about.'

'She's not ....' Vasi felt a cold horror creeping over him.

'No, no, I visited her today. The doctor is pleased with her progress. He has told her she should be well enough to leave the hospital on Monday.'

'Thank goodness.' Vasi realised he was sweating with relief. 'I'll let my father know. It was very good of you to call.' He was about to close his 'phone when the woman spoke again.

'Dimitra asked me to give you a message. She was most insistent that she needs to see you before she leaves the hospital on Monday. I'm sorry I'm telephoning you so late, but I couldn't find your card.'

Vasi gave a small smile. 'She's probably concerned about the payment for her nurse. My father arranged that and I'll let him know. Do tell her she has nothing to worry about financially.'

'Please can you visit her? She was quite adamant that she needed to speak you.'

Vasi frowned. 'I'll speak to my father. I'm sure one of us will manage to call in.'

'Can I assure her of that when I see her tomorrow?'

Vasi sighed. It would have to be his father as Mr Tsilikadis had advised him against visiting until any possible charge against him had been dropped. 'Yes, tell her my father will come in. I'm not able to do so at present.'

'Thank you. I'm sure that will put her mind at rest. She seemed to think it was urgent and was quite distraught. I had to promise to telephone you and she asked me not to forget.'

Vasi finished his e-mail to Saffron and sent it to her before he telephoned his father.

Vasilis sighed. 'I suppose I have to go in to see her as you shouldn't. I'll ask Cathy to come with me. She's probably worried about returning to work. I'll tell her she can take as much time off as she needs. It could take her quite a while to recover mentally from her ordeal. You can cope with the computer work until she's able to come back, can't you?'

'Of course,' replied Vasi, whilst he groaned mentally. He hoped Dimitra would very soon feel well enough to return to work. He did not want to be up in Heraklion at the Central hotel. When he received the results from the echo sounding he hoped he would be able to start negotiations to build a jetty, and do to that he needed to be in Elounda.

Friday 12th October

Mrs Viverakis was waiting for Costas when he arrived with the promised money. 'Are you in a hurry?' she asked.

'I've got a few minutes. Why?'

'I'd like to ask your advice.'

'What's worrying you?'

'When I was visiting Dimitra I saw one of the doctors in reception. I thought at first that he was the man I had seen at her apartment, the one I told the police about, then I realised I must be mistaken. He just looked similar. I just wondered if I should give the police the registration number of the white Peugeot and tell them the man looked like the doctor at the hospital.'

Costas shook his head. 'Better not to get involved any further. Leave it up to the police. They know their job.' He looked at his watch. 'I'd better be off or I'll be late. You're sure ten Euros is enough? You wouldn't like twenty?'

Ariadne shook her head. 'I'm going upstairs to collect Dimitra's handbag and pack some clothes ready for her to wear when leaves the hospital. She's sure there's plenty of money in her purse, provided he didn't rob her into the bargain. Ten Euros should be more than enough to pay for a taxi from the hospital to here.'

'I don't like you going up there alone. Maybe you should wait until I can come with you.'

'Don't be silly. I'll only be in there a few minutes. I'll lock the door behind me and make sure I have my mobile with me.'

'Make sure you have the instructions with you or you'll not know how to use it,' smiled Costas and gave his mother a peck on the cheek as he left.

'Why do you want me to go to the hospital with you? I don't even know the girl.'

'You met her once when Vasi was going out with her,' Vasilis reminded his wife.

'That was years ago!'

'Under the circumstances I thought she might feel more comfortable if you were with me. I don't know how women feel after they've been attacked, but they could see every man as a threat to them.'

'If she feels like that she would hardly have asked you to visit her, besides the nurse you provided should be with her.'

Vasilis slipped his arm around Cathy's waist. 'All right, I need you with me for moral support. I've never had to face a situation like this before and I don't know what to expect.'

'How long do you plan to stay? I promised to cut Vivi's hair this afternoon.'

'No longer than necessary. If we arrive about twelve we should be able to leave within half an hour. Then I'll take you for lunch at the Central and you can have a taxi home.'

'Well, if you bribe me like that how can I refuse?' Cathy turned to her husband and kissed him. 'Is there something I should take for her?'

Vasilis shrugged. 'I don't know. You know the things women appreciate when they're in hospital.'

'I know what I appreciated. Her circumstances are somewhat different from mine,' remarked Cathy dryly.

Vasi kept his e-mail account open during the morning waiting for the results of the echo sounding to be sent to him. He found it difficult to concentrate on transferring the figures from the hotels on to the weekly balance sheet and twice he had to check back where the totals did not agree.

It was a relief when he received the advice that he had a new mail in his box and opened it with alacrity. It was from Saffron and he was not sure whether to be delighted or disappointed.

'I have just read your mail and this is just a quick reply. Of course you will be proved innocent of the attack on Dimitra. I hate that Superintendent. What has he got against you? Just because you gave an employee a lift home! I feel sorry for Dimitra. It must have been a terrible experience for her. Must go – a broken leg is waiting for me!'

Vasi smiled. She would no doubt send him a long e-mail that evening. He would telephone her on Saturday; tell her the results of the echo sounding and Yiorgo's reaction to his idea. He hoped there would be no reason for him to stay in Heraklion over the weekend or that would upset his plans.

Vasilis and Cathy entered the hospital. Cathy was carrying a large bag and refused to divulge the contents to her husband.

'It may not be appropriate,' she said, 'but it was something I appreciated. It's a woman thing. You won't have to stay around. I can always get a taxi to the Central.'

Vasilis raised his eyebrows, but Cathy refused to be drawn. 'If Dimitra wants to speak to you alone I'll wait outside. Just make sure I have a chair to sit on as I may have to stand for a while later.'

Cathy was immediately conscious of the frightened look in Dimitra's eyes, which changed to relief when she saw who her visitors were.

'I hope you don't mind me coming with my husband,' she smiled. 'If you want to talk to him privately I can go away and come back later.' Cathy sat down on the chair vacated by Dimitra's nurse.

Dimitra shook her head. 'It isn't confidential, but if Mr Iliopolakis agrees I don't want anyone else to know.'

Vasilis frowned. 'If it's about paying your hospital expenses you don't have to worry. You're an employee so I consider it to be my responsibility. I shall be able to claim it against my expenses when I complete my tax return so I won't be out of pocket.'

'I'm very grateful to you, but it isn't that.' Dimitra looked at him pleadingly. 'Would I be able to come and stay at the Central when I leave here? I'll only want a small room, nothing grand, and you can deduct the cost from my wages.'

Vasilis looked at her in surprise. 'If it's the travelling to work you're concerned about it would be cheaper for you to use a taxi. I've spoken to Vasi and we both agree that you're not to return until you're fully recovered.'

Dimitra's eyes filled with tears. 'I don't want to go back to my apartment. I'm scared he'll come back.'

Vasilis shrugged. 'I don't think that's very likely. Men who commit these kind of crimes don't usually visit their victims second time.'

'Please, Mr Iliopolakis. Let me stay at the Central whilst I look for a new apartment. I *can't* go back to my old one.'

Cathy touched Vasilis's arm. 'She certainly can't return to her old apartment if she thinks the man will come back again.'

Vasilis frowned at his wife. He did not want her to suggest that Dimitra came to stay with them. 'I suppose it can be arranged.'

Dimitra leaned back and gave a long sigh of relief. 'Thank you, Mr Iliopolakis. You won't tell anyone will you? Not at the hospital. I'll tell them I'm returning to my old address.'

Cathy looked at Dimitra speculatively. She could understand the woman's aversion to returning to her old apartment, but why should she be so insistent that no one knew she was staying at the Central?

'What about your clothes and things? You'll need to go back to pack a case.'

'I'll ask my neighbour to pack some clothes for me. She's been very kind. She brought me in some clothes to wear when I leave and my handbag this morning. I can ask the taxi to stop on my way to the Central and collect it from her. I don't want to go back inside my apartment yet.'

'Why don't you ask her to send it straight to the Central?' suggested Cathy.

Dimitra shook her head vehemently. 'I don't want *anyone* to know I'm living there. It's the only way I'll feel safe.'

Vasilis shrugged. 'The staff will know you are there.'

Dimitra bit her lip. 'Ask them not to tell anyone my room number. Tell them I'm working extra hours to make up for the time I had off and don't want to be disturbed.'

'You can do that, Vasilis. In fact it would be practical for you to collect Dimitra from the hospital and take her there yourself. I'm sure the police will catch this man and once he's been detained Dimitra will feel safe again.'

'Please,' Dimitra begged.

Vasilis shrugged again. It really made little difference to him if the girl occupied an empty room at the hotel. 'I'll check that you are definitely being discharged on Monday before I come for you.'

Cathy squeezed Dimitra's hand. 'Now that's settled I'd like to offer to wash and style your hair for you. I spent a considerable time lying in a hospital bed and I always felt better when my hair had been freshly washed and dried.'

Dimitra looked at Cathy doubtfully and Vasilis smiled. No doubt his wife had shampoo, conditioner and a hair dryer in her large bag. He should have guessed.

'I used to be a hairdresser,' she assured Dimitra. 'You tell me how you'd like it to look and I'll do my best to please you.'

'I tried to wash it myself when I was allowed to have a shower, but it hurt to lift my arms up. I didn't do a very good job.'

'It isn't easy. You go off to the Central, Vasilis, and Dimitra and I will spend an hour or so together. I'll call for a taxi when we've finished. Don't forget you've promised me lunch.'

Vasi opened his e-mail that had been sent through from the echo sounding company and read it avidly. He did not understand many of the technical expressions they used, but he surmised from their report that his idea was feasible. He frowned as he read the words *'The drop in water level needs to be taken into account.'* What did that mean? He would ask Yiorgo tomorrow, he would probably know, if not a fisherman could probably tell him.

He ran off a paper copy and then the final sheet that was the bill from the company, looking at it in horror. He should have asked for an estimate before he had told them to go ahead. He hadn't even negotiated a price with Giovanni to purchase the fishing boat yet.

Superintendent Solomakis looked again at the results that had been sent through to him from the laboratories. He would ask his sergeant to pull up the records of the other assaults that had taken place earlier in the year. He doubted if they would provide him with any useful information, but he would have them to hand when he received the DNA report on Monday. If the attack on Miss Artimatakis had been by the same man the DNA should be a match, and then if that also matched the sample taken from Mr Vasi Iliopolakis it was incontrovertible evidence against him. The hair that did not match could be disregarded.

Saturday 13th October

Yiorgo steered the fishing boat carefully out of the harbour. He had received curious looks from the other boatmen who were setting up their placards advertising boat trips to Spinalonga. He kept a cautious distance between himself and the arm of land he was sailing past. He was not familiar with the rocks and currents and certainly did not want to confess to Vasi that he had run aground or holed the craft on a submerged rock. It was almost with a sense of relief that he finally cut the engine and drifted in to Giovanni's jetty, throwing the rope adroitly over the bollard and securing the fishing boat.

Annita watched her father's boat arriving and felt unaccountably sad. It looked little different from the way it had when her father had taken her and Andreas out to help him bring in his catch. Yannis had joined them in the task whilst he lived with them and they had been happy, carefree days.

Yiorgo pocketed the key to the engine and waited, uncertain whether he should stay with the boat until Vasi arrived or walk round to the house and ask for Giovanni.

'Hi, Yiorgo. Pappa said you were coming this morning. She looks in pretty good condition.' John cast an appraising eye over the vessel.

Yiorgo smiled. 'Manolis looked after her well. The engine sounded sweet and she handles easily.'

'I hope Pappa will let me take her out.'

Yiorgo frowned. 'She's considerably heavier than your little boat and with a deeper draft.'

'I'm sure I'd be able to manage her.' John spoke confidently and Yiorgo believed him. 'Are you coming up to the house? Pappa and Vasi are waiting for you.'

Yiorgo followed John across the jetty and round the side of the house to the patio.

Vasi greeted him with a smile. 'How was your journey?' he asked as Giovanni handed Yiorgo a glass of wine

'Over all too soon. You should have come with me, Vasi. You would have enjoyed yourself.' Yiorgo grinned at his friend.

'And who would have driven my car here to take you back to Aghios Nikolaos?'

'I could have taken you back in my boat,' offered John. 'We should have thought of that.'

Vasi shook his head. It would have been even more of a nightmare to him to have travelled back to Aghios Nikolaos in John's small craft. 'I need to go along to the hotel before I take Yiorgo home.'

'I have to be back in time for Barbara to go to work,' Yiorgo reminded him, wondering why Vasi had not visited the hotel earlier.

'That's no problem. We won't be long there.'

Yiorgo placed the keys he had been given for the boat on the table and Giovanni shook his head whilst refilling Yiorgo's glass.

'You hold on to those for the time being. If I haven't got them John can't be nagging at me to take the boat out by himself.'

Yiorgo pushed the keys across the table to Vasi. 'Probably better if you take care of them I'll be tempted to sneak up here and take her out myself otherwise.'

Vasi exchanged a glance with Giovanni and pocketed the keys with a nod. 'Let me know when you've spoken to Stefanos.'

'He said he could come on Monday so I should be calling you by the middle of next week. Another glass?' Giovanni offered the bottle and Vasi shook his head.

'I'm driving. Not worth taking a chance.'

John held out his glass. 'I'll have another.'

'No you won't. You're also driving. You're supposed to be going up to the taverna to relieve your mother now you've seen the boat.'

'I'll only be on the bike,' protested John.

'Makes no difference if you're stopped.'

John shrugged. It was highly unlikely that there would be a patrol car in the area. He did not particularly want another glass of wine, but he did want to be accepted as an equal of the men.

Yiorgo emptied his glass rapidly. He was the only one drinking now and guessed Vasi was impatient to be off. He took a last look at Manolis's boat and sighed. He had enjoyed himself more that morning than at any time since he had left the navy.

Vasi drove the short distance back to Elounda and along to his hotel. To Yiorgo's surprise he asked him to get out of the car and walked towards the water where it lapped gently on the small shingle beach.

'I've had an echo sounding taken of the area,' Vasi, waving his hand around to encompass the expanse of water. 'I'm thinking of building a jetty and I needed to know how far out it would have to stretch to accommodate Manolis's boat.'

'That's quite an undertaking. Is Giovanni planning to sell the boat and what would you do with it?'

'I've a couple of ideas. Do you want to hear them?'

Yiorgo nodded eagerly.

'Come into the hotel.'

Yiorgo followed Vasi through to the far corner of the reception area. As they passed the main desk Vasi asked for coffee to be brought to them and also picked up a brochure from the counter. He handed the report of the echo sounding to Yiorgo.

'That was expensive,' commented Yiorgo.

Vasi shrugged. 'Not as expensive as if I'd had a jetty built and then found there wasn't enough depth of water to use it. I asked

John to dive and take measurements of the boat and there should be enough clearance. This is the bit that puzzles me.' Vasi pointed to the last line of the report. '*The drop in water level needs to be taken into account.* What does that mean?'

'In spring the water level tends to drop. The canal becomes unusable because it is so shallow. It isn't noticeable anywhere else, but it could mean you haven't got enough depth at the end of your jetty and the boat would be grounded.'

Vasi frowned. 'Where does the water go?'

'No idea,' replied Yiorgo cheerfully, 'But it could be a good idea for you to keep an eye on the canal and when that's low have another echo sounding done.'

'Spring, you say?'

Yiorgo nodded.

'That might mean I couldn't have the trips running until the following season. I'll have to get an estimate for building the jetty, but it will take time and they have to allow for winter storms,' frowned Vasi.

'Why do you need a jetty anyway? Why didn't you leave it moored at Aghios Nikolaos?'

Vasi handed the brochure to Yiorgo.

'Boat trips to Spinalonga?'

Vasi nodded. 'The visitors all want to go out to the island. The boatmen here are making a good living, like those in Aghios Nikolaos. The visitors ask me where they can get a boat and I direct them up to the Square. I think they'd be only too pleased to be able to walk across the road and take the boat that belongs to the hotel.'

Yiorgo grinned. 'No doubt at a slightly higher price for the convenience.'

'No, I'd have to keep the prices the same as everyone else. A family on a budget wouldn't be prepared to spend an extra ten Euros just to save themselves a short walk.'

'Would you have enough visitors staying here to make it viable?'

Vasi shrugged. 'I doubt it, but there are the other hotels along this stretch. Their clients would probably patronise me. I'd also advertise it as being the original boat that took over supplies to the island. That would be a draw for some people.'

Yiorgo nodded slowly and waited whilst their coffee was placed on the table. 'So you're going to buy Manolis's boat from Giovanni? Suppose you go to the expense of building a jetty and then your idea doesn't work out?'

'I've other options. I could offer an evening visit to Spinalonga to watch the sun go down followed by a barbecue on the beach. How do you feel about it?'

'Some people would go for it, no doubt.'

Vasi shook his head. 'No, I meant how do you feel about being the boatman? Sailing backwards and forwards to Spinalonga?'

'Me?' Yiorgo looked at Vasi in disbelief.

'It won't be like being in the navy, but you'll be out on the sea most days and home for Barbara in the evenings.'

'Vasi, ...' Words failed Yiorgo and he felt close to tears.

'Think about it. You don't have to give me an answer today. Talk it over with Barbara. Provided you're both happy with the idea we can sort out the details during the winter. If the island continues to grow in popularity you'll be making a small fortune next season.'

Yiorgo shook his head, still disbelieving. 'Why are you doing this, Vasi?'

Vasi shrugged. 'A number of reasons. Giovanni doesn't want the boat and I can't bear the thought of it being sold to someone who doesn't care about it or sending it off for salvage. I think Manolis would be pleased to know it was still going to Spinalonga. Had I bought the Imperia I wouldn't have had the money to invest. As it is I've some spare capital that would be better used than sitting in the bank.'

'Suppose building a jetty here isn't feasible? The water could be too shallow.'

'Then I apply for a permit to moor the boat up at the Square. You can still be the boatman.'

Yiorgo's eyes gleamed and he leant forward and shook Vasi's

hand. 'There's one thing I would like, Vasi.'

Vasi looked at him in surprise. 'What's that?'

'I think you ought to register her under a new name. I think she should be called "Flora".'

Alecos sat in his hospital bed. When the doctor had visited him the previous day he had informed him that the heavy plasters that encased his legs would be removed during the following week and a lighter one put on. That would enable him to begin to move around and become independent.

'Once we're satisfied that you have a certain amount of mobility you'll be better off at home with your family to look after you. It's just a question of time now for the healing process to take place.'

Alecos looked at the doctor in consternation. If the hospital considered him well enough to return home there was no way he could avoid being interviewed by the bank over the discrepancies on the Iliopolakis accounts. He needed to find a way to extricate himself from the situation.

'I'm not sure if my mother could look after me. She's no longer young.'

The doctor shrugged. 'Just remember how much it's costing you to stay here in a private room. It would be more economical to return home and employ a nurse if necessary.'

Alecos sighed. However long he stayed in the hospital his problems would not go away.

Having driven Yiorgo back to his home in Aghios Nikolaos, Vasi duly reported to Inspector Christos at the police station.

'Are you any nearer to finding out who caused Mr Vikelakis's accident?' he asked.

'I'm pursuing a line of enquiry,' replied Christos noncommittally.

Vasi sighed. 'I'm supposed to be going to England in another few weeks. I don't want to have to cancel the trip through no fault of mine.'

'I assure you, Mr Vasi, as soon as we can release you from your bail conditions we will do so. Now Mr Vikelakis has been transferred to the local hospital I plan to visit him. He may have remembered some small detail by now that could help us. He may also feel more comfortable talking to me rather than an unknown policeman in Heraklion.'

'I hope so,' replied Vasi fervently.

Inspector Christos waited until the California Bar was open for custom that evening. It was not the kind of bar that he would frequent, being mainly for the young holiday makers who wanted cheap liquor and loud music. He changed out of his uniform and walked down to the waterfront where the bar was situated. It would not do for him to drive home smelling of alcohol just in case he was stopped by one of his own patrol men.

He cringed as he entered the dimly lit, noisy bar and elbowed his way forwards where he commandeered a stool. He looked around, but could see no sign of Stelios. He should have checked the man's working hours. He did not want to be sitting suffering the assault on his eardrums any longer than necessary.

'Yes?'

'Oh, a beer please.'

'Large or small?'

'Small.'

Christos waited until the tankard was placed in front of him. 'Is Stelios around?'

The bar tender shook his head. 'Hasn't turned up. At this rate when he decides to put in an appearance the boss will tell him he's not wanted anymore.'

Christos frowned. 'That's annoying. I wanted to have a word with him.'

'What's he done?'

'What makes you think he has done anything?'

The bar tender grinned. 'You've got "police" written all over you. Might as well wear a label.'

'When was he here last?'

'Thursday.'

'Not last night?'

'He has Fridays off. Look, if you only want to speak to Stelios would you mind leaving? You're not good for business.' The bar man nodded towards the room where the customers were eying Christos warily.

'To tell you the truth I'll be only too relieved to get outside. How you stand the decibel rate for the music you have playing beats me. You'll be deaf by the time you're thirty.'

'What's that?' The man cupped his hand behind his ear and grinned cheekily at Christos.

'You can have my beer.' Christos pushed it across the bar to him and it was seized upon. 'Heard that all right, I notice! Let me know if Stelios turns up.'

The man nodded. He would certainly not let the police know if Stelios put in an appearance. You didn't help them even if they had given you a beer.

Alecos went to sleep with a smile on his lips. He had the answer to his dilemma. He would ask his father to telephone Vasi Iliopolakis on Monday and ask him to pay him a visit at the hospital. He had an offer to make that he was sure Vasi would not refuse.

Monday 15th October

Superintendent Solomakis studied the DNA report that had been sent to him from the laboratory. There was no way the samples Vasi Iliopolakis had given matched the swabs taken from Dimitra or the discarded towel that had been found on the bathroom floor. The man had obviously been speaking the truth when he claimed he had not attacked the girl.

Reluctantly he picked up the telephone. He would have to call Mr Tsilikadis and advise him that his client was totally innocent of any charge against Dimitra Artimatakis. He would take the opportunity to remind him that Vasi Iliopolakis was still accused of endangering the life of Mr Vikelakis by dangerous driving. If Christos had not decided to interfere he was convinced Vasi would have been arrested and awaiting trial by now.

His telephone call made, and Mr Tsilikadis's caustic remarks about jumping to conclusions received without comment, Thranassis turned his attention back to the DNA report. He compared the information with the records he had of the other two known assaults that had taken place earlier in the year. The DNA analysis was the same in every case. Despite the other two girls having showered and not visiting the hospital immediately, swabs had been obtained with enough DNA to make analysis available.

He read their statements through again. Neither claimed to have known her attacker, yet there had been no sign of a forced entry. They were not prostitutes, one being a school teacher and the other an office worker. Nothing had been stolen by the intruder and no one appeared to have noticed him, despite the assaults having taken place during the late afternoon when it was light.

The only lead they had was from the neighbour who claimed she had seen a man at the woman's apartment the following day and he had driven away in a white car. If he interviewed her again there was just a chance that she would recall something more distinctive about him that could be helpful.

Mrs Viverakis sounded dubious when the Superintendent spoke to her over the telephone, but agreed that he could come to her home and she would go over the statement she had given.

'I couldn't come to the station,' she explained. 'Dimitra, the lady from upstairs, is coming home sometime today and I want to be here for her. I've cooked a bit extra and I can take it up to her. I'm sure she won't feel like thinking about cooking today. I can always get her a bit of shopping tomorrow and I'll make sure I'm around in case she needs anything.'

'That's very considerate of you.' Thranassis lowered himself down in the chair he was offered.

'Just being neighbourly. I'm sure she'd do the same for me.'

Thranassis nodded. 'It's fortunate for her that you were here when that young man called and you asked what he wanted. You told us a second man called the following afternoon.'

Ariadne nodded.

'You didn't ask him why he was there?'

'I would have told you if I'd spoken to him,' replied Ariadne indignantly.

'I'm sure you would, but sometimes these things can be forgotten, or you think they're of no importance.'

A slow flush crept into Ariadne's cheeks. It did not go unnoticed by Thranassis.

'Is there something else you have remembered?' asked Thranassis.

'Well, not remembered, but when I went to the hospital with

some bits and pieces, washing and night clothes things, for Dimitra, I saw one of the doctors there. Not to speak to. He was busy, but I was struck by his likeness to the man I described to you. They could be brothers, twins even, but they do say everyone has a double, don't they.'

'Do you happen to know the name of the doctor? If we spoke to him, explained the situation, I'm sure he would be co-operative and we would be able to get an accurate description of Miss Artimatakis's assailant.'

Ariadne shook her head. 'I wasn't close enough to read his name tag. I did come in to the station to tell you, and give you the car number, but you weren't there. Then I thought I could be getting a respectable doctor into trouble. I spoke to my son about it and he said I shouldn't interfere with police business.'

Thranassis stiffened. 'I am sure we would not have considered that you were interfering. You say you have a car registration number?'

'Yes. The man drove away in a white Peugeot and I wrote the number down as soon as I came indoors.'

'Do you still have it?'

Ariadne looked around her lounge. 'Well, it must be somewhere. I certainly don't remember throwing it away. Is it important?'

'It could be. If you wouldn't mind looking for it I'd be grateful. I don't mind waiting.'

'Oh, dear, I wish now that I had returned to the station when you were there and told you.' She continued to sit in her chair. 'Let me think. I came in and picked up the pen by the telephone message pad. I always keep one there. Never know when my son or daughter-in-law will ask me to get something for them. I tore it off the pad and,' she hesitated, 'put it in my purse so I would have it with me when I called at the station,' she ended triumphantly.

'So it should still be in there,' smiled Thranassis.

'I'll get my bag.' Ariadne walked through to her bedroom and returned with a bulging handbag. Methodically she began to unload the contents onto the table. Tissues, powder compact, lipstick, glasses, a packet of peppermints, odd receipts for her shopping, a letter, pen, house keys, her bank book, a mobile 'phone and finally her purse sat on the table.

She opened the zip fastener and peered inside, frowning. 'I'm sure that's where I put it. I hope I didn't give it to Costas when I repaid him the money he lent me.' She withdrew her Euro notes from the compartment and placed them on the table, separating each one to ensure there was no scrap of paper caught between them. She inserted her fingers into the empty flap and pulled out a piece of crumpled paper.

'Here it is,' she announced triumphantly. 'It had just got all scrunched up at the bottom.'

Thranassis smoothed out the paper and read the car number. According to the details the car had been registered in Athens and was approximately eighteen months old. He transferred the information into his notebook and placed the piece of paper inside also. It would be easy enough to trace the owner of the car through the licensing office, but he would drive up to the hospital and see if by any chance it was in the car park that was used exclusively by the staff.

'You've been very helpful, Mrs Viverakis. I'll leave you in peace now to await your neighbour's return.'

Ariadne looked at her watch. 'I would have expected her to have been here by now. Maybe they've decided to keep her in another day.'

Thranassis drove up to the hospital and parked amongst the cars belonging to the doctors and nurses; there were any number of white cars. He would just look for a Peugeot before he went to the trouble of memorising the number. Briskly he strode up and down until he stopped at the rear of a white Peugeot. According to the number plate it was registered in Heraklion. Just to be sure he checked the number in his notebook before walking on.

As he continued his progress up and down the rows he saw men and women emerging from the hospital, some singly and some in groups. They made their way to a car and drove out of the car park. Their duty was over for the day. Thranassis stood where he was. He was probably wasting his time. It would be more sensible to send a sergeant up the following morning to check on the cars and see if the one he was interested in was parked there. In the meantime he would ask for a check at the licensing office.

'I've been trying to contact you all afternoon,' complained Christos.

'I've been busy,' answered Thranassis tersely.

Thranassis was sure he heard a gloating note in Christos's voice as he continued to speak to him.

'I'm pretty sure we have our man who caused Mr Vikelakis's accident. I interviewed the owner of the car that had been spray painted. He claimed to know nothing, of course, but couldn't provide an alibi for the evening in question. He said he had probably spent it in his room as it was his day off. I went down to the bar where he worked and I was told he hadn't turned up for work that night. It's not unusual for summer bar workers to decide to have an evening off and then claim they were sick.'

Thranassis tapped his pen against the desk impatiently. Why didn't the man get on with it?

'I went back to the bar last night and there was still no sign of him. I called round at his lodgings and the couple there said they hadn't seen him since Friday morning. I asked them to have a look in his room and it appears he's removed his belongings. He knew we were on to him and he's flown.'

'He could still be innocent. You may just have frightened him.'

'He didn't strike me as the type who would be frightened by the police asking a few questions. I suggest we put out an alert for him and have him picked up.'

'We still don't know if he was driving the car at the time,' argued Thranassis.

Christos sighed. 'I'll go up to the hospital tomorrow and see if Mr Vikelakis can remember anything about the accident. Hopefully now his injuries are mending his memory will return.'

'His mother was adamant that he had accused Vasi Iliopolakis.'

'And Mr Iliopolakis has proof that he was in a restaurant at the time we think the accident happened,' answered Christos dryly.

'We have the evidence from the couple who were driving back from the airport.'

Christos snorted. 'A damaged car tried to overtake them at speed. That's hardly evidence.'

'I'm not prepared to release Mr Iliopolakis from his bail yet.' Thranassis spoke firmly. He was still smarting from the remarks made to him by Mr Tsilikadis. 'I'm not convinced he's innocent.'

'Very well.' Christos sighed heavily. 'I'd still like an alert put out to have Stelios Papandrakis apprehended so he can be questioned further.'

'I'll refer it to the Chief.'

'You have the authority to sign a warrant.'

'Unlike you, Inspector Christos.' Thranassis slammed down the 'phone. His case against Vasi Iliopolakis was becoming more untenable by the day.

Mrs Viverakis was becoming concerned. Dimitra had not arrived home. She had kept a vigil at her window the whole of the afternoon and there had been no sign of her. She telephoned Costas when she knew he would be home from work and relayed her concerns to him.

'She's probably just been kept in an extra day. If you're really worried why don't you 'phone the hospital and check with them?'

'I don't really like to bother them, but I suppose I ought to 'phone. That nice Superintendent said I should have told him that the doctor at the hospital resembled the man I'd seen at Dimitra's apartment and given him the car number. He made me feel quite foolish. I wish you hadn't told me to ignore it.'

Costas flushed at the rebuke. 'If it puts your mind at rest call the hospital. I've got to go. Litza's just put my supper on the table.'

Ariadne looked at the clock. It was far too early for Litza and Costas to be having their supper. It had been an excuse to curtail her 'phone call. Still, she would take his advice and call reception at the hospital and see if they could put her mind at rest.

Vasi was surprised when he received a call from Mr Vikelakis saying that Alecos wished to see him.

'I'm not sure if I should,' Vasi demurred. 'I ought to speak to my solicitor first.'

'Alecos said it was very important that he spoke to you. He said his memory was returning and you ought to be the first to know what he remembered.'

Vasi frowned. If Alecos could remember some details of his accident why wasn't he asking the police to visit him? Did he want to put Vasi's mind at rest, knowing how long it took for the police to follow through on information? It was unlike Alecos to be so thoughtful.

'Very well,' Vasi sighed. 'It's not very convenient as we have some staff off sick in Heraklion and I've had to stay up here. We're hoping they'll be well enough for work tomorrow. Provided they come in I'll drive down to Aghios Nikolaos on Tuesday morning. If I can't come then Alecos will have to wait.'

Tuesday 16th October

Mrs Viverakis had been relieved when the hospital informed her that Dimitra had been collected earlier in the afternoon by friends and she was planning to stay with them for a few days. She wished Dimitra had told her when she had visited on Friday. Had she known she would not have cooked extra to provide the girl with a meal. At least the food would not be wasted; she could eat it herself that evening.

When her telephone rang she expected it to be Costas, probably checking if she had telephoned the hospital and she was surprised when she heard Dimitra's voice.

'Mrs Viverakis, this is Dimitra.'

'How are you? I was expecting you to come back to your apartment yesterday. When you didn't arrive I 'phoned the hospital and they said you were staying with friends.'

'I'm sorry. I should have thought and telephoned you. It was a sudden change of plans. Would it be too much trouble for you to go up to my apartment and pack some clothes for me? I'm not sure how long I will be staying so I'd appreciate as much as possible.'

Ariadne frowned. 'Are you coming to collect them?'

'If you just leave a case packed up in my apartment a friend will call in this afternoon to collect it.'

'I don't have a case.'

'There are two in the cupboard in the hallway. My makeup and toiletries could go in the smaller one. I would be terribly grateful if you could have them ready by about lunch time and left by my front door. My friend will have a key to get in, so they won't need to trouble you.'

'I suppose I can,' agreed Mrs Viverakis grudgingly. She had hoped that once Dimitra had returned home she would wish to confide in her neighbour and she had been looking forward to hearing the details of her ordeal. She would certainly be watching from her window this afternoon to see who the friend was who collected the girl's belongings.

Thranassis ordered his sergeant to visit the hospital car park to see if he could find a white Peugeot with the number plate matching the details Mrs Viverakis had given him.

'Why don't I telephone and ask them? They're sure to have a record of the vehicles belonging to the staff.'

Thranassis looked at him sourly. He should have thought of that and not wasted his time the previous day wandering around fruitlessly.

'I don't want the owner to know we're interested in him at this stage. I'm contacting the licensing authority in Athens and see if they can tell me who they have recorded as owning the vehicle. Once we know the car is there and who it belongs to we'll approach the hospital.'

Makkis nodded. It would be pleasant to be out of the office and he could take his time wandering around amongst the parked cars.

Vasi entered Alecos's room hoping he would not have to spend too long with the man whom he disliked. He wanted to consult two construction engineers whose names he had found on the internet and ask them to give him estimates for building the jetty.

'Hello, Alecos. I'm pleased to hear you're recovering. Your father telephoned and asked me to visit you. He said you were regaining your memory.'

Alecos smiled. 'It can be quite interesting when your memory returns. It could mean I remember seeing you quite clearly as you forced me off the highway and into the ravine.'

'I certainly did not,' replied Vasi vehemently.

'I'm sure the police will believe me when I tell them. Of course, my memory might improve further if you bought the Imperia from me and assured the bank that the errors on your hotel accounts were due to your computer failure.'

'You're blackmailing me!'

Alecos shook his head. 'No, I'm finding a solution to our mutual problems. If the bank investigates the account discrepancies I will be disgraced and lose my job and pension. If you are found guilty of forcing me off the road you will be spending a number of years in jail and I shall be claiming compensation for my injuries. I don't think you can afford to refuse my offer.'

Vasi blanched. If Alecos did claim that he had deliberately caused the accident he would be jailed for an indeterminate number of years, whilst Alecos would no doubt think up a scheme to exonerate himself from the accusation that he had deliberately manipulated the bank accounts.

'How much are you selling it for?'

Alecos grinned maliciously. 'I thought thirty percent more than I paid for it would be a fair price.'

Vasi gasped. To pay that for a hotel that needed considerable structural repairs was extortionate.

'The choice is yours. If you agree I suggest you go to the bank and arrange for a transfer into my account for the full amount. I'll give you a letter of authority for my solicitor asking him to transfer the deeds into your name once the amount is in my account.'

'What's your rush? Why can't it wait until you leave the hospital? We can both go to the solicitors and the usual procedures can be followed.'

Alecos shook his head. 'It all depends upon how quickly my memory returns, doesn't it? You have this afternoon to think my offer over. If you haven't agreed by Friday my memory of the accident will have fully returned and I shall swear that I quite clearly saw your face grinning at me as you rammed your car into mine.'

Vasi glared at Alecos venomously and left the room. He really did not have a choice.

Makkis used his mobile to call Thranassis at the police station. 'The car is here. What do you want me to do now?'

'Wait there until I arrive. I have the name of the owner and we'll have a word with him. He may have an innocent explanation for calling at the girl's apartment; in which case he'll not refuse to give us a DNA sample.'

Doctor Melanakis entered the small room that was usually reserved for breaking bad news to relatives confidently. 'How can I help you?' he smiled.

'Just a couple of questions. I'm sure I'll not need to keep you for more than a few minutes. You are the owner of a white Peugeot and the registration number is,' Thranassis consulted his notebook and read out the number plate details, whilst Makkis stood near the door.

Doctor Melanakis nodded. 'Have I violated a parking restriction somewhere? My car has certainly not been involved in an accident.'

'You were driving that car on the afternoon of Tuesday the ninth of October?'

'Yes.'

'And again on Wednesday the tenth?'

'Yes. I drive it every day.'

'And on those two occasions you called at an apartment where a Miss Dimitra Artimatakis resides?'

Doctor Melanakis frowned. Surely Dimitra had not complained about his behaviour to the police? The other girls had been far too frightened to do so. He had left Athens a year earlier after the unfortunate death of a girl. She had screamed so loudly he had been forced to place his hand over her mouth to quieten her. Since then he had been more careful, and indulged in violence less often. On the occasions when he had been unable to control his sadistic pleasure any longer he had threatened the girls that he would return and they would experience worse treatment at his hands, leaving them too terrified to name him as their assailant. He had to extricate himself from suspicion.

'I called on her to advise her that Mr Vikelakis was to be transferred down to Aghios Nikolaos. She was not at home on either occasion.'

Thranassis raised his eyebrows. 'Do you make it a habit to call on friends or relatives of your patients at their homes?'

'Not usually, but Miss Artimatakis had stopped me on a number of occasions to enquire about the progress of her friend. I did not want her to call at the hospital and find he was not here. She would have expected the worst and I wished to prevent her from the unnecessary distress.'

'Very considerate of you.'

'Is that all?'

'Not quite. Unfortunately Miss Artimatakis was assaulted by an intruder. A neighbour thinks it may have been you she saw leaving the lady's apartment on Monday the eighth when the assault took place.'

Doctor Melanakis paled and he no longer looked at Thranassis. He would have been able to keep control of himself with Dimitra if she had not inflamed him further each time he saw her. His reaction was not lost on the Superintendent.

'Just so we are able to eliminate you from our enquiries I'd like you to give us a DNA sample.'

Doctor Melanakis shook his head. 'That will not be necessary. I had nothing to do with it.'

'I am afraid I have to insist, Doctor. You're refusal to co-operate could be construed as deliberate obstruction to a police enquiry.'

Doctor Melanakis licked his dry lips. 'She invited me in and made overtures to me. If she claims I forced her that is untrue. The sex was consensual.'

'So you did not force yourself upon her against her will?'

'Certainly not.'

'Then it is even more important that you give us a DNA sample. It would obviously eliminate you from our enquiries. It is quite simple. Just a saliva sample will be sufficient.'

Doctor Melanakis looked at the door. Makkis had now positioned himself in front of it. There was no way he could leave. He knew it would take four days at least for the results of the test to be returned to the police. He would be out of the country by then, and he would make sure it was somewhere that did not have an extradition agreement with Greece.

He shrugged. 'If you insist. I have nothing to fear.'

Tuesday 23rd October

Vasi sent a long e-mail to Saffron.

He explained that Alecos had blackmailed him into buying the Imperia hotel at an inflated price.

'I had no choice. If I refused he said he would tell the police that he had recognised me as the driver who had pushed him into the ravine. I am sure he has no idea who actually caused his accident. I also had to declare to the bank that the problems with our hotel accounts had been due to the programme we had on our computer.

It is all lies, of course, but what could I do? I did not want to end up in prison. It was such a relief when I reported to Mr Christos to be told that I was no longer under suspicion.

I have told my father and we are moving all our bank accounts. Stavros Tanakis, the manager, was most upset and offered all sorts of inducements, but my father would have none of it. Giovanni has also said they will also move theirs and he said I should pursue Alecos through the courts, but it would take so long and I am sure I would not win. Alecos can always claim loss of memory and who can prove otherwise?

Unfortunately I have had to alter my plans. I cannot possibly afford to build a jetty at the Elounda hotel now. I am negotiating for a mooring berth at the Square in Elounda and have asked to have Manolis's licence transferred into my name. At the beginning of the season I will buy a scooter for Yiorgo so he can travel up each day from Aghios Nikolaos. I still have to work out the financial details with him. He will have to pay me a percentage of his earnings to cover the running costs, but I will be very fair with him.

I think now Giovanni is regretting that he did not keep Manolis's boat and run trips to the island, but he is putting a good face on it. He says the money I paid him will allow him to build another self catering unit ready for next season.

Dimitra is still living at the Central. She is determined to find a new apartment and she has changed her mobile number. Apparently she did know her attacker, but did not think she would be believed if she accused Doctor Melanakis and was also frightened that he would return and inflict more damage on her. I could hardly believe that a doctor could be responsible, but she said Superintendent Solomakis would also be charging him with two other assaults when they caught him. He has disappeared and no one knows his whereabouts.

I have not had the opportunity to talk further with my father about the ideas for turning his house into a holiday centre. I would like to do so before I visit you in London so that we are able to make some definite plans.

My bail money has been refunded and I have been told that I am free to travel wherever I wish. I am longing to see you. After all that has happened here in the last few weeks it will be good to get away from Crete and have other things to occupy and interest me. '

Saffron read the mail with relief. Despite knowing that Vasi was innocent it was so good to know that the police believed him to be also and he was a free man again.

November 2007

'Saffie, it's Vasi.'

Saffron felt her heart give a little jump of excitement.

'Saffie, I am so sorry. I cannot come to England.'

'What do you mean? You cannot come? You were told you could leave Crete, that you were no longer under suspicion. It was all arranged. You have your ticket.' Saffron spoke wildly. 'Why have you changed your mind?'

'I haven't. Listen, Saffie, it is not my fault. Cathy has had an accident. It is serious this time. She fell and has broken a bone in her pelvis. She is in so much pain.'

Saffron nodded. She knew the effects such a break could have.

'Oh, Vasi. I am so sorry. Poor Cathy. Is she in hospital?'

'They only kept her overnight to take x-rays and assess the amount of damage. She returned home the next day with orders to rest and move around as little as possible. Pappa is with her, of course, and Rebecca is going to stay with them to help, but I have to manage the hotel.'

'It's the end of the season, Vasi. The hotels are closed.'

'Not the Central. That is open all year round. We host conferences from Athens. I am needed here.'

Saffron felt close to tears. She had not realised how much she had been looking forward to seeing Vasi again.

'You are not cross with me, Saffie?'

Saffron swallowed hard. 'Of course I am not cross with you. I am disappointed.'

'That is good that you are disappointed. I, too, am very disappointed, but you understand that I have to stay, to help my father. He is distraught. I cannot leave Crete until Cathy has recovered.'

'It will take her at least two months,' Saffron frowned.

'So maybe you could come here?'

'I can't.' Saffron shook her head. 'The winter months are some of our busiest. So many people have falls when it becomes icy. No one is allowed leave between mid November and the end of March.'

'So when will I see you? I want to see you so much and I have something very important to ask you.'

If you have enjoyed reading Alecos, you will be pleased to know that the next book – John – is planned for publication in June 2013.

See overleaf for a 'taster' of what is to come.

JOHN

November 2007

Vasi sat at the desk is his father's study, the computer open before him. He studied the page carefully. He was not poor by most peoples' standards, but he was certainly in debt to the bank. He had only managed to repay half of the loan he had taken out to refurbish the hotel at Hersonissos after Stelios had used it as a brothel. Now the premises were closed until the following year he would still have to continue to pay the bank the arranged monthly amount and also a retainer fee to his manager if he wanted to continue to employ him.

The decision he and his father had made to take their hotel accounts to a different bank meant the loan arrangement he had was not as favourable as before. Having bought Manolis's boat he would not have contemplated having an echo sounding of the bay with a view to building a jetty had he known he would be forced to purchase the Imperia hotel. He had also promised to buy Yiorgo a scooter so he could travel to Elounda from Aghios Nikolaos to run the boat trips to Spinalonga. The mooring fees for the boat he had paid in advance and he could delay purchasing a licence to carry passengers until the following year, but his expenses added up.

Ownership of the Central hotel had been signed over to him some years ago as a gift from his father and he was loath to approach him for any financial help. Fortunately the Central had made a good profit and should continue to do so during the winter months as the hotel was booked for conferences. To his relief there were no major repairs or refurbishments needed there.

He and his father conducted their accounts in different ways. Vasilis took his percentage from the hotels he owned at the end of each season, whereas Vasi preferred to take a monthly amount and hoped to be able to add a sizeable amount to his bank balance from the final profit when the season finished.

The percentage he expected to receive this year was already earmarked as a repayment towards the loan he had needed to take out for the useless Imperia hotel. He had bought a new car, not knowing how long the police would impound his original one and now he regretted it. He should have had more patience and waited; having had his damaged car re-sprayed the new car sat in the garage totally unused.

His visit to England was booked and paid for. He would only need to have spending money whilst he was there, but John had said he and Nicola had found the city expensive. He closed down the computer with a sigh. He would sell his new car and that debt could be cleared. Once he had returned from England he would look at his accounts more closely and see if he could negotiate a more favourable interest rate for the loans with his new bank.

He stretched and yawned. It was too early to go to bed. He thought about 'phoning Yiorgo and decided against it. If Barbara was not working Yiorgo would suggest that Vasi drove into Aghios Nikolaos and they met up for a drink. That would only cause trouble between Yiorgo and his wife.

The evenings seemed to stretch interminably before him now Saffron had returned to England. Usually when the season ended he was busy making plans to refurbish the hotels, but this year he had made any necessary arrangements earlier, thinking he would be devoting his time to designing and supervising the building of a jetty.

Finally he decided he would go out into the garden and spend some time with the dogs before checking their water bowl and locking the house for the night. Vasi pulled on a jumper and picked up two chewed balls from beside the door. He would play with the dogs for a while and it would not matter how excitedly they barked they would not be disturbing anyone.

An hour later he returned to the house, still feeling restless. The dogs had chased after the balls as he threw them, returning to drop them at his feet until he had become tired of the game before they had. He had filled their water bowl a second time for them and watched whilst they lapped eagerly until deciding they had drunk sufficient.

As he opened the patio door he could hear the telephone ringing. He frowned. Who would be calling the house at that time? It was probably someone trying to sell him something for the hotels. He ignored it and went into the cloakroom and washed his hands to remove the dogs' spittle from the balls.

As he returned to the kitchen he heard the end of the answer 'phone message. 'Vasi, do pick up if you're there whatever you're doing. It's urgent.' He heard his father sigh at the end of the 'phone and then the line went dead.

Vasi tapped his pockets. Why hadn't his father called him on his mobile? Where was his mobile? Surely it hadn't fallen from his pocket whist he had been playing with the dogs? He looked around the kitchen wildly. It could be anywhere outside, but why hadn't he realised he had dropped it? He would have to wait until daylight to search for it.

He picked up the telephone and dialled his father's number at the apartment. There was no answer. Obviously his father and Cathy were out somewhere for the evening. He screwed up his face in concentration in an attempt to remember his father's mobile 'phone number, relieved to hear it ring and have his father's voice on the other end.

'Pappa, it's Vasi. What's the problem?'

'Where have you been? I've been trying to call you on your mobile for the last half an hour.'

330

'I'm sorry. I think it must have fallen from my pocket when I was playing with the dogs. What's so urgent?'

He heard his father take a deep breath. 'I'm at the hospital. Cathy had a fall earlier this evening. I had to call an ambulance. She can't move.'

'What! Has she damaged her spine?'

'We don't know at the moment. They've taken her for x-rays. Now I've spoken to you I'm going back inside to see if they have any results. You can't use a mobile inside. I'll come out and call you again as soon as I have any news.'

'Call me on the land line. I'll wait by the 'phone,' promised Vasi. Now he had to stay up he suddenly had an overwhelming desire to go to bed. He would have to do something to occupy his time until his father had telephoned again.

He walked back into the study. He would open up the computer and look again at the various attractions London had to offer. Already he had a long list, but there could be something he had overlooked. The first thing he saw as he sat down at the computer was his mobile 'phone. He was both annoyed and relieved. Now he could call his father and ask him to use the mobile when he knew the results from Cathy's x-ray.

Vasi sighed with frustration when he was told the number he was calling was switched off. He had no choice but wait up until his father's call came, but at least he would not have to search the grounds for his mobile the following day.

It was almost an hour before Vasilis finally called and Vasi answered with alacrity.

'How is Cathy?' asked Vasi immediately.

Vasilis sighed deeply. 'The doctor says she has broken a bone in her pelvis. That's why she is in so much pain and can hardly move.'

'What can they do for her? Are they keeping her in hospital?'

'They say they'll keep her in tonight and she can return home tomorrow. She will have to stay in bed and rest until the injury has healed. They've warned me that it will take some weeks.'

'Poor Cathy. It could have been a good deal worse, of course.'

His father continued as if Vasi had not spoken. 'I'll need you up here to run the Central. I won't be able to leave Cathy.'

Vasi swallowed. 'How long will you want me to stay in Heraklion? I'm due to go to England in ten days.'

'You'll have to cancel. I'm sorry, Vasi, but Cathy needs me and I need you to be on hand here during the conferences. You can always go to England later. I'll see you tomorrow. Call me from the Central and when Cathy's home you can come over and we'll discuss the bookings and the arrangement requests that have been made.'

'Yes, Pappa,' Vasi answered miserably. 'By the way, I've found my mobile.'

'Good.' The line went dead and Vasi guessed his father had returned inside the hospital to be with Cathy. He dropped his head in his hands. Why did Cathy have to have an accident now? Once he had seen Cathy and spoken to his father again he would have to 'phone Saffron. It was possible that his projected visit to London could take place a couple of weeks later than scheduled.

'Saffie, it's Vasi.'

Saffron felt her heart give a little jump of excitement.

'Saffie, I am so sorry. I cannot come to England.'

'What do you mean? You cannot come? You were told you could leave Crete, that you were no longer under suspicion. It was all arranged. You have your ticket.' Saffron spoke wildly. 'Why have you changed your mind?'

'I haven't. Listen, Saffie, it is not my fault. Cathy has had an accident. It is serious this time. She fell and has broken a bone in her pelvis. She is in so much pain.'

Saffron nodded. She knew the effects such a break could have.

'Oh, Vasi. I am so sorry. Poor Cathy. Is she in hospital?'

'They only kept her overnight to take x-rays and assess the

amount of damage. She returned home the next day with orders to rest and move around as little as possible. Pappa is with her, of course, and Rebecca is going to stay with them to help, but I have to manage the hotel.'

'It's the end of the season, Vasi. The hotels are closed.'

'Not the Central. That is open all year round. We host conferences from Athens. I am needed here.'

Saffron felt close to tears. She had not realised how much she had been looking forward to seeing Vasi again.

'You are not cross with me, Saffie?'

Saffron swallowed hard. 'Of course I am not cross with you. I am disappointed.'

'That is good that you are disappointed. I, too, am very disappointed, but you understand that I have to stay, to help my father. He is distraught. I cannot leave Crete until Cathy has recovered.'

'It will take her at least two months,' Saffron frowned.

'So maybe you could come here?'

'I can't.' Saffron shook her head. 'The winter months are some of our busiest. So many people have falls when it becomes icy. No one is allowed leave between mid November and the end of March.'

'So when will I see you? I want to see you so much and I have something very important to ask you.'

'What's that, Vasi?'

'It is not something to ask over the telephone. I will ask you the next time we are together.'

'Vasi, that's not fair. Please tell me.'

To be continued .....